THE CHALICE AND THE SWORD

BOOKS BY ERNEST RAYMOND

NOVELS

A London Gallery *comprising:*

We, the Accused	*Was There Love Once?*
The Marsh	*The Corporal of the Guard*
Gentle Greaves	*A Song of the Tide*
The Witness of Canon Welcome	*The Chalice and the Sword*
A Chorus Ending	*To the Wood No More*
The Kilburn Tale	*The Lord of Wensley*
Child of Norman's End	*The Old June Weather*
For Them That Trespass	*The City and the Dream*
A Georgian Love Story	*Our Late Member*

Other Novels

The Bethany Road	*Mary Leith*
The Mountain Farm	*Morris in the Dance*
The Tree of Heaven	*The Old Tree Blossomed*
One of Our Brethren	*Don John's Mountain Home*
Late in the Day	*The Five Sons of Le Faber*
Mr Olim	*The Last to Rest*
The Chatelaine	*Newtimber Lane*
The Visit of Brother Ives	*The Miracle of Brean*
The Quiet Shore	*Rossenal*
The Nameless Places	*Damascus Gate*
Tell England	*Wanderlight*
A Family that Was	*Daphne Bruno I*
A Jesting Army	*Daphne Bruno II*

BIOGRAPHIES, ETC.

The Story of My Days (*Autobiography I*)
Please You, Draw Near (*Autobiography II*)
Good Morning Good People (*Autobiography III*)
Paris, City of Enchantment
Two Gentlemen of Rome (*The Story of Keats and Shelley*)
In the Steps of St. Francis
In the Steps of the Brontës

ESSAYS, ETC.

Through Literature to Life
The Shout of the King
Back to Humanity (with Patrick Raymond)

PLAYS

The Berg
The Multabello Road

THE CHALICE
AND THE SWORD

by
ERNEST RAYMOND

CASSELL · LONDON

CASSELL & COMPANY LTD
35 Red Lion Square, London WC1R 4SG
Sydney, Auckland
Toronto, Johannesburg

First edition 1952
First edition, second impression 1973

I.S.B.N. 0 304 29161 7

Printed in Great Britain by A. Wheaton & Co., Exeter

872

FOR

CHRISTOPHER PATRICK RAYMOND

AUTHOR'S NOTE

FATHER DAWBENY in this tale is an entirely fictitious character. But I should be failing in a duty of gratitude if I did not acknowledge that I have been helped in his creation by a study of two famous ministries, long closed now, in a part of London very different from the Potters Dale of this book, and in a time very different from our own bewildered and menacing age. Not a single incident in this story happened in real life, but, even so, some of its older readers may suspect that they know certain facts which have inspired its author ; and they will be right if they are remembering the great apostolates of Father Alexander Heriot Mackonochie and Father Arthur Henry Stanton in the dingy and sometimes desperate streets about Holborn.

For preserving me from error in certain legal and ' criminal ' phases of the story I am particularly grateful to my friends, Mr. E. G. Robey and Chief Superintendent Hawkyard, M.B.E., of Scotland Yard.

PART I

CHAPTER ONE

ERNEST MATTERS and Sophie, his wife, came round the curve of the hill. It is probable that neither of them, though they had lived in this area of London most of their lives, was conscious that they were coming round a hill. The tall, terraced houses on the crown and sides of Ledbitter Hill divert the eye from the easy-sloping pavements ; and, anyhow, does any Londoner notice the swell of the earth beneath the crowding houses unless it is at least as steep as Ludgate or Highgate Hills. For example, does any resident of Ledbitter Hill, even for a moment, see it as it was only a century ago ; a hill on a farmland with trees on its summit, sheep on its flanks, and larks and linnets in the sweet, smokeless air above ?

Nevertheless, Ernie and Sophie, hurrying along the wide curve of Connell Crescent, which sweeps from Montebello Road to Potters Dale, were walking round the low ground at the base of the hill. In the old days, when Ledbitter Hill was a tree-capped hummock on the farm of Thomas Ledbitter, Esq., Potters Dale was the wet, flat, couch-grass region that lay in the west ; but in the 1850's, or thereabouts, London, marching in power across a great high road from wealthy and royal Kensington, planted handsome houses all over the hill ; and the poorer people, driven in front of the prosperous men, or assembling to gather their rich refuse, spread like a silt on the dead flats of the Dale.

They are high, ornate houses on the hill ; they are Kensington's grand Victorian efflorescence, as bombastic as it was brief ; for there is more indigence than wealth in their lofty chambers now. They are palaces that have failed.

As for the Dale—well, enough for the present to say that the great Charles Booth, in his seventeen volumes on the life and labour of London, underscored the streets of the Dale dark blue for extreme poverty and the ultimate black for something worse. A certain parallelogram of streets make a dark and deplorable patch on his map. He went so far as to call it a 'Special Area'. Even to-day it is a queer fragment of West London.

It was to this queer fragment that Ernie and Sophie were walking. They were walking fast as if hastening to some show, and the man's walk seemed all the more eager because he was small and a little lame, dragging one leg hurriedly after the other. His right leg, you might say, had something of the character of a child hurrying to keep pace with a stronger and more active brother. Sophie seemed to be hurrying, too, because she was short and plump, and haste is perhaps more clearly seen in short, round legs, broad, round hips, and a full, heaving breast. It may seem strange that they looked as if hastening to an entertainment, because it was Sunday morning, and not yet half-past ten.

Before them the curving street seemed empty of all but the pale sunlight. The high houses with their pillared porticoes had their doors tight-closed ; the milk bottles waited patiently on the tops of the steps ; the dustbins stood against the area railings, their rounded lids askew ; and Saturday's litter lay asleep in the gutters. In the distance a door banged and a Salvation Army man came down his steps with an enormous silver horn ; across the road a woman in an apron swept the water from her cataract of steps across the pavement and into the gutter ; but for the most part the workers, who now possessed these lofty houses, were observing Sunday with a ' lay-in '. The quick steps of Ernie and Sophie echoed in an empty road.

They were in fact going to a church, and this was not usual with them. It was not usual with any of the exceedingly cheerful but unredeemed people who lived in and about the Montebello Road. But it had happened that Ernie, standing at the Craven Arms corner of that teeming and bawling street-market, had learned from another unemployed man that there were ' goings-on ' at a church in Potters Dale, and that the services there were ' as good as a show '. And Ernie had said, ' I've always wanted to see one of them sort of services. What's the name of the church ? '

' St. John the Prior's, Potters Dale.'

' St. John the Prior's ? I see. Well ; tell you what.' Ernie
was a little man who liked his joke. ' St. John won't be the
only pryer there next Sunday. I shall go round and do some
prying myself. I shall make old Sophie come along, too.
Do her good to go to church once in a way. We'll go together,
first time in fifteen years. In fact, let us pry.'

And now he was explaining for the ninth time to Sophie,
enthusiastically, ' Sfars I can make out they got a minister there
who's f'rall practical purposes a Romer Catholic. The services
are abs'lootly Romer Catholic.'

' But it's still Church of England, isn't it ? '

' Oh, yes, it's still C. of E., but, according to Harry, that's
about all you can say about it. He says the minister's gone
that far that, if he ain't careful, he'll be copping it.'

' Why, what could they do to him ? '

' Put him in prison.'

' Down' talk so silly. They don't put ministers in prison.'

' That's all *you* know.'

It was all Ernie had known till the day before yesterday when,
unemployed and bored, and ready to absorb at a street corner
some ancient history, he had listened to Harry Seaman, and
received the backwash of the old Tractarian tide which had
swept across London a hundred years before.

' They done it before now,' he assured Sophie. ' And they
could do it again.'

' What's the minister's name ? '

' I wouldn't know, lady ; but Harry says he's got all the
money in the world and he's spent thousands on that there
church. Comic what some people'll spend their money on.
Come on. Step on it. Fresh, this morning, ain't it ? You'd
never know it was the middle of June.' He ran his index finger
under both nostrils, first one, then the other, and wiped the
accrued moisture from it on the lapel of his jacket. ' Yes, it
was on the ribs, down and out, more or less, till he come along.'

' What was ? '

' The church. His church in Greig Street. It was abs'lootly
on its uppers—more'n what we are.' And Ernie laughed at
his joke. ' Christ ! 'Sever so nippy for June.'

' Yes, it always is on a Sunday morning. I don't know why.'

' It's because there's nobody much about. Takes a lot of
people to warm a place up.'

3

All the way Connell Crescent was curving round and dipping gently ; and as it dipped on the earth's surface it dipped in social quality. The houses became a little smaller, narrower, and less ornamented.

But now the broad and graceful curve swept into Hambledon Road—Hambledon Road as straight as a railway over a prairie and seemingly almost as long. It ran straight into the misty sunlight of the great highroad, straight into the spacious region of the great mansions and the parks ; and you could see that the houses at that distant end of Hambledon Road, standing so close to gentility, were still the houses of gentlemen.

Now, there is a remarkable thing about the long, straight Hambledon Road, and it is this : it turns its back on the west. Resolutely it looks east, keeping its eyes on the respectable slopes of Ledbitter Hill, and striving to forget the lower ground behind it. Only a couple of narrow, unwilling, ungracious turnings lead down into this low ground. And this perhaps is natural for Hambledon Road 'keeps up appearances,' and behind it— immediately behind it—is Potters Dale.

Nothing of this, of course, did Ernie and Sophie perceive. They turned into the first of these narrow, ungracious streets— which amounts to saying that they passed through the surly gates of Hambledon Road into the Dale. Heddle Way this short street was called, and it still dipped ; but at its foot there was no more dipping. Thenceforward all was flat. They were in the Dale.

No question about this part having been built for the pros- perous and inherited by the poor. It was built for the poor. For the very poor. Here on these dead levels were long streets of low two-storied houses crossing each other like a grid. A few terraces of three-storied houses stood about the grid, but they seemed even poorer, and certainly sadder and more de- pressed than their little neighbours, because they had attempted more, and their estate was fallen. Everywhere there were public-houses ; public-houses at every corner ; it was said that there was a public-house in the Dale for every twenty-five dwellings. Ernie and Sophie had never heard of Charles Booth and his ' Special Area ', underscored blue and black, but they were walking in it now. They were working their way through the grille of low-built streets : Quennel Street, Greig Street, Welcome Street, Morrow Street, crossed by Purvey Close,

4

Becker Street, Queen's Walk (inaptly named) and Thyatira Place.

'It's Greig Street we're after,' said Ernie; and in another minute, 'Here it is, see.'

Here was Greig Street, straight and low-built as the rest, and there, almost in its centre, on the south side, was the church of St. John the Prior's. It was a small, gabled Gothic affair, built in the sixties, with a three-arched porch before it, a rose window above, and a turret, like an ornamental pepper-castor, at each corner. Its London-grey bricks were banded with courses of red brick, but all the bricks were now approximating to the same neutral dun, and all the white stone dressings, on arches, gable and turrets, were crumbling away like old dried cheese. An alley ran up its left side to a vestry like an outhouse, and beyond the alley stood the Church Hall. The Church Hall was the only tall building in the road. Tall and square, its cornices were on a level with the ridge of the little church's steep-pitched roof.

§

Ernie and Sophie went into the church. It was empty. Like many people eager for a show, they had started too soon and walked too fast. Ernie moved to sit in front—'in the nine-pennies,' as he said—but Sophie whispered 'No,' and with a firm, if nervous, hand guided him into a back pew.

'Hell . . .' he protested. 'Shan't see much here.'

'*Tsh!* . . .' warned Sophie, perceiving that not the oath only, but his very voice was out of place in this silence.

Ernie sat down obediently and looked around him. An array of small candles burned quietly in a corner before a brightly-painted statuette; sun-shafts, piercing the coloured windows, laid lozenges of various hues on the dun-brick wall; a single hanging lamp burned golden before the altar; the rest was dusk. This jewelled dusk seemed one with the silence. Only after a while did Ernie notice that a clock was ticking loudly over the west door. It was not in him to liken this enclosed stillness to a portion of the timeless stillness, or to think that that ticking, warning clock stood over the exit into the world of time; but he did feel something; he did notice the contrast between the two and apprehend dimly some queer

5

significance in it. He had his part in the immature poetry of the poor.

Now his eyes were on the high altar under its lofty baldachin. Six unlit candles, each tall as a man, stood on its retable, and behind them hung a huge crucifix with gilded rays branching from it, as if it were the sun itself.

'Crikey!' he muttered. 'It's just like places I seen in France. Right up close to the Line sometimes.'

'*Tsh!*' chided Sophie, in the tone of a wife who could no more trust a man to 'behave' than a mischievous child.

Ernie sniffed—and sniffed again. 'Smelt this in France, too.'

'Incense,' Sophie informed him because, while confident that they 'didn't ought to be talking,' she could not hide this piece of knowledge, this gleam of light, under a bushel.

'Where?' demanded Ernie.

'*Tsh!*' Having said her piece, she extinguished the talk.

The clock ticked on, and they sat side by side, alone. Suddenly Ernie turned an ear towards the altar. Somewhere out of sight a voice had begun speaking; a man's voice; it was saying, reciting, something rapidly, monotonously, at a level pitch and without pause or end. On and on, unanswered, went the voice—on and on—and Ernie turned and grinned at Sophie. 'Can't turn it off now he's started. . . . Can't find the switch.'

'*Tsh!*' repeated the anxious woman.

Slowly, at intervals, people came in: children noisily; a few old people stiffly and heavily; a few young men self-consciously; several young women with far more ease and confidence. And all, before taking their seats, genuflected towards the altar—the children with quick formality; the old grey people with difficulty; the young men hurriedly; the girls with an obvious joy in this devotion.

Just when the church was still again a large, handsome, elderly lady, in silk and pearls and a mink coat and with a high white coiffure elaborately and expensively dressed, entered and made this reverence towards the altar. It was the deepest, longest, and best-enjoyed genuflection they had yet seen.

'Caw-lovey, should we ought to 'a done that?' Ernie inquired, and was again discouraged from speech.

The elderly lady carried her jewels and her fur to a lowly place at the back, sank on her knees, and stayed on her knees,

6

gloved hands clasped, white head bowed. She was evidently very devout.

But look: a very tall black figure stood before the altar arranging things upon it; a figure looking very long and slight in a close-fitting cassock with brief cape and taut cincture. He finished his soft, busy movements up there, turned round, and came down towards the people. And Ernie gaped.

Almost he gasped.

'Who's he like?' he was thinking. 'I seen someone like him before. Who was it? Lord 'a mercy, who?'

He was a minister, no doubt; and he came closer, giving a faint, shy smile now and then to someone in the congregation. Who? Like, and yet not quite like. Hair black, face thin, skin pale beneath the waving black hair, nose high-arched and prominent ('like a duke's at least,' thought Ernie, probably remembering stories at school of the Iron Duke), age between fifty and sixty—who was it he favoured? Someone not so thin and not so old. But he was a relation, surely? Even an elder brother perhaps.

He must be all of six foot two. But while his face was lean and hollowed to the point of gauntness, his long body seemed no more than slender and graceful. The eyes of Sophie, watching at Ernie's side, thought it an elegant figure—'ever so elegant in that perfectly-fitting cassock with the little cape and tight sash.' She thought he moved beautifully up and down; and she noticed, what Ernie would never have noticed, that, even though he was 'rising sixty,' he had still the large dark eyes of a wondering child.

'Who the hell . . .?' Ernie dug and dug in the deeps of memory. He dug; paused and frowned; and dug again. 'Someone . . . someone I was afraid of.'

The priest was now wandering round the aisles, giving the same shy smile to this old woman or that little girl. Once he went out into the porch and gazed up and down Greig Street. He seemed to be looking for a few more worshippers; and Ernie thought he came away disappointed.

The elderly lady had lifted her splendid white head and was watching him—watching him wherever he went.

Now another figure was before the altar; a black and white figure this time; a tall, square-shouldered youth in black cassock and laced cotta. So far as the deeply interested Ernie

7

could distinguish his features, he was a lad with a straight nose, broad brow and a fullness and affluence of fair, brown hair. With his good height, good shoulders, good nose, and hair almost gold, he was a very good-looking lad. But now one fact shone in the sun-rays slanting down towards the altar: the young man thought the world of that almost golden hair. He wore it long, too long, and one couldn't be sure that it hadn't been artificially waved or set like a girl's; anyhow, it had been greased and dressed and brushed up over the ears to make a treat for the audience this morning.

Thus robed and carefully polished, he was carrying a long taper and lighting the high candles on the altar. When he had achieved this, not without some interesting difficulties, he came down into the body of the church to light the candles on a side-altar, walking with a studied slowness, softness, and grace, and obviously much preoccupied with his performance and his appearance. Ernie watched him all the way; he considered the brief cotta hanging loose and spreading wide over his middle; and then, whispering out of shut, unmoving lips (a trick he'd learned in a House of Correction), he demanded of Sophie, 'What's he want a maternity smock for at *his* age?' to which Sophie responded, 'Oh, don't be awful, Ernie,' and then tittered.

'Well . . .' Ernie, pleased with his joke, considered the cotta further. 'I mean—wha'd you say? He quite fancies himself in that get-up, don't he?'

'*Will* you stop?'

'Where did he get that hair?'

'Ernie!'

The tall priest had now disappeared. A bell was ringing above the roof; the church clock ticked on. It struck; other clocks struck in the Dale; and now everything began to happen. A light, hidden under the baldachin, flooded the great crucifix —one hadn't realized that it hung in a dusk before. The bell stopped; the organ played; a little procession appeared from somewhere beside the altar—first a gentleman carrying a silver something on a jingling chain; then the golden young man carrying a crucifix, with a small boy on each side of him carrying a candle; then the tall priest with a cotta over his cassock, and lastly a short, fat priest in a wonderful heavy garment embroidered with gold. The tall dark priest seemed to treat the little fat one with great respect, almost holding up his skirts

8

for him as he ascended to the altar and generally dancing attendance on him.

'Then he's not the boss,' concluded Ernie. 'The boss is the one in the bedspread.'

A pillar of smoke was rising from the altar towards the flood-lit crucifix—rising like the smoke from a fire of leaves on a still autumn day. The priest in the green garment was swinging the jingling silver vessel ; a smell as of burning pine needles and resin drifted towards Ernie ; and he thought of a forest in France twenty years ago and of a soldier's fire smouldering among the bivouacs.

He was very proud of having been a soldier in France in 1916.

'Caw love-a-duck ! ' he murmured, watching the grey-blue smoke. But in truth he was moved. 'It's rather lovely,' he thought to himself. 'A bit of all right, if you ask me.'

And he watched and watched. The two priests kept bobbing up and down and moving this way and that ; the gentleman kept swinging his incense-thing like a pendulum ; the boys, with or without their candles, moved in pairs or in line abreast with military precision ('they got a good sergeant-major,' thought Ernie 'and I wouldn't put it past that tall, dark minister being the R.S.M. and the little fat one the C.O.') ; the organ sang on ; the people sang, too, seemingly indifferent to all that was happening up there ; and the sun shafts, with the dust-motes gleaming and dancing within them, poured down upon it all.

Once the whole congregation sank down to its knees ; and Ernie, finding himself so prominently erect, started to go down, too, but the anxious Sophie stayed him with her hand, which was just as well, because now all the people were up again. This embarrassing incident was hardly over before the tall priest deserted everybody up there and came down into the nave while everybody was still singing—just as if he were feeling sick and falling out on parade. He mounted the pulpit, and as the pulpit was on the north side, he stood in the bright sun-light streaming through the clerestory windows.

'Got it ! ' exclaimed Ernie beneath the singing, and he said it so emphatically that Sophie glanced up. 'Lord, of course ! It's the Colonel he's like. Might be his older brother. But it's probably only a coincidence. Can't see any of the Colonel's family getting up to these games.'

§

The singing ended; the people sat; and the priest who looked very tall in that low pulpit, raised its brass lectern as high as it would go, and read out a few announcements. Then, picking up a stole and kissing it, he put it about his neck and began to speak.

He spoke gently and, as he supposed, chattily, but without ease. It was as if some shyness inhibited ease, or some ineradicable sense that he was different from his audience, the son of a proud house and pupil of a great school while they were children of the Dale, stood as a barrier between him and them, and he had to force his love for them through this barrier; and he *was* forcing it, with these shy, awkward smiles. But, even so, his gentleman's English, his ' seven-and-sixpenny words,' as Sophie called them afterwards, were too often above the heads of the people. He was no great preacher, certainly; he was too constricted in utterance, and had no arts of delivery nor any feeling for elocution. Sometimes he was not easy to hear. He was successful only—but then very successful—when he bent his head to talk to the children. Beneath the pulpit was a square block of children : boys and girls of the Sunday school, boy scouts and cubs, girl guides and brownies. Shedding for their sakes all the seven-and-sixpenny words, he told them stories, so that they tittered often and sometimes roared with shrill laughter—which surprised Sophie much and somewhat shocked her.

He had been speaking of parental love, and of the power for self-sacrifice which it gave to mothers and fathers; and now he told the children the tale of an Indian squaw, not seventeen years old, who, when the encampment had been attacked by a hostile tribe, was found spread above her baby with her arms outstretched and every bullet that had come their way in her body—but the child alive and safe beneath her. He told them of a young Chinese father who, as a crowded ship went down, lashed his child to a floating board, kissed him and sank, lest his weight were too much for the board.

Not less than the children Sophie was staring with captured eyes. She was thinking of the only child she'd borne, the little boy they'd lost at three years old. She remembered how she'd flung herself on the little dead body, and not for hours had Ernie been able to lift her from it and draw her away.

That was long ago now. She looked at the acolytes who'd come down into the nave to hear the sermon, little fair-haired, smiling, blunt-nosed English boys of eleven and twelve, and she thought that Micky, if he'd lived, would have been like them, and how proud she'd have been to see him in a red cassock and white cotta like that.

Now the priest was talking to the adults again. With a brightening of the large dark eyes, and a fervour kindling within him so that it overcame the constraint in his speech, he asked them, ' How many thousands of men and women have, at the touch of God, found within themselves a love for their weaker fellows as strong and self-sacrificing as anything you feel for your children ? ' and to illustrate this he spoke to them of Father Damien, who had discharged his priestly task among the lepers on a Hawaiian island till he died among them, a leper and their fellow.

' And if even such noble human love as this is as a drop to the ocean compared with the infinite and all-embracing Divine Love, then how deep, how awful, how beyond all human imagination must be the passionate need of God to come and labour and suffer among us ! My friends, if ever you begin to feel this longing to offer yourselves for others, you will begin to understand why the Divine Love emptied itself of all its glory and became like one of us, that it might suffer the utmost we could suffer.

> ' Oh, wondrous depth of Love Divine
> That He should bend so low.'

That was all.

§

Ernie and Sophie, since they had been watching the other people for instruction, passed out of the church behind all the rest. Ernie limped out behind Sophie to meet the sunlight of Greig Street and the clean Sunday air. And directly the sun-light justified speech he began, ' Caw-lummy, Sophie ! That cove was——' but she interrupted him, saying, 'I liked it. I liked it, I *must* say. I liked all he said a lot. It kind'a made you understand things——'

'Yes, but listen, Sophie——'

'I tell you what I didn't like : that young man who lit the candles and carried the cross. He's too beautiful by half, and he knows it. Anyone could see he was thinking most of the time about himself and the sort of figure he was cutting up there. Acting, he was ; showing off his beauty, to give us a treat.'

'Yes, and he wants his hair cut ; but listen, Sophie : I wonder what that preacher's name was. You know my colonel in France—I've told you about him often enough—well, this cove's related to him, or I'll eat my boots. He's the dead, spitting image of him, only older and as gentle-like as the Colonel was tough—caw-lummy, the Colonel'd take the hide off you if you was up before him, or if you didn't turn out the guard properly. I remember once when I was on sentry duty and had to turn out the guard he come along and I got a bit flustered—because I was a bit afraid of him, I don't mind admitting—and I yelled, "Turn out the *guards* ! " The Colonel just stopped still and stared at me while I shivered, and then he bawled, " Wha'd you mean, man ? It's 'turn out the *guard*'—not 'the guards.' The guards are a fine body of men." Which was a bit rude to us all, wa'n't it ? Caw, he had a tongue like a saw-bayonet. Caw, his lang'widge, sometimes was like a five-nine exploding. It fair took the skin off you, if it didn't blow your head into the next trench.'

'It's not nice to talk like that,' suggested Sophie.

'Don't you believe it ! It's all right as long as you're issuing it out to the troops instead of getting it issued to you. It's fine then.'

'Still, people have no call to talk like that to people,' Sophie persisted. 'Not to anyone, they haven't, I don't think.'

'And that shows you never been a Colonel or a Sergeant in a Great War. The boys understood they got to be swore at a bit because there was no time to parly-voo with them when the Jerries were likely to come to tea at any minute. But they *did* think the Colonel said a shade too much sometimes.'

'He sounds a bully to me,' Sophie commented.

'No, but the boys liked him, and I'll tell you for why. If ever the Jerries attacked, or it looked like they would, he was there with the boys in front, not saying much, but just there—just walking up and down the trench. And d'you know why?'

But Sophie was gazing up the street, and she burst out, ' Will you only look at that now?'

The large elderly lady with the white hair and the mink coat was walking away in the distance, and a big blue limousine had come silently round a corner, where apparently it had been modestly hiding, to meet her. A uniformed chauffeur stepped down, opened the door for her, and packed her in with rugs. The car moved silently away.

' Who's she, I wonder,' said Sophie.

' Oh, that old cow. Yes, I saw her in church. The queen's first cousin, I should think. That's a Westminster Straight Eight, that car. Cost a coupla thousand at least.'

' Yes, and that fur coat put her back another thousand.'

' We *are* seeing life. But as I was saying, Sophie, he'd be up there in the trench, walking up and down, with his Sam Browne belt and his Russian boots and his revolver holster all shining like one o'clock—because he was a dandy—not half—and liked his reputation as just about the best-dressed officer in the brigade. There he was, just waiting for the Jerries ; standing in along of the boys, instead of staying back in the Battle Headquarters. He was there the day I stopped my packet, and I'm not likely to forget that. It was like this——'

' Hush ! Someone's coming.'

' Think I could ask 'em what his name is ?'

' Don't suppose there's no harm in it.'

Out came the tall young crucifer, looking very different in his grey flannel trousers, bright brown sports jacket, and grey cap pulled daintily to one side of his head so that a wing of the almost gold hair could be brushed up on the other. They saw now that he was no more than nineteen and had the paleness, and a few of the pimples, of adolescence.

' 'Scuse me, chum,' said Ernie, limping up to him, ' but who was the gentleman who preached ?'

' He ?' The young man seemed to be surprised at such ignorance. ' Why, the vicar, of course.'

' Oh, then he *was* the boss ?'

' The boss ? Yes, of course.'

' Well, why did the other bloke wear all the glad rags ? And why did the boss act up to him like a plumber's mate ?'

'Because the "other bloke," as you call him'—obviously this high church young man didn't like hearing a priest referred to as a 'bloke'—'that bloke happened to be the celebrant.'

'The—pardon?'

'The celebrant. The celebrating priest.'

'*I'll* say he did some celebrating up there,' agreed Ernie.

'Now, Ernie!' Sophie chided. 'Don't be profane. The young gentleman may not like it.'

'Oh, I don't mind,' laughed the young man. He was now correcting Sophie, in her turn. 'It's only the prots who're afraid to joke about religion. That was Sung Mass and Sermon. We used to have proper High Mass with deacon and sub-deacon in dalmatic and tunicle, and a ceremoniarius, but we can't do it now; we haven't the help. I've been ceremoniarius myself sometimes.'

Ernie, as shrewd as he was ignorant, could see very well that this young man was exhibiting his ecclesiastical learning and trying to dazzle the unscholarly with long, unintelligible terms; so he declined to please him by asking what the hell a ceremoniarius was. Instead he asked, 'Well, what's his name?'

'Father Grayson.'

'Oh . . .' It was a word of disappointment. Ernie had expected another name.

'He comes to help the vicar sometimes. We can't afford an assistant priest any more.'

'Oh, but I mean the vicar. What's *his* name?'

'Father Dawbeny.'

'I knew it!' Ernie triumphed. 'I told you so, Sophie. He's his brother, betcher life. Well, now, did you ever? What d'you know?'

The young man, unaware of what he was taking about, smiled a good-bye and walked on. The smile was friendly and attractive and disclosed another trait than conceit.

'Say,' said Ernie, whispering like a conspirator, 'd'you think I could nip in and ask if he's related to Colonel Dawb'ny? I just *must* know if he's his brother. Gawd almighty, I'll never forget the Colonel at Murder Wood when I got my packet. He was there in the trenches because Jerry was coming. Just walking up and down, dressed like an army tailor's model and spreading out the platoons to keep touch as the lads got knocked out. Of course, Murder Wood wasn't its real name ; it was Meurthe Wood, or some daft name like that, but the boys called it Murder Wood, and that just about fitted it. There were none of its trees left, only stumps and stakes, and no grass or nothing, only the dried-up earth and a stink like a butcher's shop when all the meat's gone off. The boys always said that the Colonel saved the whole line that day, because the battalions on each side of us were caving right in, and we didn't budge. He wouldn't let us. No, he just walked up and down and saw that we didn't—walked up and down with his hands joined behind his back, dangling his stick against his Russian boots, which his batman had polished up to the nines. Of course, he was a swell in peace-time, and I'll say he looked it. He was an On'rible. Son of an Earl.'

If ever a title had a capital letter, Ernie gave ' Earl ' one then.

' Yes, he was Colonel the On'rible Piers Lygon Dawbeny, *what, what,* and they said that his family owned half of Cumberland, with a tidy heap of mountains thrown in. . . . Yes, his old man, the Earl, owned about forty-five mountains and whenever he was in the mood to, could give one of his nippers a mountain for an Easter egg.'

' Good law' now,' said Sophie. ' I always thought mountains kind'a belonged to everybody.'

' Oh no, *oh* no! " denied Ernie with conviction. ' These 'ere mountains belonged to the Earl, the Colonel's old dad, and he could hand them around as he liked.'

' Well, go on about the Colonel and Murder Wood.'

' Yeah, all the Colonel owned or cared about that day was Murder Wood, and lemme tell you he wasn't giving it away to anyone. He may have been a terror for discipline back in rest billets, but he was quite different when Jerry was coming. Then he just walked up and down, giving the boys a smile now and then—not much more because he wasn't much good at talking to us common fellows—but they thought the world of him then. Yes, they fair worshipped him.' Just as a child's talk deals only in ' millions ' and ' tons ' and ' miles,' so Ernie preferred the largest terms. ' Oh, yes, and that day when I got my blighty, he'd a bandage round his head because he'd stopped a splinter the day before. And it was a nasty wound, too, but he only got the M.O. to bandage it up and give him his anti-tetanus, and back he come to the boys because Jerry was expected to call. And I can tell you it was the neatest bandage you ever saw, under his tin hat. When I stopped my blighty just here '—Ernie touched the leg that made him lame—' they bandaged me up and put me in an officer's sleeping-place, which was just a shelf cut in the trench wall. Law-love you, it was like a grave with one side missing. And I laid there and saw the Colonel passing every quarter of an hour, hands behind his back, and swagger cane smacking his boots. Once he stopped and give me a smile and asked how I was. I said, " O.K., sir. Not too bad," and he fetched out a fag-case—gold, mind you— gold like his wrist-watch and his pocket-pencil—and he give me a fag and lit it for me. And he said, " We'll soon get you away, lad. Never worry." Next time he come along his stick was under his arm, and he was dangling his revolver behind him because he thought Jerry was coming. And just as he passed me a nine-inch shell burst behind the parados and covered him with dust, and, bless you, he drew a silk handkerchief from under his sleeve and dusted himself down, while he says to me, " You all right, lad ? Good ! Don't you worry. Nobody's going to have this trench." That was the last I ever saw of him, because when the attack was over—and did they shift us ? Not on your life—not with the Colonel there—I was got away and evacuated back to Blighty for good and all. But I've never forgotten the——'

' Tsh ! Here's the minister.'

The vicar's voice, just behind them, was speaking to an old woman who was putting the hymn-books back on a shelf. He came out, in cassock, cape, and sash, just as they had first seen him ; and a heavy, short-legged dog with a black, sad, crumpled face followed him. Seeing two strangers whom he'd noticed at the service, he gave them his rather wan smile, as if a little afraid, or shy, of them.

Ernie took courage and spoke. ' 'Scuse me, sir, but might I ask you something ? '

' Certainly.' Again the embarrassed smile. ' Down, Squaller ! I know you've heard your mass and want your lunch, but you must wait. I've got to talk to this gentleman.'

This address to the dog so surprised Sophie that she was emboldened to ask, ' Was he in church, then ? '

' Oh, yes. He insists on coming. He stays in the sacristy

and keeps perfectly still and quiet, which must be a strain for him because he hates singing, and when I turn on the wireless at home he usually howls.'

'The pet!' exclaimed Sophie, stroking his ears.

' 'Scuse me, sir,' continued Ernie, 'but would you be related to a Colonel Dawb'ny who used to command the 10th West Londons in the war? Because I was with that battalion in France. I was only with 'em a short time because I copped it at Murder Wood in '16. But I remember the Colonel well, and I thought you favoured him. We boys liked him a lot, even though he could be a holy terror back in billets.'

The vicar, a foot taller than Ernie, looked down at him with that small, twisted smile. 'Yes, colonels get like that. A pity, isn't it! What is your name?'

'Matters, sir. Ernie Matters.'

The vicar, frowning slightly, appeared to be searching among his relatives for a Colonel Dawbeny. But he smiled and shook his head. 'No, Mr. Matters.'

Mr. Matters! How civil, thought Sophie. What a gentleman he is.

'Oh . . .'' Ernie was heavily disappointed. 'I'm sorry, sir, but I thought you were so like him.'

'That was over twenty years ago, wasn't it?'

'Yes, I suppose it was. Twenty-two years ago. And it seems like yesterday.'

'No, I'm not related to him, Mr. Matters.'

'Well, I'm sorry to have troubled you, sir.'

'Not at all.' The thin smile broadened a little. 'You see, I'm hardly related to him, because I *was* Colonel Dawbeny.'

CHAPTER TWO

YES, strange. The colonel of Murder Wood into the priest of Potters Dale. No wonder that little man, Matters, had gaped. Matters? Ernest Matters? No, he had no recollection of him. But twenty-two years was a long time, and people changed. Yes, changed.

Father Dawbeny, still in his cassock, sat in his sitting-room above the Church Hall. The heavy dog with the crumpled face sat beside him, sometimes looking up at the thinker and presumably thinking too behind his absurd, appealing eyes. Those bloodshot eyes looked grateful, and the two forepaws padded happily, when the thinker fiddled absent-mindedly with his companion's ears or stroked his neck.

The room was large and long. Once it had been a club room. The pious Lord Hobart who built the church and hall had intended these upper rooms for a boys' club or a girls' club, but the church had no such harvest now as it reaped in the Victorian sunlight, and the ground-floor rooms were all that were needed for parish purposes. So Father Dawbeny had made the upper rooms into a clergy house, and in these latter and straitened days, when they could afford a curate no more, lived there alone. It was convenient for a clergy house, only the alley to the vestry separating it from the church.

This long upper room with its bare boards and distempered walls still looked like a club room. The only things that conflicted with its communal character were the two old Victorian arm-chairs by the fireplace, in one of which Father Dawbeny sat, the Persian prayer-rug between them, and the many well-kept books on the cheap deal shelves. Two plain deal tables, one large, one small, stood on the bare boards; the large one, a trestle table, held a typewriter, a telephone, and a scatter of papers; the small one the remains of a meal which the father had just prepared for himself. Several cane-seated chairs (brought up from the assembly room below for Bible-class purposes) stood against the walls where the bookshelves would admit them. On the wall behind the long trestle table hung a large map of the Potters Dale and Ledbitter Hill areas, with the parishes outlined and shaded in contrasting tints. The room could well have been a battalion orderly room behind the Line in France—except for a small crucifix over the mantel-shelf, which assuredly no orderly room would ever have hung up for the encouragement of the Adjutant, or the reproof of defaulters.

Everything in it was extremely tidy and neat—as tidy and neat as the padre's long cassock.

Yes, 'strange the metamorphosis'—from what poem, learned in childhood, came that line? 'Strange the metamorphosis.' Its cause—or should he say its occasion?—was a thing too private to tell to anyone. It was a thing done in an extreme of solitariness. Who would have understood? Not Brother Bob, the present earl, nor his sons and daughters. They could not understand Uncle Piers even now. Not Cecil, his sister. No : silence for ever.

As he thought of Earl Bob, his mind travelled from Potters Dale to other and lovelier dales. He saw the soft, green fall of Emberdale in Cumberland, with the long sheet of Emberdale Water in its bottom. And at the far end of the water he saw a battlemented hall, Castle Strathpenny, the seat for three hundred years of the Earls of Strathpenny. It incorporated still a portion of the old towered and crenellated stronghold from which the mediæval lords of Strathpenny strove to keep the moss-troopers out of their green straths and off the breasts of their stony fells. All around the castle, curtained with pines and larches, rolled the fells and vales and mountains, thirty thousand acres of them, with hill farms, lowland farms, hæma-tite iron mines, and slate quarries—and all a part of the Strath-penny Estate. And all beautiful—except perhaps the blast furnaces and iron works nearer the sea. Pleasant to remember wandering, a happy boy, over the fells to the peaks of the family mountains, and exchanging friendly words with the farmers, his father's tenants, or with the shepherds plodding in the alpine pastures above the timber line and the drystone walls. Often he had helped farmers and shepherds to save their sheep in a snow-storm, or to dig them out before they were smothered. He had loved and been proud of that rescue work. Sometimes he had climbed with the Strathpenny Rescue Team to the black and splintered precipices where a mountaineer lay with a broken limb.

The Strathpenny Mountain Rescue Team! It had been the creation of his brother and himself when they were enthusiastic lads of eighteen and seventeen. Long before other men formed these teams in the valleys Bob and he had conceived, organized, and equipped this company of young volunteers, mostly the farmers' sons and the younger shepherds, who passed a first-aid test and formed a pool of mountaineers from which a rescue party could be promptly drawn when news of disaster came down the hills. And they had given to this young fellowship the very name adopted years after by all such Samaritan companies: 'Mountain Rescue Team.'

From the Strathpenny mountains to Greig Street, Potters Dale. From Castle Strathpenny to this bare room. Yes, strange.

§

Who would understand if he tried to tell of that awful hour when the choice before him was 'Kill . . . or forgive? Go bad . . . or turn good? Hate all . . . or love all?' No half-way to healing then: the pain was too great. Compromise, and the pain was back. 'Hate all men . . . or . . . love all men everywhere?'

1920; and he forty; and Ursula had raised within him such a power of love as he had never imagined himself capable of, in his careless, selfish, philandering years. Ursula . . . nineteen . . . Lady Ursula Burne . . . daughter of the Marquess of Retford, forsooth, and she looked like a small pretty child in a nursery who'd put up her hair for fun. Ursula, Ursula . . . the name now, after eighteen years, lifted him from his chair, so that the dog's great head, which had been resting on his knee in sentimental appeal, was flung off like a parcel forgotten.

Ursula, so alight with childish affection, so ready with protestations that lovers must be faithful to each other and have no secrets and tell no lies! He, looking down on to her childish face so far below him: 'If you cannot trust the one you love, you may as well die.' She, looking up at him with bright eyes:

20

' Of course, of course.' And he, like a million fools before him, had believed that she, because she was his woman, his choice, was different from all other women—pure as a Victorian heroine, trustworthy as Cæsar's wife. And all the brilliant protestations had been lies—not at first, not at first, for she had loved him then, but after Kemble Reeves had appeared—after that pleasing and secret cad had looked at her and wanted her and whistled to her to come. Then, oh, sick and awful days when he had begun to suspect, and had worried her with his questions, and she had protested that he was silly to doubt her: shameful days when he had spied on her ; dark, dreadful evening when he had followed behind her to Kemble's rooms and waited all night for her to come away—waited through the dark hours, waited in the cold London morning, and walked straight up to her as she came creeping, slinking, from his door. How many hearts had died in such agony as his that long black night and early morning . He said burning, branding, scorifying things to her, there in the empty London street—no officer or man in the worst of battles had heard such words from him : words of fire, words of filth. ' Bitch on heat,' ' Whore,' ' Piccadilly drab ' and ' Ten shilling street-woman ' were left to scald her memory as he ran from her. He ran—ran to a wilderness, out of men's sight, three hundred miles away, the wilderness he knew. It was early in the morning, and he dragged out his car and raced it along the roads to the north—raced it with a lunatic's hand—so that it was early evening when it stood, radiator steaming, on the drive of Castle Strathpenny. Mother, Bob and Cecil were at home ; his father in London for a debate in the Lords. Wonderful his acting before mother, brother, sister, and servants : Ursula, that little cheat, could not have done better. Not a word to anyone. Jokes at the dinner table. Jokes with the servants. Witticisms with all. Witticisms sometimes bitter, sometimes gay and laden with laughter. Billiards. A grip of iron on his agony.

But in the morning, very early, out before anyone was astir— out and wandering over fells and mountains. Wandering all day—past the happy holiday-makers, past the rock-climbers setting out for the Ridges. ' Kill . . . or forgive ? Go bad . . . or turn good ? Hate all . . . or love all ? ' No other healing.

That day, whether standing on empty crests or dropping into hollows and toiling up again, he knew a strange thing : that the wounded love for a faithless child could become—if he would let it—a love for all the world. And that there was nothing else for him to do. This second love was crying to him, ' Come, come ; and be at peace.'

How could its cry be so strong ? There had been but small evidence of its strength in his forty years of life. There had been dim perceptions, of course, many times before, of a beauty and joy in selfless service—what man did not see such momentary gleams ?—but he had quickly turned his eyes from them. In the war he had held it his duty to attend not only the padre's parade services in the open meadows, but his Holy Communions in tent or field or ruined room ; but the attendance had been a somewhat formal business, a duty to his men rather than to his God. In the parade services he had stood in front of his men ; at the Holy Communions he had knelt behind them all—why ? He could hardly say. Possibly to express to them that, however they stood on the parade ground, they were equal in rank before God, and the greatest among them should be as their servant. And sometimes, kneeling behind his men and hearing the words of prayer or Scripture, he had felt an uprising of love for them, as for a flock, and had seen the calm and sweetness of a life of service.

So likewise to-day on his home mountains : holiness and service were crying to him, Come, come, and be happy again. Why, in states of turmoil, did words always form themselves unsought ? Where did they leap from ? As he toiled up to Scafell Pike the words of some man's prayer that he'd read somewhere, or heard somewhere, stood in his mind: ' Break me, and make me anew.'

Some small happiness, a gleam along the dark horizon, brightened before him as he wondered if God so loved him that he had thus broken him. He stopped in his climbing ; he stood still among a cataract of boulders and scree under the summit rocks ; stood with hands behind him and face uplifted to a clouded sky in which a curlew was flying and complaining ; and he repeated the prayer, ' Break me if you wish and must . . . break me.'

§

No half-way to healing. Compromise, and the pain was back. Only an extreme of self-offering changed miraculously the pain into something that felt like happiness, and even more than happiness—a beginning of exultation. Besides, he had always craved perfections, whether in his dress or in his house-rooms, or in the movements of his men on the drill-ground, and he could feel content with nothing but the utmost now. A missionary like Father Damien among the lepers? A doctor giving his labour free in the slums? A Brown Brother of St. Francis with a guest-house (built at his own cost) for all destitute and foot-weary wanderers?

No; something less than these: he was forty, and had neither the time nor the talents for long training as a doctor; he was not good enough, with his sins still strong within him, to take the vows of a monk. One course seemed possible, since the training would not be long: that of an unpaid curate in a parish of low streets, bringing his wealth to the poor, the abject, and, best of all, the vile. . . .

Father Dawbeny was walking up and down that long upper room as he gazed into the past; and the dog's unhappy eyes followed him. Only occasionally did the dog, sitting there on his haunches, beat a fore-paw impatiently. He seemed to know that, just as he must keep quiet during Mass and not howl a descant during the hymns, so he must stay still on his haunches when his master had gone into a solitariness. He sat watching him.

It had not been an easy task to shift that vision on the hill-side from its unstable base of emotion on to a firm base of will; not an easy journey from the sand to the rock; not a struggle in which he was not often beaten to his knees. At first he had been very happy. Extraordinary the peace and satisfaction of a life whose one grand purpose was to obey at every moment the love within. The life itself seemed to prove that this love within was God. And if it was That, how wonderful to be united with Something that, unlike the things of this world, every one of which must sooner or later fail you, was permanent, unchanging, *perfect*. He learned now that he was getting far more joy out of the world than when he was a man of the world.

So it had been at first, but as the figure of Ursula receded, and the pain of her name lost power, the battle swayed, the breastworks gave, and sometimes the position looked like falling. How often came the overwhelming desire to backslide into comfort and good living and worldly ambition. But, always obstinate, always grimly resolute, always of an iron and formidable will, he had stiffened that will to steel—and stood. Stood, yes ; but was the battle won even yet ? Eighteen years since that day on the hillside, and he alone knew how easily the old sins could jump to life in him : pride and aristocratic contempt, and covetousness for beautiful things, and anger, and a tongue with a sting like a serpent's. He had only to think of these things to feel them stir in their sleep. Let the will fail, and they would rise and throw him.

The will must not fail. Hands clasped behind him, he went to the long trestle table and looked across it at the wall-map which included his parish. Parts of it were underlined in black where the Council had condemned whole terraces of poor houses. After a time he undid his hands, grasped the table edge, and, kneeling down, laid his head upon his arms.

The dog waited upon his haunches till this solitary business was over.

CHAPTER THREE

Two mornings afterwards, having said Mass, Father Dawbeny went from the sacristy to the Church Dues chest by the west door. Unlocking it, with no more hope than usual of finding within it any offer of help, he was pleased to see one folded slip lying on the bottom, like a single ballot-paper in the box. He took it out and read :

> ' *I* (*Mr.*, *Mrs.*, *or Miss*), Mr. Ernest Matters,
> *of* 73, Dryfield Street, W.2.,
> *undertake to pay, so long as I am able, the sum of*
> one shilling *weekly*
>   . . . *monthly*
>   . . . *quarterly*
>   . . . *yearly*
> *towards the expenses of St. John the Prior's, Potters*
> *Dale.*'

Affection and pity touched his heart : Ernie Matters must have talked it over with that plump little wife of his and come back to the empty church yesterday with that form filled in. Dryfield Street ? That was a turning off the Montebello Road, some way from here. But if Matters and his wife were to be new members of his congregation he must go and call on them as soon as possible. Why not this evening, when the little man would be at home from work ?

So that evening Father Dawbeny, with the dog padding before, behind, and beside him, walked along the same road that Ernie and Sophie had taken : round the rising curve of Ledbitter Hill and down the gentle droop of the twisting Montebello Road. The Montebello Road was the only serpentine street among these straight roads and crescents, because it was once the old winding cart-track to the Montebello Farm.

Here was Dryfield Street, straight as all its sisters : a long road of three-storied houses designed in the sixties for small middle-class people, but possessed to-day by the poor. No. 73 ? More than half-way down ; but here at length it was. Its door stood open, and Father Dawbeny on the threshold saw a narrow passage with some worn fragments of differently patterned carpet on the splintering boards, some clouded milk bottles against the skirting, and a bundle in a dirty sheet, waiting, no doubt, to be carried to a bagwash laundry. An ageing perambulator stood at the dark vista's end, with another bundle in it, perhaps also intended for the laundry. Not in eighteen years had he, once the master of a thousand men, conquered his nervousness at a poor man's door. His hand shook as he knocked ; his knee trembled as a fat, staring woman in a soiled pink overall came quickly, inquisitively, from the back parts. He could understand why she was peering at him. He was not in his cassock, nor even in a clerical collar, but in a very well-tailored dark suit, and he knew she was wondering what so well-dressed a gentleman could want. In the inmost chamber of his heart he was never quite at ease about his one remaining concession to the old craving for perfect things : his well-made cassock and his well-made clothes.

' Mr. Matters ? ' he inquired.

' Oh, yes, that's right. But he's on the top floor. You should'a knocked three times. One for each floor, see.' She turned her head to the stairs, lifted up her voice, and sang, ' Mr. *Matt*-ers ! Mr. *Matt*-ers ! '

' What ho ? ' came Ernie's voice down the stairs.

' Gen'lman to see you.'

' See me ? ' He was limping, thumping, down the uncarpeted stairs, his head and eyes in advance of his shirt-sleeved body because he was eager to see who the visitor was.

' Gaw-crickey ! Mr. Dawb'ny ! Lummy, I almost saluted. This gentleman was my colonel in the Great War, ducks.'

' Well, I never ! ' said the woman.

' May I be allowed to come and see you, Mr. Matters ? '

' '*Course*, sir. Of course. Come up, if you don't mind us a bit untidy. And " *Mr.* Matters " ! And " May I be allowed ? " That's good, sir. *Sophie !* Mind that there tread : it's broken. *Sophie*, here's the colonel. Go slow, sir. She's not quite ready for kit inspection yet.'

They were winding up the stairs, Ernie first, then the father, and lastly the dog, confident of a welcome. They went up through a close smell of dust, dry sweat and staled, stagnant air ; and Father Dawbeny shut his lips tight and held his breath as he met a sour, urinary smell from a door on the first landing. On the second landing a broken window had been patched with a ragged square of packer's cardboard, and he swung his eyes from it. All such things offended his fastidious taste and hurt his eyes that craved beauty ; they had done so for eighteen years and always would ; sometimes they laid a headache across his brows ; but he went on through them.

' Here we are, sir. Come on, Sophie, turn out the guard. D'you remember how you once told me not to say " Turn out the guards " because the guards were a fine body of men ? '

' Yes, I'm afraid I made that joke more than once.'

Through the crack in the front-room door he could see that Sophie's idea of turning out the guard was to thrust everything unsightly beneath the bedspread or behind the cupboard door. Ernie led the way into the room.

' Now then, Sophie ! Jump to it ! Gran' Rounds. Spring to attention smartly now. Come along : for inspection port arms ! '

The only porting of arms she did was to pull down the sleeves which had been rolled up round her plump arms.

' Don't mind me, Mrs. Matters,' begged Father Dawbeny. ' I hope I haven't come at an inconvenient time.'

' No, sir. Pleased to see you, I'm sure.'

The room, fairly big, was obviously the whole of the Matters' home. A double bed filled part of it, and the stained and faded blue bedspread was now like a relief map of the Himalayas or the Andes, so many unpresentable things had Sophie hustled beneath it. A gas cooker stood on one side of the fireplace. On the mantelpiece were two cheap and gaudy vases such as Ernie might have won at a shooting booth on a bank holiday, and a row of birthday or Christmas cards bright with spangling frost and coloured plush. Above the mantel, between the wedding group and a portrait of Ernie in khaki, hung a large engraving which showed a guardian angel with hand out-stretched over a child near a precipice. But the most noticeable thing in the room was a footbath standing on a naked table and still breathing steam.

' I'm afraid we're not really fit to receive you, sir,' said Sophie,

27

' but I was doing a bit of washing.   But don't worry about that.
I done it all now.   I'm sure we're very pleased to see you.'

' The missus not only does our washing, but quite a tidy lot
for the ladies she obliges,' explained Ernie.   ' It's she earns the
money now.   I get nothing, I just loaf, that's all.'

' Oh, but it's not his fault, sir.   I'm sure it's not for want of
trying.   Would you sit here, sir.'   She pushed forward a chair.
' He kep' on trying for a long time.'

' I've almost given up trying now.   I help Sophie what I
can, but I'd like a regular job again some day, I must say.'

' Lie down, Squaller !   At *once* !   You don't mind the dog,
Mrs. Matters ? '

' *Mind* him ?   O' course not, the pet !   What kind of dog
is he ? '

' Ah, I wonder.   Nearer a mastiff than anything else.   But
let's leave that, in case he's sensitive about it.'

' And his name—what's his name ? '

' I just call him Squaller ;   first because he used to squall if
I left him alone, and secondly because it's a corruption of
Squalor.   There was a certain squalor in his habits as a
puppy.   At one time I thought of calling him Barrie.   Barrie,
because he makes short, sentimental tails.'

The joke was wasted—lost like the waters of the Tarim river
which dry up and sink in the sands of the Taklamakan desert.
Neither of them had ever heard of Sir James Barrie, the writer.
Discomfited, he promptly changed the subject.   ' I got your
Church Dues paper, Matters.'

' Yes . . . well . . . see . . .'   Ernie was a little embarrassed,
too, by the memory of this document.   ' I saw them papers
by the door and I thought for old times' sake . . .'

' But listen :   you're not to give me anything you can't afford.
These are bad times for us all.'

' Reckon we can afford a bob.   Tenny-rate, we'll afford it as
long as we can.'

' Does this mean you'd like to be members of my congregation ? '

' Yes,' answered Sophie, because Ernie seemed ashamed to
admit it.   ' We liked it.   We liked it ever so much.   I've always
had a feeling I'd like to go to church—my dad was chapel—
and Ernie was disposed to when he knew who you were.   Can
I make you a cup of tea, sir ?   Yes, a cup of tea.'

Father Dawbeny knew that the best courtesy was to accept. 'Thank you very much. I certainly will, if you'll have one with me, Mrs. Matters.'

'Well, yes, I don't mind if I do.'

'Law! "Mrs. Matters"! Call her Sophie,' protested Ernie. 'That is, if you don't mind.'

'I should be greatly privileged if I might. Thank you, Sophie.'

Ernie, seated on a chair, hands on knees, was staring at him. 'Fancy you sitting there, sir. I can't believe it. And fancy you having been in the Dale all these years. How long, sir?'

'Twelve years in the Dale, Ernie.'

'Ah, he's got round to calling me Ernie.' So Father Dawbeny had—with a great effort. 'You didn't do that in France, sir. No, it was "Jump to it, Private Matters! What the hell do you think you are?"'

'That was twenty odd years ago. What have you been doing all these years?'

'Mostly jobs in the catering line. I been a kitchen porter at one big hotel and a plateman at another, and I was a head barman for a time at the Roebuck, Kensal Green. But the best job I ever had was waiter at a big London club—you probably know it—it was full of swells—lords and things—the Royal Cavalry Club, Carlton Gardens. *Some* job that. I was a mutt to lose it. It was my last steady job, too. There's nothing for me now.'

'Oh, surely there is. Perhaps I can help you.'

'No, sir.' Ernie's lips set firmly; he was joking no more. 'Not for me. There's heaps of good lads, and they'll get anything that's going before I do.'

'But why do you say that?'

Ernie remained silent, lips set, eyes averted. The silence was awkward, and Father Dawbeny who had not in a dozen years enabled his love for the poor to conquer his shyness in their presence, dredged desperately for words. But it was Ernie who spoke—abruptly, almost angrily. 'I done for myself, see.'

'No, no . . .'

'Yes. That's what I said. Done for myself.'

Sophie, her hand on the kettle, put in her counsel. 'I should tell the minister, Ernie. He's different.'

'You can tell me anything.' Father Dawbeny managed to

produce his awkward but humorous smile. 'That's largely what I'm for.'

'Yes, and I think you ought to tell him, Ernie, if you're going to his church.'

'O.K., then. I got into trouble, and I mean : that finishes you.'

'You mean you——'

'Yes, I took some money at that club, and they pinned it on me all right, and I got my stretch.'

'A *stretch* ? A year for a first offence ! But that was stiff, wasn't it ? '

'That's right, but it wasn't a first offence. The old split had to cough up my previous cons—only two of them—but the beak called it a bad criminal record and sent me up the stairs. Committed me to Sessions, that is.'

'I know,' nodded Father Dawbeny, who was proud of understanding the esoteric language of his many thieves in the Dale.

'And there I got my stretch. That was six years ago. And I've never had a decent job since.'

'And he's never done anything wrong in that six years,' put in Mrs. Matters as she brought the cup of tea to her guest and handed him sugar and milk.

He sipped the tea. 'I appreciate immensely, Matters, that you should have told me all this.'

He did not like to ask what the previous convictions had been, but Ernie, now sure of a safe confidant, was as ready and eager to talk about his ' troubles ' as any man or woman about a recent illness. He'd begun by betting, he said ; a mug's game, because he'd lost money, run into a blooming minefield of debts and had to borrow from Harris and Bauer in the Montebello Road, ' at fivepence per month per pound, which, I don't mind telling you, mounts up.' He couldn't pay them, and in a desperate moment he'd pinched some of the silver plate at the hotel. He'd been bound over that time, but . . . well . . . ' there was a second time ; it was when Sophie's one and only kid was dying, and she had no job, and we couldn't get much tick, and oh, I felt mad and took a couple of pound notes at the Roebuck —it's as easy in a pub as drawing the beer—and for that I got a carpet. The last time—absolutely the last time—was when I got angry with the swells at the club, who seemed to have everything when Sophie was ill, and we could hardly pay our rent or keep up our insurance, and . . . well, there was the piles of money in the open cash-box and no one in the coffee-room to see . . .' Ernie sighed as he remembered it, and all that ensued. 'So there you are,' he added more cheerfully, getting up from his chair as a man might get up, by sheer will-power, from his despondency. 'There's nothing for me now, and, of course, it don't help being lame. But I'm not saying it's that. It's my own fault.'

Father Dawbeny felt that outgoing of love which nowadays always poured from him towards a sinner. 'Perhaps not wholly your fault.'

'Yes, I mucked things up for myself.' The sinner was now looking out of the window. 'I got myself in prison twice, and now nobody'll trust me any more. No one in the whole wide world.'

Silence; and Father Dawbeny gazing at Ernie while he pondered for a period. Then he spoke. 'How would you like to be a verger?'

'What?' Ernie swung round. 'Pardon?'

'It's simple. I'm offering you the job of verger at St. John's. I have only an honorary verger at the moment.' The father's thin smile widened, but some invincible reserve in him never allowed that smile to attain its full breadth. 'You'd have to clean the church plate, receive the wedding fees, and keep all the Sunday collection money in the safe till we can bank it. I'm offering you the job because I have perfect trust in you.'

CHAPTER FOUR

It was only to a few, only to those who wouldn't scoff, that Ernie told the story, but when he did so he always spoke of it as 'a blooming miracle.' He told them how the father in his sermon, the first sermon Ernie'd heard in twenty years, had said they could always ask God to do something for them if they always added 'but only if it's according to Thy will,' or some words like that; 'and so I done what he said,' Ernie would continue, half laughing at himself. 'I asked Him, before we got up and come away, to give me a steady job, but only if He thought best, and, Crikey! there was the father at the door two days after. It was a blooming miracle, say what you like.' When he said this to the father, the ex-colonel, ever embarrassed by praise, found himself resisting too much praise even for his God and muttering in deprecation, 'No, no; that's nothing, Matters. It's just that I happened to need help.'

Father Dawbeny had done more than make him his verger. He had made Sophie his housekeeper, and given them a bedroom and a kitchen among the upper rooms of the Church Hall. For neither job could he pay a large wage, but Ernie and Sophie were better off, and happier, in the Church Hall in Greig Street then they'd been for many years.

And one week-day, at seven in the morning, Ernie, proudly wearing the cassock of a verger, was in the vestry learning his duties. St. John's being but a small church, the vestry and sacristy were one. In the small square room, on a dais, stood a long, deep vestment-and-linen chest, furnished like an altar with crucifix, two candles and a large framed card of ' Prayers Before and After the Celebration of Mass '—*Orationes Ante et Post Celebrationem Missae* : Father Dawbeny loved the dignity of the Latin. From a corner a crowned and gilded statue of ' Mary the Mother of Jesus ' looked down upon the chairs, table, and hanging surplices. Every piece of furniture, from chest to chairs, was exactly in its right place and at its correct angle, as if in obedience to a drill-book. And every piece shone with polish as if on a king's parade.

Ernie's teacher was the tall, good-looking, self-conscious youth with the near-golden hair who'd boasted to them of having been a ceremoniarius in his time. Devoted to Father Dawbeny and Anglo-Catholicity, he had been acting for some months as honorary verger because the income of the church was now so small. It was only when listening to Ernie's unhappy record and observing his hopelessness that Father Dawbeny had suddenly decided to pay a verger's wage out of his own pocket.

Denys Flackman was this young man's name. He had been christened Dennis, but he always wrote the name ' Denys ' because it both looked more poetical like that and enabled him to declare that St. Denys of Paris was his patron saint, to whom he prayed. Ernie, sharp-eyed creature of the London pave-ments, had no difficulty in perceiving this young Mr. Flackman's pride in being the expert instructor with the greenhorn, the ' old boy ' with the ' new boy,' and his joy in confusing an ignoramus with incomprehensible terms and shocking him with his extreme catholicity. In the course of the instruction Ernie had some horrible and heating moments when he suspected that the fluent young man was considering himself better educated than and socially superior to him, Ernie—to him who was old enough to be his dad and had been in foreign parts and fought in the Great War, whereas this little apprentice at the gas-works, nineteen years old, had probably never been further afield than Brighton sea front with a gas-fitters' outing. That this lanky stripling with the flowery hair, who looked rather like a sunflower on a stalk—or a stick of celery—should try to come it over him ! One day he'd tell him where to get off—but not just now, not this morning, because he didn't want to offend the father. But Mr. Flackman had it coming to him. Gas-fitter ! Gaspipe was more like it. And one day Ernie'd turn the gas off at the source. Or, better still, close it down at the nozzle.

But when Mr. Flackman, who was going to serve at Mass, had draped his long figure in cassock and surplice, and tidied his gold-silk hair before the hanging mirror, he looked impressive, and Ernie was reminded, unpleasantly reminded, of the junior subalterns in the war from whom he'd have taken no sauce if he'd met them in civies, but from whom he had accepted a powerful deal of sauce when they wore the Sam Browne and single star of an officer.

'Now look, Matters,' said Mr. Flackman, standing before the vestment chest—and to hell with him for calling him 'Matters' like he was his boss—'you must lay out the vestments so that they come to the priest's hands in the right order—because, of course, he's saying the *Veni Creator* to himself. That means—look—first the chasuble, then the maniple, or fanon, as it's sometimes called—lay it like that so that he can kiss the cross on it—then the stole, then the girdle, then the alb, and then the amice—like this, so that he can kiss the cross.'

'I see,' said Ernie, hoping he did.

'Fine.' His teacher complimented him, just like he was a school kid. 'Well now, have you got the sacred vessels right? No—good Christopher, no !—you must put the purificator on the chalice, then the paten with an unbroken host, then the pall and veil—and, of course, the veil has to be of the right liturgical colour—then the burse, and make sure the corporal's in the burse. Got it?'

'I think so. First the goblet and plate——'

Mr. Flackman sighed. Most offensively. Like an escape of gas. 'The chalice and paten,' he corrected.

'All right. I see, chum. Then this thing, and this here, and this . . .?'

'Yes, and mind : don't forget the corporal.'

'No, it don't pay to forget the corporal,' said the old soldier, trying to make good in humour what he lacked in ecclesiastical scholarship.

There being nothing more to do till the celebrant arrived, Mr. Flackman sat down on a chair and fingered some faint golden fluff on his lip hopefully. Ernie sat, too, and rested his thick, coarse hands on his knees.

'How long'a you been verger?' he asked.

'*Honorary* verger,' Mr. Flackman hastened to correct him. 'I've been honorary verger ever since our real verger had to leave. I took the job on honorarily because the church hasn't really got the money to pay a full-time verger.'

'Hey, but then !' interrupted Ernie. 'Who's paying *me*?'

'Well, what do you think? The father, of course. Out of his own pocket.'

'Well . . . but . . .' Ernie demurred.

'Don't let that get you down. We should've had to have a proper verger, sooner or later . . . I think. . . . And your missus is acting as his housekeeper, isn't she ? '

'Yes. And *I* help with the housework too,' Ernie submitted, for his own peace rather than Mr. Flackman's.

'Well, that's fine. Fine for everybody. You knew the father long ago, he tells me ? '

'I'll say I did ! Before you were born.' One for his High and Mightiness there ! 'We were in the Great War together.'

'Oh, yes. I knew that he was a soldier in his unregenerate days. What was he like then ? '

'He was my colonel, and you could 'a knocked me down when I see him in the pulpit there.' And Ernie began to pour out some of the enthusiasm for the Colonel which he was wont to discharge over Sophie, but Mr. Flackman, more disposed to speak of his own enthusiasms, banked the flow with a 'Yes . . . yes. . . . You know his brother's an earl and his family has a castle up north, and a——'

'I knew it before you were born——'

'—and a big house in London. They got all the cash they need. I wish I'd as many pence as they've got pounds. And he's given it all up. There's nothing he mightn't have had. He could have had all the luxuries he wanted, and all the high society—yeah—and all the women . . .'

Ernie, who'd been biting a broken thumb-nail, looked up in surprise at that word ' women ', coming from that musing, white-robed figure in this quiet and dim religious place.

'Fancy giving up everything like that—everthing he could have had.' It was plain that Mr. Flackman was fascinated by the earldom and the big houses and the wealth. 'It's pretty wonderful. I don't think I could have done it. No, I don't think I could, but I should have liked to be able to. I should like to feel I'd done something like that. Thousands he's got rid of in a dozen years or so. Thousands.'

'But how ? What's he spent it on ? "

'Oh, on this church, which he's practically rebuilt and refurnished since he came—he's always buying beautiful things for it —and on his Costers' Club, as he calls it, in Becker Street—that's cost him a tidy penny—and on helping people. Yes, I don't mind telling you, Matters, there's no priest like him for a hundred

35

miles around. He's no great guns in the pulpit, as you've seen, but he's wonderful as a confessor, because he makes you feel he has no condemnation for you, whatever you've done, but only love. In fact, he's best with individuals. They say penitents come to him from all over the country ... Yes, I'd give something to be like him.'

This was said so obviously sincerely that for a moment Ernie's feeling for the young man turned right over, and he wondered if he wasn't going to like him. But unfortunately Mr. Flackman was soon demolishing this new liking beneath further avalanches of ostentation and instruction.

' Of course I don't approve of all he does. Take this matter of confession, for example. I hold it the one sure test whether you're a Catholic or not. In my view he should regard it as compulsory in anyone who's going to serve in a really Catholic church, but he won't hear of it.'

' Well, thank God for that.'

' You haven't a director, I imagine ? '

' A what ? '

' A director. A spiritual director.'

' Oh, yes, I have : Sophie.'

Mr. Flackman declined to be amused. ' Yes, he's a great man, and I'd do anything on God's earth for him, but I must say that in some ways I think he's timid.'

' Timid ! *Timid!* Caw ! ' All Ernie's power of scoffing was in that syllable. ' You should just'a seen him in France.'

' Oh, I'm not talking about his physical courage, my dear chap—' to hell with his ' my dear chap '—' I mean he's timid about putting on the full Catholic ceremonial. We've got the six points, but he won't go further.'

Ernie wondered what the six points were, and Mr. Flackman waited for him to ask. He did not ask.

' You know what the six points are, I suppose ? '

' Not sure that I do. No. Isn't it about time he come? It's twenty past seven.'

' They are incense, lights, vestments, mixed chalice, wafers, and eastward position.'

' I see,' said Ernie. ' I'll tell Sophie.'

' Well, there he sticks. The real trouble, of course, is that he likes everything to be beautiful, but if his ideas of what's beautiful are different from those of Catholic tradition, it's the Catholic rules that go overboard. Well, that's Private Judgment, isn't it ? '

' Sounds like it, Brother.'

' Yes ; it's not Catholic. It's just his own species of protestantism. I've told him so. What's your other name, Matters ? '

' Ernie. Yes, that's it . . . Flackman.'

' You know my other name ? '

' Dennis, isn't it ? '

' Yes, but for God's sake remember it's spelt D-e-n-y-s. Same as San Denee of France. He's my patron saint.'

' Who ? '

' San Denee.'

' Oh, I see. San Denee. O.K.'

' I don't know who your patron saint can be.'

' I'm not all that certain myself.'

Since neither knew this particular saint, there fell a moment's silence in the sacristy. The footsteps of the priest were not yet to be heard in the alley-way coming towards the vestry ; only the footsteps of women in the church coming towards the side-chapel. And only a few of these, and some very old, and coming very slowly.

So Denys considered how further to shock this new, ignorant, and patently protestant verger.

' Gee, I'm looking forward to next Thursday,' he said.

' Why, what's the matter with next Thursday ? '

' Don't you know ? It's August 15th.'

' What's funny about August 15th ? '

' It's the Assumption of the B.V.M. I shall go to All Saints, Margaret Street, where they do things properly. Father Dawbeny isn't doing anything particular about it. And it's a Primary Double of the First Class ! And naturally a Holy Day of Obligation—as of course is the Immaculate Conception of the B.V.M. I doubt very much if he believes in the Assumption *or* the Immaculate Conception of the B.V.M.'

' Shame ! ' declared Ernie. ' And do you ? '

' Naturally I do.'

' Go on ! There now ! And you go to confession, I suppose ? '

Denys's eyes shifted suddenly away. ' Of course I do.'

Ernie wondered.

'I used to go at first to Father Dawbeny, but now—now I think that on the whole it's better to go to someone far away. Most people think that.'

His eyes had remained apart from Ernie's, so that Ernie continued to wonder. 'Sez you!' he gibed.

And Denys became wordy. This doubt of Ernie's he wrapped about with layers of words. 'No. I do, *really*. You should have heard my old man and Mum when I first told them I was going. They're Plymouth Brethren—the strictest prots in the world—and were they horrified? But the father came round to see them, and in half an hour old Mum had fallen for him and was saying, "Well, I suppose the lad must do what he thinks best." And what do you think old Mrs. Bigland next door said? She said, "Don't worry, Mrs. Flackman, ducks. Mr. Dawbeny's ever such a nice gentleman, and he'd never let your boy confess to anything wrong." Ha, ha, ha. A scream, wasn't it? And little she knew! I thought I'd die at some of the things I'd have to confess. You see, I'm a hot-blooded chap—' and here Denys began to speak with some eagerness of the sins to which a hot-blooded chap was liable. The watchful-eyed Ernie, listening keenly, even raptly (the subject was interesting) discerned with some amusement that this pale and unripe young acolyte, sitting there in his holy robes, was as anxious to discuss the difficulties of a highly-sexed but religious chap as the distressing protestantism of Father Dawbeny; that he was as proud of his high sex as of his high churchmanship; and that he was as ready to shock him now with his sexual adventures as before with his extreme catholicity. Talking there with a strange mixture of penitence and pride, he had just worked his way into the story of an adventure in some shadowed street—a story in which, it must be allowed, Ernie was deeply interested—when a door of the church closed sharply, and the priest's footsteps approached. They were followed by the padding footsteps of his dog. Ernie, sharply disappointed, felt that he'd have to guide Denys to the end of this story at a later date.

'Good morning, Denys. Lie down, Squaller. Good morning, Matters.' Not for all the hidden love he bore him could Father Dawbeny maintain with ease the habit of calling him 'Ernie.' 'Denys' he could manage because the lad was only nineteen; and 'Sophie' because she was a fresh and smiling woman; but not 'Ernie.' Not to a man of forty. Not yet. And he was ashamed that his love should be so inarticulate, such a blunted instrument, so hampered by the habits of the past.

Denys rose at once to help him vest, to say the Preparation with him, and generally to impress the new pupil watching. He adjusted the alb on the priest's long figure, drawing it through the girdle to within an inch of the ground; he straightened the amice and chasuble ; and then knelt at the left side of the robed priest. Father Dawbeny mumbled, 'In the name of the Father...' and his server made a large and soulful sign of the cross, all over his brow and breast—large enough and slow enough to be seen by the watching protestant.

' I will go unto the altar of God,' said Father Dawbeny, holding the sacred vessels before his breast.

' Even unto the God of my joy and gladness,' responded the server.

' Give sentence with me, O God, and defend my cause against the ungodly people . . .'

Ernie watched server and priest passing out of the vestry into the side-chapel, and thought, as he stared at the priest's magnificent green and gold chasuble, patterned with an orphrey in the shape of a cross, ' My Christ ! And that's the Colonel ! What do you know, chaps ? What do you know ? '

And he fell to tidying up the sacristy.

CHAPTER FIVE

WITHIN a few weeks Ernie was well established as verger, sacristan, clerk, and cleaner ; and Sophie as housekeeper and cook to Father Dawbeny ; and all three of them were well content. Sophie had no more charring and washing to do, and Ernie was as pleased as a boy with his tasks about the church, though inclined to make fun of the cassock which he had to wear at times of Divine Service. Father Dawbeny was better served than he'd been for months, and happier in their manifest devotion than he could have told to any man.

Ernie, having fully learned his part, sometimes served the father at Mass, and he said his prayers and was secretly surprised that prayers could make one feel so peaceful and happy. Sophie likewise : she spoke no more of her inward thoughts than Ernie, but she was finding a simple happiness in following in the religious footsteps of her new master, and of her husband. Denys Flackman, having yielded up the post of honorary verger, came sometimes to serve, but—and this caused Ernie to ponder—at ever longer intervals. Ernie never heard the end of that backstreet story. The year turned, and it was 1939.

Such was the happy state under the roof of the Church Hall when, one Saturday morning, as the father sat at his table in the long upper room, typing his Weekly Paper—St. John's could no longer afford a parish magazine—Sophie peeped round the door and said, ' Mr. Custance to see you, sir.' Father Dawbeny immediately rose. ' Oh, come in, Custance.' And in came a young priest of short stature and round habit, with soft features and full chin to match his soft but well-protended paunch. He was of so round and smooth a figure that when the tall figure of Father Dawbeny, looking all the taller for his long cassock, stood opposite him and shook hands with him, you might think of the Crown jewels and imagine the sceptre shaking hands with the orb. Young ? Well, thirty-three, but he seemed young to Father Dawbeny who was now fifty-eight.

The Rev. Oliver Custance was the recently appointed vicar of a neighbouring parish, St. Luke's, Ledbitter, on the slope of Ledbitter Hill. A large church with a high and pompous Corinthian front, and the pure Low Church gospel preached within—the wags used to say it was as lofty as it was Low, just as St. John the Prior's was as low as it was High—St. Luke's had been popular and crowded in the days when comfortable people lived on Ledbitter Hill, and even now, though in the ever-increasing religious drought its congregation had drained to a mere puddle, it was better attended than St. John's on the flat land below. Oliver Custance had been appointed by the Bishop in the hope that a young energetic man would bring some of the life back into St. Luke's, though of course the days of its pride were gone for ever.

He was a bustling young man with a strong desire to do this, but less because he loved souls than because he wanted the bishop's approval and the consequent preferment. By bustling about he had added thirty or forty people to his congregation and a hundred and more to his electoral roll. It was much easier to get them on to paper than into the pews, but, after all, it was the paper and not the pews that bishop and archdeacon saw.

Now Father Dawbeny may have loved Ernie and Sophie with an inarticulate love, and felt a like love for all the rough costers in his club and all the abominable sinners in his streets, none of whom would come to church, but he could not love Oliver Custance. At least, not without a great Christian effort. He loved him in theory only (so he told himself) finding it extremely hard to do anything but dislike very heartily this plump and pushing young priest. In a secret closet of his mind his nickname for the man was ' Piggy ', and there were times when, the ex-colonel's lips being in command rather than the priest's conscience, those lips had muttered aloud to his bare walls, ' I can't stand the fat little pup.' And there was one time of great exasperation when the lips had been so frank as to denominate him a dirty little bastard. For which deplorable lapse he had given himself no absolution until he'd done a suitable penance.

Father Dawbeny told so little of his private thoughts that few realized that his eyes saw a very great deal. They were large, clear, greenish eyes under dark, meeting brows, and they saw most that was going on in the round head and under the brown, waved hair of Oliver Custance. He saw the ambition dressing itself up as service ; he saw the desire for numbers, not directed towards the glory of God but to the glory of Oliver Custance ; and he saw the jealousy of himself, Father Dawbeny—not indeed of his power to draw large numbers into his church, because that didn't exist—but of his considerable reputation in the streets outside the church. Custance could go nowhere without hearing mention of Father Dawbeny, who was an Earl's son and had given up everything to live like the poorest among the people of the Dale. Father Dawbeny saw that Custance was jealous of the Earl, of the family wealth—and of the sacrifice. He knew that Custance, even while pretending to agree with the praise of Father Dawbeny, contrived whenever possible to inject a dram or two of derogation.

Sometimes the young man's hypocrisy and self-assertion, which he supposed to be hidden but stood so clearly before Father Dawbeny, so chafed the ex-colonel that if that late officer with the stinging tongue were not to come alive again and speak words of power, the only possible compromise was to indulge in satirical comment behind a disarming smile. Feeling this unfortunate dislike of Custance, the father made his welcome this morning more than usually warm. ' Come in, my dear fellow,' he said ; and that was more than he could manage as a rule with those he loved. It was his dislike that enabled him to be demonstrative.

' I am not disturbing you, Dawbeny ? '

' Not a bit. You're welcome at any time. Sit down and take a cigarette.'

But damn him for calling him ' Dawbeny ' like that.

They sat in the two armchairs by the fireplace, Father Dawbeny first lighting the gas-fire which even at full pressure could hardly warm that large bare room on a March day. Privately the father was very severe with himself in the matter of warmth and cigarettes but this austerity was a matter between himself and God ; with a guest he shared his gas-fire and put him at ease by smoking a cigarette with him.

Custance glanced at the long, bare, littered table. ' Preparing your sermon for to-morrow ? '

' No. I have to start that on a Monday. If I didn't, I should be worrying all the week. I've been sixteen years in Orders, Custance, and still find preaching a worry.'

'Good gracious, do you?' Clearly Custance had—or wished to appear to have—a high confidence in himself as a preacher.

'Yes, I can never conquer a fear that my memory may fail in the pulpit, and my mind become paralysed, so I have to make copious notes and have them at hand. I'm still a slave to my notes though the people may not perceive it, because by Sunday I almost know the discourse by heart.'

'Indeed? I hardly ever use a note.'

'Well, you're a fortunate man,' said Father Dawbeny, and doubted whether he wasn't also a liar. 'I came so late to the business. A soldier's life is a pretty inarticulate one.'

'But didn't you have to talk to the men of your battalion?'

'No, only bark at them.'

'Are you getting a good congregation now?'

'Alas, no. Forty or fifty on a good day, and of course the children. We get less and less as the years pass. Sometimes it seems a losing battle.'

'Oh, I don't think so. I'm increasing my congregation.'

'Well, that's splendid. How many do you get?'

'Oh, two hundred or so in the morning, and rather more than a hundred at night.'

Father Dawbeny mentally knocked off thirty-three and a third per cent of these figures—with the possibility of a larger discount—and even then arrived at a figure much larger than his own. 'I call that good for these parts.'

'It looks few enough in a church built for fifteen hundred.'

'Never mind. You're going up.'

Custance could be generous when praised and instantly conceded, 'Yours is a more difficult parish than most.'

'Perhaps.'

'It's about one of your parishioners that I've come. Do you know an old fellow called Howden in Cremona Road?'

'Old Bert Howden and his case house? Gracious, yes!'

Custance was somewhat disconcerted. He had wanted to shock his brother priest with the words, 'You know he keeps a brothel,' but Dawbeny had fired this gun for him, and, so to say, in his face.

'You knew that his house was a brothel?'

'Certainly. I know him well. A very bad old man, of whom I'm rather fond. Unfortunately his isn't the only such establishment in Cremona Road. I always think Cremona Road is

43

typical of this part of London. It's an example, produced to extremes, of something we can find all round us.'

' How do you mean ? '

' Well, with its high, pretentious houses, it looks the only good street in my parish, and it's the worst. It's the widest road, and the lightest—and also the darkest.'

As he said this he saw the long, broad thoroughfare running right through the western end of his parish, down by the railway and the dead-ends. He saw the long terraces of high houses which flanked it ; sly, secretive terraces behind rank garden strips. He saw the few reticent shops at its corners, and the wide sky above it, which always seemed to make it so queerly and menacingly quiet. He knew that some of those houses, once the homes of the fairly well-to-do, were now common lodging houses charging eightpence a bed, and that others let off their furnished rooms at seven or eight shillings a night, and say half-price for ' short times ', and no questions asked. He saw the side streets on its west side which ran to the dead-end walls of the railway with the Communist slogans painted on them, and the side streets on its east side which, as he knew, had houses with ever-open doors and rooms available for two shillings a night. Some of these little side-street houses were as annexes to the main establishments, such as Mr. Howden's, in the main road. Chapels of Ease to the Mother Church. If there was a ' red lamp ' district in this part of West London, it was here, along and about Cremona Road.

' I can tell you quite a lot about old Bert Howden,' he went on. ' An impressive-looking old fellow with his distinguished grey locks. But he got three months some three years ago as a " rogue and a vagabond "—in other words, a pimp—and four months a little later for keeping a disorderly house. Probably he had other sorts of convictions in his early and less reputable days. His present mansion in Cremona Road was watched by the police for some time, and he walked very delicately, but I've no doubt he's up to his games again.'

' He certainly is. Are you aware that he's far more than a bawdy-house keeper ? He's a procurer.'

' Oh, *no* ! ' This time Custance had certainly achieved his desire and fired a gun that shook his host. ' We can't have that.'

' Yes, a procurer, and, what's more, a procurer of girls under age.'

'Custance, how can you know this?'

'I'll tell you. Yesterday evening I went into the church to take a churching, and I saw a woman kneeling in the nave. At first I thought it must be my parishioner waiting for me, and I went towards her. She heard me and lifted her head in a frightened way and sat up immediately as if ashamed. Then I saw she was a stranger and a much younger woman than the one I expected, and that she'd been sobbing bitterly. I tried to say something, but she cried out hysterically, "No, go away." I asked if I could help her in any way, but she just stared. Stared and stared and said nothing. I begged her to wait for me, but when I'd finished the churching in the chapel, I came out to look for her and she was no longer there. I imagined she'd fled but I found her lingering by the church door. She was now amenable and came back with me into the church. There she told me all. She poured out everything to me.'

'Yes?' Father Dawbeny saw that the young Custance was not a little proud of his triumph with this Magdalen, but it was no moment to think of Custance. Custance was not the important one now.

'She lives in Howden's house—officially as a lodger who has a small daily job in a café, but she's really there for Howden to bring the men to at night. She was terrified by some hell-and-damnation sermon at a Salvation Army street meeting, but she didn't go with her trouble into their Citadel because she was afraid of being recognized, so she wandered out of the Dale and into my church, not with the idea of telling anyone anything, unless it was God. However, as I say, she told me everything, everything. She told me, whether you believe it or not, that—if I may so put it—Howden's *spécialité de la maison* is girls under age. There's one there now. He first got her there as a "domestic help," but soon demoralized her so that he could get his friends to her and, in view of her age, charge them handsomely.'

'Do you believe it?'

'Why should she invent it? It was only incidentally that she told me. But you haven't heard all. The worst for you has yet to come.'

'And that is?'

'One of Mr. Howden's customers within the last weeks has been a server at your church.'

45

Father Dawbeny kept a silence behind tight lips ; then said, ' Evidence, please ? '

' Howden knew his young visitor by sight and name and made a fine jest of it among the women.'

' Do you mean that he came to the young girl ? '

' That I don't know. Maybe not. But he's definitely a customer of your Mr. Howden.'

' How did she come to tell you all this ? '

' She threw it at me when I mentioned coming to church—not angrily, but because she couldn't understand. I asked if she knew his name, and she told me.'

Instantly Father Dawbeny thought of the Church's unbreakable rule that no name of a third person must ever be asked or given in the confessional. But perhaps Custance hadn't thought of himself as a confessor in this case—so say nothing and spare him.

Custance, disappointed that Dawbeny did not ask for the name, presently gave it him. ' It was a lad called Flackman.'

It was the name Father Dawbeny had foreseen, because at one time he had heard Denys's confessions, but he said nothing in reply. He obeyed the rules and revealed nothing by word or look.

' What do you propose to do ? ' asked Custance.

Father Dawbeny gazed at him, frustrated. ' What can I do ? '

' Throw him out, I suppose.'

' Oh, no. Surely not that. That can't be the answer.'

' What ? Would you keep him serving at the altar ? My dear fellow '—even in this troubled moment Father Dawbeny felt a small and unworthy irritation that this young man, twenty-five years his junior, should call him ' my dear fellow '—' my dear chap, the boy must be a very unwholesome creature.'

' That may be. But what were we at that age ? '

' Not like him, I hope.'

' Are you so sure ? Our opportunities were brighter, so perhaps our sins looked less sordid.' He was not seeing his visitor now ; he was seeing a tall youth of twenty-two, not himself, but his son—his son by a married woman, born in the war years, and accepted by the mother's husband for the wife's sake and the child's—his bastard son, tall and dark and beautiful, whom he might see and speak to sometimes, but to whom he must never disclose his paternity. ' I think we were driven and confused, and not very strong. Were you not so ? '

' I was never the customer of a brothel.'

' Then you were better than I.'

' But do you mean that you'd go on letting him be a server ? '

' If he came and confessed to me I might impose a period of penance away from the altar. But at present I know nothing.'

' You know what I've told you.'

' I do not. I regard that as buried under the seal of the confessional.'

Custance felt a rebuke here, and he did not like rebukes. He stammered in the attempt to justify himself. ' I've told you what I've told you because the youth's doing you no good. No good at all. My book, *The Ceremonial of the Altar*, says quite clearly that servers should be such as are not likely to cause scandal to the faithful by evil conduct away from the altar. It says it quite clearly.'

' I prefer an older book.'

' Pfah ! . . .' Custance didn't like this answer, but was at a loss for a moment to rebut it.

And Father Dawbeny got up, walked around, halted before his visitor's chair, and smiled down on him that his words might not hurt. ' Isn't this old stuff, Custance ? " Why eateth your master with publicans and sinners ? And he answered, They that are whole need not a physician, but they that are sick." '

Despite Father Dawbeny's deliberate smile, the young Custance disliked this veiled suggestion that he was an inadequate exponent of Christianity, and he instantly capped Father Dawbeny's scripture with one of his own. ' I seem to remember St. Paul giving the Corinthians very emphatic instructions what to do in such a case.'

' I remember, too.'

' He said they were to deliver such a one to Satan.'

' He did.'

' Well——'

' He said all that. He said, If any man that is called a brother be a fornicator, with such a one do not eat. Put away from among yourselves that wicked person.'

' Well, how do you get over that ? '

'I suppose by refusing either to believe in it or to obey it.'

'Good God ! Good heavens, Dawbeny ! ' Custance was hot now, and stuttering. 'Do you set yourself above St. Paul ? '

'I set my Master above him, and if I have to choose between the two, I choose Him.'

'Then do I take it——' began Custance.

But Father Dawbeny interrupted, 'As I understand Him, He did not, like St. Paul, turn towards the sinner with punishment, but towards God with reparation and atonement.'

'Then I do take it that you don't consider the whole of the Bible as the inspired word of God ? '

'Custance, doesn't St. Paul himself in one place hint that in some of his statements he may not " have the spirit " ? '

'All right. Leave St. Paul out of it. What about our Lord taking a whip to the people who profaned the temple ? '

'Oh, that whip ! ' Father Dawbeny stamped a foot beneath his cassock. Now he, too, was hot, and feeling the hot words flaming up in him. 'What a relief that wretched whip is to some of you who feel a blood-lust to punish ! I tell you I can forgive a layman who cries out that we should be tough with our criminals and use the cat on this man and that boy, but in a minister of Christ it is a treachery. And they abound, such ministers ; they abound, they abound. I can only hope that the Christ I worship was mis-reported on that occasion, and on other occasions when His words seem too harsh for me——'

'Good *God*, Dawbeny ! '

'The Christ I follow is the one Who said we were to forgive our brother till seventy times seven, and to cast no stones till we are stainless ourselves, which is never ; that is the only one I can worship because it is the only one I can admire. You cannot worship unless you admire.'

'But, in heaven's name, what are you saying ? Where do we stop if we reject everything in the Bible that we don't like ? ' Custance, angry at being disagreed with, furious at being disapproved of—' blood lust to punish ! ' 'Treachery ! '—was digging in his brain for further supports to his argument. 'How about " No whoremonger hath any inheritance in the Kingdom of Christ " ? Eh ? '

'True enough ; but shall we help him back towards his inheritance by kicking him out ? '

'You don't believe in excommunication then ? '

' Certainly not. Nor in anathema either. Nor in the Com-mination Service.'

' Oh, well, if you're a law unto yourself, we know where we are.'

' My dear fool—forgive me—in religion every man is alone and a law unto himself.'

' I don't agree. I don't agree at all. Nor would most of my friends.'

' All right. Keep your own view. No doubt but that ye are the people and Wisdom shall die with you.'

' Of course, if you're going to be offensive——'

' My way, as I see it, will quite possibly keep him ; yours will as certainly drive him away.'

' Well, I think that all you say is very sentimental.'

Father Dawbeny was just about to exclaim, ' The devil you do ! ' but he got control of his tongue, and he answered instead, ' Yes.'

Just ' Yes ' ; a crisp plea of ' Guilty.'

Custance, impatient of any more, rose too, and stood facing him. The dog, who had been lying with his great frowning face between his paws, watching, caught the infection of the quarrel and got up to join in. He barked and barked. Custance tossed an irritated head at the noise and, his vocabulary disordered by anger, could only say again what he'd just said, and say it more violently.

' To say there can be no excommunication, or no stern punishment, seems to me spineless sentimentality.'

' It does, does it ? Well, I congratulate you on finding a new adjective. The usual one is " maudlin sentimentality " or " sloppy sentimentality "—Get out of it, Squaller ! Keep out of this. Or " woolly sentimentality ".' The control was slipping ; the heat rising. He felt the warmth on his cheeks and guessed that his usually sallow face was now the colour of copper. ' I know that lad. I know him as you don't. I know that he is a mess, as I was at his age, and as you were not. I know that he is a hypocrite at times, but I don't think he wants to be. So when he comes to me to serve I shall presume that at that moment he is penitent, and I shall bring forth the best robe and put it on him.'

An extraordinary thing about Father Dawbeny, which he often observed in himself, was that, whereas his love was inarticulate, his anger and hate, when they possessed him, could be quite remarkably eloquent. When the fire kindled he spake with his tongue, and with power.

' To me,' said Custance, still justifying himself, ' all such nasty little hotch-potches of vice and piety are peculiarly revolting types.'

' And to me there's a glory round about them.'

' A *glory* ? '

' Yes, a glory, because the God of all the universe invests them with His love.'

Wild words, uttered in anger by a combative man, but, even as he spoke them, he saw that they were words of vision, too. And he was pleased with them.

Custance, obviously beaten on this ground, and therefore angry, hastened quickly back to a safer terrain. ' I don't understand you. You call yourself a Catholic, and you pick and choose what you believe——'

' I don't know what I call myself. I only know that such vision as I have learned from my Master tells me that the worse a sinner is, the more I walk with him.'

Custance had no immediate answer, and Father Dawbeny, now striding up and down, had the floor to himself—except in so far as the dog had it and barked. ' Christ's vision, unless I'm all wrong, was that we've got to rise above all cheap and easy vindictiveness, all censorious eagerness to punish, because angry punishment never did anything to heal a sinner yet, and all so-called " righteous indignation ", because it's inevitably *self*-righteous. Can't you see it ? Can't you *begin* to see it ? Can't you see that what He gave His life to teach us is that we must be done with the old self-righteous instinct to say " Get out ! I want nothing more to do with you ", and eager instead to say, " Come. I, too, am a sinner ". No, of course you can't. How many clergy can ? The bishops are always the first to advocate indignant and rigorous punishment. Get out of it, Squaller ; and stop that filthy row. " Condign punishment " I think they call it. And they're blind. Blind to the vision.'

So he might say, but his next words were to be a betrayal of the vision, and he could see this, but couldn't stay them. ' Excommunicate ! Excommunicate, ha ! The only people *I'd* like to excommunicate are all the professional priests who set up as interpreters of Christ and are blind or indifferent to His vision ;

and that means about seventy per cent. of the clergy of my church and ninety per cent. of the Church of Rome. They are far worse enemies of the Church than a few erring boys, because they obscure the vision.'

Every word was a betrayal, and he knew it ; every word was the opposite of all that he was advocating because every word was a savage and punishing lash across the face of Custance. He stopped in his words, and in his tracks, and stood still, hands and knees slightly trembling.

And Custance made it quite clear that he knew he'd been lashed. His face was as white as Father Dawbeny's was copper-coloured, and the father knew that he had made an enemy of a young man who would never forgive this description of him as a ' professional priest', doing more harm to the Church than good. His sullenness would be the greater because he would know in the depths of his heart that the description was true.

' Oh, well,' he said, moving towards the door, ' it's for you to do what you like in your own parish.'

' On that point at least we are agreed.' Father Dawbeny stood perfectly erect as he said this, and perfectly still. His will had mastered that momentary trembling and bound it hand and foot. ' Thank you.'

' I've said what I came to say, and there's no need to continue this.'

' None whatever. Again agreement.'

' All right. I'll be going.'

' If you wish to. I wouldn't want to detain you from your work.'

' Worthless work, it seems ; or worse than worthless. Well, never mind. Good morning, then, Mr. Dawbeny.'

' Good morning, sir.'

He watched the young priest go. Shame and penitence, surging up in him, insisted that he should call him back and apologize ; but the devils of pride and anger held his limbs and his lips, so that he could not move or speak.

§

Nothing for it now but mortification. He knew—all the vision in him which he believed to come from God told him that the only way to the life he sought was through mortification. And three hours of mortification there were in that upper room : spiritual mortification only, but violent, very violent. Pride was a demon that fought and spat and would not die —*did* not die in fact, though he battered it to the ground and held it to the ground as he shaped in his mind a letter of apology to the young man. ' You've got to do it, Piers. Piers Lygon Dawbeny, you've *got* to do it. So jump to it. Now ! At once. You've got to write to the dirty little bastard—to your brother, I mean.' And he wrote. He wrote with one foot, as it were, pressing down on the still active demon. He forced his pen to apologize for his ' ill-temper this morning and his really intolerable discourtesy,' and to offer his young brother his friendship at all times, and his co-operation. As he wrote those words ' friendship ' and ' co-operation ' the demon died, and he was happy, immensely happy, to sign the letter, ' Your affectionate brother in our Blessed Lord.'

The answer did not come quickly ; and he waited for it anxiously, looking for it first in every handful of letters that Ernie or Sophie brought in to him. And when at last he saw it he opened it before all others. And he read : ' Dear Mr. Dawbeny, In our conversation last Saturday morning you gave me to understand that my ministry was an injury to the Church to which I have devoted my life. Since that is your view, I do not see how you can wish to co-operate with me in such work or that there is anything to be gained by continuing this correspondence. Believe me, Yours truly, Oliver Custance.'

CHAPTER SIX

MONDAY morning, and early. Father Dawbeny, having medi-
tated on Custance's story all through Sunday, now directed his
steps towards Cremona Road and the home of Mr. Howden.
He wore neither cassock nor clerical collar, for he would not
embarrass so great a sinner as Mr. Howden and bring down
laughter upon him. The March day was mild, and he wore
a grey flannel suit with brown shoes ; and the shoes fitted as
well to his feet as the well-shaped suit to his tall figure, for
they, too, had been made to measure.

The dog padded after him, or in front of him, or stayed to
consider an item in the gutter or the contribution of one of
his predecessors to the base of a lamp-post.

To reach Cremona Road he had to pass through a large
part of the Dale. First, Greig Street, his own street, that long,
low uniform road where only the gable of his church and the
cornice of his Church Hall broke the skyline. At this hour
many women were on their thresholds, cleaning the steps or
standing in talk. Some were young women, some middle-
aged, some old ; some, usually the younger, wore coloured
overalls with scarves about their heads ; others, usually the
older, and for no reason that he'd ever understood, wore their
husbands' old grey caps ; but whether young or old, they had
all, now that they were securely married and housed, abandoned
the effort to be beautiful. Their faces were mottled or pale
and drawn, their hair wispy, their stockings awry. He did not
pass one who came to church, but all greeted him with smiles
and ' Good morning, Father.' Some children, off to school,
did not hesitate to join him and walk or skip or dance at his
side. At the far corner of Greig Street he raised his hand in
greeting to old Mr. Jim Fowler, who stood in his yard among
the stacked or parked barrows that he hired out (at an average
of sixpence a day) for costermonger stands in Becker Street
and Brickmaker Street.

Here he turned into Cartwright Street, a road of small shops, none of which had graduated from old-time glazing bars to plate-glass. Some were in such a small way of business that their names and trades were home-painted on their fascia boards. Many, as he passed their doors, smelt of the dust and grime within. Always, walking along this street and looking up at those names and trades, he thought how well they reflected the struggling lives and small, striving joys of the people in the Dale : Wardrobe Dealer . . . Second-hand Furniture Mart . . . Meat Pies . . . Ferdie's Fish Bar . . . Lemans Buy Second-hand Jewellery . . . Turner's Herbal Remedies. . . . Our Pets . . . Rag and Bottle Merchant . . . Jenkyn's Twopenny Library . . . Delicatessen Stores. And at every second corner a public-house, large or small.

Out of this long, grey, dusty bazaar he turned into a brief street of three-storied houses ; it was the latter end of Morrow Street. No shops, and little movement here ; no women on the steps or children going to school ; all the stucco houses, blackened by the town's stale breath, wore a grey-black mantle like a sub-fusc suit, and seemed mute as eye-witnesses to a felony who will say nothing to the police. A drab and rather sinister end to Morrow Street, and so a fitting approach to Cremona Road.

And here was Cremona Road : broad highway beneath broad span of sky. Here were its terraces slyly withdrawn behind their narrow gardens : terraces of tall, ornamented houses whose creators (like other parents) had expected better things of them ; and how dismally they had failed these aspirations ! Their large windows and ornamental architraves stressed the aspirations ; their stucco fronts, mapped with cracks, flakes, rents, and heavy falls, stressed the failure. Not all were like this ; one or two had been lately re-painted, and the old aspiration was temporarily alive and shining again. But others were worse than this : their façades so disfigured with cracks and sores, so chipped and peeled and chunked away, that they reminded him of the old paper-seller in the station entry, most of whose features a disease had eaten.

But because of its width of sky it was brighter than the other streets—brighter to the eye, that is ; what to some other and nameless sense ? Father Dawbeny never knew whether his apprehension of lurking evil in certain places was induced by stories he'd heard about them, or whether evil was a real thing, an actual and positive thing, apprehensible in the air. Well, whatever it might be, here before him was Cremona Road, stretching away to the north, and through other men's parishes; becoming respectable as it climbed slowly out of the Dale; and keeping its shadowed reputation mainly in that sector which was under his pastoral care.

On his left the truncated side-streets ran to the dead-end walls of the railway, most of which, though they oozed a green sweat on this low-lying ground, had been turned by the Communists into huge blackboards for the display of their symbols and slogans. Hammer and sickle, chalked or white-washed on the grey-green walls, stood at the end of each street, and the whitewash ran down the bricks like white blood from a sore.

No. 9, Lamplough Terrace: that was Mr. Howden's home. And Lamplough Terrace was the third of these long, ulcerous rows. Father Dawbeny turned on to its private pavement between its deep areas and its strips of railed garden. Sparrows, who neighbour all men, no matter how evil, cheeped in gutter and garden. True sons of God, they made their song to shine on the just and the unjust.

No. 9. There was surely nothing wrong about the cipher 9, but here it seemed dubious, ominous, as unholy as 7 and 3 were sacred. And yet the house was cleaner and less cracked than any near it. Apparently Mr. Howden and his trade were prospering. Going up its ten steps, Father Dawbeny thought with a grim smile that, just as his little building in Greig Street was a temple of the hungry spirit, so this high, ugly house was a temple of the hungry body. And Father Howden the pastor of his flock.

The door was open and he could see into the entrance hall. It was less narrow and loftier than most he looked into, but —was evil a thing in the eye of the beholder, or was it really there?

No knocker on the door; so the visitor relied on his knuckle. Tappity-tap. It was enough: it brought a large face and a head of magnificent grey hair round the side-post of a door on the left; and Mr. Howden came forth. Old Bert Howden was a corpulent man, rather too short for his large head and large features. The abundant grey hair, reaching almost to his collar, gave him the appearance of a famous platform musician or celebrated philosopher : had you been dim-sighted you would have thought him venerable. But if clear-sighted you saw the blood-veined, peering, suspicious, hole-and-corner eyes, the buttoned-up lips, the ill-shaved grey stubble beneath them, and ceased to venerate. His eyes were brown, but had the quality of seeming red ; each in its moist setting looked like a pale red sun in a November mist. Some women, however, seemed able to venerate him. He must have been nearly sixty, but within the last two years the West London magistrate, Henry Fisher, had made two affiliation orders against him, and would describe him to Father Dawbeny as ' your local Don Juan.'

He came forth in a good blue suit—or, rather, in the trousers and waistcoat of a good blue suit. The waistcoat, open, showed that the trousers stayed in place only by constricting the globe of his stomach. Evidently he had not long been up and about. It was not yet ten o'clock, and perhaps business at his counter had been brisk during the night.

The red and rheumy eyes peered suspiciously at the figure in his doorway ; recognized it ; and at once put on a bright light of welcome—which did not, however, hide the suspicion. ' It's you, Father ! Haven't seen you for ages. Given me up as a bad job ? '

' No, no,' said the father, since it seemed the best thing to say.

' No, never lose heart. But I'm afraid I don't get to church much. You see, I——'

' Could I come in ? '

' It was me you wanted to see, was it ? ' he inquired, staring at the caller ; and for a moment Father Dawbeny wondered if the old pimp supposed he'd come to negotiate with one of his ladies.

' Yes, Mr. Howden.' So bad was old Bert Howden, so full must his heart be of guilt, that one must not hurt him by omitting the ' Mister.' Obviously the worse the sinner, the greater the courtesy.

' Why, come in ! . . . Yes, of course . . .' This after a few seconds of hesitation. ' Always pleased to see you, Father.' If ever words sounded like a courteous lie these did.

' And the dog ? Do you mind him ? '

' '*Course* not. I love dogs. Come on, doggie. I love all animals. Mrs. Howden's out. You know : shopping : Monday morning. Come in here.'

Father Dawbeny surmised that Mrs. Howden was not strictly Mrs. Howden. There had been three Mrs. Howdens during his twelve years in the Dale, and each, he would say, had been more like a golden and full-blown rose than the last.

As he went in he glanced up the stairs ; then set his lips and suppressed all thought—lest he partook of other men's sins.

' Not as tidy as it might be, perhaps, Father, but you know how it is in the morning.'

The large, lofty room was furnished as a dining-room with some fine pieces, but it was spoiled by two high screens, which Mr. Howden hastened to close around a double bed. Presumably Mr. and Mrs. Howden lived and slept here, so that all the other rooms in the house could be earning good money. A good husbandman likes to see every inch of his small plot of earth working hard in rain and sun. This husbandman now whipped some feminine garments off a chair and thrust them behind the screens ; and his visitor grinned inwardly : here was Howden pushing other things—like his sins—behind the screens.

' Well now, Mr. Howden——'

' Sit down, sir, and come off the " Mister." It makes me feel old. All my pals call me Bert. *You* call me Bert.'

Father Dawbeny felt a strong recoil from calling him Bert : he tried to, but couldn't. His love was not equal to it.

' Well, now, this is what I wanted to——'

' Yes, I was named after Albert Edward, Prince of Wales— I mean Edward the Seventh. That dates me, doesn't it ? I was born in 1881.'

' Then you're the same age as I am.'

' You don't say ! ' It was clear that he imagined he looked younger than this parson, even as Father Dawbeny was hoping that he, with his dark hair and slender figure, looked younger than this grey and rheumy old man. Both men were disappointed. ' Yes, I'm fifty-eight, Father. I don't lie about it.'

' I'm fifty-eight, too.'

' Yes, well—and how's trade with you, Father ? Going strong ? '

' I'm afraid not. Not in these times.'

' You surprise me. Everyone I meet says you're Absolutely It—and then they don't go to church ? Is that it ? "

' The second part of that statement is exactly it.'

' Well, fancy ! I'm not much of a church-goer myself, but the way they talk, you'd think—— Of course, if I went any-where it'd be to your church. Sometimes I've thought of coming along. Not that I hold with all you get up to there, incense and all. You won't mind my saying that, will you, Father ? I've always been a good Protestant. And one should be honest about one's religion, shouldn't one ? "

' Undoubtedly. I want to be honest with you now——'

' I say, Father, just do tell me one thing. Is it true what Joe Palmer says, that on Palm Sundays you have a procession and go round the church on a donkey ? He swears you do.'

' That's a very old yarn, Mr. Howden, and the answer's simple : there's never been a donkey at any service of mine—unless it was when your informant attended.'

' Don't think I was suggesting it was wrong ! Not at all. I was just interested. Church matters interest me. I mean, why shouldn't you ? Palm Sunday's Palm Sunday, the day our Blest Redeemer entered Jerusalem.'

' Perhaps it wouldn't be wrong, but I think it would be exceedingly inconvenient, and even, unless things went well, a little insanitary.'

' Yes, I see that. Yes, of course there's *that*. Still, it was the day our Blest Redeemer entered Jerusalem. I know my Bible, you see. I went to Sunday school when I was a nipper.'

His suspicious, watching eyes and his shifting in his chair showed that all this talk was a temporary diversion, a little smoke screen behind which he could assemble forces to defend a position which was certainly weak.

Father Dawbeny did not want to be diverted. ' Mr. Howden, this is what I wanted to see you about——'

' He's a nice dog, that. What make would you call him ? Something between a bulldog and a bloodhound ? I wonder you don't lose him, the number of dog-stealers there are around here. There's a regular trade in it. Shocking, I call it. I mean, people love their dogs, and sometimes a tyke is the only pal a poor man's got. It's cruel to steal it from him. And it's cruel to the dog, too, come to that. I don't hold with cruelty, I never did. Least of all to poor dumb animals——'

' Mr. Howden——'

' Good doggie, come here—here's a morsel for you—see, he

comes to his old Uncle Bert all right. I always find that dogs like me.'

' Mr. Howden, I want to come to the point. I've been told something about you which——'

' About *me* ? ' Mr. Howden's eyes looked up from the dog's ears : there was resentment in them, and instant repudiation. He did not realize that in putting these righteous expressions there, he showed his certainty that anything said about him would necessarily be bad. ' Oh, no ! '

' Yes. And if it's true, it's very, very serious.'

' Who's been saying things about me ? ' His lips set in great indignation, such indignation that he forgot to be respectful. ' Come on ! Who ? '

' We know, Mr. Howden, that you've had two terms of imprisonment for keeping a disorderly house.'

' No, only one. Just one for that.'

' I was letting you down lightly, putting it like that. The other term was for living wholly or in part on the earnings of prostitution.'

' That's what they called it, yes. Such nonsense.'

' That's what it was.'

' Oh, no, sir. No, Father. I don't admit it. One can't always know what women are up to, can one ? And in any case it seems to me that their lives are their own, to do what they like with. I'm not an interferer. Live and let live, I say.'

' Mr. Howden, what's the good of these pretences ? Parsons aren't fools.'

' Oh, I never said that ! Never ! That's putting words into my mouth. I like parsons as a rule.'

' You did exactly what the police said, and you know it.'

' Well . . . it was a long time ago. And I paid for it. I paid my bill. I don't think I've such a bad record. I'm fifty-one, and only been in prison twice.'

' You were fifty-eight a few minutes ago.'

' Yes—what did I say—fifty-one ? Fifty-eight, that's right. Born in 1881. It's the " ones " that got me mixed up. I remember the old lady's jubilee. My mum and dad took me to the first and held me up to see it. Just by High Park Corner.'

' Didn't you have some earlier convictions in your youth ? And haven't you a real good file at the Yard ? '

59

'Yes, but—just *think*—that's yurs and *yurs* ago.   No point in bringing that up.   The second jubilee in 1887——'

'Let's leave 1887 for the present and concentrate on 1939.'

'O.K., Father.'

'It's come to my notice that you're using this house in the old way.'

'Who told you that?'   His eyes said sadly, How humans can lie.   'The nosey-Parkers around here!   Who's been blackening——'

'You can't expect me to give you names.   And it's no good pretending to be injured.   Seven or eight rooms of this house are used for the purposes of prostitution.'

'If that's so I must look into it.   Yes : I suppose I must. But I don't like interfering.   What I mean is, Father, we're men of the world, and women are women—especially in these parts.   I've got some lady lodgers here, I admit ; but they're no chickens, and I reckon they're old enough to look after themselves.   I don't go out of my way to make trouble.   I'm a peace-loving man.   One wants a little peace at my age. And I believe in liberty. '

'Never mind your permanent ladies.   I'm thinking of those who lodge with you for one night only.'

'Well . . . yes . . . there are some like that . . . Certainly . . . sometimes . . . but I don't care to ask questions.'

'They don't come unaccompanied?'

'Maybe not.'

'Give up pretending to innocence, Mr. Howden.   You know that you're breaking the law, and the police could——'

'Come to that, you break it, too, if all they say is true.   Incense and all ; and I don't get at you, though I don't really approve.'

'All right.   I'm ready to take my chance of going to prison. Are you?   Are you prepared for me to tell the police what I know?   You with that file?'

'You'd never do that !   You're no copper's snout.   I can't see you coming the copper on any one.   I remember a story about you, Father ; a good story.   I remember how young Stan Archer, old Walter's kiddy, maced some blouses off a stall in Becker Street, and a cop saw him, and he ran away and dashed into your Church Hall.   He'd been one of your servers once, I think.   Server !   He served himself all right that time.

And look, Mr. Dawbeny, what did you do when he told you a copper was streaking after him?'

'Well, what?'

'You let him out of the back door. Of course you did. And shut the front door. And when the cop comes hammering at the front door and you open it, he says, " I'm sorry, Father, but we've traced a dirty young sneak-thief to your house, and would you tell us where he's gone and help us find him?" And what did you answer, eh?'

'I really forget.'

'The Dale hasn't forgotten. They talk about it still. You said, " Officer, I've got to preach a sermon to-morrow, and I've got a Mothers' Meeting this afternoon, so if you'll write my sermon for me and take the mothers, I'll do *your* work for you." That was the real *you*, Father. It was the act of a gentleman who knows what life can be like for the poor. But strictly it was —I looked the matter up—it was compounding a felony. That's what it was : compounding a felony. No, you're no copper's nark. *Noh.*' He shook his head, so confident was he of this.

'I'm not compounding any felony of yours, Mr. Howden.'

'Felony?' The sad, bloodshot eyes said that this was no word to apply to such as he. 'What if the poor girls do come for—for what you think? I can't see that it's a felony if I sometimes shut my eyes. Lord Nelson did. The poor girls have got to live, and, you see, you and I have different ideas of what they're entitled to do with their lives. There's nothing wrong in having one's own views. I respect yours, even if I don't agree with them. They'd starve, these poor girls, if there weren't understanding places like mine. D'you ever think of that? Starve! You've got a heart, you know, and so have I. They haven't got nice flats up west and, generally speaking, their landladies, who haven't got a heart between them, won't let them bring a gentleman in.'

'The felony I'm speaking of is far more serious than that.'

'What d'you mean?'

'At least one of the girls in your house, so far from being " no chicken," is under age.'

'There's no one in this house under age.'

'She was under age when she first came——'

'As a domestic help,' corrected Mr. Howden. 'As a domestic help.' He said it as one begging his accuser to be reasonable.

61

But Father Dawbeny was not going to be reasonable. 'She was under age when she was first sold by you.'

'Sold! I don't know what you mean. Sold! I like that! She came as a domestic help. One can have domestic help, can't one? A large house, this. And in any case I took her to be eighteen.'

'You know, then, to whom I'm referring?'

The suspicious eyes watched to see if he'd said anything unwise. They waited while brainwork went on behind them. 'Of course I do,' he allowed at length. 'Florrie. Little Florrie Garside.'

'Well, Mr. Howden, we're not having this. Just hear what I have come to say. Either you hand this girl over to me and I will look after her, or the police will come and fetch her— and you, too.'

The blood rushed up and discoloured, mottled, Mr. Howden's putty-soft cheeks. Rage glowed in his eyes. The rage seemed hot enough to dry up their moisture. 'I'm doing nothing, and I'm not yielding to threats. I'm not that sort. I've done nothing wrong. What the girl's done is *her* business. Besides— Christ!—you said you were not a fool; I'm not either. Even if I'd done anything wrong you couldn't prove it. Not that I have—I don't admit that I have.'

'I shall prove everything.'

'How?'

'I shall persuade the girl to give evidence.'

'Come off it! Come away. Try another. What corroboration would she have—I mean, if she wanted to lie? I know the law, I do. No one can be convicted of—of what you're suggesting—on the evidence of one witness. What corroboration could she get?'

'Plenty. Counsel, whom we shall employ, will extract convincing corroboration from her, and the police will get plenty from your neighbours on either side and across the road. All the respectable ones will tell all they've seen from their windows; they're usually only too ready to. And, finally, I shall be the corroboration. I shall tell everything that you've said to me. I know the law, too, and I know that anything you've said can be used in evidence.'

'Such as what? What've I said?'

'That you took her to be eighteen. That's a commonplace

give-away. And that what she's done is her business. And that you sometimes shut your eyes. And so on. Plenty more.'

' You'd tell all that to the cops ? '

' Most assuredly. In this case I am happy to be a copper's nark.'

' God ! To think that of *you* ! And what if I bring evidence to show that she needed no procuring at all ? That'd settle it. That'd settle all you could do. No, I'm not taking any threats from you. I never procured no one. You go and do your damned worst. I'll take my chance.'

' You mean you give up your last chance of keeping out of prison. It won't be four months this time, but two years or more. If the girl was between thirteen and sixteen you can get two years, and if we can find evidence of other girls—and we'll search the earth for it—you can get two years for each of them. We'll mount up a sentence for you of four, six, eight years.'

' You will, will you ? Go and do it. I'm doing just nothing.' Mr. Howden's fury had got the better of his wisdom. He had risen and was storming about the room. ' I knew nothing about the girl—not her age, nor nothing. I'll get a good mouthpiece who'll chew up anything the cops and you can put up against me. I can afford it, I don't mind telling you. There's not much that girl didn't know when she came here. If you ask me, she was ready for anything.'

' I'm remembering all those words, Mr. Howden,' said Father Dawbeny, walking from the room towards the front door, while the raging but worrying Mr. Howden followed him, and the dog, glad that the interview was at an end, ran ahead of them. ' And I suspect they'll be more than enough to hang you.'

§

He went straight home, at a quick step, to the Church Hall and his upper room. He shut the door on himself. He lifted the telephone receiver and dialled a number. Promptly, quietly, a voice answered him : ' Ledbitter 1113, Police Station, Lutine Street.'

' Could I speak to Detective-Inspector Morrison ? '

' He's gone, sir. He's D.D.I. now at King Street.'

'Is he? Good for him! Well, could I speak to his successor?'

'Inspector Glower? Yes, sir.' *Click*, and another voice, 'Hello?'

'Could I speak to Detective-Inspector Glower?'

'Speaking.'

'My name is the Rev. Piers Dawbeny, and I'm the vicar of St. John the Prior's. I used to know your predecessor well. A good friend of mine.'

'Oh, yes sir. And we know of you.' It was a good, Scotch voice.

'Nothing against me, I hope?'

'Oh, no, sir; thank you very much. Nothing as yet.'

'Nothing as yet? Well, that's comforting. Inspector, there's something I'd very much like to report to you.'

'Is it something you can tell me over the phone?'

'Hardly . . . No, I'm afraid not. Should I come round and see you?'

'Well, I'm a bit busy this morning. We're hot on the track of a shop-breaking gang and hope to have them in at any time now. Old clients of ours. Could I come and see you this evening? Will the matter wait?'

'Oh yes. It'll keep.'

'Then this evening about six . . .'

And at six that evening the new Detective-Inspector came up the stairs of the Church Hall, led to the padre by Ernie, who was much interested and impressed by this caller. Ernie showed him into the father's room. 'Inspector Glower, Father.'

'Thank you, Ernie. Shut the door. Come in, Inspector.'

Father Dawbeny, rising to welcome him, was surprised by the slightness of his frame and the mildness of his face. 'Glower'—never was a man less well named. There was no natural glowering in this man's kindly face. With his dark thick hair, his hollows under the cheek-bones, and his gentle, contemplative, almost pious eyes, he might have been a new youthful elder of a Scotch church, instead of an elder at the police station. A Scotch church, because his enunciation had the clearness and measured beauty of Scotch speech, every vowel differentiated and every consonant sounded. 'Glower'—when you could see that, as a rule, he had a half-smile on his bony face! Father Dawbeny was further impressed by his youth, and said so.

'You're very young to be a detective-inspector, aren't you, Mr. Glower? Sit down and have a cigarette.'

'Not all that young, sir,' demurred the inspector, sitting down.

'Well, perhaps it is that I'm getting old. They say the first sign of getting old is when the policemen look too young to you.' Father Dawbeny lit his cigarette for him.

'I completed twenty years' service three days ago, sir.'

'Then you're forty at least, I suppose.'

'About that, sir.'

'And you look thirty ! Evidently an unexacting life, a detective's. Well, I'll tell you everything I've got to tell you.' He looked at the door to see that Ernie had shut it on them. He lit himself a cigarette so that the Inspector might feel at ease with his. And he sat in the opposite chair and crossed his long legs under the cassock. 'I'm going to come the copper, good and proper, on a venerable parishioner of mine.'

CHAPTER SEVEN

SULLEN and stubborn, his lips clamped together like pincers,
Mr. Howden told himself that he was not going to be bullied by
any copulating parson.   No filthy interfering parson was going
to come and sort *him* out.   Believing what he wanted to believe,
what he needed to believe, he persuaded himself that the man,
with his threats, was just ' shooting his face off.'   ' He can't
do anything.   It was all talk.   These parsons think they can
do anything.   But I bet all the gold in the Bank to the two-
pence in his poor-box that he can't mix anything for me.   The
evidence isn't there.   And the answer's there : she acted of her
own free will ; she didn't need no procuring.   No—nah !—he
he was threatening ; just threatening.   And I'm not such a fool
as to be taken in by threats.'
Nevertheless, beneath this parade of self-assurance, the found-
ations of his house were shaken.   His house needed some stout
beams to shore it up and hold it still.   Like many who live at the
receiving end of the Law he knew a good deal more about the
Law than those who dwell in the placid fields on its silent and
inactive side.   He knew, for example, that a man could get,
not only two years, as the padre had said, for procuring a
woman to leave her usual place of abode and frequent a brothel,
but could also, at the Court's discretion be sentenced in addition to be privately whipped, the number of strokes, and the
instrument to be used, resting on the decision of the Court.
Whipped.   But no !   they only whipped younger men ;   not an
old grey-haired gentleman of reverend appearance, and a considerable property owner.   But it was true what the padre had
said :   if the prosecution could rake up more than one charge
against him (and Mr. Howden could think of one or two available incidents in the past) the old judge could impose consecutive
sentences on each count.   Hell !   Mr. Howden hastened to
shore up the shaking house.   First, and with promptitude—and
with a fine show of indignation—he got rid of the girl.   ' Lying

66

to me about your age ! You might'a got me into serious trouble. Don't you know the Law ? ' And when the girl replied, ' I never lied to you. You knew perfectly well how old I was. You told me to keep quiet about it,' he was exceedingly angry and raised his voice : ' How dare you say such a thing ? Don't you ever say such a thing to anybody, or you'll be getting put away too. They'll treat you as a young person in need of care and protection, and that means some approved school or other. Don't you forget that.'

The trade in which Mr. Howden worked as a small master was as well organized, below ground level, as the drains, mains, or post office wires that run under London, and the girl went all the way from Cremona Road to Arturo Fattore who lived and did business, not in little Italy (which is Soho) but in Canning Town, near the docks and the ships.

If that functioning interfering parson had really shopped him to the police, then Mr. Howden, who'd often been as a mouse in the skirting beneath the cats' eyes of the police, suspected that observation was being kept on No. 9 Lamplough Terrace. Did he not remember—with indignation—that dirty, lousy cop who gave evidence against him three years ago ? ' I kept observation on his house, your worship, and on the night of May 7th I saw the woman take four different men into the house in the space of five hours.' The liar ! Four ! Was it likely ? Why, three would take some believing. So Mr. Howden, pretty certain that the police would keep obbo and record what they observed —with advantages—warned all his lady customers to ' bloody-well keep away,' and if a lady, unadvised of this warning, came to his threshold with a gentleman partner, he waved her from his sinless door with a large white hand as innocent of stain as a magnolia bloom in the first blush of summer. ' No, no ; go away ; go away. What nonsense ! This is a respectable house.' He said it fairly loud, and hoped that the busies heard him.

Mr. Howden's splendid grey hair and his aqueous, rust-red eyes were often at his front-floor window, looking out for a busy at watch in the street or behind some lace curtains across the road. He could see no one, but you never knew. Some loafing lad standing in the lee of a door to light a fag ; some long-coated man pretending to consult a rent book or to be the insur-ance bloke from the Pru ; some coster pushing a barrow covered with flowers (a good disguise, this, in Potters Dale) ; a rag-and bone man driving past in a pony shay and sending his cry up to the house windows—you never knew ; the busies were up to all sorts of games, the dirty spies.

Sometimes when he was in the street, engaged upon what for the present, and *sine die*, were lawful occasions, he would espy the long, cassocked figure of Father Dawbeny in the distance, moving like a tall black pillar, with his sooty-faced dog padding happily behind, and he, Mr. Howden, went with some speed round the next corner. Best not remind the father of Mr. Howden ; and, in any case, a greeting would be awkward after the set-to they'd had last time. He waited till the father was gone from sight, or, if that cassock came nearer he went quickly and softly, like a child at hide-and-seek, out of that street and into another. At other times he met the dog first and hastily turned about and scuttled into obscurity.

But two months, four months, six months went by ; no police came near him ; and confidence and comfort grew and spread and began to flourish in the heart of Mr. Howden like plants refreshed after a drought. If the minister had grassed him, and if the cops had acted on the information, they'd evidently been quite unable to ' make it stick.' It was just as he'd said : they couldn't collect enough evidence. If they'd failed to visit him in six months, that was proof that they were pursuing the case no further. Cops liked to act while a crime was hot, not when it was six months cold. Mr. Howden felt safe again, and much pleased to have been right in what he'd said to that functioning interfering parson.

§

If Mr. Howden did not know what action the minister had taken in the matter of No. 9 Lamplough Terrace, neither did he know of things which had come into the life of Father Dawbeny and had no connection with No. 9. On a Sunday morning in July of that year, at fifteen minutes to eleven, the huge and handsome, if furtive, Westminster Straight Eight limousine which Ernie and Sophie had admired and wondered about on their first visit to St. John's, came as usual into the Dale, silently and smoothly, and halted a good furlong from the church, keeping modestly out of sight round a corner. Mr. Howden himself could not have kept more modestly out of view round a corner. The large uniformed chauffeur stepped down from his driving seat, opened the saloon door and suffered the car to unload not only the large elderly lady with the white hair and the pearls but also a thin little grey man in very good clothes and a thin little grey woman whose features and figure and equally good clothes suggested that she was his sister. These three expensively dressed persons, so alien and inappropriate to these pavements, left the shy car and turned the corner into Greig Street, while the chauffeur got back into his upholstered place, shut his door quietly and rewarded himself first with a cigarette and then, when his lady was far enough away, with the *News of the World*. As usual he would have an hour to wait while his mistress said her prayers and sang her hymns in this extremely unpleasant part of London.

'Where in pity are you getting us to, Beaty?' demanded the thin little man, as he looked along Greig Street. His utterances were quick and sharp like a dog's barks. 'A more depressing place I can't imagine. So this is where she comes to church, Peggy. No accounting for tastes.'

'You wait till you see him,' advised the large lady. 'He has the most lovely face. Stern and beautiful. That's his church bell going. St. John the Prior's. You wait.' In her enthusiasm she was a pace ahead of both of them, like a child proud of her show-piece and eager to lead them to it. 'Prudence Elgar calls him St. John the Divine. And, incidentally, he's got the sweetest little verger who's rather lame. The little man goes dot-and-carry-one about the church in his little cassock and gown or his little amice and alb. When he follows behind Father Dawbeny they look like father and son. Or like a king and his page-boy. Everyone calls him Ernie, except me. I wouldn't dare call him anything except Mr. Matters, with the utmost respect.'

'Funny that one can live so close to places like this and not know of their existence,' said the man, glancing around. 'Can't have come more than a mile along the top of the park. You never know what's hiding behind the houses of a main road.'

'It doesn't look as though many people were going to church,' said the little thin woman, trying to keep abreast of their guide. 'Shall we be the only people there?'

'I'm afraid you won't find very many, Peggy. They get less

69

and less. It's such a shame because it's a quite beautiful service. He's always kept it perfectly beautiful. Chiefly at his own expense.'

' And at yours,' barked the man.

' A little. But, you see, he's spent nearly all he had now. On the church and on that silly great Costers' Club. And that reminds me, John. Just you put something very handsome in the plate. The poor man needs it.'

The three persons hurrying towards the church were, in order of size : Lady Guttree, widow of the ninth Earl of Duncombe ; Lord Guttree, her bachelor brother-in-law and the present earl ; and Lady Marjorie Ungar-Bateman, his unmarried sister who lived with him and kept his houses. Lady Guttree, eyes alight with high purpose, had this morning left her home in Upper Hyde Street, collected her brother-in-law and sister-in-law from Guttree House, Brook Street, and brought them in her car from this region of palaces to this congregation of poor streets, hidden behind the main road, a mile from their doors.

' It must be a heart-breaking business, working in these parts,' said Lady Ungar-Bateman. ' I'd die rather than live here.'

' And with his background too ! ' agreed the enthusiastic guide. ' Have you ever seen Strathpenny Castle ? Or the Strathpenny Estate ? Thirty thousand acres of mountains and lakes. I always see the mountains behind him when he's preaching. You know his story, of course ? He was madly in love with Ursula Burne—and what a couple they'd have been, he so dark and beautiful, and she so lovely—the tiniest but most exquisite little thing ! And money ! She'd all the money in the world. But they parted quite suddenly—no one ever knew why. Just an announcement that the marriage between the Honourable Piers Dawbeny and Lady Ursula Burne would not take place. And Piers Dawbeny just disappeared from Society overnight. He was next heard of in a theological college. A theological college at forty ! '

' Get's 'em like that sometimes,' snapped Lord Guttree.

' At first he was a curate at the Eton and King's Mission in Somers Town, and then came here as vicar, and here he's been ever since.'

' Much better have made the grand tour, or gone off and shot tigers,' suggested Lord Guttree.

' And he's never married since,' gushed Lady Guttree with rich appreciation of the romance. ' Never married anyone else.'

' Much better have married the housemaid, and got it out of his system.'

' Now do behave yourself, John, and don't be flippant. You're going to church. And you've got to try and like him. Do please like him. I'm quite determined to have him at Duncombe. I'm living for the day when he comes to us. Think what he'd look like after silly, fat old Mr. Cullis. He'd be an ornament to the church, the parish, and the whole countryside. Not that Mr. Cullis wasn't a gentleman—after all, he was Eton —but he never looked like one. In his ordinary clothes he looked like a village grocer, and in his vestments like a charwoman. I can't think why Fingal ever instituted him as rector.'

' A lay patron, my dear Beaty, doesn't institute a rector. He offers him a living.'

' Oh, well, it comes to the same thing. The Bishop or the King, or whoever it is, has to do what the patron tells him. I must have my Piers Dawbeny. He looks a duke—or, rather, he looks like what a duke ought to look like, and never does. He'd be perfect in the picture. Fingal spent thousands on the restoration of that church and its ornaments, and Mr. Cullis, as an ornament, spoils them all. His chasuble's always on one side, and his alb all rucked up, and his trousers and boots showing. Father Dawbeny has the most perfect sense of appearances. Wherever he is, he's always beautifully groomed—it's about the only luxury he still allows himself—and he has a passion for beautiful things. It's *too* pathetic, Peggy : he wanders about the antique shops in the Brompton Road, looking at beautiful things and coveting them, but he'll only buy them for the church. He allows himself nothing.'

' Well, I think that's absurd. Why shouldn't he have beautiful things, if he likes them ? '

' You don't know anything about it, Peggy. You've no vision. He thinks he ought to live like the people around him—if he's to win them at all. He's got to be in with them in everything. Poor darling, I don't suppose he's really happy about his good clothes. I'm always so afraid that one of these days he'll cast them off. We can't have that. " Father Dawbeny of Duncombe." Think how it sounds ! Perfect ! '

'But why should you suppose he'd come?' barked Lord Guttree.

'I feel sure he would. He simply loved the little church when I had him to stay at the Dower House after he'd been ill. There are not many village churches with full Catholic ceremonial. He said it was the most beautiful country church he'd ever seen, and how wonderful it must be to have such a church and to live in such surroundings. He said he'd often thought he'd like to end in such a place. And he's tired out now, anybody can see. Worn out. And well he may be ; I looked him up, and he's fifty-eight, and he's been in one or other of these ghastly parts for fifteen years. Surely he's done his Time. Fifteen years ! That's all a reprieved murderer's asked to do. It'd be a work of mercy to get him out. But hush now : do stop talking. Here we are.'

They passed into the church.

§

An hour later the chauffeur stubbed out his cigarette, put away the *News of the World*, and sat waiting in a quiet reverie. The time for his resumed service was at hand. And in fact, though he could not see this from round his corner, two of his passengers had come out of the church and were waiting by the porch.

Lady Guttree was still within, having a ' word ' with the Vicar. The word endured for many minutes, because Lady Guttree's talk could rush like a waterfall in the Strathpenny mountains— as the Vicar had been known to say, after he'd been bathed in its spray. All the rest of the congregation (and that was not many) had passed through the porch before she came hurrying out.

'Hasn't he a beautiful face?' she inquired of her brother-in-law.

'A good-looking fellow enough,' allowed Lord Guttree.

'Oh, but he's much more than that. Those huge dark eyes, like a little wistful boy's ! Do you wonder that Prudence calls him St. John the Divine. And the way he moves ! The way he moves about the church ! '

'That's merely the old Guards officer. Properly drilled.'

'No, it isn't. It's nothing of the sort. It's his deep feeling for art. It's his profound sense of beauty. Every movement in the service has to be perfection.'

'Who's the beautiful young man who was serving him?' asked Lady Peggy. 'The young Apollo with the spun-gold hair?'

'That's Denys Flackman. Isn't he loathsome? Like one of those Greek statues, and as revolting. More so, really, because he's eaten up with conceit, as anyone can see. But ornamental, I suppose. And he's absolutely devoted to Father Dawbeny; there's that to be said for him. Perhaps he's better than he looks.'

'It's certainly a beautiful service,' Lady Peggy continued. 'I'd never have expected to find anything like that in a slum like this?'

'Beautiful for those who like that sort of thing,' suggested Lord Guttree.

'But *John*,' Lady Guttree reproached him. 'How could you not like it if you've any feeling for beauty? And he says he'll come to luncheon. Tuesday—you said Tuesday, didn't you? There'll be just you and Peggy, and Archdeacon and Mrs. La Roche, to keep it ecclesiastical. And please, both of you, be as attractive as possible. I want him to like you. He's got to like you. And don't you get into any theological arguments, John. You don't know anything about it. You're just an ignorant old prot. And mind you look your nicest: the sort of patron a really conscientious parson would give his eyes to possess. You can look like that, if you try.'

§

As Lord Guttree had said, it was no great distance from the low roofs of Potters Dale to the lofty roofs of Mayfair. Father Dawbeny, dressed in his best for a luncheon party, turned out of the Dale and walked along the high road north of the parks. He walked alone. Squaller, the dog, had not received an invitation, and in any case he knew a countess's vestibule from a church vestry, and was not likely to remain uncomplaining during a lunch, as he was trained to do during a Mass. He was left howling at home, and Father Dawbeny had had to hurry out of the Dale from his reproachful eyes and those heart-rending whines.

In Upper Hyde Street he came to what Lady Guttree called her 'little house in town.' To Lady Guttree it may have seemed little after Guttree House in Duncombe, or even the Dower House in Guttree Park ; to Father Dawbeny the word 'little' may not have seemed amiss after Strathpenny Castle and the Strathpenny home in Belgrave Square ; but to Ernie Matters and Denys Flackman it would have seemed a fine and some-what frightening mansion for the 'nobs'. An eighteenth-century house, it was a hundred years older than the long, low, uniform terraces in the Dale. When Upper Hyde Street was rising by the park, the Dale was but a marshy netherlands of coarse grass and wheel-cut farm tracks, north of the turnpike road. It had not even a name then, for the potters and brick-makers had not yet set up their kilns and shacks along the rutted roads.

A manservant received the father's hat, stick, and name and led him up a gracious white staircase to a spacious white drawing-room. 'Mr. Dawbeny,' he announced, for Father Dawbeny, when asked his name, was always too diffident to decorate it with the word 'Father.'

'Ah, come in, Father !' Lady Guttree, on the other hand, always rejoiced to use the title 'Father.' 'Come and meet the others.' And she introduced him to Mrs. La Roche, the Arch-deacon's wife, nearly as large and well-attired as herself; to Peggy Ungar-Bateman ; to Lord Guttree, 'my beloved brother-in-law ' ; and to Archdeacon La Roche, 'whom probably you know.'

Archdeacon La Roche, Vicar of St. Erkenwald's, Aubrey Place, and Archdeacon of North London, said, 'How do you do ? I didn't catch the name. Oh, yes, of course : Dawbeny. Lady Guttree was telling me. And where is it you work ? '

'Potters Dale.'

'Oh, yes ; that's west of Ledbitter Hill, isn't it ?—just outside my archdeaconry. I know young Custance—Oliver Custance, at St. Luke's, Ledbitter. He's making some impression there, I'm told. A very live wire, isn't he ? '

'Yes, he's doing excellent work.' Father Dawbeny hoped that this effort at generosity justified the lie. 'His parish touches mine.'

'Does it? Does it really?'

Tales of Father Dawbeny of Potters Dale, which ran among the poor for miles about his parish and made him something of a legend among Anglo-Catholic youth in distant parts of England, had not come the way of Archdeacon La Roche, who moved in the fashionable world. Neither a 'slum priest' nor a 'Catholic,' he was 'fashionable' and 'broad'; and he looked both, with his pewter-grey hair tastefully arranged above a round, clean face, his gaiters swelling about neat, shapely calves, and his silk apron taut as a cumerbund across an ample stomach. He was sipping a golden cocktail as he spoke, and the chaste little graven glass seemed perfectly in place within his soft, plump fingers.

Not that Father Dawbeny refused a cocktail when a footman came to him with these golden drinks on a silver tray. In his bare upper room he allowed himself only a glass of beer at the end of the day; but in the first forty years of his life he had delighted in, and considered himself a connoisseur of, good wine and good food, and this morning he had decided to allow himself an hour or two among the old delights. One could not set oneself up in self-righteous contrast with the other guests, and so this indulgence was justified—or so he hoped, with occasional doubts. And certainly the cocktail was good.

'Well, now——' Lady Guttree glanced round and saw that all glasses were empty. 'Shall we . . .?' and she led them down the white stairs to the cream and green dining-room.

The room was everything that Father Dawbeny would have loved to possess. A thick cream and green carpet ran to the cream-panelled walls; an oval swing-leg Chippendale table, with cabriole legs, stood in state in the centre of this creamy-green lake; it was set about with riband-backed Chippendale chairs; its glistening oval top was garnished with lace, silver, cut-glass and pink roses; against one cream wall stretched a long sideboard-table, with carved scrolled legs, and carved rail; and above this handsome counter hung the only picture in the room, a life-sized portrait of the late Earl Guttree in the robes of a Lord Rector of McGomme University.

Father Dawbeny coveted it all; it was even a faint pain, a continuing ache, to look upon it and remember Greig Street.

The hostess, splendidly executive, directed them to their chairs with a diamonded hand cupped like a waterlily : her brother-in-law opposite her ; a parson on her either side ; and the two ladies, Mrs. La Roche and Lady Peggy, between the priests and the earl.

A meal of exquisite foods began.

The cocktails had been strong ; more than one had been sipped by the guests upstairs ; the wine, now circumnavigating them, was old and potent ; the butler refilled their glasses directly they were empty, which was not seldom ; and soon the talk was running fast and high. If it could be said to be running like a rapid-swelling tide, then Lady Guttree was the mid-stream flood, the Earl and the Archdeacon the slightly tardier flows on either side ; and the two ladies the slow, following water under the banks.

Mrs. La Roche had just said to Father Dawbeny, 'That Potters Dale of yours must be full of the most dreadful people,' and he had smiled and said, 'Yes, yes, thank God,' when Lady Guttree called down the noisy table to her brother-in-law, 'Shall we tell him now, John?' and silence fell upon all.

The Cream of Sorrel had gone by and the sliced chicken and Salade Chiffonade was coming round in the hands of butler and footman.

'Yes, now, I think, John, don't you? We got you here on false pretences, Father ; it's a trap. We really, my brother-in-law and I, want to know if you'd accept——'

'Not quite so fast, Beaty,' Lord Guttree interrupted. 'Mr. Dawbeny and I would have to discuss the matter very fully first.'

'Oh, well, you know what I mean. John and I have been wondering—perhaps I ought to say *he* has been wondering, because I'm only the old dowager—whether you'd consider the offer of Little Christ Church, Duncombe, when our silly old Mr. Cullis retires in October.'

'Good heavens!' Father Dawbeny laid down the knife and fork which he'd just begun to address to the sliced chicken. Taken by surprise, his defences were breached, and a flood of desire poured into him. He saw the little Sussex church at the edge of the park, seven hundred years old, but maintained in state by the Earls of Duncombe. He had thought it lovely and lovable when he'd seen it, and prayed in it, during a week of convalescence at the Dower House. Outside its timbered churchyard the country sloped down to a hollow where the silver Deenrush meandered by among carpets of green ; beyond the valley the country mounted to a noble skyline broken in places by lofty woods. It was autumn when he had seen it, and the grassy slopes were a brilliant green in contrast with the crimson and copper and amber leaves of the crowding trees. Here were hills which you could climb and summits along which you could wander ; they were not his Strathpenny mountains, but they were England, as only England could be. The whole scene, as he saw it in that moment of surprise, called to him to come. It called, ' Will you not come ? You are tired, and you have done enough. You are getting old, and when a man gets old, he longs to strain no more, but to rest in the things he knew as a child. You have lived long enough among strangers who are a different people from your own people, and speak a different language. Come and enjoy for a little, because there are not so many years left, the habits and the words and the thoughts of your own people.' Could it be that God had sent this offer to him ?

These thoughts had rushed like a veil between him and Lady Guttree's talk, so that he was only pretending to heed it, but now he heard it more clearly.

' It was my suggestion to John. I remembered how you had loved the little church and said how wonderful it must be to have a church in the heart of the country, where the service was still what it was seven hundred years ago, and where there was a congregation trained to expect nothing else. We want someone who can feel like that about it, don't we, John ? '

' Well, of course, I'm not the high churchman my brother Fingal was, Dawbeny. I didn't have the advantage of being married to Beaty and taken in hand by her. I've never been a ritualist, but——'

' He means an Anglo-Catholic,' Lady Guttree apologized.

' —but, of course, I've let Cullis go his own way, undisturbed by any interfering layman. And in any case Beaty is the power in the church. For my part, quite frankly, I find all this ritual more of a hindrance than a help.'

' I'm afraid I agree with you, Lord Guttree,' admitted the Archdeacon as he and all the company set about the chicken and the jellied vegetables.

77

'Oh, no, surely not!' pleaded Father Dawbeny. 'Not if you understand what its uses—and its only uses—are. It's a means—a means, merely—and nothing more.'

Lady Guttree watched him with some doubt in her eyes. Was this sound Catholic doctrine?

'Means to what?' demanded Lord Guttree.

'To two ends, as I see them. One directed towards God and the other towards man. First and foremost to express our veneration and honour——'

'Yes, but "God is a Spirit,"' quoted Lord Guttree, anxious to defend his ground, '"and they that worship Him must worship Him in spirit."'

'That's it. That's the point,' endorsed the Archdeacon.

'Certainly, certainly. That is primary. But He is also Beauty and Perfection, and we must worship Him with beauty and perfection.' When Father Dawbeny spoke of beauty he always spoke with some fire; and now all were gazing at him as they ate. His language was well hewn and effective because he was recalling it from sermons he had written; and it held their eyes and their ears. 'Isn't this it: we bring to His worship the most perfect beauty we can, saying something like, "This is the best we can do in our adoration and love; this is all the beauty we can bring to meet with yours, but here it is, as perfect as we can make it." And Catholic ceremonial is pretty perfect because it has been worked upon with love for two thousand years.'

'And the other aim?' inquired Lord Guttree, less argumentative now, because impressed. 'The other end?'

'The other end is to teach the old faith more effectively than in any other way. Our old church is wise with two thousand years of life, and she knows that the people are best taught a truth by having it dramatized before their eyes. We all learn best through our eyes.'

'Well, there's something in that,' conceded Lord Guttree.

'Yes, there *is*,' agreed the Archdeacon. 'There's something in that.'

'And I think I see another end. Not so important, perhaps, as these two, but—very important to me.'

'And it is, Dawbeny . . . ?' Lord Guttree encouraged him.

'To bring some beauty that is perfect into the grey days of the poor. . . . Some haunting beauty . . . You know, even

78

in Greig Street, we hunger after beauty. And the strange thing is we want it to be flawless—perfect.'

'You argue well, Dawbeny. Why doesn't Cullis explain things like that?'

'Because he's a silly old fool,' offered Lady Guttree.

'Well, it's all very tentative, Dawbeny, but are you at all interested in coming to Duncombe?'

'I am enormously attracted by the idea, but I must think and think.'

'Try to persuade him.' Lady Guttree, far ahead of her brother-in-law, was already offering the living. An able hostess, she had turned to the Archdeacon to bring him back into the talk. 'Can't you as an archdeacon give him his marching orders? He has all the military virtues, and he'll do it if you tell him it's his duty to go and sacrifice himself among us. Tell him it's "his not to reason why"—and all that. Go on.'

'I'm afraid he's not in my brigade,' smiled the Archdeacon. 'You'd better apply to his divisional commander, his diocesan.'

'And who, pray, is that?' asked Lady Peggy, since she hadn't spoken for a long time.

'The Bishop, dear lady. Perhaps the Bishop'll order him to abandon his present position and advance upon Duncombe. Thank you; I will.' A footman was offering him a further helping of the chicken and jellied vegetables. 'This is an excellent dish.'

Abandon the position—the words had been lightly uttered, but to Father Dawbeny, listening, they came like a cold cloud, dimming the dream-window through which he had looked upon the green slopes and autumn-rusted woods of Duncombe.

'Yes . . . thank you . . .' The Archdeacon was now encouraging the butler to refill his wine-glass. 'That'll do,' he insisted, lifting his hand in something like a benediction and farewell to the butler, now that the wine was as high in the glass as any butler was likely to put it. 'No more. . . . Yes, I sometimes feel I'd give my soul to be done with the everlasting labour and strain of a London cure and to rest in peace in some country parish.'

Give my soul—a careless phrase, but would he, Piers Dawbeny, be giving his soul if he abandoned the Dale and sought refreshment and peace in Duncombe?

'Well, at present,' Lord Guttree reminded them, 'we're only asking Mr. Dawbeny to bear the matter in mind.'

'And I can only say—indeed, I might have said it with advantage a little sooner'—Father Dawbeny smiled apologetically upon them all—'that I'm very sensible of the honour you've done me in even considering me.'

§

Here the entry of the sweet provided a brief entr'acte in the talk and when the curtain went up on it again the skilful hostess saw to it that the entertainment was changed and the subject a new one. This new subject was the theatre. She spoke of plays in town, and the company fell to discussing those they had seen. In this talk Father Dawbeny took but a small part, though he had allowed himself now and again a cheap and lonely seat in an upper circle. He said little, preferring to turn his eyes from one speaker to the next and to study the human comedy before him. A little of this watching and this listening, and he was appalled, he was revolted—his desire to love the human race was damaged even to wilting and a temporary death—by the abundant slanders with which his hostess bespattered the name of almost every actor, actress, playwright or manager, immediately it was mentioned. She was incapable of not alluding to any small scandal that had ever been associated with such a name, and if Lord Guttree, who was the only one who dared correct her, suggested that it was gossip and no more, she denied this because it spoiled her story—'Everybody knows it, John'—and even invented (so Father Dawbeny suspected) details to sustain the good story. 'Oh, *he*,' she would say. 'Of course, he can't act for toffee, but he's a pretty boy, and there are always reasons, unconnected with acting, why Norman Costello chooses his juvenile leads.' And 'Oh, *she*. It's notorious how she gets her good parts out of old Sir Joseph Coyne. She pays her price. He exacts his price out of many of his younger actresses, you know : a kind of *droit du seigneur*.' And 'Oh, that old pansy. Christopher Tullet is his buddy, and when I've said that I've said everything.'

And in this universal massacre she was undiscouraged by the

Archdeacon, and abetted in it, obsequiously, by the Archdeacon's lady ! To most of it, to one decapitation after another,
the Archdeacon was agreeing, sometimes accompanying the
agreement with a sorrowful head-shaking and other manifesta-
tions of clerical distress at the sins of theatrical mankind. 'The
soft, fluent toady ! ' The words formed in Father Dawbeny's
mind—and might God forgive them ; but it was a good phrase.

Lady Guttree had a high reputation for wit, and she cheerfully
sacrificed any famous name to it. Let the name make a good
story for a witty woman, and it was hastened to the sacrifice.
One of the wickedest things, it seemed to the listener, was the
way she took some remark of her victim, which he had obviously
intended as a jest, and represented it as a serious statement,
so that she could make a guy of him. 'Just to show you what
a detestable man he is, I'll tell you two stories about him.'
She was speaking of a young man who had made himself of
great reputation by a series of popular broadcast talks on
philosophy. 'When Prudence Elgar told him his moustache
was too long he said, " No, I'm growing it long because it makes
me look like Robert Louis Stevenson, only better looking."
Did you ever hear anything so conceited ? And when his
window-cleaner was talking through the window with him,
saying how he'd enjoyed his talks on Hegel, he said, " But what
do you know about Hegel ? You're only a window-cleaner."
Did you ever hear anything so outrageous ? '

Father Dawbeny could stand this wickedness no more. ' Oh,
but, Lady Guttree,' he protested, ' the man was obviously joking
in both cases. It's just inconceivable that any man would say
either of those things except in fun. In the first case he was
laughing at himself, and in the second case he was being affable
with the window-cleaner, and chaffing him.'

' Oh, no, he wasn't ! Oh, no, he wasn't ! ' she declared
emphatically, because it spoiled the story. ' He was serious.'

' Well, if you can believe that, Lady Guttree, you can believe
anything.'

He had said it with a smile so that it should seem part of the
fun, but inwardly he sighed. This unscrupulous old lady with
a good heart for her friends, but a murderous tongue for everyone else! She had attended his church and listened to his
teaching for several years, and the essence of Christianity had
not touched her. Oh, but one must be patient, patient with

the blind. Patient, patient with the intolerant and the censorious and the self-righteous and the cruel. Patient with the sycophantic and the servile and the cowardly, like this deplorable old archdeacon and the lady attached to him. But he wasn't feeling patient ; the fire was kindling within him ; he was restive in his seat ; and when a little later Lady Guttree turned to him brightly (because she was enjoying the talk) and said, ' You aren't saying much, Father,' he answered with only a quarter of a smile, ' I've kept silence for a very simple reason.'

' And what's that ? '

' Because the poor man hasn't had much opportunity,' suggested Lord Guttree.

' But that's rubbish. Are you trying to say I've been talking too much ? Nonsense. What's your good reason, Father ? '

' Because I desire no part in this massacre.'

' Massacre ! Who's massacring who ? '

' You, Lady Guttree——' And that's the end of Duncombe for me, he thought.

' Me ! '

' Yes, you—with some help from the Archdeacon and Mrs. La Roche.'

' Oh, my dear Father ! ' She acknowledged this with a humorous little scream. ' What an awful thing to say ! I might do a little massacring, but not the Archdeacon.'

' Well, are there not at least a dozen good names lying dead in the dust ? And has the Archdeacon lifted a hand to save them ? '

' But they were dead already,' she objected, taking the rebuke in good part—though the Archdeacon's face was white. ' I've said nothing that everybody doesn't know.'

' Everybody may know it, and I may still decline to believe any of it.'

' But why not ? Just because you want to be charitable.'

' Oh, no. Simply because the evidence isn't good enough.'

' But if everybody knows—— '

' All you mean by " everybody knows " is " everybody says," and they're not the same thing.'

' Quite right ! Quite right, Dawbeny ! ' endorsed Lord Guttree with delight and fervour. He, too, was bright with wine. ' Absolutely right, my dear boy. Tell her the truth for once in a way. It'll do her good.'

' Oh, dear . . .' sighed Lady Guttree in perfect good humour, enjoying her punishment.

' I've very little faith in your " everybody ", Lady Guttree. " Everybody " may occasionally give us a true biography, but usually he—or should I say " she " ?—is a master of historical fiction.'

' Good ! Excellent ! ' laughed Lord Guttree. ' Let Beaty have it.'

' And I think it's wicked to take people's obvious jokes and use them as evidence against them, that they're vain, or pansies, or imbeciles, or something. I don't think I shall ever make a joke again. It doesn't seem safe.'

' There you are, Beaty. And it's true, what he's saying. That's just what you always do. Continue, Dawbeny.'

' The trouble, Lady Guttree is that it's disastrous to have such a reputation for wit as yours. It's a Moloch which demands the life of every one who's mentioned. Into the fire with him ! And, really, that's a form of murder for selfish gain. Isn't it ? '

' Certainly it is. It is exactly that, Beaty. Murder for selfish gain.'

' Oh, well . . .' said the good-humoured lady, undisturbed. ' I suppose I'm a bad old woman.'

' You certainly are,' declared her brother-in-law. ' Dawbeny, I begin to think you must certainly come to Duncombe and teach us all not to murder our neighbours.'

CHAPTER EIGHT

So far from having lost by his outspoken words all hope of being offered the incumbency of Duncombe, Father Dawbeny had made a considerable impression on its patron, Lord Guttree, a far greater impression than that gentleman had expected. Lord Guttree, however ill-informed a churchman, had the desire of his kind to be a conscientious patron and to find a good padre for his people. He had been impressed, not by any nonsense about a 'stern and beautiful face,' but by a quality which he thought he perceived in Dawbeny, a quality that was quiet and humorous, fearless and forth-right. He had much preferred him to the sycophantic archdeacon. So a week or two later he invited him to lunch at the Travellers' Club, and in a corner of its library, safely hidden behind the white Corinthian columns and pilasters, he said to him after talking of twenty other topics, 'Well, Dawbeny, I really do want to offer you this living. I offer it to you here and now. Will you accept the charge of Little Christ Church, Duncombe? Don't think you need answer at once, my dear fellow. Take your time. But I very much hope your answer will be Yes.'

Father Dawbeny carried this question back to his upper room. He sat musing upon it in his big chair, while he fiddled with the dog's ears ; often he walked up and down with it, and stood before his long trestle table, hands behind his back and eyes resting on the litter of papers belonging to St. John the Prior's. Sometimes he went to the window and looked out at Greig Street.

He had gone into that extreme of loneliness in which, twenty years before, he had turned away from all his past and given himself to a new vision. 'Which way, O Lord? Duncombe or the Dale?' Standing by the window, he saw himself as a soldier under authority, ready to surrender any position and march elsewhere if he felt sure the signal had come from the Commander. But had it so come?

Ambition had no part in the problem. From that moment when he turned away he had felt a drive towards some life-work so quiet and unobtrusive as to be almost silent. All desire for a spectacular career and the acclamation of the world had died in him then. That he had won a kind of fame among certain specialized and very limited circles all over the country, he knew—though it is probable he didn't know how widely strewn that reputation was—but he certainly hadn't laboured for it.

But if ambition had no part, his longing for beauty and rest was strong indeed. The appeal of Duncombe, its church, its parsonage and garden, and its quiet hills, was almost overpowering. As a labourer who has toiled for a dozen hours longs for his chair and his pipe at the end of the day, so he longed for the rest which was proposed to him. Only he knew how tired he sometimes felt. Sometimes he wondered if he had really ' worn himself out.' Sometimes, not less subject to nervous fears than other men, he suspected that he had a ' tired heart ' ; and, like other men, he did not dare to ask his doctor, lest it was so. Though there were other times—times of deep depression—when he felt quite ready to die.

To accept this refreshment in beauty and this healing in rest —would it be wrong ; a turning back in his path ; a retreat ; a concession to those two deadly sins which had their roots in him as in all men, sloth and covetousness ? He seemed to hear the voices of a hundred friends saying, ' No, Piers. No, Father. You can push asceticism too far.' But did they, bless their friendly hearts, know what they were talking about ? Were they not speaking of something they had not begun to understand ? Why had every saint in every religion—and that was simply to say, every expert and profound scholar in the spiritual life—always felt this drive towards asceticism ? Why had some even chosen an absolute poverty ? Asceticism ? Mortification ? The words made clever sceptics hot and angry. They did not begin to see that the aim of mortification was not death but life ; not less life but more ; it merely meant death to all earthly trammels so that the soul might shake itself free, brace itself for the new and sunnier road, and really begin to live.

Plenty of mortification for him out there in the Dale ! The mortification of working and working with ever-lessening encouragement and less and less of visible result. The mortification of ever accepting this discouragement with a smile of welcome. He left the window and walked towards the crucifix over his mantelpiece. He stared at it, hands behind his back. What had *that* to tell him? Simply that discouragement could not exist if dedication was complete. The measure of success was in the degree of one's dedication, not in the number of people at one's services or in any visible results which God allowed one to see. *He* had only one man and three women at the end.

Then what? Was it Duncombe or the Dale? He might gaze out of the window at Greig Street or stare at this symbol on his wall, but neither gave forth an answer.

§

So Father Dawbeny's thoughts in these days were straying always to Duncombe and its pleasant hills, and not once did they visit Lamplough Terrace in Cremona Road. It was not so with the thoughts of Detective-Inspector Glower, seated in the D.I.'s office at Lutine Street Police Station. His thoughts had been constant visitors to the Terrace, and one morning they were there, waiting with much interest alongside of young Jerry Sadler, a plain-clothes patrol on probation, who was keeping observation on No. 9 in that terrace. Seated at his desk, with his dark hair, thin hollowed face, and gentle eyes clouded with thought, a pencil between his fingers tapping a tom-tom beat on his blotting-pad, he looked, as Father Dawbeny had thought, less like a senior, briskly efficient and sometimes stern policeman than a young elder of a Scotch kirk, or even, perhaps, in this contemplative mood, the minister himself, composing his sermon for the next sabbath. At thirty-five minutes past ten, one of the two telephones on his desk rang.

He picked up the receiver. 'Yes?'

It was Jerry Sadler who had been put through to him. 'It's O.K., sir. He's come home. He went into the house and shut the door on himself, so it looks as if he's staying for a bit.'

'That's fine, Sadler. We'll punt round now.'

He went straight out of his little office into the large C.I.D. office, and called to a sergeant seated at one of the six little tables, 'Come on, Cundle. Our client's waiting for us.'

Detective-Sergeant Cundle (Hughie to most in the station)

rose immediately and went to his hat on the rack by the door. He was a young man, only recently promoted, but a big and powerful lad. On this occasion Inspector Glower needed a sergeant, not only to memorize any words that Mr. Howden in his exasperation and unwisdom might let fall and to note down the same at the earliest opportunity in his note-book, so as to corroborate the Inspector's versions of what had been said ; but also to stand on guard over the captive while he himself made an interesting journey through every room in the house.

The two men went down the steps and sat themselves in the car, which was standing against the kerb. They sat in its back seat because the Inspector wanted to advise and instruct this young sergeant whom he considered to be still *in statu pupillari.*

' Well, Hughie,' he began. ' I'm glad to be pulling this boy in. It's a Right Job, if ever there was one. He's a very bad old man. We've established that at one time he had quite an efficient organization for offering facilities to women and to the men in search of them. And generally speaking he got a pound from the men and a pound out of every five earned by the women. Well, like my fellow criminals, Hughie, I don't love ponces, pimps, and procurers. We have our standards, we criminals.'

' He'll get his full two years, I suppose ? ' asked the Sergeant, less to learn the answer than to show that he knew the maximum sentence.

' Two years ! Three penn'orth's more my idea.'

' Three years ? '

' Yes, and even possibly five.'

' But how can he get five, sir, when the maximum—"

' Oh, very simply, Hughie. Consecutive sentences on each count, if his record's bad enough. And C.R.O. assure me he's plenty of form. Good and plenty. And this time we've got him by the short hairs. We've established that this girl was no prostitute when he got hold of her. Her moral character was quite good enough. Probably she was no timid and blushing rosebud, but she was no worse than a hundred others till old Howden did his work on her. It's a blazing case of procuration. Look, Hughie, you will stay with him while I turn over his drum. I need hardly tell a first-rate copper like you that you're not to *encourage* him to talk, since he'll have been cautioned, but—*but*, my boy, if he does show a disposition to

87

become chatty, well, take what the gods give you. Good lord, we'd never get anywhere if we went out of our way to shut their silly mouths for them. It never ceases to surprise me, Hughie, the way even our oldest clients, who ought to know better after all the years we've been advising them, become chatty in the C.I.D. office when the formalities of arrest and charge are over and their finger-prints are being taken or particulars about their wife and family are being noted down. I suppose the atmosphere suddenly seems more friendly. Nobody asks them to give themselves away but they feel an urge in their unhappy state to chat with someone. I tell you one thing this old bastard'll say. They all do on this charge. Extraordinary the way humans move like flocks of birds, all saying the same thing all over the country, though they've no contact with each other. He'll say, " She looked eighteen to me." It's never seventeen or nineteen ; always eighteen. Right-ho : you stay with him and keep your ears open and your memory as sticky as a fly-paper, while I search the house. We've enough evidence to pin this pretty little button-hole on him, but I shall be quite pleased to collect a little more. I want to put such a play-pen round the old baby as he can't get out of, this time.'

' What do you expect to find, sir ? '

' Oh, I don't know. You never know. Letters, diaries, ten beds slept in last night.'

' I see. Yes, of course . . .'

' None of it's really necessary, perhaps. The girl's evidence and the padre's should do the trick for him. He said some very unwise things to the padre.'

' How did you induce the girl to speak ? '

' The padre did that. I doubt if we could have done much without him. When we traced the girl to Canning Town, he and another padre sought her out. He asked me to leave her to him, and I thought it was best. She'd been afraid of a policeman, but, as far as I understand, no sinner's ever been afraid of Father Dawbeny. Strange : he turns his own form of heat on—I wish I knew where he got it—and they melt. What happened I don't know. All I know is that he rang me up after a week or two to say he'd got her at his vicarage—or whatever he calls that old barn of his—it's about as bare as a police station—and that he'd persuaded her to tell everything. I shall never forget it when we went round to the vicarage, Gracie and

I—' he was alluding to Policewoman Grace Lane. 'The poor kid sat there trembling in the padre's chair with him sitting on its arm and holding her hand and sometimes patting it, or standing up and laying his arm along her shoulders. Whatever old Howden may say, she didn't look sixteen to me. She was terrified, but the padre persuaded her that we were on her side all the way and only anxious to help her, and I promised her that we'd conceal her name at the trial and in the meantime put her in a place of safety, where she'd be very happy. Actually she's with old Nancy Harbord and her new husband —oh, but you don't know Nancy, do you. She was matron at Gayne Street when I was a young constable there, and we used to call her Nannie. Nannie'll mother the kid all right and never throw her past in her face. She'll make a good girl of her, I shouldn't be surprised.'

'But excuse me, sir: how can you conceal her name?' The young sergeant had seen another chance to exhibit his knowledge. 'She's not a juvenile offender, and it's not a case of blackmail.'

'It can be worked, my boy. I told the padre we couldn't claim it, but we could ensure it. The old beak and the old judge'll play. So will the reporters. They always do. The old Judge'll say, "We've no power to enforce concealment of this young girl's name, but at the request of counsel for the prosecution, and in the young girl's interest, I hope you will agree to suppress it." And not a paper in England will give her name. Extraordinary chaps, these press boys: they've no scruples about some things and the highest standards in others. Besides, they're the most sentimental people in the world—after us cops.'

The car had stopped. Like Lady Guttree's long limousine it had stopped shyly round a corner, in Morrow Street. The two detectives got out and walked rapidly to No. 9 Lamplough Terrace and up its steps. Its door was not open as when Father Dawbeny stood on the threshold, so Inspector Glower looked for the bell. In Cremona Road's more dignified days it had been a doctor's house, and there were two bells: day and night; also the mouth-piece of a speaking tube.

The Inspector smiled as he pressed the day-bell. 'I daren't think what the night-bell's for, Hughie, but don't you ever come ringing it. And don't you go sending any love-talk up that tube.'

The door was opened by a spacious woman in a dirty green overall. Her grey hair was tied up in a blue scarf, and the broom which she'd just been plying leaned against the passage wall. This was certainly not Mrs. Howden who was always garish and golden. Presumably a charwoman.

' Could we see Mr. Howden? ' asked the Inspector courteously.

' Oh yes . . . I think so . . . I'll go and see—'

But it was not necessary for her to go and see, because Mr. Howden had heard the bell and the voices, and, being an ambitious man, who ever dreamed of good things for himself, and ever placed the happiest hopes on a door-bell ring, he had come out of his front room in the hope of good news. He came hurriedly, but his hurrying diminished to a slow-march, as he saw two men on his threshold. He'd had previous experience of two men on his threshold. And as his fine grey head came forward to let the moist, red eyes make a keener inspection of their faces, he recognized one of them. And this recognition caused his eyes to stare, his lips to shut, and his march to halt.

' Yes? ' he inquired, each grey eyebrow lifting high into his forehead as if he were at a loss to understand what they could want of him.

' You are Mr. Albert Howden? '

Choosing to assume a perfect peace of mind he put a cheerful note into his voice. ' Yes, cock.'

' We are police officers. I am Detective-Inspector Glower of Lutine Road Station—'

' Don't I know that ! '

' —and this is Sergeant Cundle.'

' How do you do? ' said Mr. Howden politely.

The Sergeant nodded at this greeting, briefly and non-committally, but said nothing ; and Mr. Howden was left without any information as to how he did.

' What is it you want, Inspector? Is it something I can do for you? I will if I can.' He said it in the tone of a good citizen who was always ready to do his duty and render all aid to the police. ' But come in. Don't stand there. You'd better come in here.' Torn between a desire to see the last of them and a desire that the street should see nothing of them, he turned towards his room. ' Forgive me if it sounds rude, but I don't like police on my doorstep. It makes people talk. And the things they'll bring themselves to say ! ' He led them into the bed-sitting room where he'd received Father Dawbeny but, having no great love for these two visitors of to-day, he did not trouble to hustle any embarrassing litter behind the two bed-screens. He just shut the door. He shut it because the char-woman was making it her business to sweep near by. 'Won't you sit down?' he invited, not very cordially, but pushing forward a chair.

'No.' The Inspector declined the chair crisply. 'Mr. Howden I have been making inquiries into an allegation that a Miss Florence Garside was kept in this house——'

'Florrie? Yes, I did have a Florrie Garside. A domestic help. Yes, that's right. Correct.'

'Let me finish. Kept in this house for purposes that you know all about——'

'Purposes?'

'All right : purposes of prostitution, and as——'

'Who on earth told you that? You don't believe that, do you? Good God!' He was indignant at the things people would say. And at the things police would believe.

'And, as a result of these inquiries I am going to arrest you on a charge of procuring this woman.'

'Oh, my . . . *lord*!' It was said almost in pity for the police, as the Inspector continued his recitation, giving the dates between which the misdemeanour was alleged to have been committed.

'I never heard such stuff! Prove it. Prove it if you can. I'll get out of this if it costs me every ha'penny I've got. I've got two thousand quid in the bank, and I'll spend every ha'penny of it, till I've made some of you sit up. That girl needed no procuring, whatever she's done. Whatever she's done, she's done of her own free will. And whatever she's done, it was none of my business.'

'And I must caution you that you need not say anything, but that——'

Mr. Howden did not wait to hear the rest of this. He'd heard it all before. 'I can't look after the morals of every girl who comes to work in my house. And I knew nothing about her age. She looked eighteen to me.'

'I've said nothing about her age.'

'Oh, haven't you? But that's what you were thinking.' Mr. Howden perceived that his skate had slipped on this difficult

91

ice, and he must recover his stance. 'Police always think the worst.'

'Certainly, when they have every evidence to warrant it.'

'There isn't any evidence. You're just trying to spruce me. All you cops do that, even after you've done the cautioning. And before the beak you talk as though you'd never done such a thing in all your lives. It's illegal. It's cheating.'

'Stay with him, Cundle, while I search the house.'

'Here! What the hell! You can't start turning over my house.'

'Can't I? That's news to me. If you like, you can be getting ready while I'm doing it, because you're coming along with us.'

'I can't come at once. I've got a lot to do. I shall want to talk to Mrs. Howden. I've got to explain to her what it's all about.'

'I'll send an officer round to tell her you're detained in custody. You can see her in court to-morrow.'

'Yes, and see her I will, to some purpose. I'll arrange a few things with her. I'll get her to see my solicitor about all you've done. I'm not at all sure that you've any right to search my house without a warrant. I *own* this house, did you know that?' The suggestion appeared to be that such prosperity was proof of innocence. 'And if there's any wrongful arrest here, you're *for* it. You've got it coming to you. I can write to my Member of Parliament about it. I know him quite well. I talked to him after the last Labour Party meeting here and told him I was a Christian Socialist, and he said——'

'Keep an eye on him, Cundle.'

And the Inspector was gone.

'Gawd's Christ!' exclaimed Mr. Howden. Not to the sergeant, but to the room so suddenly and rudely deserted.

It was uncomfortable for both the sergeant and himself. Neither wished to talk. So they stood apart, the sergeant looking all the time at Mr. Howden, and Mr. Howden looking only occasionally at the sergeant. Much of the time Mr. Howden looked at the curtains on the window or the pictures on the walls, as if unaware there was anybody else in the room.

At last he decided it would be safe to remark, 'I suppose it was that bloody parson who worked this for me.'

No answer from the sergeant: only a shrug.

92

' Eh ? Was it ? You can tell me that much.'

' You probably know more about that than I do.'

' That's what *you* say. I guess I know who's behind this. And, my God, I'll sort it out for him if I'm right. It's an outrage. Yes, if you want to write something down, write that down.' He was pacing the room, and he stopped. ' Well, I suppose we can sit down ? I suppose I can sit in my own house ? '

He sat ; the sergeant did not ; and there was a pause. But perhaps sitting down lessened the tension and the formality and, as the Inspector foretold, he felt a desire in his present unhappy state to talk to someone.

' I hope you've got a flounder (taxi) out there,' he began. ' I've no use for walking through the streets with a couple of cops. People turn round and stare.'

' We have a car there.'

' I bet you have.' He ruminated, his humid eyes reflecting the brilliant window at which he was gazing. ' Yes, that parson. He's done the dirty on me. And I've never been anything but decent to him. I've said fine things about him sometimes, and now he goes and shops me—for something of which I'm as completely innocent as he is,' he quickly added. ' My God, if ever I get a chance to pin something on him I will ; and I don't think you'd blame me, would you, guv'nor ? He tries to put me away. Call that Christian ! . . . Not that *I've* got anything on my conscience. . . . Yeah, I don't suppose he's been all that good all his life . . . do you ? '

' I don't imagine he's done anything criminal.'

' I don't know.' Mr. Howden was not at all sure. ' Parsons do get up to games. You read about it every day. They have opportunities . . . like doctors. I remember one who got his half-stretch for—well, you can guess what.' Mr. Howden, as a man of refinement, preferred hinting at, to speaking of, such a thing. ' And there was another in the Ville—it's no good hiding that I was there for a little some time ago—you'll know all about that. Gaw blimey, you never let a man forget anything. Once we've been inside you won't ever leave us alone. . . . No. Mr. the Honourable Piers Lygon Dawbeny hasn't heard the last of me yet. He says it's all wrong if a bloke hits you to hit him back ; but that's where he's wrong himself. That doesn't just make sense. If a man hits me he gets it back —with a little thrown in.'

So he chatted on till the Inspector returned, of whom he demanded sarcastically, 'And what do you think you've found, Officer? Anything up there belongs to my guests, and not to me. So you've been wasting your time and the ratepayers' money.'

The Inspector did not deal with these points. 'Put your hat on,' he ordered, 'and come along with us.'

'O.K., Officer.' Mr. Howden rose from his chair. 'But somebody's going to pay for this here before I've done.'

CHAPTER NINE

THIS was the year 1939, and the month of August. And in the fourth week of that month a shock hit the world, and the world trembled beneath it.

That week-end was hot and close, with the menace of thunder in the still air. A storm crashed and detonated over London on the Saturday night, and the air lightened and freshened, only to pack close again, with still mists in the mornings and oppressive heat at noon. A few warm showers fell, and then all was still again, the pavements drying quickly under the canopy of low, warm cloud.

And on the Tuesday, the 22nd day of August, Father Dawbeny, having said Mass to Ernie and one old lady, seated himself at his table where his coffee and toast awaited him. He opened his *Times*. And he read : ' It was announced in Berlin late last night that Germany and Russia have concluded a non-aggression pact, and that Germany's foreign minister will fly to Moscow to sign it to-morrow.' And he was only one of millions the world over who read this report, and read it again, and stared, and could not believe. He protested, ' No. *No!* '

On the Ides of March, five months before, the dictator of Germany, Adolf Hitler, had snatched up a new kingdom between dawn and nightfall, and put threatening arms about another. He had hoisted his hideous Nazi flag above the former royal palace of Czechoslovakia, and put his armies on three sides of Poland. In so doing he had stepped out of his plausible Pan-Germanism and announced a new era in history —or, rather, a return to an old era, the era of conquest and enslavement, for the people of these old kingdoms were not Germans, but neighbours of a different blood. On that day the Peace of the World was as Cæsar on the morning of the Ides of March.

However, these Ides had gone, and Cæsar still stood. He had received a stab, but apparently had accepted it, contenting himself with the announcement that it should be the last of its kind. In the Commons Britain's Prime Minister had pledged to Poland all the support in Britain's power if her independence was attacked, and so, in his turn, inaugurated a new era in European history, since Britain was now pledged to defend not only her buffer states across the Channel, but a state on the far side of Europe. And with the months it seems that the Peace was now fully convalescent after that savage assault. By August Britain had eight hundred thousand men under arms ; her fleet was at sea ' on exercises', and a British and French mission was in Moscow for staff talks with Russia. Let these talks prosper, and there was a chain round the mad German. Like Mr. Howden, he would be in a play-pen from which he couldn't well get out.

So on that hot week-end England felt itself at peace and able to play. The Canterbury Cricket Week had begun, the Promenade Concerts were flourishing in London before crowds of excited boys and girls, there was a music festival in one town, a summer conference in another and a carnival and flower show in a third. Even the Channel swimmers were at sea. And Father Dawbeny was thinking of nothing but Duncombe.

On the Monday morning, depressed by the emptiness of his church on the previous day, he wandered about his room, hands in his cassock pockets, asking himself, Surely he could do as good work at Duncombe as here in Potters Dale ? Might he not even hope to reach more hearts among those simple country people than among these restless and worldly-wise children of pavement, factory and slum ? Or was he just finding reasons for indulging his desire to rest ? To surrender and retreat. What was the answer ? Where was the answer ? He knelt on one knee by his long trestle table, resting one elbow on it, and his brow on his hand. ' Give me some sign, O Lord. I do not know. I have tried to see Thy will, but I cannot see it clearly. Give me some sign. May I go ? '

That was on the Monday after church, when the weather was hot and depressing, so that his heart was almost as empty as St. John's had been yesterday, both morning and evening. And now on the Tuesday morning, having forgotten all that, he was reading that the ally of his country had gone over to the enemy, and protesting his disbelief. ' No. *No !* '

With the disbelief went a great fear for his country. Sipping the coffee, munching the toast, and tasting neither, he thought, 'Doesn't this mean the greatest threat to England for nine hundred years, since William of Normandy made ready to conquer us?' With this enormous desertion to the enemy the scales of power had thumped down heavily on his side. Hitler's scale was now full of might. All hope of a blockade that might deter him from marching, or entangle his limbs if he began to march, was at an end: the whole of the east was open to him for sustenance, and full of corn and wine. The chain around the madman was broken. One side of the play-pen was down, and the infantile tyrant could easily push over the rest and start smashing up the house of Europe, and all its ancient treasures, just as soon as he liked. No hope now that he would listen to reason, when he must be confident of victory. France and Britain could not—and must not—yield to his insolent demands, and therefore war was but a few days, a few hours, away.

Father Dawbeny trembled, but it was not with fear. It was with an old excitement, an old exultation. War?

But how could Britain and France survive against a Germany aided and sustained by Russia? He read on. He read that the Prime Minister had summoned his cabinet to an emergency meeting and that Parliament would be recalled to pass an Emergency Powers (Defence) Bill. He felt a thrill at the words— and the word 'Defence' he spelt as 'Defiance.' In these moments, as he munched and sipped and read, he had not the least consciousness that he was a priest. His response was the reaction of a soldier, uncomplicated by bookish analyses of the economic or social causes of war. His heart, unmindful of the cassock about him, thumped with three life-long loves: love of excitement, love of fighting, and love of England. 'Hell!' He was not even using the language of a parson as he rose smartly from the table and stood quite still and very erect. 'If we have to go under, may we go under, fighting. And God grant that I may find a place to fight in.' The Nazi louts in possession of England and forcing his kindly, tolerant people into their crude and brutish moulds! The English people 'made to sweat for Germany'! That was what they boasted. Might he lie dead on some battlefield before he saw such a thing. 'Sweat we will, but in fighting them over every inch of our soil, and then digging their graves. "Six foot of English earth for a grave"—that's all they'll have of England.'

Duncombe? It was forgotten. It was too small a spot of English earth when he was thinking of the whole of Britain, from the heel of Kent to the outer Hebrides. All that day he was talking of war with Ernie or with parishioners in the streets; or he was reading the papers in his own room and planning the defence of Britain. The next day he saw that his dignified *Times* had allowed itself two-column banner head-lines: *Cabinet and the Crisis*, *British Pledge Reaffirmed*, *The World Astonished at Nazi-Soviet Pact*. To another headline, *Jubilation in Berlin*, he responded, ' Don't jubilate too soon '; and reading another, *Emergency Powers*, *Safety of Realm*, he trembled with resolution and pride. The following day it seemed that all over the world the events were converging upon the dread point of explosion. Berlin announced that Poland's preparations had ' assumed a sinister character.' The *casus belli*? Poland called up half a million reserves. France ordered partial mobiliza-tion and warned all unnecessary civilians to leave Paris. In England Parliament granted dictatorial powers to the Govern-ment, so that it could take all measures to meet the threat. All museums were closed, that their treasures might be removed; many liners were held in port, lest they should be needed as troopships, and school teachers were recalled from their holidays to London, that they might be at hand to conduct the evacuation of its children.

Father Dawbeny, having read of these matters, rose from his fireside chair to stand a little, and pace a little, and think. And as he rose his eyes fell on a little Churchman's tear-off calendar on his mantelpiece. It said, ' August 24th, St. Bartholomew's Day.' Since it was evening he tore off the date; and, as he looked at the little pad of remaining days, he thought, ' Where are we now? Does the end of England lie somewhere within that pad of days? What waits in the calendar of God? '

§

He went to the window. The street below was empty and quiet because of the warm, close, thundery air. As his window was high and the street's houses low, he looked across many of the roofs and chimneys of his parish. And, so looking, he saw what form the assault would take. Partial destruction of London from the air by high-explosive bombs, fire bombs, and gas bombs. Gas by bomb and spray and cloud. This was what *must* happen, because the enemy must strike at England's head and brain, so that all her muscles of government might be paralysed. And if that were done and England lay helpless before the enemy, what then? Why, then *vae victis*. And *vae victis* meant the murder of all those selected by the conqueror's secret police: socialists, communists, liberals, Jews. Especially Jews. Beneath those roofs and chimneys were many socialists, communists and Jews. Remember the communist slogans on the railway walls.

It was then that the memory of Duncombe came back to him. Came back to be laid aside at once and for ever. He laughed to think that he would go there. His question, 'Which way do I go?' had been answered for him, and by those efficient people, the dictators of Europe. They had dispersed the fog in his mind, and his road was now as clear as the street below the window. And he did not flatter himself that it was merely the self-sacrificing duty of a priest that bade him stay in the Dale, *for he no longer wanted to go.* He couldn't imagine himself going. No, not till this battle for the soil and the soul of England had reached its issue. He wanted to be in the war and the danger, fifty-eight though he was. His heart lifted in excitement as he perceived his part in the war. The people under those roofs might not come to his church, but they loved him—no moment for modest words now—these good-hearted and sentimental people loved him: he knew it. Whatever he was within the walls of his little failing church, he was a power outside it. He would help them to fight.

Not for months had he felt so happy. His whole nature seemed united—'like the country at this moment,' he told himself. No quarrelling parties within him; all for the State; never before in his sixteen years as a London parson had the priest and the colonel been so perfectly at one.

He laughed again in his joy. 'Well, that problem's settled.' And he went quickly from window to door and called for Ernie.

§

'Yes, Father?' Ernie came limping up the stairs from the assembly hall below, which he had been sweeping and cleaning.

'Let's have Sophie, too,' called the father, very cheerfully. 'We've serious business to discuss.'

'Sophie!' Ernie summoned his wife with a loud voice from the sink in which she was washing up after their tea. 'The father wants you.'

Sophie came along the passage rubbing her damp hands on the sides of her overall; her kitchen was on the same floor as the father's two rooms.

'Now, sit down, Sophie,' invited the father, advancing a chair with his usual courtesy. 'And you, too, Ernie.'

Sophie sat on the chair, uncomfortably upright, as she always did on the chair of a gentleman or a lady.

'Well, the question, children'—no one was more surprised at this word 'children' than the father himself; never before had he been so gay and free with these two good friends—'is what are we going to do. The war will be on us in a matter of days.'

'Oh, do you really think so?' Sophie frowned in dismay. 'Oh, I can't think that.'

'You listen to what the father says,' enjoined her husband; and it was as if he wanted to add, 'The Colonel knows better than you or me.'

'I can't see how it can be avoided,' said the father. '*We* can't back down and dishonour our pledge to Poland——'

'Good Lord, no,' agreed Ernie.

'—and Germany isn't going to back down and do what we tell her, when she has—or thinks she has—all the trumps in her hand.'

'*Thinks* she has,' Ernie preferred.

'Oh dear!' sighed Sophie, and added, 'No, I suppose not.'

'Don't worry yourself with supposing,' recommended Ernie. He, too, had been a soldier and could expound these military matters to a woman. 'There's not a hope in hell.'

'Well . . .' Father Dawbeny raised his eyebrows and smiled at them. 'What do *you* propose to do?'

'How do you mean, sir?'

'Well, there's no doubt about me: I've got to stay here. But you haven't.'

'Why not?' asked Ernie simply.

'Why—because you're free to go. There's nothing on earth to keep you.'

' Oh, yes, there is.'

' What ? '

Ernie's lip was sullen, as if his driving thought were anger with the insolent enemy instead of that thing which one did not utter aloud : loyalty to a friend and master. ' If you stay, we stay.'

' No, wait a minute, both of you. This is not a light decision.' And he told them what he thought would happen : explosive bombs, fire bombs, gas. He mentioned the proposed evacuation of the children, the expectant mothers, the blind, and the cripples ; looking away at the word ' cripples,' lest Ernie suppose he was alluding to him.

When he had finished Ernie announced from his sullen mouth, ' I'm not running before the bastards—if you'll pardon the word, sir.'

' Certainly I will. I've been using it once or twice myself.'

' *Ernie !* ' Sophie chided.

' Well, if *you* won't go, Ernie, what do you say to sending our Sophie away ? ' Never ' our Sophie ' before ; and his happiness was heightened by this sudden and wonderful release from the old fetters. ' Give us your views on that. Briefly.'

' Send her away ? But where the—where in heaven to ? '

' Oh, I can manage that all right. I'll send her just as far from danger as she can get.'

Both stared at him, waiting for some elucidation.

And he explained. ' To my brother in Cumberland.'

' To the Earl ? ' Ernie sat astonished. ' To his castle ? '

' To one of his farms, I thought. There she could have the time of her life, eating the best food, drinking the country air, walking in the woods, climbing the mountains. Heaven knows what food there'll be in London.'

' See me climbing any mountains ! ' scoffed Sophie.

' It was there that I had it in mind to send you, Ernie,' he added very deliberately, lest Ernie should wish to reconsider his refusal.

' But who'd look after the church, sir ? '

' I'd find someone—or I'd sweep it out myself.'

' No, sir. No, thank you. I'm stopping if you're stopping.'

' And you, Sophie ? '

' It's very kind of you, sir. But I don't see as how I can go if Ernie don't. I shouldn't like to.'

'And I'm not going if the father doesn't,' repeated Ernie. 'Not on your life.'

'No . . .' Sophie assented, but with less emphasis.

'It's not that we're bloody—that we're heroes, sir. Don't you think that.' At all costs Ernie must disavow any such imputation. 'It's just that Sophie and me've lived in London all our lives, and I reckon we'd both be more miserable in the country than in London with the bombs. Besides, I don't know that it's going to be so awful. He knows he'll get what he gives. And, any old how, one can die but once.'

'Do you really mean this? Understand: I quite definitely recommend Sophie to be sensible and go. I recommend you to tell her she ought to.'

'Much good it'd do my telling her. She don't do anything I tell her.'

'Sophie, will you be sensible and go? I repeat, they'll try to bomb the heart out of us ; they'll try to disrupt our railways and demolish our docks——'

'Yes, they'll do that,' agreed Ernie, another military expert.

'—and God alone knows if we'll be able to feed the millions in London. We're going to be besieged.'

Sophie sat with her hands clasped in her lap. But her silence was not long. 'I wouldn't go, sir, if Ernie wouldn't.'

'Then we all sit tight? Is that it, children? Is that it, Ernie?'

'Yes, sir : sit tight and let him do his damnedest.'

'*Ernie!*' Sophie again chided.

'Nothing to get hot about, Sophie. That's what the Colonel used to say to us in Murder Wood. Yes, " let him do his bloody damnedest "—those were his very words.'

'Oh, *Ernie* !'

'Remember Murder Wood, sir?' Ernie rubbed his hands happily. 'This is quite like old times. This is fine. May I say something, sir? Something I was thinking the other day?'

'Certainly you may.'

'Well, I was thinking, Things are funny, they are. When you used to shout my head off because my puttees were crooked or my tunic undone, I couldn't say anything back but, law-love-you, I thought all the more.'

'I'm sure you did, Ernie. And what did you think?'

'Well, I used to think, If the ruddy 'Uns come to-morrow

102

over that there parapet, I shall say, Come inside, Jerry. We can't be worse off under your Kaiser than what we are under our Colonel.'

' Oh, Ernie ! ' Sophie rebuked him. ' You shouldn't say things like that to the father.'

' No, but I used to think it ; really I did.'

' Well, you've no call to mention it to the father now.'

' It's hardly necessary for him to mention it, Sophie, because I used to get the impression that the men were thinking exactly that. I felt their thoughts behind me as I went out of the trench.'

' Law, yes, I used to say to your back as you went out of the trench, Yah, you may be Somebody now, old cock, but this 'ere war won't last for ever, and when we're both in civvies, if I meet you in the old Montebello Road, I shan't half tell you a few things I'd like you to know. But there ! we met just off the old Montebello Road and I never said none of them.'

' Say them now, Ernie. It'll probably do you good. Besides, I should like to hear them.'

' No, I don't feel like saying them now. And anyhow, there isn't time. Jerry may be knocking us up any moment.'

' And you no longer feel like saying, Come inside ? '

' Only if it's Come into our cemetery, brother, where we'll put you up and make you cosy. We've room for you and all your mates, so come along. You really think he's coming, sir ? '

' I do,' said Father Dawbeny tersely.

' Soon ? '

' Yes.'

' O.K., then. I'll go and get my best suit on and be ready to receive him, like. Come, Sophie. We're expecting Company. Any minute now.'

§

The children marched out of the Dale on the following Friday. In ragged threes, their teachers leading them, the children marched to the fleets of buses or to the great stations where the long empty trains, steam up, awaited them. According to the

Great Plan, half a million children would be out of London by the evening ; to-morrow the expectant mothers, the crippled, and the blind would follow them ; by Monday evening three million of the helpless would have been extracted from the threatened city.

From as early as six a.m. the children had begun to assemble in their school halls or church halls. Father Dawbeny, coming from his daily mass at seven thirty, saw the children approaching his assembly hall. They were coming along Greig Street from Cartwright Street, Becker Street, Purvey Close, and Queen's Walk. They came excitedly in twos and threes ; or, less excitedly, as single, solitary, units ; and each child, obeying the Great Plan, had a gas mask slung across the breast, a label in his left lapel declaring his identity, a loaded bag or suit-case in one hand and an overcoat or waterproof on the other arm.

Some of the bags were heavy, dragging the children down to one side. Those of the children whose parents had no suit-case to give them carried sacks over their shoulders like sailors' kit-bags, or stuffed pillow-cases like bundles for the laundries. Father Dawbeny's eye warmed, especially at the sight of those who came alone ; and he thanked Heaven for the cartons of chocolate and butterscotch, stacked high in his hall, which a pleasing and unexpected bank-balance had enabled him to buy. Ernie and he had calculated how many cartons would be required if every child in the Dale was to have a bar of chocolate and a stick of butterscotch, and had then fetched these supplies from a wholesaler in the Montebello Road, bringing them home on a barrow hired from old Jim Fowler's yard.,

Many women were standing about the doors of his Church Hall, mothers and their friends ; and they smiled at him, or tried to, and some attempted a joke as he went in.

The large hall was loud as a playground with the voices of children and teachers, the children chattering or shouting, the teachers calling out their instructions. The teachers, each with a brassard around his arm, were placing their charges in groups or inspecting their kits if they were already marshalled. Were their gas masks properly in their containers, the spare clothing and the food-for-one-day in their bags, and the identifying labels in good order ? Had they their postcards ready to send to their parents ? No one knew where anyone was going, whether to the country or to the sea ; and these postcards were to tell their parents to-morrow where they had arrived. One small boy had brought a tin bucket and spade, in case it was the sea.

From his own hall Father Dawbeny walked to the big L.C.C. school in Thyatira Place, and this time Ernie limped behind him with the barrow. Squaller the dog, padded along with them both, now behind the barrow, now alongside of it. On the barrow were the cartons, and Ernie who so loved to remember his days as a soldier shouted to loungers on the pavements, who stared at this odd procession of long, cassocked priest, loaded barrow, following dog and limping verger : 'Up come the rations.' Father Dawbeny walked in front of the barrow, silently. Was it fancy, or were the distant streets, was the vast spread of London, unusually quiet ? It might be so, for the normal bus services and train services had been curtailed, and the people had been asked to keep away, when possible, from roads and tubes and terminuses till half-past five that evening. As far as possible the roads and railways were to be kept clear for this exodus of the children.

He was at each school in time for the children's departure, and he handed out to each child the church's parting gift. A few of the teachers offered some disapproval of this, some questioning whether it was according to the Plan, but he told them that the Home Secretary and the Minister for Education had telephoned him personally that morning, instructing him to do precisely this ; and he went on with the distribution, ordering every third child in his fiercest military manner, 'Don't you dare to eat this till you want to.'

He returned to his own Church Hall in time for the departure there. A head teacher shouted to the grouped children to be ready to march, and Father Dawbeny walked out on to the pavement and stood in the sunlight to see them pass. Ernie and Sophie stood with him. A teacher at the head of each column, the children marched out, labelled and loaded : gas masks slung, coats on their arms, bags in their hands or sacks on their shoulders. To Father Dawbeny standing on the pavement and smiling down on them, they called, 'Good-bye, Father' or 'Good-bye, Fah'ver ; ' but he only nodded to these farewells with tight, smiling lips. He could not speak. Some of the boys, since male human animals are by nature clowns, strove, so far as their weighty bags would allow, to imitate marching soldiers with high-swinging arms and thrust-out chests ; and Ernie, no less of a clown, though thirty years older, called out, ' Pick up your feet there ! Smarten up now ! Chins up ! What do you think you are ? A lot of school kids going to the sea ? '

Sophie just wiped her nose and, since her handkerchief was at hand, touched her eyes with it and smiled.

By noon that day all were gone ; and then indeed the streets of the Dale were quiet. Quiet and oddly dull. Father Dawbeny, looking down upon them from his upper window, smiled as he remembered a line from *The Pied Piper* : ' It's dull in our town since my playmates left.' After a time his ears discerned the rumour of London's traffic around this area of silence ; and he saw in imagination all the great roads out of London with the buses and charabancs streaming away from the capital, freighted with waving, shouting, singing children ; and not these caval- cades only, but the trains of vehicles from public schools, private schools, reformatories, orphanages and hospitals.

And there below him were the quiet streets, waiting. It was Friday, September 1st, and at dawn that morning as the world knew, the Germans had marched into Poland across all her frontiers ; by now Danzig was in their hands ; and Upper Silesia would be theirs by nightfall. War was certain. And the streets were quiet and waiting. He looked up at the empty sky : it was clean and carefree and innocent.

PART II

CHAPTER ONE

THE October morning was cold, and Father Dawbeny gazed into his small gas-fire, with his notebook on his lap ; but he was seeing nothing around him, and writing nothing, for he was plunged deep into the business of a sermon.

More than a month had passed since that week-end when the children marched away and war fell upon England ; and in those few weeks things had happened that astounded and confounded the mind. All Poland had been rubbed out like a pencilled map, and not by Germany's fingers only ; Russia had erased her half. And then these two states, one Fascist, one Socialist, had shaken each other's hands over the agreed demarcation line between their two new satrapies. This done, the question of Poland settled by her annihilation, Russia and Germany had proposed peace to the world. And the Communist party in England, not disobedient to the heavenly vision from Moscow, had swung, in an incredible face-about, from fervid support of a righteous anti-fascist war to the new party line, a no less fervid agitation against it. 'Stop the War!' The new slogan, in dribbling white paint, was on all available walls in the Dale.

Peace ? Stop the war ? Condone a ruthless rape and take the safety offered ? Everything in Father Dawbeny, as he sat with his notebook, cried, 'No.' And if 'No' was the right answer, the only honourable answer, then it was his duty to play his small local part in the war and preach it to his people. He must combat the Communist campaign in the streets, and say to those who would listen to him, 'Not " stop " but " stand ".'

But were his surging instincts right ? He was always able to take his brain aside from his instincts and make it examine them sternly. How far were they such as he could preach without hesitation in his Master's presence ? Yes, how far ? He was deep down in that lonely and lightless place, that locked room, where his great personal decisions were made. And, shut in there, he could achieve humility and large doubts of himself in the face of Truth. Give Truth another name to-day : Humanity; he could almost see Humanity before him as a symbolical figure —and was it other than the gracious figure of his Master ? It was in this presence that he must make his decision.

These surging emotions—what were they ? Love of England —never so deep as now—but was love of country ever much more than an extension of self-love ? Pride in England, but wasn't pride always suspect ? Anger and vindictiveness against all crude bullies and torturers—but did anger and vindictiveness ever work anything good ? The old love of war's high drama— this was the most suspect of all. A haughty scorn that any men should think him and his people stuff for slaves—with this alone could he find no fault.

Stand ? Or stop ? Still his vision was clouded. He had no undimmed view that it would be right to say to his people, ' War to the end, no matter what agonies it may inflict upon the world, no matter what degradation it may work in men's characters. This I deem to be the wish of God.'

But the alternative ? ' Abandon our declared purpose and treat for peace ? ' Nothing, no, not God Himself, could persuade him to utter that. Rather than speak that—silence. But not to speak it was weakly to accept the war, silently to countenance it. If you were going to countenance it at all, do it strongly, not skulking. Proclaim it with conviction and pride.

Now as he sat there, brows furrowed, hand fingering his note-book or knocking his pencil against his teeth, he was justifying to himself the conviction and the pride, his longing to take the side of war. War to an end that was either victory (which seemed impossible) or annihilation (the more likely)—but at least annihilation in the trench we had chosen. Was it not a war to save for others, both now and in future time, all the things that Christians believed in : mercy, brotherhood, kindness, human rights, preciousness of every human soul—and peace itself ? Was it not a war against those who declared proudly that they spat upon all these things ? Was not the appalling thing about this present enemy, not that his methods were evil, but that Evil was his religion ? It was a war, not against Germany, but for the soul of Germany ; a war against those who were defiling her soul, even as Howden defiled the souls of children. He had not hesitated to set the law marching against Howden. No peace with Howden. No peace with Hitler.

'No. I can believe nothing else. Very good then.' He stood up ; and his standing was an unconscious symbol. 'I shall tell them to stand. I shall say, Hate war but accept it. Take and accept it proudly and humbly. I shall tell them to be ready to lose all they have, and all they hope in life, if by so doing they can save manknid. That is *my* party line. I have chosen it. Forgive me if I am wrong, O Lord.'

§

He went straight down to the hall below where he heard Ernie at his morning's work. 'Come on, Ernie, I want you to help me paint a notice.' For some time St. John the Prior's had been too poor to pay for the printing of Jumble Sale, Whist Drive and Social Dance advertisements ; Ernie and he would print them in red and black paint and paste them outside hall or church. They were getting quite adept at this sign-writing, showboard-writing, and bill-sticking. This time he was going to paint something more than a double-crown poster ; he was going to hang a long calico banner right across the three-arched porch of his church, and the words were going to be as large and terse and striking as the Communist slogan on the railway walls. Once you have made your choice, put all hampering doubts behind you and strike with all your strength. His brain beat and raced as he sought for words to answer that slogan, 'Stop the War !' It raked in memory for Bible words ; and finally it found them. And he and Ernie painted them in red on the white calico and took ladders (Ernie with joy) and hung the announcement along the front of St. John the Prior's : 'Sunday Next, 11.0. Sermon by the Vicar, " Prepare Ye War ".'

§

He had no great hope that it would bring him a large congregation : his Jumble Sale, Whist Drive and Church Social advertisements drew people in plenty through the doors of the Church Hall, but Service and Sermon notices fetched few but the faithful into the church itself. On this occasion, however, he was powerfully helped by his opponents, the communists, who, as he always maintained, were the worst tacticians in the world, whether in Moscow or in Potters Dale. They never perceived that their loud and bullying methods tended always to achieve the opposite of their aims. They saw his notice and, lapsing always into fury if their sacred faith was attacked, they painted their counter-notice on every available wall : ' Sunday Next, 12.0. Stop the War Rally, Greig Street.' And they canvassed the streets with news of Father Dawbeny's action and their reply. Father Dawbeny saw their notice and grinned.

And on the Sunday morning, when he crossed from hall to church, he found such a congregation waiting him as he saw only at Watch Night services on the last day of the year. The church was not full, but something more than two hundred people were in the pews. A number of them were men ; and there were some young men loitering about outside, communists probably, who would come in when the clock struck.

But Father Dawbeny's sermon was not the excitement of that Sunday in Greig Street. It said little that the people did not agree with and expect to hear, and want to hear—except the few communists at the back. Having first explained that the words, ' Prepare ye war ' were better translated ' Sanctify ye War ' he told them very simply of his own struggle and its issue ; how he had laboured in thought, but nothing, nothing could make him believe that to ' stop the war ' before the Nazi tyrants released their gains and foreswore their aims, would be anything but treachery to humanity all the world over and down much of future time. His close was solemn, and the people listened, staring and very still.

' You agree with me now, while it is easy to agree, but the trial, the testing of your agreement, has not come yet. It will come, and will you agree then ? It will come first from the air, and you may see your own home—not your neighbour's—ruined ; you may see someone you love lying mutilated or dead. Then will be the time to stand. In that day, if it comes, try to say, Let our homes be ruined, let ourselves be killed, but let our beliefs stand. The instinct to defend our country rises easily in us all ; it is a true instinct, and let it strengthen you in that day ; but strengthen yourselves also, and still further, by thinking that you are defending, not your country only, but the true and real country of all mankind, which is the Kingdom of God.' Behind him on a column, as he preached, hung a crucifix ; and for a second he turned and looked at it silently. Then, facing the people again, he said ' I am asking nothing less of you than that you should prepare yourselves to lose all you have, and all you hope in life, if by so doing you can save mankind. I am saying that, to save mankind, you should scorn to save yourselves.

> ' Long years ago, as earth lay dark and still,
> Rose a loud cry upon a lonely hill,
> Whilst in the frailty of our human clay
> Christ, our Redeemer, passed the self-same way.'

§

As Father Dawbeny, still in cassock and biretta, left the vestry and came down the broad alley between church and hall, he heard many voices in the street, one manifestly haranguing a crowd, the others chattering among themselves or calling out their interruptions.

He halted in the alley-mouth and looked towards them.

Half-way down Greig Street was another flagged alley, parallel with his own, and at its corner a considerable crowd stood around a young street orator, mounted on a small portable lectern. At the side of this lectern another youth held a poster aloft on a pole : ' Stop the War ! ' The speaker had a young, squarish flat-featured, but not unattractive, face beneath a thick mop of russet hair—the russet of bracken in November. This rusty tint clashed with the soiled, crimson, high-necked sweater which he wore beneath a loose copper-brown jacket. Rather did the crimson of his angry young face match this jersey, instead of the thick reddish hair. The hair bunched up and out from the square face like a huge head-dress of fur. His shoulders were high and thick too, one seeming higher than the other. Yes, an appealing figure, thought Father Dawbeny, if only the young face, between the high hair and the high shoulders, had not been flushed and distorted with anger.

One thing was surprising : all the time he was speaking, he kept both hands in his jacket pockets and used only his thick body for emphasis, thrusting it forward over the lectern where another man would throw forth an arm.

Father Dawbeny stayed in the alley-mouth to listen, his hands playing with one another before the cincture of his cassock. He considered the young man's audience. Not a few of them were youths in slack, grubby jackets and polo sweaters like the speaker, and of these one or two had thin beards of soft, innocent, newly grown fluff. With them were a few girls whose lank hair, untended skins and careless clothes showed that they were superior to the bourgeois notion that women should make themselves fair for men. But besides these palpable young communists there were men and women who'd come from their doors in Greig Street, and others who'd been in his church a few minutes ago. Especially had the men from his congregation stayed to hear the loud speech, or to see some fun.

Loud, virulent, and spitting were the words which the young voice sent down the street. 'It defeats me, absolutely defeats me that you can be such mutts, such saps, such poor, uncritical numskulls, as to believe everything your oppressors and exploiters tell you, and to do everything their lackeys, the politicians and parsons and pressmen, bamboozle you into doing. Don't forget it : these newspaper editors and parsons are only the dogs they get to bark for them. And you do everything the dogs say, like a pack of silly sheep. This is a war for humanity, is it ? You fall for that boloney ? A war to save mankind ? Oh, no : I'll tell you what it is : it is a war for loot ; a war between two gangs of imperialists for markets and colonies and profits. That's all ! It's the 1914 war over again ; an exploiters' war, in which they use you, the workers, as their pawns in the fight for all the nice things that empire brings them. And what are those things, you ask ? '

Father Dawbeny went a few steps nearer the voice, to hear the answer, and his dog, released from holy walls and Divine Service, went frisking and barking at his side. 'Stop, Squaller ! Down ! Hold your foolish tongue. I want to hear.'

The dog desisted, and looked sensitive and hurt at this rejection.

'What are those things, you ask ? I'll tell you : they are profits, privileges, access to raw materials, fields of investment, and cheap coolie labour. This war at present is just a quarrel between Britain and Germany to determine who shall dominate most of the globe, but mark my words : the Americans will soon, very soon, be sharpening their knives and coming in for their share of the carve-up. And whoever wins—mark you this—they'll league together afterwards to defend the interests of their capitalist class against the world-wide Socialist revolu-ion. Yes . . . that's it. Oh, don't you see, don't you *see*,' he screamed, and his mouth dripped, but he did not lift a hand from his pocket to wipe it, he only shook his head as a horse does, to fling the spittle from his lips, ' don't you SEE : there's nothing in this war for you except the chance of death and mutilation now and the certainty of oppression hereafter. Well—I don't mind—if you want to die in the front line—or here in your houses—for the Bank of England, that's *your* funeral. If you want to drench the soil of France—or the soil of Greig Street —with your blood to defend the rich man's profits and privileges, and his right to exploit your fellow-workers everywhere, O.K., fine, go and do it ; but at least see what you're doing. They've already shipped 150,000 of your mates over to France, all of them cheering as they went, poor, deluded fools. Go and join 'em, if you want to. I'm not stopping you. I'm only just telling you that what you'll get out of it is this and no more : the fixing of your chains on your backs by one capitalist power or the other. And whether it is British capitalism or German capitalism, does it matter much ? Is there much to choose between them ? Of the two I'm not at all sure that I don't prefer the Nazi brand——'

But this was too much for his audience—or for most of it. A low, guttural roar of protest swept up towards him.

' No, wait ! ' he commanded, but still only throwing forth his thick body to impose his will upon his hearers. ' Wait while I explain. I've no use for Dr. Ley, the so-called Leader of the German Labour Front—he's probably as big a scoundrel and hypocrite as any of your so-called leaders over here—but he did speak a word of sense when he said that a task before the world was the utter destruction of the Western plutocrats and of old-type capitalism everywhere. He couldn't have expressed my own views better. After all, in Germany, until we declared war on them, the Nazi Socialists *had* smashed the power of the industrial magnates and forced them to produce what they were told and pay the wages they were told and take only such profits as the State allowed. Had we anything like that in Britain ? Not likely ! I have little doubt that Great Britain is the most reactionary force in the world, and that Nazi-fascism with all its faults, is relatively progressive, compared with Anglo-American capitalism——'

Again a roar of dissent which broke like a wave into derisory laughter.

Father Dawbeny walked towards the orator, his blood rising. Relatively progressive, this regression into aboriginal savagery! But he walked slowly. He was angry with the words, not with the young man. He couldn't help liking the young man. He could see that, however wild and exaggerated his words, however blind he might choose to be to the devilries of Nazism and the comparative decencies of Anglo-Saxon Liberalism, he was driven to his present unpopular and risky task by some faith and vision within him. Like many another humble rank-and-file communist—or like Father Dawbeny himself—he was ready to spend himself to exhaustion for the sake of some distant 'kingdom' which he would never enjoy.

'Like it or not, it's what I say: your real enemy is a terrible thing called Monopoly Capitalism, wherever it is to be found, and Anglo-American capitalism is the very head and front of it. I tell you again that, whichever side wins, the victors will turn their power against you, by the simple means of marching against the only country where your fellow-workers are at last in control, the only country where a socialist state has been established in majesty and power—the Soviet Union——'

'Rubbish!' called a voice, and another echoed it, but with a shorter Greig Street word.

'It's not rubbish. Didn't you see it at Munich? Only a year ago as I speak? Are your eyes never going to open? At Munich didn't your Prime Minister and his henchman from France aim, not at defeating the German Nazis, who were their natural allies, but at diverting them from the capitalist lands of the West to the one Socialist country in the East? Didn't they help and encourage Hitler, giving him all the arms of Czechoslovakia and a free way through that country so that he should march against their real enemy, the Soviet Union? But Comrade Stalin wasn't having that. He nicely outwitted them. They thought themselves clever boys, but Comrade Stalin was just that bit cleverer. He did a deal with Hitler, and turned the Nazis' faces west again, where the real enemies of the people were. About turn, Mr. Hitler! And he was perfectly right.

He knew that he had to defend for the people—for you and the workers everywhere—the one and only country where your mates have won power.

'This is no " people's war " ; there has been only one real " people's war " ; and that was in Spain, when the same robber gangs set out to overthrow a people's republic, and when your masters here saw to it that the Spanish people got no help. I supported that war, comrades. I went and fought in it. I— I was wounded in it. But to this war of the imperial gangsters I say just what they said about the people's war : " Not a ship, not a gun, not a plane, not a hand's turn of work——" '

It was at this point that his smouldering, flaming eyes saw Father Dawbeny, whose biretta and black cape showed above the heads of shorter men. The sight of him there stirred both defiance and fear so that his words became even more violent.

'No, your enemy is not there in Germany, but here in England. Your true war is here. And your opportunity is here. Remember what Lenin said, " The government's danger is the working class's opportunity, and a revolutionary class in a reactionary war cannot but desire the defeat of its government——" '

'Wait ! ' interrupted Father Dawbeny, and all eyes swung towards this sudden voice. Fortunately he was so tall that all could see him and watch him and listen. 'Just a moment, comrade. If Comrade Lenin said that, he must have said it during the first war, 1917 or thereabouts—twenty-two years ago, and he'd be the first to tell you that it's completely undialectical, unscientific, uncommunistic, to apply what may have been true then to a completely new set of circumstances a generation later. It's un-Marxian, and I can't say worse than that, can I ? '

' 'Ear, 'ear,' called some of the crowd, not that they understood what he was talking about, but that they gathered he was against the young man and in favour of the war. And they wanted some fun.

'I don't know much about Communism,' continued Father Dawbeny, smiling, ' but I seem to know more than you do.'

' *What ?* ' Infuriated by this insult, as he conceived it, the young man struggled with an answer, stuttering, spitting. ' Lenin laid down the principle which applies to all time. He said— he said——' and here, to make his point and win it, he drew his right hand from his pocket and stretched it out towards Father Dawbeny. It was gloved, and stiff as wood ; an artificial limb. Its unmoving fingers were in a half-clutch and seemed unable to point at the interrupter or to clench in a furious fist.

'Hothead he may be,' thought Father Dawbeny, 'but at least he's given his right hand for the things in which he believes.'

'Lenin said——' stammered the youth, holding quite still this rigid, brown, extended limb—' he said, "The proletariat in every country must work for the overthrow of its own bourgeois government, and never mind other governments. It must work to——"'

'All right,' Father Dawbeny interrupted again. 'Let's all work for the overthrow of our present bourgeois government by the Nazis. And after this overthrow, what ? '

'Yes, *what* ? ' shouted the people, excited by this duel. The father in his cassock, with his biretta on the back of his head, son of an earl, and presumably a scholar, and once a high officer in the army, was no unimportant challenger to have entered the lists. 'Yeah, ah'ter we been beaten, what ? '

The boy's answer was glib. Glib, since it was a lesson learned by heart. 'A general revolution, and a people's peace. Not a rich man's peace ; a people's peace.'

'And that's what you really think you're going to get ? ' asked Father Dawbeny.

'He's off his chump,' someone at the back provided.

'That's what I'm going to fight for, and that only.' The orator put the shameful limb back in his pocket. 'Not for Britain, not for Germany, but for the Proletarian Revolution.' He turned from the father to the crowd in an effort to detach them from this too successful critic. 'The proletarian, friends, has no country ; that's the first axiom of Communism and the first thing we've got to get into our heads——'

'And it's nonsense,' submitted the critic, quite jovially.

'He has no country except one, and that one country is the Proletarian Revolution. That is our only fatherland.'

In Father Dawbeny the passionate need to answer was burning up all shyness and raising with this combustion a high steam-pressure of words ; but he controlled himself and said only with merry eyes, 'Comrade, will you allow me your platform for one minute ? '

116

' No ! ' cried the boy, now just angry and sulky.

' Yes, yes ! ' shouted the people, partly because they wanted
to see fair play, but more because they wanted to see the fun.
' Yes, yes . . . Yah, boo ! . . . You aren't afraid of him, are
you ? Gahn ! Let him up ! Fair's fair.'

The boy, angry as a child, yielded to the clamour and stepped
down, and Father Dawbeny stepped up into his place.

' Hurray ! ' greeted the people, much enjoying this Sunday
morning's entertainment. ' Cheerioh, Father ! How are you
this morning ? Give the silly drip something to think about.'

' He's not a silly drip, my good friends. I think he's terribly
mistaken in his views, but he is at least inspired by a great
ideal.' This unexpected beginning produced silence—a serious
silence, with all eyes trained on the speaker. ' The original
inspiration of the communists was a completely noble one, and
far nobler than the motives of many who attack and revile
them. It was a passionate desire to set the people free from
poverty and exploitation and war. It longed to see all people
everywhere, no matter what their country, free and equal as
brothers. Some of the first communists—yes, and some of the
young communists in our day like our friend here who went
to fight for the people in Spain—have served that ideal with a
selflessness that the martyrs of my own church could hardly
surpass and that thousands of church-goers might envy.'

' Dope ! ' sneered the young communist, standing at the
platform's side and fearing in a moment of illumination that
this urbanity might be more successful with the audience than
any hot and violent words. Similar jeers, ' Dope ! ' and ' Bah ! '
and ' Soft soap ! ' came from his group of supporters, the girls
being particularly shrill.

' Well, if you won't trust my sincerity, Comrade——' Father
Dawbeny looked down at him—' Comrade what ? What is
your name ? '

The boy tossed his red-thatched head and declined to answer,
so the humourists in the crowd answered for him. ' Joe Stalin
. . . Karl Marx, sir . . . Harpo Marx, more likely . . .' But
a lad on the other side of the platform glanced up at the speaker
and gave him the real name. ' Anton Bax, sir.'

' Anton Bax. Fine. Well, if you won't trust my sincerity,
Comrade Anton, and if my other comrades down there won't,
perhaps the rest of this audience will. I want to say simply this.

117

First, that you're very silly to fly in the face of a natural instinct, love of country and to say that it shouldn't exist. It will always exist very powerfully, and it will beat anyone who doesn't come to terms with it and enlist it on his side. Secondly, you believe —or you want to believe, because it is the new faith lately delivered by Moscow to the saints—that if your country's government can be brought down you will get a " people's peace." You will get nothing of the sort, my lad. You will get what your Dr. Ley, leader of the German Labour Front, promised you. You quoted him as saying that the Western plutocrats must be routed and capitalism destroyed. Have you forgotten something else he said ? He said that the people of Britain must be made to sweat for Germany. Are you taking that ? *I'm* not. Are you lads taking it ? '

' *No !* ' A most satisfying roar.

' I say the Nazis have got to be routed because I'm on your side, Comrade Anton. If there *is* a class struggle, as you say, then so far as my arm is of any use to them it is on the side of the poor and the weak and the exploited. There's a lot in me that merely wants to fight for my country which I love, but there's even more in me that wants to fight for you and all working men everywhere. And, as I see it, there's only one choice left to us in this late and terrible hour : either to fight for Britain, where there's still some freedom to fight for the workers, or to fight for Germany, where there's none. And you, by striving to break down our will to fight for Britain, are not being neutral, but fighting your best for Germany.'

' Hear, *hear* ! ' and ' Yah ! *Shame !* ' and ' That's the stuff to give 'em ! ' The acclamation was universal, except in the little band of communists. Perhaps the loudest ' Hear, hears ' were Ernie's, who had finished his tasks in church and arrived in his cassock on the skirts of the crowd. And here he was delighted to shout and root in support of the home team.

' Now, my good friends, the position is just this : if we throw all we've got into the fight we may *perhaps* win ; but if we spend ourselves discouraging and disheartening people, the Germans will certainly win. And if that happens there'll be no Proletarian Revolution in Germany because the Nazis will be more firmly enthroned than ever, and there'll be no revolution here because there'll be no time. We are living in the days of motorized armies. Break our will to fight and the Germans won't be here in months or in weeks, but in days. It took them only a few days to overrun Poland. Look down that street—*our* street —*your* street—do you want to see the German bullies coming down in their tanks and armoured cars, with their machine guns on their knees? Revolution, forsooth! What would you oppose to those tanks and guns? Fists? Boots? Why—so much as spit at them and you'd have forty bullets in your chest. I want to save this good-hearted but silly lad from the consequences of his folly. You chaps may get only Dr. Ley's whip, but he and his like'll get the concentration camp and torture and maybe the axe. My dear Comrade Anton, and you boys who think you agree with him, run your hands along your silly necks and ask yourselves if you want an axe there—not in a few years' time, but in a few days.'

' Do 'em good! ' suggested a few blithe voices. ' Let some light into 'em.'

' Please.' He raised a hand for silence. ' Comrade Anton says there's no difference between Britain and Germany, and if anything Germany is the more progressive. Did you ever hear such—" bull," I believe you call it, but I prefer on the whole to say " cock-and-bull ".' This drew laughter because ' bull ' was an abbreviation of a very crude army phrase. ' There may be exploitation in these islands—and I'll fight against it with you—but we have priceless and precious liberties here that they spit upon in Nazi Germany. An English docky may be fired if he slacks, but he's not imprisoned. An English editor may chafe beneath the pressure of his millionaire owner, but he's not turned into a human tape machine. Comrade Anton may be jeered at when he attacks the government, but he's not executed. I say there's more than a difference of degree between our victory and theirs; there's a difference of kind; a difference between life and death. Lose this war, and it's death to all your working-class hopes; defend Britain with all you've got, and all you are, and you'll be defending a piece of ground on which at least there's hope of building better things for you all one day.'

A billow of cheers, many sincere, some merely merry, broke over him as he stepped down. This street meeting was his, captured, its communist organizers broken, non-suited, dismissed from the case. And he thought, ' How much better I speak when I trust to the passion of the moment than when

I give long preparation to an address. Why can I never make the venture of faith and do this with my sermons?'

But the lad, Anton Bax, was not one to suffer a non-suiting. He stepped up as Father Dawbeny stepped down. To hear himself and his sacrosanct faith made fun of, and the fun cheered, was not a thing he could stomach without belching choler and hate.

'Watch out!' he cried; and now his gloved artificial hand was thrust well forward—stiff as timber, stiff as a branch in winter, and shaped like a clutching, gathering hand. 'How dare *he*—how can he have the face—to stand up here and say he's on your side in the class war? Look at his class! Doesn't he come from the gangster class of earls and barons who for a thousand years have held our land by the power of their knives and their guns, or of their paid, suave toughs in Parliament? How dare he stand up here in that uniform—the uniform of the Church which for a thousand years has been the mortal enemy of the people, fighting against all education and science and progress? For a thousand years and more the priests have been the uniformed flunkeys of the ruling classes on whose money they depend. Are you blind? Listen to others, if you like, but not to him. Not to any priests anywhere. They may not be conscious of what they are doing, but the plain fact is that they're paid by their bourgeois masters to stupefy the people with soft and comforting words. But never mind. They'll not be here much longer to block the people's progress. All religion is but the reflex of the economic fact that there are masters who must oppress and people to be oppressed. When we change all that, religion will be relegated to the rubbish heap of outmoded things.'

'Listen, comrade.' From his place on the ground Father Dawbeny persisted in smiling. 'Hot abuse like that is nearly always proof that a case is lost. I am no flunkey of any class.' He turned his eyes from the communist to the crowd, and as he was taller than any they were able to watch him as he spoke. 'May I be allowed to say this to you all: it was religion alone that put me, and all I possess, on your side. And when I'm weary and lazy and ready to give up the struggle, it's religion alone which gives me the power to go on.'

With that he turned away and walked towards his home.

'Yes, but——' began the lad, Anton Bax, running up to him.

'No, no ; not now.' He raised a deprecatory hand. 'We've each said our piece, and you are hot. Heat never produces anything much but hate. Some other day, my boy. Good-bye.'

The little high-shouldered communist lad walked back to his friends, throbbing with defeat ; and Father Dawbeny heard him say, as Ernie and he walked back to the Church Hall, 'If that man wants war he can have it.'

§

Walking back, Ernie told him that young Anton Bax, who lived in Tyre Street, had been christened Antony, but had changed his name to Anton because it sounded Russian. And Father Dawbeny was reminded of another lad, Dennis Flackman, who had become Denys because it looked more picturesque and was the name of a saint in France.

CHAPTER TWO

THE broad sky above the Dale and above the vast spread of London remained empty of menace. Clear or clouded, it neither revealed nor hid any high-flying flocks of terror-laden planes. The ground below waited for the sky to speak. The houses, factories, stores, and temples waited. Brick air-raid shelters stood along the gutters in the Dale ; notices affixed to lamp-posts pointed to air-raid trenches in Potterdale Park ; and in those streets where the basements were deep, stencilled signs stood at every few yards : ' Air Raid Shelter.' In back gardens ' Anderson ' shelters humped their backs over home-made ' funk-holes ' like the earth dwellings of a troglodyte people. The enormous gas-holders by the railway had wrapped themselves in cloaks of brown, green and yellow paint and hoped they looked like autumn landscapes in the heart of London. In the low, bright autumn suns the cables of the barrage balloons, shooting up into the sky from Potterdale Park and from the gardens in the handsome Ledbitter squares glistened like the wires of flying fairies on a pantomime stage. And sometimes Ernie, looking up at the last migrant birds flying out of London as out of a doomed city, would address them, ' Now, mind all them wires, boys.' The balloons floated on the tops of the taut cables like silver seed-pearls in the sky, and Ernie, watching some urchins hurling their toy aeroplanes into the air with ever-springing hope—for some of the children had come home—would admonish them as he admonished the birds, ' Now, then, chaps, mind all them balloons.'

Unwatched from this neutral and impassive sky, the business of war ran on. Convoys of army lorries and trains of artillery rattled along the highroad south of the Dale, usually travelling eastward to the docks or to the flat seaboards which an invader must attempt. Father Dawbeny, standing at the entrance to the Dale and watching them trundle by would marvel at the pink-cheeked youthfulness of the soldiers and ask himself, ' Did we look like that in 1914 ? '

At night the Dale, church and all, lay submerged in a sea of blackness. No window light, save in a forgetful or unlawful moment, gleamed in these fathoms of blackness. Sometimes the pin-prick point of an electric torch trailed and bobbed about this sea-bottom, as some policeman pounded his beat, or some worker came home. Or perhaps some lounger at a corner, trusting that no policeman was in the neighbourhood, struck a match and let it flame with brilliant defiance over his pipe-bowl—to be saluted, perhaps, by the voice of an unseen warden, ' *Put that light out!* ' Occasionally the narrow pin-light from a car's headlamp pierced a pilot tunnel through the limitless dark. The darkness was full of sounds and voices ; and sometimes a whistle—two or three whistles—started one's heart up, like a motor engine, and one waited for the air-raid sirens to wail their warning into the night.

But nothing happened. Each month, with its nights and days, was like a chain of black-and-white dominoes ; and no enemy came. Not even when the disobedient moon, contemptuous of policemen and wardens, came up from under the sea and bathed the whole of London in its brooding light.

In this unlooked-for tranquillity the normal business of the city went on. The business of justice went on. In No. 2 Court of the Old Bailey Father Dawbeny stood in the witness-box and gave his evidence against Albert Edward Howden, who watched him from the dock with his lips set in a straight, malignant line. And Howden, standing between his prison officers, heard his sentence. Seven years ! ' You will go to prison for seven years.' *Seven!* Stunned, almost paralysed, he turned round, at a peremptory touch from one of his guards, to go down to the cells ; and as he went he looked through the glass panels of the dock at Father Dawbeny, who was rising from his seat behind the reporters. Father Dawbeny met his eyes, and saw more hate gleaming there than ever he'd seen in human eyes before. Down in the cells below, Howden, his tongue loosed by fury, hissed at his warders, ' Seven years ! Seven bloody years ! It's a long time, mate, but I'll see that parson-nark when I come out. I shall be an old man then, but not too old to pay my bill. I'll lay he's done things in his life, but no one's ever got up a case against him, because he's a rich man with friends in the House'a Lords. He's been able to get up a case against me

123

because I'm only a working man. But he's got it coming to him. Let him wait.'

The business of the Church went on. Never in his fourteen years at St. John the Prior's had its vicar conducted so many weddings. At least once a week it seemed he was standing at his altar step before a bridegroom in air-force blue or khaki battle-dress and a childish bride in a cheap white frock and veil. Always these girls of the Dale were in white, for they were resolved, war or no war, Hitler or no Hitler, to have the white wedding of their dreams. In peace-time his heart would rush out to these young couples, overdressed boy and white bride, but now, in these death-shadowed days, the outgoing of his heart was almost a physical pain. The words of the service took on a new meaning as he spoke them, and never had they so charged his voice with sincerity and benediction. 'Thy wife shall be as the fruitful vine upon the walls of thy house ; thy children like the olive branches round about thy table . . . Yea, thou shalt see thy children's children, and peace upon Israel.'

§

This odd, eerie, ominous state-of-the-nation, neither peace nor war, was blasted in the spring. And blasted more terribly than the most timorous had feared. April and May changed the pattern of nations as it had not been changed since Charlemagne stretched his kingdom from the Elbe to the Ebro. Forty-eight hours, and the new Emperor of the West, the Nazi Fuehrer, had overrun Denmark ; five days, and he had conquered Holland ; one week, and Belgium was so much spoil behind his advancing armies ; two weeks and the *grande armeé* of France, its pride for centuries, was broken and scattered and impotent. The British army, three hundred thousand men, had been, literally and exactly, driven into the sea, but fortunately, every available English boat, large or small, pleasure-craft or river tug, was in the same sea, waiting for them. Still, the British army was routed, disorganized and disarmed, and the enemy had his airfields along the whole fringe of the Continent, within twenty minutes' flying distance of London. Hitler announced that he would enter London on August 15th.

'Well, Ernie,' said Father Dawbeny, ' what now ? The little gentleman is coming on August 15th. Do you still feel that you and Sophie wouldn't enjoy a visit to Cumberland? It's a lovely country, with plenty of meat and butter and eggs ; and I doubt if the war will ever reach as far as that. I can promise you you'd be very comfortable on one of the Strathpenny farms.'

' *You* going, Father ? '

' Good gracious, no ! '

' Then what are we talking about ? ' The subject was closed. ' August 15th. That's the Feast of the Assumption, isn't it ? I remember Denys talking about it and saying as how you didn't keep it properly. He had a mighty fine opinion of himself, Denny. He thought he knew how to run a church better than all the bishops put together.'

' That's true of most young Anglo-Catholics,' said Father Dawbeny. ' They have the Truth, and the rest of us are still in our sins.'

' Assumption ! ' Ernie had seen the chance for a joke. ' It's *some* assumption on Hitler's part ! August 15th. What the hell! There's still the old L.D.V. to reckon with.' Ernie, despite his lame leg, had been accepted in the Local Defence Volunteers a few days after their hurried formation. The L.D.V. demanded no medical inspection, and Ernie was considerably more active and mobile than some of the old gentlemen who had crowded to the police stations and been cheerfully enrolled. ' There's a million of us L.D.V. boys.'

' Yes,' laughed Father Dawbeny. ' And how many rifles ? '

' Well . . . there's other weapons besides rifles,' submitted Ernie, but doubtfully, as if he were not quite sure what they were. ' And there's seven hundred square miles of London and its suburbs. Seven hundred ! If he has to fight us in every street—and like hell he will !—we shall be there—it'll take him ten years to get really comfortably settled down. August 15th, 1950, p'raps he'll be in Buckingham Palace ; and p'raps not. Do you ever hear from Denys, sir ? Heard anything from our late Honorary Verger ? '

' No. Not a thing. Not a sound since he came and said good-bye when all the men between twenty and twenty-two were called up. Last October, wasn't it ? He promised to write, but . . . not a sound. Perhaps he's in Africa.'

'Perhaps he's dead,' suggested Ernie.

August 15th, the Festival of the Assumption, broke over the Dale, dry and warm and clean, with the enemy no nearer than he had been two months ago when France laid down her arms. At seven o'clock Father Dawbeny went out into the quiet and empty morning to celebrate Mass. On entering the side-chapel, vested in white-and-gold chasuble, with Ernie in cassock and surplice for his server, he perceived that there were a few more people than usual kneeling there : five or six women, two old men, and behind them all in the hindmost seat a solitary figure in khaki with his head cupped in his hands. Father Dawbeny's movements were always in strict accord with the Ceremonial drill-book, and so his eyes were kept lowered on his sacred vessels as he walked at a quiet and even pace to the lowest step before the altar and made his inclination to it. And the stern drill-book did not suffer him to turn and face the people till the stillness and mystery were gathered into the chapel, and established there beyond the power of men, and he was speaking the Comfortable Words. 'Hear what comfortable words our Saviour Christ saith unto all that truly turn to him. Come unto me all that travail . . .'

It was then that he saw the upturned face of the soldier at the back. The face was Denys Flackman's.

The service over, and he and Ernie back in the sacristy, he set down the vessels, hastily removed his chasuble and maniple, and, still in alb and stole, hurried back into the church to see Denys before he left. Ernie likewise abandoned his duties and, having doffed his surplice but not his cassock, followed the father. Denys was standing by the step of the chapel, waiting for them. He looked wonderfully handsome in his battle-dress which he'd carefully brushed and pressed, and with his fair hair oiled and smoothed for attendance at church. After months in camp and on the parade grounds his cheeks were fuller, his eyes clearer, and his skin cleaner, fresher, and better coloured than in the old days when he loitered in the streets of the Dale.

'Well, Denys,' Father Dawbeny greeted him. 'Where have you been all this long time ? '

'I was billeted in Sussex till the Spring, Father, and since then I've been in camp at Camberley.' Had his eyes swung away as if this answer did not really account for his long absence ? 'Hallo, Ernie.'

'Hallo, San Denee. Good to see you again. We thought you was dead. It must be a year since we seen you. Law, how you've grown!'

'Well, anyhow, we're glad you've come at last,' said Father Dawbeny. 'Haven't you had any leaves all these months, so that you could come and see us?'

'Oh yes, one or two, but you know how it is. A seven days' leave now and then, and perhaps a forty-eight-hour pass occasionally—there's not much time to do anything.'

Clearly he was a little ashamed of, and did not know how to explain, his neglect. Father Dawbeny, perceiving his discomfort, said nothing, lest he should be further distressed. But Ernie, less tactful, less subtly compassionate, didn't hesitate to declare, 'Denny, you ought to be ashamed of yourself.'

'Well, I suppose I'd better make a clean breast of it. You know what the Army is, Father.' Denys's eyes shifted away. 'I got in with a lot of fellows who had no use for religion and especially with one chap who was a public schoolboy and Oxford and all that, and enormously clever—we became pals, and he got to like me a lot and I got to agree with him. He used to argue that the dogmas of the Church were just so much incredible superstition to the contemporary mind'—Denys was plainly proud of this phrasing—'and that the sacraments were just so much primitive magic and witch-doctoring. He used to make out that the day of religion was nearly over, and there was no future in it.'

'Judging by the state of the world,' laughed Father Dawbeny —laughing that he might not show the slightest shock at this apostasy, 'I should say there's no future for mankind without it.'

'That's right,' said Ernie.

'You can give the word what meaning you like, but unless Man finds *some* sort of religion soon, he's finished. He'll destroy himself. Or so it seems to me.'

'And to me,' said Ernie. 'That's it.'

'Yes,' agreed Denys, 'but I kind of lost my faith listening to this chap, who was one of the best, Father——"

'I can quite believe it.'

'——and I gave up going to my duties. So when I got home, I kept away from you—kind of afraid.'

'You need never be afraid of me, Denys, whatever you've

done or not done,' said Father Dawbeny, picking up an end of his white stole and passing its golden fringe through his fingers.

'No . . . but I didn't want to be persuaded back again. And I knew you'd persuade me, if anyone would. I was glad to be shut of everything and free, absolutely free, to do whatever I fancied.'

'That happens to most people sometimes.' He continued to smooth the fringe of the stole. 'And now you've come back to us?'

'Yes. . . . yes . . .' His eyes wandered round the church. 'This is my last leave, you see. Embarkation leave.'

'Oh? The Front?'

'Yes. Africa, I imagine, because we're entraining for Liverpool. I've got to be back in camp by Reveille the day after to-morrow, and I shall take the late train to Camberley. Yes, it's Africa all right.' And he began talking about Africa and how they would travel round the Cape, how they might get shore leave at Cape Town or Durban, how the army was obviously being built up in Egypt for some big offensive—plainly talking about anything rather than what he'd come to say.

Father Dawbeny perceived that he was postponing and postponing what he'd come to say ; and he tried to help him.

'This is very interesting, Denys. Is there anything I can do for you or your people?'

'Yes, Father . . . I thought . . . I thought I'd like to come and make my confession before I go.'

At the word ' confession,' Ernie, not so unsubtle that he didn't perceive when to take himself off, quietly and unobtrusively withdrew.

'To me?' inquired Father Dawbeny.

'Yes, if I may . . .'

'Here I am, my boy. When would you like to come?'

'This evening, Father?' The boy's voice stuttered as he said it. 'Then I could make my communion in the morning before I go.'

'Perfect.' Father Dawbeny said it with a smile.

'When's best for you, Father?'

'After Evensong this evening? How's that? There'll be no one there—there never is, alas !—but we could say Evensong together.'

'Yes . . . that will do. Fine . . .'
But he was obviously very much afraid.

§

So Father Dawbeny came into the church at six o'clock that evening ; and it was as he had said : no one else was in the chapel—not even Ernie, because it was Thursday and his 'afternoon off.' Ernie and Sophie were at the 'pictures.' Only Denys was there. And the priest and he said their Evensong together, exchanging versicle and response in this strange place of stillness among the murmuring streets.

Then Denys left the chapel and, crossing the nave, went into the shadows of the north-east corner where there was a little prayer-desk against the wall and a chair before it for the confessor. There were no enclosed confessionals in St. John the Prior's—just this prayer-desk and chair, and in the old days Denys would deplore this ' timid protestantism ' of the vicar.

Father Dawbeny, after allowing enough time for Denys to say his ' Prayers before Confession ', came slowly to the chair, took up the violet stole that hung over its back, and put it first to his lips and then over his surplice. Seated in the chair he said his own prayer just loud enough for his penitent to hear. ' Be present, O Lord, with our supplications, and graciously hear me who am the first to need thy mercy. Not for my own merit but of Thy grace hast thou appointed me minister in this work. . . .'

He ceased . . . and waited.

Denys spoke his words. ' Bless me, Father, for I have sinned.'

Turning slightly towards his penitent, Father Dawbeny said, ' The Lord be with thy heart and in thy lips that thou mayst humbly and faithfully confess thy sins in the name of the Father . . .'

Having said this, he sat very still in his chair against the wall ; as still as one of those seated statues of Peter in Rome.

And the boy began his confession. ' I confess to Almighty God, to Blessed Mary ever Virgin, to blessed Michael the Archangel, to blessed John Baptist, to the holy apostles Peter and Paul, to all the Saints, and to you, my father, that I have sinned exceedingly, in thought, word, and deed, by my fault, by my own fault, by my own most grievous fault.' Father Dawbeny, sitting there, could not stay the thought that, even in his manifestly real penitence, Denys must use the full Roman Confiteor and gently beat three times upon his breast as he said 'my fault, my own fault, my own most grievous fault.' 'Since the time of my last confession which was two years ago, I accuse myself of the following sins.'

There was no doubt that he was striving in great earnest to make his confession complete. He began by enumerating offences of thought which a Catholic was instructed to consider sins against God and the Church, but about which Father Dawbeny, in his private, heretical, and pitying heart, was inclined to wonder if they were sins at all. He spoke rapidly of losing his faith, doubting the word of the Church, talking lightly of sacred things, uttering the holy Names in his oaths, and joking about sex. And the ex-professional soldier in the surplice found it difficult to think of these as sins. Then Denys spoke of less venial offences : attending mass at one period ' to keep up appearances,' and pretending to a faith which he no longer held ; then swinging to the opposite pole and feeling shame for the religion he had once practised and deliberately attacking it so that he could seem clever and stand well in the eyes of others. He spoke of bragging and boasting before his mates, of telling many lies to them, of joining them in drunken bouts, and of listening to and laughing at their stories of their sins. So he came to those sins of his own, to confess which was to set the heart hammering in opposition to the will. But his will was master and drove him on. He was stammering now, and speaking very fast, for these sins were flooding his cheeks and brow with shame. Not that the priest saw these crimson flags, for his eyes were staring straight ahead of him into the dusk of the church. But he knew they were there, and behind his unmoving lips he prayed hard for the boy, ' O God, help him, help him.'

Denys was speaking of impure thoughts and desires, of delighting in reading and thinking of unclean things, and of sinful acts committed ' by himself, and many times with others.' Here he paused, and Father Dawbeny knew it for a pause of fear, a pause in hope of more courage. It seemed to last for a whole minute and more, and that clock over the west door ticked louder and louder. But Father Dawbeny stayed completely still. Let there be no sign of impatience, no hint of disapproval. Only that prayer : ' O God, help him. With thee all things are possible.'

And Denys spoke of sins on the open heaths of London, in lonely country places and in the basement rooms of empty houses—sins which, if discovered, would have put him in the hands of the police.

Still not a movement from his confessor, not a sign of condemnation, not one breath of distaste. The boy had done it bravely, and his priest felt only a great and almost unbearable love for him. Sitting there like the seated statue, he was picturing him tormented with desire in his young loneliness and feeling driven out to the lonely places. Driven, helpless, once the fire burned within him.

Of course Denys had kept these worst sins to the last and was now hurrying away from them. As over some plank that enabled him to escape from a scorching and searing pain he was stumbling quickly over the familiar words of the Confiteor's close. ' For these and all my other sins which I cannot now remember I am heartily sorry, firmly purpose amendment, and most humbly ask pardon of God, and penance, counsel, and absolution of you, my father. Therefore I beseech Blessed Mary ever Virgin, blessed Michael the Archangel, blessed John Baptist, the holy apostles Peter and Paul and all the Saints, and you, my father, to pray to the Lord our God for me.'

Instantly—before offering counsel or allotting a penance— Father Dawbeny rose to say the words of absolution. Instantly, lest the boy should think him shaken by what he had heard or in any doubt whether to give absolution. Over the boy's bowed head he said the words of comfort, ' By His authority committed unto me I absolve thee from all thy sins,' and then sat down again and, speaking gently, said, ' You can be certain, absolutely certain, that these sins are forgiven and though they may trouble your conscience sometimes, they need no longer be springs of fear or raise in you any sense of apartness from God. The special penance which I shall tell you to say will be the 103rd psalm, and as you say it, believe every word of it, especially the words, " Look how high the heaven is in comparison with the earth, so great is his mercy towards them that fear him. Look how wide also is the east from the west, so far hath he set our sins from us." You have never in your life been nearer to God than at this moment. Thank God for this complete forgiveness, and forgive everyone else always—even when their sins seem to you unpardonable. Practise this complete forgiveness, day by day, whenever you can, remembering this day. Now I want you to be happy, forgetting those things which are behind and pressing forward to the mark of your high calling.' Drawing upon his own experience he enjoined him to achieve a morality that was not the fruit of emotion but wrung out of intellect and wrought hard by constant thought and practice. ' You have the intelligence to do this ; you have the courage ; you have a strength of will that can master your weakness ; and you have, so clearly, a dislike of sin and a love of virtue. Also you have affection (that is clear to me). Cultivate these splendid things, your courage, your will, your dislike of sin, and your affection ; and let your affection be such that it prevents you from ever injuring or defiling anyone again —especially those that are younger than you.'

Then the last prayer, so aptly fitted to these last words of counsel : ' May the Passion of our Lord supply all the defects of this thy confession ; may it supply to thee strength in every good work, grace to overcome all thy temptations and perseverance until thou reach the land of everlasting life ; ' and the Blessing ; and the Dismissal : ' Go in peace, for the Lord hath put away thy sin.'

Denys left the prayer desk and went back into the dim-lit body of the church to say his penance. And Father Dawbeny went into the sacristy, where he waited lest Denys was ready to meet him again and talk of commonplace things. But the boy did not come, and time passed, and at last he went to the door and looked into the church. He saw Denys lingering in doubt by the west door, but the moment the boy heard his confessor's step, he turned and hurried out of the church, afraid to face him. His flight was so obviously a flight of shame that Father Dawbeny wondered if he would ever see him again.

CHAPTER THREE

In the next month, at five in the evening of September 17th, it came : the enemy appeared in the hitherto inviolate sky and his malice fell upon London. This opening barrage in the full daylight was the overture to ninety nights of bombardment from the air.

For ninety nights, between dark and dawn, the ground and the sky fought each other. The sky let fall its screaming explosive bombs, its fire bombs which descended lazily like luminous worms wriggling downward, and its parachute flares which drifted to the roofs with a slow indifference, illuminating as they came a whole target area. Red, orange and green, with their sparks dropping faster than they themselves could sink, these flares were as beautiful as they were evil. Sometimes, loitering down through a darkness that should have extinguished the Dale, they re-created it, clear and solid and bright under the sky ; the Dale existed for a while in their light, and when the light went out, ceased to exist.

The ground saluted this insolent invasion with a fury of guns. All the guns in London, all the guns around London, turning their throats to the sky, spread a canopy of irate and bursting shell-fire over their city. In the lightning of their flashes the Dale, once again, would exist for a half-second and then cease to exist. From every quarter the searchlights ransacked the sky, and if one found an enemy aeroplane it held it in its unsparing beam while the others swept round to share in the capture and fetter the prisoner in new chains of light. Then up these trembling but resolute beams went the tracer shells, small golden rods sliding idly towards the victim. At other times the searchlights could not find their quarry, and one and another of them would shut off, like memories suddenly lost ; and the guns would place their exploding shells, like a chaplet of sparkling gems, around some aeroplane located but unseen. Did the guns kill their victim, his fall to the earth was like a long ropeworm with a head of fire and a tail of smoke.

Beneath this nightly battle raging in extended order over the fields of the air and among the hillocks of cloud the rescue-workers of London raced in their lorries and ambulances to some blazing home or tumbled factory or lurching church wall. Here they laboured like shadows in the clouds of brick dust or of reeking, suffocating smoke : air-raid wardens, rescue and demolition squads, firemen, stretcher parties and mobile medical units. Each ' incident '—as officialism with dignified understatement called each focus of disaster—was cordoned off with ropes and lanterns, and somewhere within the cordoned area the incident officer's control post announced its position by two blue lamps on a pole.

The Dale was a part of this London floor so wantonly beaten from the sky, and at every incident Father Dawbeny was of the company within the cordon. He had no official rank or character, but after the first few days it had been tacitly accepted by all, by wardens, police, firemen, stretcher-bearers and ambulance girls, that the father had the freedom of every incident. If any strangers asked what right he had to be digging in the rubble, crawling through the wreckage, clambering along a dizzy cornice (he had a head for mountains and rescue work) to some upper chamber miraculously suspended in the air, or administering first aid to a casualty extricated from the ruins, the local wags would inform them that Mr. Dawbeny was an honorary fireman, rescue man, stretcher-bearer, doctor, nurse, and street sweeper. A.R.P. headquarters had given him a blue siren suit like those the wardens wore (and the Prime Minister), but it was rather too small for his tall figure, so that his wrists and ankles extended far beyond its limits as he laboured. Still, in this comfortable and business-like garment he spent his days, ready for every call, and wearing always with it his clerical collar, so that the dazed or the dying could recognize his office. Generally they recognized his face and smiled and were glad.

Now, forty years later, he thanked Heaven for his first-aid training and practice, on tumbling screes and precipitous shelves, in the old days of the Strathpenny Mountain Rescue Team.

If the cordon was there before him he went through it as of right, but quite often he was at the place of disaster before the cordon arrived. In the beginning he had been followed by Squaller, the dog, but after the first few nights he refused the dog further permission to attend the incidents, and Squaller was shut up on the Church Hall, howling to heaven that he'd been left out of the battle. He added his melancholy wails to the uproar of the night, and the guns tired and the Germans tired before his wails.

Never before, despite the suffering to which he must minister, had Father Dawbeny been so at peace within himself. He was at peace because both parts of his nature, the priest and the late soldier and leader of men, were working at full pressure. Before the enemy came he had often been disheartened by the sight of a mere twenty people in his pews, and a mere five or six in his choir, but now, night after night, and half the daytime, his ministry was stretched over the whole of the Dale. The people saw him in the streets with bloodshot eyes, sunken cheeks, and dark, unshaven chin, his blue siren suit grey with the dust of last night's work among the rubble ; and before that year of 1940 began to die, and the great London blitz with it, ' Father Dawbeny ' was something of a legend in the Dale, just as Colonel Dawbeny had been a legend on the Somme. The simple people of the Dale, and not least the sinners among them, were always ready to believe big things and to praise abundantly ; and Ernie went amongst them as an unconscious but splendid publicity agent for his master, reporting his deeds, with exaggerations, to everyone in shop and pub and street. ' I seen him at this game before,' he would say proudly, and would thereupon exaggerate Mr. Dawbeny's heroism both in Murder Wood long ago and in Becker Street last night. ' Yes, the Colonel's in his element now if you ask me. He likes conducting a battle. And this is the Battle of London, ain't it ? Well, this is our stretch of it, and so far as the Dale's concerned he'll never let it budge an inch before bloody old Hitler.'

When asked by admiring listeners, ' Does he ever sleep ? ' Ernie would make a good story of his answer and say, ' Oh, yes, he gets an hour or two of a morning when everyone else is comfortably settled in the rest centre or the hospital or the mortuary.' It may be true that no man is a hero to his valet, but this priest was certainly the pride of his verger.

Praise him the people might, but no more of them came to church ; rather less, if anything, because whole terraces of his parish, whole blocks of buildings, were dead and their inmates scattered. He could walk about his parish and see these murdered homes in every street and perhaps a whole square block, where the demolition squads had been at work, transfigured into an open and trampled waste of rubble. Forster Place, a brief, truncated alley which, because blind, had always been a children's play-street—they had held their Silver Jubilee Party there, with flags and bunting festooned across it, and the long trestle tables spread under the flags—was a dead street, every house blasted and uninhabitable. Its gay spirit was gone. In Simon Street the tenement buildings with their balcony access had received a direct hit and their floors hung down, almost perpendicular, between their sharded walls. Vicar and verger would stand and look at them and speak of Ypres.

The church stood unshaken. Here and there its walls were pock-marked or gouged where bomb splinters had sprayed them ; a few of its leaded windows had been bent by blast, but apart from these minor lesions it stood among the ruins like an ark riding a storm. So firmly did it stand on its base that the people became superstitious about it. They believed (or chose to believe) that it was being preserved miraculously. There was no sense in this fancy because they could see another house of God, St. Anne's, on the north border of the Dale, a stark, oblong ruin ; but among the more untutored people the belief persisted and spread, so that some of them, directly the bomb-bursts sounded near, would run into the church from the houses across the road or those in the next street. Because of this the church was kept open day and night during the great blitz ; and when October passed into November, Ernie would stoke up its furnace to have it warm for the shelterers. On nights when the assault was close to the Dale, Sophie would be there, in the verger's cubby-hole, making cocoa on the gas-ring for lonely old women sitting in the nave, mothers walking up and down dandling their babies, and the children playing hide-and-seek among the pews.

All through the blitz a banner streamed across the three-arched entrance, not now advertising a sermon, but proclaiming some slogan to hearten or amuse the people. The vicar had been stirred by the placard pasted on the refuse vans of the borough, 'We Can Take It,' and his first slogan, painted red on white by himself and Ernie, was simply a repetition of these admirable words. But as the bombardment of the rain washed all its scarlet brilliance away (the vicar's and verger's paint couldn't take it) they amused themselves inventing slogans of their own and blazoning them before the parishioners as long as the rain would allow of it. They never achieved, in the vicar's view, the simple perfection of 'We Can Take It,' but some of their slogans are spoken of in the Dale to this hour. 'The Dale is Ours' was one; another, 'We are the Hitch in Hitler's Plan'; another, 'Potters Dale *v.* Pottersdam'; and another, after fifty nights of it, 'Potters Dale Still Going Strong.' It became quite a fashion for the older people and the young couples to take a walk to the church and see what flag he was flying this week to embolden or divert them.

§

As far as is known the Rev. Piers Dawbeny of Potters Dale conceived and put into practice the idea of 'fire-watchers' long before the State thought of it. At any rate that is what they still like to believe in the Dale. It came about like this. The church was open day and night, not only to receive any shelterers, but to take in and store any furniture that could be saved from bombed or burning houses. Soon both aisles— never needed now, alas, for worshippers—were stacked with beds, mattresses, tables, chairs, curtains, vases and cheap but treasured ornaments. After a while more floor space was needed, and the stacked furniture invaded the west end of the nave so that only an area before the chancel steps, some sixty feet square, was available for worshippers—but again, alas, it was enough. Much of the furniture belonged to strangers who'd never set foot in the church: Jews, costers, orientals, burglars and even, to the vicar's amusement, some of Mr. Howden's profession. Father Dawbeny, mounting his pulpit, would see it all around him and think with pleasure, but never say aloud, 'I was a stranger and ye took me in.'

But what if a fire bomb fell through the roof, or half a dozen of them? One morning Father Dawbeny, staring at his verger with a grim smile, posed this question: 'What if we burn? Eh, Ernie, what if we burn?'

'It'll be the best blaze we've had yet,' suggested Ernie, looking at the piled furniture. 'Yes, the fire's nicely laid.'

' But it just mustn't burn, Ernie. We mustn't let it. These are the people's treasures, and we're responsible for them. We can't have the Fuehrer putting a match to it.'

' If he does it'll burn just lovely. They'll see it from Richmond to Southend.'

' It shall not burn.' What a slogan ! Almost as good as the one he and Ernie used to see on the walls of French villages : ' They shall not pass.'

' It shall not burn. That's our motto, Ernie. The incendiaries shan't pass. We'll stop them on the roof. We must have a permanent watch in the church and on the roof when the siren goes ; we must divide the nights into watches as they do on a ship. S.S. *St. John's*. The whole congregation, the whole crew, has got to come into this, with you as first mate, Ernie ; you as Jimmy the One.'

Those were days, brave days, when you could persuade people to anything, and this idea of saving the church and the people's treasures was one that Father Dawbeny, because it inspired him, could put over to the congregation with eloquence, humour and power. The Parish Church Council was small ; it consisted of Ernie and Sophie ; Miss Maud Ayer, the organist ; Mr. Eric Sandeman, the greengrocer ; Mr. George Legg, the second-hand dealer; Mr. Andy Wayman and Mr. Jack Frisk, both street traders, Mr. Harry Benson, a casual labourer ; Mr. Charlie Shotts, the rag, metal and old clothes merchant (or marine store dealer, as he preferred to be called), and four women who said little at the council meetings, but were of great use because they were always present and so enabled a quorum to be formed. All of these enrolled in the proposed watch. The rest of the congregation did not number many more than the P.C.C. itself, but they all responded to their vicar's appeal, and he quickly had the fifty watchers he required. The air-raid wardens willingly trained them in the use of the stirrup-pump and in the disabling and disposing of incendiaries; and now in the church porch there was regularly a notice headed, ' It Shall Not Burn ' and giving the week's rota of watchers.

As a matter of fact no incendiaries ever did touch the church, and Ernie suggested that this was because the enemy had been advised that bombs would be wasted on St. John the Prior's. ' His briefing officers tell the Fritzes before ever they take off for London that there are chaps on our roof waiting to catch their bombs. That's how it is, you see. They don't lay any of their eggs on us.'

And so the church stood, a small, safe, lump of pity and consolation in the heart of all this conflict, suffering and death, and therefore necessarily (or so its vicar liked to think) a symbol and proof of something in the heart of man.

§

The London blitz died suddenly at the end of the year. One great fire raid on the city, like the last uprush of fevered, wild-eyed life in a patient before he dies, and then an extraordinary quiet ; then, incredibly, nights of silence and peace. Days passed, weeks passed, and the sky above London stayed empty. And beneath this empty vault Potters Dale lay like a small-scale relief map of London as a whole : much of it still standing, some of it jagged ruins or hunks and chunks of houses, parts of it an open and sprawling waste. You could even liken the little church of St. John's, standing intact among the ruins and waste, to its great mother church of St. Paul's, which still raised its dome haughtily and defiantly in the heart of the ravaged city.

§

Father Dawbeny, much uplifted by this stubborn endurance of England's ancient capital, spoke with quite extraordinary eloquence to his few people one Sunday morning under a tranquil sky. He was always eloquent when he spoke of England, or, come to that, of fighting. London, he said, was the only undefeated city in Western Europe. London alone had declined to surrender. Hitler, as the world had foreseen, had attacked the head and brain of Britain in an effort to paralyse the whole country ; he had put forth all he could, and he had failed. The hitch in his plan for world conquest was complete, and London was the hitch. London had fought him to a standstill, said the preacher with unmistakable glee, a glee that he didn't often allow into his eyes or on to his lips. London had looked into the blazing eyes of the Fuehrer, and he had dropped his first. And Potters Dale was an honourable part of London.

One effect of this hitch was to turn the enemy's discomfited eyes away from Britain, away from the West altogether, and towards the East. At dawn on a June day, without a declaration of war, with a treaty of non-aggression between them, and without the semblance of a dispute to justify it, Germany attacked Russia all along her frontier from the Baltic to the Black Sea. The Russians responded with violence enough to occupy most of the enemy's mind and power, and Britain was left in an uneasy and watchful peace. It was not till the dark of a late July night, at two in the morning, that the air-raid sirens wailed again. For the first time in fifty days they cried all over London, and their chain of lamentations had hardly sunk down into the darkness before the bombs and the incendiaries were falling upon the roofs, here, there, and everywhere, as if the enemy's mind was to instruct as much of London as possible that Britain was not forgotten. Only a few incendiaries fell on the Dale, and only one of these achieved much ; but this one achieved the whole of its hope. It fell through the roof and staircase of a three-storied house in Bolney Street, and in a matter of minutes set the dry, rotting staircase ablaze, so that no escape was possible for the people on the upper floors.

Eleven people died, five adults and six children. The number of children would have been greater if a mother had not thrown out her two babies into the waiting arms of men who had escaped from the ground floor. The smoke and the heat had almost overpowered her as she flung the second child, and, her last maternal service done, she fell back into the mercy of the smoke, which gave her sleep before the flames could touch her.

Father Dawbeny arrived soon upon the scene, with an excited Ernie limping behind him. He came in a grey jacket and trousers drawn over his pyjamas, and with his chin darkly bristling. Ernie came in a buff mackintosh, flying open to reveal his pyjamas. But, the father having slept through the sirens, to be awakened by Ernie, they were not at their places quite as quickly as usual, and they found the wardens, firemen, and ambulances already on duty before the house, and all the inhabitants of the street standing against the cordon ropes or on their doorsteps. The tall, roaring flames were now changing into a gush of smoke and flying sparks, and there was no chance, even if there had ever been one, of his reaching and ministering to the dying. All he could do was to assemble the dazed and silent people from the ground-floor rooms, and from the next-door house which was now alight, and to lead them away to a rest centre. He was so terribly moved by the story of that young mother and by the thought of the six dead children that he was able to say to his little company, ' Come, my dears.' For once his love was able to express itself in words.

And he led them away through the first of the light ; seven women (the men having remained) and eleven children, two of the women carrying the babies whose young mother was now dead, after having flung them into the arms of the world. He led a child by either hand, and Ernie limped ahead of them all to prepare their reception.

Father Dawbeny thanked God that he had his own rest centre to take them to. There were two rest centres near at hand, one in the big L.C.C. school in Thyatira Place, the other, a much smaller one, in the basement of his own Church Hall. Here some thirty beds always waited for the homeless beneath bright counterpanes that had mostly come from America in their ' Bundles for Britain.' Stout brick walls before the ground-level windows protected these sleeping rooms ; further baffle, or blast, walls stood within the rooms to protect the beds ; and at intervals stout brick pillars reinforced the ceilings. The rooms above, including the big assembly hall, were furnished as dining-room, reading-room and kitchen ; and here the evicted refugees might live for many days because it was often difficult to find homes for families with many children. To his own Church Hall, then, Father Dawbeny brought this large family, and having seen them into the gentle charge of the Deputy Supervisor (who was Sophie), went off with Ernie to make the tea. Cups of tea were always the first ministration. There was no one else to do this because these long weeks of calm had justified a relaxation of duty at the centre. Besides, it was only four o'clock.

The people settled and comforted, and Ernie left to jolly them all, especially the ' kids,' he returned to Bolney Street. It was daylight now, and the two houses were giving forth little but a lazy smoke. The firemen were still playing their jets on to the walls of the adjoining houses ; the wardens were still standing by their blue lamps, talking together and making notes; and by the two ropes that cordoned off the area the people still stood at gaze and muttering their indignation. He passed through the cordon and stood near the wardens, not caring in his shyness to disturb them with a parson's questions till their present work was done. He had been there perhaps half an hour when he became conscious of a loud and continuing voice, apparently aimed at an audience somewhere beyond the crowd on his right. Turning his face, he saw that a mob-orator had mounted the steps of a house to take advantage of the people's indignation and present an impassioned argument before them. He had now quite a large audience on the pavement before him. Father Dawbeny drew down his dark eyebrows in an effort to see the speaker more clearly. Yes, it was his old opponent, the little thick-set communist, Antony Bax: Comrade Anton, in fact. There was the massy, high-brushed rust-red hair, the high, round shoulders in the loose tweed jacket, the high-necked jersey (but black this time instead of crimson) and the body leaning forward from the waist to stress his point, because the hands were thrust out of sight into his pockets. His excited voice was so hoarse and rasping that many of his sentences could be heard.

'Look at that, *look* at it!' His head and body jerked towards the smoking houses. 'And have no further doubt, my friends, what your task is. It is to do all in your power to support our government in this war against Hitler. This is the one supreme business of us all. I am no sentimentalist, as some of you know, but I have no hesitation in saying now that if the words "Sacred Task" and "Holy War" ever applied to anything, they apply to this duty to smash Hitler and his fascism and wipe it from the face of the earth——'

Good Lord! Had one really heard aright? Was this really Comrade Anton? Father Dawbeny strolled towards him, stepping over the cordon, and the shouted words became yet clearer.

'We communists have only one purpose now: the final and absolute defeat of Germany. I only wish I could go and fight in this sacred cause, but I was disabled in an earlier phase of the same battle—in Spain five years ago—and I'm not much use to anyone now. But at least I can do this; I can do something; I can speak in the streets and call upon people everywhere for a mighty and unwavering effort in support of our soldiers; I can tell them that all those who stop to argue about the rightness of the war, all those who are too slack to labour as they should, and, worse still, all those who try to sabotage the war-effort, are traitors, not only to the British people, but to all mankind. Show them no mercy.'

'Well, well . . . !' thought Father Dawbeny, coming to the rim of the audience, and standing there to hear more. 'Is Saul also among the prophets?'

He was in time to hear an interrupter shout merrily, 'Thought you was against the old war, mate?'

'So I was . . . but . . .' The speaker halted, a little disconcerted. 'So I was, friend, but surely you know by this time, surely you aren't so ignorant that you don't know by this time—' at all costs one must stamp on a heckler like a beetle—'that the Communist Party always adjusts its political line to the concrete situation of the moment. The concrete situation has changed from that of yesterday. Our policy was correct in the circumstances then, but those circumstances no longer exist.'

'Gahn!' scoffed the heckler. 'That one won't wash, mate. Try another.'

Comrade Anton leaned his body forward, cheeks and neck afire. Any scoffing at the sacred faith always ignited him. 'If you can't see that the face of the world was changed in a dozen hours, between dawn and dusk, on a day one month ago, I'm sorry for you.'

'What day, cocky?'

'*The Twenty Second of June*,' screamed the young orator in contempt. 'At dawn that day—in case you've forgotten—Germany attacked the Soviet Union. I think I'm correct, friends—' he turned towards the rest of the audience to enlist them against this blasphemer—'that it was June 22nd. We are agreed, are we? Good. And now use your imagination, all of you. Forget him. Never mind him. Listen. How can you pause to argue or doubt when at this moment, as you listen to me, thousands of tanks, thousands of planes, and millions of men are hurling themselves against the one and only Socialist state in the world—in history? Say they get through—but, by the living God, they won't!—but imagine they get to Moscow as they got to Paris, why, then the only country where the workers have taken control, and are at last, at last, building a society free from exploitation and oppression, will have been obliterated. The greatest event in the history of mankind, the Russian Revolution, will have been undone. But if you have not imagination enough to see what this would mean to you workers and wage-slaves in England, then let me tell you this : once the Soviet Union is overthrown, all that might of guns and planes will be turned against *you*, and then that *there*—' he jerked his head towards the smoking houses—' will be but a foretaste of the meal you'll have to swallow. Russia is fighting to save *you*—and me—they are dropping dead on their steppes and in their streets as I speak, laying down their lives that we may be saved ; and therefore I say, mobilize the entire British people so that we may give the enemy the maximum of war ; I say, give him the war on two fronts that he's always dreaded, and give it to him now ; I say, give him what he's given us. Give him *that* ! ' Now that stiff, gloved, artificial hand had sprung from his pocket and was pointing—no, not pointing for the fingers were half-clenched and motionless—but extending itself towards the still smoking houses. ' Give him all that and much more.'

' That's the stuff ! ' cried one or two enthusiastically. ' Now you're talking.' Their cheers drew people from the cordon where there was little now to see but drifting smoke and standing firemen. And the more the people came towards his voice, the more they drew others. ' Yeah, that's about the size of it. Like hell it is ! Give him the whole boiling works. Exterminate the whole bloody lot of them. That's the idea. That's the idea every time ! '

The support of the audience, and the swelling of the audience, further excited him. Nevertheless he whipped the rigid hand back into his pocket as if regretting that he'd exposed it. ' Somewhere under that smoke, friends, are the ashes of children : six little mites, full of joy and hope when they went to bed last night, and now—ashes ! '

' God damn their souls ! God rot them, I—— '

' Don't wait for God to do anything. If you wait for that, you'll wait till Kingdom Come. *We've* got to do it. I say, bomb their cities too. Bomb them without mercy. Hesitate no more, but for every ten bombs they drop on our homes, drop a hundred on theirs. Give them no respite till Berlin and Hamburg and Essen and Cologne are as flat from end to end as that waste of rubble at the end of the road there—' the hand was about to spring out and point at the distant wilderness, but he restrained it in time. 'Let's have no more sentimental nonsense about bombing military objectives only. Bomb him precisely as he bombs us, and do it ten times worse.'

The cheers for this, from people fresh from staring at the smoking deathbeds of little children, were all that he could want, but they lay on Father Dawbeny's heart like a hot iron, searing it. The young man had not recognized him in the enlarging crowd. Last time they had met he had been in his long cassock; this morning the collar of his grey coat was turned up over his pyjama jacket, his chin was dark and unshaved, and his cheeks, though he did not know it, were smudged with blacks from the smoke.

'Let him drink of his own poison, till he cries, Enough ! Bomb and obliterate his cities. And do it now. At the moment there's no other means of saving Russia—and ourselves.' He added 'ourselves' almost as an afterthought. 'Look, look again at those two homes ; think that *your* children may be next ; and say to yourselves, " He's asked for it, and he shall have it." And have, not only what he's given us, but ten times, a hundred times, more.' Now he brought out his left hand, which was of flesh and blood and glanced at the watch on his wrist. 'Well, friends, it's seven o'clock. I must go to work.' Suddenly, with a smile, he had changed from a human furnace belching hot words, to an ordinary pleasant working boy. 'I'm a clerk in a firm of Research Engineers, and I don't mind telling you that we're engaged on important work for the Admiralty and the Air Ministry—leave it at that. Enough said ! Careless talk costs lives. Our hours in war time are from eight-thirty to seven, but let me tell you I'm ready to work from eight till midnight if they want me. Good-bye, all. Work hard too. Work your guts out and win the war.'

Cheers accompanied him as he came down the steps, smiling, and Father Dawbeny heard voices saying, ' Good lad, that. He ought to stump the country and say that sort of thing in places where they never seen a bomb.' Or, 'He can't half talk, can he ? But it's the stuff. Give 'em what they give us and a hell of a lot more. I agree. I agree absolutely.' One or two of the people were now standing about Comrade Anton on the pavement and talking to him, and Father Dawbeny went up to speak with him too. The young man recognized him after a brief stare and his eyes surveyed him uncomfortably. Father Dawbeny put a smile in his own eyes that the lad might be at ease. 'Good-morning, Comrade. You remember me?'

'Yes. It's Mr. Dawbeny. I didn't see you there before.'

'I was listening.'

'Oh, were you. . . ?' The boy waited; perhaps for praise. It did not come, so he asked, 'Did you agree?'

'Most heartily with all you said about winning the war and saving the Soviet Union, but not—we seem fated to argue with each other, don't we?—not that we should fight it with methods like those.' He pointed to the ruined, smouldering houses where the children had died. 'Are you really advocating that we should do *that* to him?'

'Certainly I am!' Instantly friendliness had slid from his face like a lantern-picture from a sheet, leaving him pale like the sheet. The sacred faith, the untouchable Party Line, had been challenged; it was apparently being disapproved of; and now only hate and intolerance could appear on the sheet. 'I'm advocating exactly that.'

'Yeah! Of course he is!' said some of the standers-by. 'And quite right too!'

'Oh, no, no,' said Father Dawbeny to them all. 'You can't want to torture children to death. No, Comrade, you're simply not thinking. You're not using your imagination.'

This was not a statement the comrade could stomach, he who imagined that it was other men who were the romantic, unthinking self-deluding fools, and himself, as a student of that supreme science, Dialectical Materialism, the real clear-headed thinker. 'It's because I use my imagination in a way no one else does that I don't think of the present moment only or of individuals either——'

'No, my boy, that won't do. You have pity, you have kindness and a love of your fellows, or you'd never have given your-self heart and soul to the party which you think can save and help them. You have a gift for oratory; surely you're not going to use it to advocate torture and torment for people of your own working class and their children.'

'I certainly am, if that's the only way we can win the war. What you don't see—' for a second the old proud aristocrat, seated within Father Dawbeny, leapt to his feet, saying, 'Damn this upstart puppy telling me what I don't see,' but he was persuaded, with some difficulty, to be seated again and go to sleep or, better still die—' what you don't see is that individuals don't matter—I don't matter—you don't matter—it's only the future of humanity that matters.'

' Exactly ; and if we abandon pity and decency we betray the future.'

' I don't agree. We've got to meet utter ruthlessness with utter ruthlessness. It's the historical necessity of the moment. It's the only way to win the war.'

' Of *course* it is,' said the standers-by. ' Stands to reason.'

Father Dawbeny sighed, and his heart sank. He turned towards these mutterers. ' It's the only way to lose it, men. If we adopt the enemy's filthy creed and exult in it, crushing down the pity and decency we were born with, he will have won the war, no matter what army is on top at the end.'

' Have some logic,' cried the boy (and ' Damn him ! ' whispered the old aristocrat, not yet asleep, and certainly not dead). ' You accept the blockading of Germany, which starves children —where's the logic ? '

' Yeah, where's the logic, mister ? '

' There may be none. But sometimes the wisdom of the heart is larger than logic.'

' Bah ! Sentimental bourgeois nonsense ! The silliest, sloppiest sentimentality ! I'm going. I've got work to do. I know nothing about your sort of pity. We talk different languages. Pity may be an absolute for you ; it's not for me. The only morality for me is determined, moment by moment, by what the World Revolution demands. And at this moment in history it demands that we win the war.'

' Yeah. 'Course it does.'

' Would you *lose* the war ? ' demanded the boy, pleased to have the support of these voices. ' Are you ready to lose it ? '

' Yes. Rather than do *that* deliberately to a single German child.'

The boy turned away. ' Well, all I can say is, you seem to me a pro-German.'

' Yeah,' muttered some of the listeners who did not know him, or who had no love for him. ' That's about it. Bloody proGerman.'

' No, my boy. No, men. Not pro-German, but pro-every man in the world. And certainly pro-every child.'

'Then call off the blockade. Call off the whole war, I should. Bah! I must be going. You were all for the war the last time we met.'

'Yes, strange, isn't it? A little while ago you had no interest in my war, and now, if this is the way you want to fight it, I have no interest in yours.'

'Damned pro-German,' muttered the listeners who were hostile; and he heard them as he walked away. 'Lucky if he don't get his house smashed up, one of these days, and his Greig Street shop too, like that hairdresser's in Nore street. He'll shoot his tongue out once too often, one of these days.'

CHAPTER FOUR

THAT was the beginning of his sorrowful loss of heart in the war. Not that he didn't daily crave victories for his country, but that a distress sat at his heart, a dull pain of disappointment at the new unmoral ferocity with which she appeared to be fighting. Nowadays he had to keep the eyes of his mind away from the war because the things he saw could wound them so. It seemed that Comrade Anton's voice, and no longer any voice in his own heart, was the new voice of England ; preaching the doctrine that England must compete with Nazidom in the markets of inhumanity and outbid it.

He would sit in his chair by the empty grate and fiddle with the ears of his dog, meditating and melancholy. And always the text for his meditation was those last words of his to the young communist, ' You had no interest in my war, and now I have no interest in yours.' He would tell himself, ' I was fighting in defence of love and compassion ; he is fighting to destroy them.' Or he would invert this and say, ' I was fighting to destroy the Nazi creed of hate and ruthlessness ; he is fighting to establish it.' And either he would stay in the chair and fondle the dog's head, defeated ; or he would rise and walk to the window, as if there were some light there, some help across the sun-washed roofs or beyond the blue-grey, luminous mists at the end of the street. He never spoke of the war in his pulpit now.

§

The distress, festering within him, came to a bursting head in the spring of the next year—and he spoke. In the spring of that year it was plain to him that Britain's Air Force was no longer even pretending to bombard only military and industrial targets, but was deliberately obliterating whole cities, area by area, and

149

that the people of England, *his* England, were glorying in this work. This new technique of utter ruthlessness, sparing none, culminated in the Thousand-Bomber Raid on Cologne. Nonsense to pretend that a thousand-bomber raid could be anything but an obliteration raid, but it was being presented to the nation as something to be proud of, something to stir and delight the heart. The Prime Minister announced to the House that this triumphant achievement was the herald of what Germany would receive henceforward city by city ; and the House cheered, and no one chose to remember his execration of the Germans five years before, for bombing the Spanish city of Guernica almost out of existence. No man mentioned Guernica. The Chief of Bomber Command proudly echoed his chief. ' We are bombing Germany city by city, and ever more terribly, in order to make it impossible for her to go on with the war. That is our object. We shall pursue it relentlessly, till the heart of Germany ceases to beat.' And finally a bishop in the Midlands, whose cathedral had been destroyed, declared that Britain was now morally justified in these retaliatory raids.

Then Father Dawbeny rose. He could take no more. The abscess-wall burst within him. A bishop, a *bishop*, to say such a thing. He went to the window and the light. Blue, pearly mists had fallen into the faraway channels of the streets, and the slate roofs, reflecting them, had turned a brilliant blue. Pale pink clouds dreamed over the Dale and were as beautiful in the serene air as chimneys, cowls, and aerials were ugly. All the buildings he could see from his window were cut four-square by the low flood-lighting of the sun. Up from the street came the characteristic sound of the Dale : the clattering hooves of a pony dragging a dealer's trolley over the setts. It rattled away towards Ledbitter Hill, and the cry of the dealer went with it, ' O'rags o'lumber. Any rags iron lumber. O'rags o'lumber. '

Hooves and cry died in the distance.

He, Piers Dawbeny, who was he compared with the Prime Minister or with a bishop or with a great captain of the war ? These few poor streets were the whole of his province, and his influence did not pass, or hardly passed, beyond the sun-flushed mist, blue as watered milk, that closed each vista's end. The mists were around him like a curtain. But such as he was, he must speak. Never had the burden of duty lain so surely on his heart.

And never had his vision been so clear. It had been a little clouded when he preached the war ; there was no cloud anywhere now. And because of this, because he saw his road without one shadow of doubt touching it, he felt of a sudden completely at peace. If he must sacrifice all the praise and hero-worship he'd won in the blitz, well, he was going to do it. Without further question. The old stern, iron will was on the bridge again, and at its side the old secret craving for perfection ; and in this cause he need be ashamed of neither. On to his manifest task, no matter what came to him. It might be that, in their present mood, the people would salute him with hisses and hootings, or even perhaps with stones, but his lips were tight set and he was at peace.

In his mind he saw his congregation : a few people dotted about on one side of the nave, and a large block of children on the other. Those people ; those children ; he must give them the truth of which he was so certain. A command uttered three thousand years ago was sounding again in that quiet London room. ' These are the words which shall be in thine heart, and thou shalt teach them diligently unto thy children.'

Two days later, a streamer, painted by himself and Ernie, swung across his three-arched porch : ' Has the Enemy Come ? '

No one could see what it meant, and when he entered the church on the Sunday morning he saw that quite a few, besides the faithful, had come to learn what it meant. Here was nothing like the congregation for his ' Prepare ye War ' sermon, which the local Communists had so obligingly publicized, but this was a gathering larger than any he'd had since that day three years ago.

When he went to the pulpit and looked down upon the people, while the last of the Creed was being sung, he saw Lady Guttree in her usual place with Lady Peggy Ungar-Bateman beside her. He saw all the usual worshippers and a number of other faces well known to him in the streets but never before seen in his pews ; and he saw the children.

Thou shalt teach them diligently to thy children.

He was well prepared with his sermon. Quite unable to trust himself to the inspiration of the moment, he had written it over and over again, and read it over and over again, and now knew it almost by heart. And never had he felt less nervous, because never so sure that he was called to say these words. He knew he would speak easily, because the whole of his nature—

his sense of duty, his pride in the battle, and his adamantine will—would be behind the words.

He gave out no text, and his first words were spoken in conversational tones. ' How proud we were a year or so ago when it became clear that we had baulked the enemy's plan to invade us, when we knew that our young men in the air, by fighting him sick, and ourselves on the ground, by enduring all things till he wearied, had taught him that he had best not come our way. And he did not come. He could not. Britain alone has been spared the sight of his tanks, guns, and other engines of war defiling her towns, ravaging her villages, and murdering her people. He did not come.'

He felt the congregation thrilling with pride at his words. But then, suddenly, after a significant halt, he changed his tone His tone now rang with doubt. It sounded the first notes of alarm. 'He did not come, we say. But is this really so ? Or has he perhaps come in a different shape ? In a spiritual instead of a bodily shape ? Is he, after all, and in spite of all, sweeping over our country, defiling it and murdering, not our bodies, but our souls ? In simpler words, must it be said that we are no longer resisting him but surrendering to him because we are accepting—yes and welcoming—his hateful creed and practice of ruthlessness, frightfulness and inhumanity ? And to that question I answer with a great sickness in my heart, Yes. To this extent, and in this sense, he has come.'

A fidgeting among his hearers ; a restlessness as of indignation rising.

But relentlessly he went on. He reminded them that the faith for which their little church stood in their streets was nothing less than this : that God had created all men in His own image including every single one of their enemies ; that, therefore, he was the Father of all Germans, even the most corrupted of them, and ' we, my dear people, are their brothers. We cannot escape it, and we should not want to. Ninety nights of bombing by these our brothers has not shaken this little church, and so long as I am its minister, nothing else that the enemy can do, not the foulest things, shall shake it from its faith or drive my Master out of it.'

That fidgeting again ; and a sibilant stuttering of offended tongues ; but this opposition before him only stirred up the old fighting instinct, so that he put heat and defiance into his next words. That was their creed, he said, however uncomfortable they might find it in their present mood of resentment. That was what he had been commissioned to preach and would always preach. Their leaders, their newspapers, aye, and their bishops, might be putting out a different doctrine and glorying in it, but he, for one, was not going to say his Amen. Quickly he recovered himself and remembered that he must speak in gentleness and love, not in anger and pride. And he said gently, 'Did you glory in that thousand-bomber raid on the unarmed people of Cologne? Yes, you did. You were told to, and you did. But it was in your thoughtlessness. You do yourselves less than justice if you think you are no better than that. What if you had walked through the ruins of that city the morning after? How if you had looked down upon children gasping in torment; mothers wailing over their tortured infants and helplessly seeking to comfort them with kisses; old people racked in an agony of lacerated flesh and smashed limbs, and resting their bewildered eyes on you—you who have ordered this—as you pass by? Come. You know the truth of yourselves. You know that, nowhere on this earth, could you see with your eyes a fellow-creature in an agony of torn limbs without running to minister to him, never caring for a second whether he was born in Potters Dale or in some similar corner of Cologne. Ask yourselves here in this little church of yours before this your altar: Do you *really* believe in this mass-torturing of fellow-creatures from one-year-old to ninety? Which Master do you serve? Him of Berlin, or Him of Nazareth? In this church we shall serve the one we call our Lord. I am your priest and, as your priest, I lead you in imagination along the streets of every enemy city where, deliberately and of set purpose, we have bombed, not only the military targets and the industries, but the unarmed people. And I say, look down upon these helpless victims—don't turn your eyes away—look down upon them lying there gashed, dismembered, blinded '—he did not intend to spare them, for love at times must heal by fire—' and remember that, wherever they were born, they have the same capacity for excruciating pain as you or me or these little children here. And look down upon the dead. Look down upon every slain body of the hundreds lying there, and say to yourself—say it till its meaning is clear to you: " Lord, if Thou hadst been here, my brother had not died." ' He deliberately repeated the words, ' Lord, if Thou hadst been here, my brother had not died.' And then said simply, ' In this church He is still here.'

§

The sermon over, he returned towards the altar, with his face from the people. But even as he went, he heard them going. Before he could read one of the Offertory Sentences, he heard the steps of many departing towards the west door. He had never heard such a thing before. Presumably one or two of the angered visitors had set the example, and others had followed it. The footsteps of departing people—it was a parable. The strangers in the church had heard his hard saying and would not stay for more. Possibly some of those who had hitherto been faithful were now following the feet of the strangers. When he turned again to face the people he saw a church rather emptier than it had ever been. All the visitors had gone or were going ; Lady Guttree and Peggy Ungar-Bateman had gone, and one or two others of the faithful. But some were still with him.

§

It was Lady Guttree who had led the march from the church. She had marched out like a commander, her face a flying red banner in front of the march. Lady Peggy had followed, two paces behind, like her adjutant or her orderly. Others, catching the pleasant infection of this patriotic indignation had streamed after these two leaders in a straggling and (in respect of the last units) hurrying company. And to their backs Father Dawbeny said the first of the Sentences : ' Let your light so shine before men that they may see your good works . . .'

Out on the pavement Lady Guttree waited for her sister-in-law to come abreast of her and then, careless who heard, nay, hoping many would hear, said loudly, ' Thank God we didn't have *him* at Duncombe. Our people at Duncombe are loyal. We don't want them corrupted. Brothers ! Brothers to those brutes and murderers ! '

Lady Peggy laughed. 'All the same, Beaty, I wish you hadn't stamped out of church like that. It made me sweat all over.'

'I wasn't going to let all those people think I gave any countenance to such traitorous stuff. We've got to set them an example. I did it for their sakes, partly—and as noisily as possible. Such hopelessly illogical and sentimental stuff! How can you make war humane? Either we believe in this war or we don't; and if we do, we can't fight it with one hand behind our back, while *he's* using both hands and both feet. I'm sorry in a way for the German people, but they've asked for everything they're getting. They've always enthusiastically supported their leaders in making war, so long as it's been in other people's countries; now let them feel what it's like to have it in their own. I say, it's a kindness to them in the long run. That's the last time he'll see me in *his* church. I've never been so disappointed in anyone in my life. And he's had the last penny of *my* money.'

In her anger she walked quickly to her big limousine round the corner, and her arrival there took the large and comfortable chauffeur by surprise; he had not expected her for another half-hour and was obliged to swing up from a semi-recumbent position, thrust the *News of the World* down the side of his seat, button up the top buttons of his trousers and the lower buttons of his waistcoat, fling a cigarette, only just lit, out of the window, and alight on the pavement and stand by the open door of the saloon in the attitude of one whom no untoward event had disturbed.

'Take us home, Holt,' commanded his lady. 'We shan't be coming this way again.'

'Yes, my lady,' he acknowledged with a bow and inwardly commented, 'Something's bitten the old heifer where it hurts.'

Word of the sermon ran along the Potters Dale grapevine and blossomed in homes, pubs, and barbers' saloons. 'He said we were no better than the Germans. Did you ever hear the like?' It ran up Ledbitter Hill and reached the home of the Rev. Oliver Custance, Vicar of St. Luke's. And though Mr. Custance would not admit it to himself, he was glad in his heart that the much-lauded Father Dawbeny had now antagonized the people of the Dale. He was glad when opportunities presented themselves of saying to his parishioners with a slight

155

shake of his head, as though it distressed him to disparage a brother priest, ' I'm afraid I must confess I think it was a bit of a publicity stunt. He's been preaching more than one notoriety-seeking sermon lately. I can't say I approve of these methods ; they savour too much of the Salvation Army. I hope I'm not being unjust to him, but I can't help thinking he's reduced to making desperate attempts to get more people into his church. His congregation's getting smaller and smaller. We're none of us perfect, and there's always a temptation to ministers to get people into their churches or chapels by making a loud noise. Fortunately we're going up, in St. Luke's. Either it's that, or he's venting his disappointment on the world in general. I must say that for some time now Dawbeny's looked very sad and melancholy. He gives me the impression of a tragically disappointed man.'

Word of the sermon reached Comrade Anton and the boys and girls of his cell, which met as a rule in his room in Tyre Street. And Comrade Anton was not less pleased than the Rev. Oliver Custance that Father Dawbeny, who in the past had so successfully deluded the people that religion was a good thing instead of a damnable drug, had at last laid his flank open to a powerful assault. Always the reputation of Father Dawbeny had been a stout breastwork against the Party's attack against the churches. The people, no matter whether they'd ever seen the inside of St. John's or not, would always reject any derogation of its vicar. John Scully, the fruit vendor, might be the spokesman of them all. ' Don't care what you say, mate, but if Mr. Dawbeny isn't one of the best, I don't know who is. All I know is that he's a dam-sight better bloke than I am, and—if you don't mind my being personal—I wouldn't wish to offend you—have an apple, see—a dam-sight better bloke than you are, or ever will be.' Or Sam Hughes, the coster. ' Oh, no thank you, chum. It won't wash with me, chum ; ta. I'm not a religious man myself, but I am a member of his club. And it's a bit of all right, his Costers' Club. No religion shoved down your throat, but everything nice for the boys. A bar too ; he don't mind us having a pint or two after we've been yelling ourselves hoarse in half the streets of London. He'll have his pint with us sometimes—a bit shy, perhaps, but trying his best to be like one of us common chaps. No, he's a gentleman. Sorry.'

So it had been yesterday ; but what now ? Now at last

there was a chance to undo that reputation. The people, sentimental fools as they were, and always ready to swing from extremes of praise to extremes of blame, were in a mood to believe anything against the father now. Comrade Anton bade his boys and girls go forth and whisper everywhere that Father Dawbeny had said, ' The British are ten times worse than the Germans.'

That this was a deliberate distortion of the father's words did not disturb the young communist, or seem immoral to him ; rather did it fit very well with his idealism and his devotion. Objective truth was not necessarily a good thing, in his view ; and certainly it was not an absolute. He had emancipated himself from such a bourgeois notion. The only ' good thing ' to him, as he'd said to Father Dawbeny, was that which helped forward the World Revolution. And the Party Line of the World Revolution, at this tremendous moment in history, was total war against the fascists who, exactly as the sacred books of Marx and Lenin had foretold, had attacked the Revolution in its only home, the Soviet Union ; and all devoted communists had conditioned themselves into believing that anyone who opposed this Line was either a fascist or an unconscious agent of the fascists and must be discredited, defamed, and, if possible, befouled. Befouled with all the mud available, and if there was not enough mud to hand, with lies. The boys and girls went to their work in the streets and workshops with the zeal and the joy of self-dedicated missionaries. The men and women of the Salvation Army Citadel could hardly have gone with more devotion about the work of Man's salvation. And soon Father Dawbeny, walking in the streets of his parish, saw a new slogan painted at the very entrance to Greig Street, on a ruined wall, ' DOWN ALL FASCIST PRIESTS.' He saw it again, many times, on the grey-green railway walls by Cremona Road. ' DOWN ALL FASCIST PRIESTS.'

§

But once again Comrade Anton, striving to injure the father, only succeeded in bringing help to him. The ripples from this sermon would have washed no further than the districts around the Dale if Comrade Anton hadn't contrived to get a venomous little paragraph about 'the Rev. the *Honourable* Piers Dawbeny, brother of the Earl of Strathpenny' and 'his sabotaging of the People's War' into the Communist news-sheet *The World To Be*, which carried a regular column under the heading, 'Our Fascists.' This paragraph, on the morning of its publication, attracted and held the eyes of a man seated in a spacious, comfortable and handsomely furnished office in Amen Street, St. Paul's Churchyard; a man with a splendid crown of black, curling hair, a fine Jewish nose, and brilliant dark eyes—as handsome a Jew, in fact, as had ever been born in all of Israel's five thousand years. Nothing in this man's costly dark clothes, stiff white collar, and clean soft hands to suggest that he was a communist and a fighter in the class war against the capitalists. He was, however, a very keen socialist and, while he liked good living and handsome furniture around him, devoted much of his time and wealth to endeavouring to bring similar good things to his poorer brothers. Believing with fervour that love and humanity were the only tools for reshaping the world, he was a fascinated student of the Communist publications : *The Daily Worker, The Labour Monthly,* and *The World To Be,* because their spleen and violence so horrified him. And as he read of a certain priest in Potters Dale (where on earth was that?) who from his pulpit had denounced the deliberate massacre of civilians, he exclaimed to the empty room, 'What! Is there then a Christian among the Churchmen?' and, reading the agreeable paragraph a second time, added, 'But, by the Lord Jesus and all the other prophets of Israel, this is a man after my own heart.'

Two days later his car, as large as Lady Guttree's limousine, sped by the Parks towards Potters Dale. One could imagine the two cars passing each other, one leaving the Dale in disgust, the other approaching it in delight. His car wandered about the Dale looking for Greig Street, and at last, enthusiastically aided by various residents, found it in its place with the little church of St. John's standing intact among many damaged or derelict houses. He tried one of the church doors under the three-arched porch. It was on the latch. He went in and saw in the dim spaces before the altar a limping man with a bucket and mop, washing the tiles of footpace and sanctuary.

He walked softly towards the man and explained how he'd read in a Communist paper, *The World To Be,* a rancorous

attack on a recent sermon by the Vicar. At once Ernie's loyalty
fired up and, resting on his mop with the altar rail between him
and this visitor, he was loud and loquacious in his defence of
his vicar, explaining exactly what he had said in the sermon
and how wickedly he'd been misrepresented. He told him of
the communist slogans on the walls and how, without the
father knowing it, he'd gone round and painted them all out :
'Yes, two can play at that game.' And he mentioned how
'wonderful-like' the sermon's close had been, 'Lord, if you'd
bin 'ere, my brother'd never've had this done on him,' and
how Sophie had cried.

'I'm sure he's perfectly right,' said the Jew.

'Of *course* he's right,' affirmed Ernie, as if the father's rightness
was never a subject for argument. And lest this Yid didn't
know, he expounded that the Vicar was an 'On'rible, the
brother of an earl, and that he was absolutely fearless when it
came to a fight, 'yielding never an inch to nobody'—as he,
Ernie, ought to know, because he'd been with him in the Great
War. 'He was my colonel in the Great War.'

'Well, could I see Mr. Dawbeny, do you think ? ' asked the
Jew.

'Not to-day, sir,' Ernie apologized. 'He's in retreat.'

'He's *what* ? '

'In retreat, sir.'

'But I thought you said he never retreated ? '

'Well, no, but what I mean is, he's gone on a retreat.'

Still the Jew didn't understand, and Ernie explained that a
'retreat' was a kind of quiet time for parsons, with prayers
and sermons and the Lives of the Saints all day, and that this
here retreat was at Keble College in Oxford.

'I see. And for how long is he going on this retreat ? '

'Couple'o days, sir.'

'Right.' The Jew felt for his pocket case and drew out a
card, and with a gold pencil wrote on it, 'I should be so pleased
if I might come and see you one evening.' He handed the card
to Ernie. 'Would you give him this card when he advances
again ? '

'Righty-ho, sir. He'll be back to-morrow.'

'Thank you.' The Jew then wandered round the church,
staring at the statues with the golden lamps burning before them,
at the beautiful pieta by the west door and at the brightly

coloured Arundel prints on the walls, and admiring the care with which everything was cleaned and polished and kept beautiful. And so he came to the west door again and went forth to his waiting car. Once he was gone Ernie was not above looking at the name on the card. He read :

> ' *Mr. Ben Ostrion*
> *Ostrion, Hart and Company*
> *Amen Street*
> *St. Paul's Churchyard.*'

CHAPTER FIVE

On the evening of the following day Father Dawbeny returned, and Ernie showed him the card which he'd laid on the long table. Father Dawbeny picked it up. 'Ben Ostrion. Ostrion, Hart and Company. Good gracious, those are the publishers. One of the largest and wealthiest houses in England.'

'Yes, he looked as though he could afford to buy his fags,' agreed Ernie. 'He was a Jewish gentleman with a car as big as the Assembly Room downstairs. And a chauffeur and all.'

'Oh, he's a Jew all right, and of a very famous family. What could he want with me?'

'He'd heard of your bombing sermon.'

'I shouldn't think he'd heard much good about that. By the time it reached Amen Street it had probably been transformed into a traitorous diatribe worthy of the Tower. Perhaps he's working for M.I.5 and came to take me to Brixton Prison.'

'No, he said he agreed with everything you said.'

'I see he's pencilled his telephone number, so I suppose he expects me to ring him. Wimbledon . . . that must be his home address. One of those enormous mansions by the Common, I suppose.'

'Yes, he asked for you to ring him,' said Ernie, and seeing his master approach the telephone, went out tactfully.

Father Dawbeny dialled the Wimbledon number and imagined the luxurious room or hall in which the distant bell was ringing. A distant click, and the bell was answered by a child's voice : the voice of a girl who could be hardly more than eleven or twelve. 'Hallo!' said the voice in the friendliest way. It was like the voice of a happy schoolgirl greeting her vicar in the street. Or should he say of this child her rabbi?

'Hallo, dear.' He could always use endearments with children. 'This is Father—this is Mr. Dawbeny speaking. Is that the house of Mr. Ben Ostrion?'

'Yes, this is Daddy's house.' The voice turned away from

the telephone. 'Daddy, it's a Mr. Dorby . . . Dadd*ee* ! Oh, where is the man ? Just a minute please ; he won't be long. Ben Ostrion, *will* you come ? A Mr. Dorby wants to speak to you."

Now, at some distance from the telephone, came a male voice, rich, deep, and strong. 'Who ? Who ? Dorby ? Oh yes, Dawbeny. Hold him tight, Naomi. He's important. Don't let him get away.'

'Daddy's just coming, Mr. Dorby.'

'So I hear, Naomi.'

'Golly ! Did you hear ? Naomi's not my real name. It's Leah, but I've never liked Leah since I read she had weak eyes. That finished me off absolutely. I always liked Naomi because she was kind to Ruth. And I think Naomi's rather a peach of a name.'

'So do I, Naomi.'

'What's your name ? '

'Piers.'

'Oh, I like Piers. We've been doing *Piers Plowman* at school. In soppy old English Lit. Where are you speaking from ? Where do you live ? '

'At a place called Potters Dale. In Darkest London. Among the burglars and thieves.'

'Lucky you ! Is it very bad ? '

'Oh, no. Parts of it are excellent.'

'Are there any murderers there ? '

'Not at the moment, I'm afraid. We've had some in the past and I daresay we shall have some more in soon.'

'Have you ever met a murderer ? '

'Alas, no, Naomi.'

'I wondered what they were like to talk to. I'm never likely to meet one in Wimbledon. It's the stuffiest place ever. We're all so frightfully well behaved.'

'I see. That must be rather a strain.'

'It is. Oh, here's Daddy. Here's Ben Ostrion, of Ostrion, Hart and Company. No, don't snatch, Daddy, I'm talking. Here's Daddy, Mr. Dawb'ny. He's always a bit slow after a big dinner. We've only just finished dinner, and now I've got to go to bed. Isn't it rather foul ? '

'Well, don't go, my dear. Tell him I absolve you from going.'

'That won't do any good. He's one of these strong types.'

'*Good* evening.' The rich male voice had taken over. 'Delighted to know you, Mr. Dawbeny. What an awful child.'

'Not at all, sir. A child of great charm. Is she half as beautiful as her voice?'

'No, pretty hideous, really—go away, angel daughter—but she has her points. I've got three others like her, God forgive me, and two great louts of sons. This is Ben Ostrion speaking,' he added somewhat late. And from that moment it was plain that Ben Ostrion desired to do the speaking. His deep voice, as pleasant as it was fluent, poured forth, across or under the Thames Valley and the half of London (according as the telephone wires went over or under ground) his approval of the sermon, the whole story of his visit to the church and his illuminating conversation with the verger, and his conviction that Mr. Dawbeny had a jewel in that fellow. 'He thinks you're the cat's whiskers.'

Father Dawbeny managed to intrude a question. 'But how did you know anything about that ill-starred sermon?'

Clear, unmistakable, in that well-managed and seemingly superbly sane voice, came the answer, 'I came across it in the world to be,' and for a moment the listener wondered in some alarm if Mr. Ostrion was some spiritualist crank trying to enrol him in the true church. It required two or three more minutes of Mr. Ostrion's expositions before he perceived that *The World to Be* was a journal, and felt relieved. Relieved because he wanted to like this Ben Ostrion with his fervent voice and charming daughter. Ben Ostrion was now narrating all that the verger had said about 'being on the Somme with the Colonel,' and how he himself had been in the Desert of Sinai at that time with the 126th Brigade—'a good place for a little Jew-boy, eh?' This led the two voices—enjoying their talk under, or across, London—into a well-informed analysis of the discomforts of the various war-fronts in 1916; a rehearsal of the various places where Captain Ostrion and Colonel Dawbeny had found themselves in '17, '18, and '19; and a somewhat nostalgic comparison between ' *our* war—that old, unhappy, far-off thing and battle long ago,' and this present unhappy affair. So they got back to the sermon. 'I want your help, Mr. Dawbeny—or do I call you Father'—here there was a brief interruption while they dealt with their ages and agreed that, even if Ben Ostrion was only forty-nine and a dozen years younger than the father, he was probably as wise, because all Jews matured quicker than Gentiles and were ten years older than their chronology would suggest. Then back to business. ' I want your help. I'm publishing a pamphlet at once—which amounts to an appeal to the Allies not to sully their noble Cause, and throw away its moral strength, by adopting the revolting methods of the Nazis. I'm getting contributions from Tories, Liberals, Socialists, Communists, and from Catholics, Anglicans——'

' Communists ? Not Communists, surely ? '

' Well, ex-Communists. There are plenty who've seceded from the Party because of their late ludicrous and tedious somersaulting. I want a contribution from you on the lines of that sermon.'

' Do you want to lose all your public and go bankrupt ? '

' If necessary, yes. Of course. Naturally. This is important.'

' But who cares what I think ? Nobody.'

' Don't you believe it ! I've been making enquiries about you, brother, and you're much better known than you imagine.'

' You wouldn't think so, to judge from my congregation. Thirty beloved loyalists, and there an end.'

' Never mind. It's not given to us to see what our words are doing. They get around. Yours arrived in Amen Street and delighted a sinner there. I must say it's a treat to find an Anglican padre who sees the whole Christian vision and is not afraid to state it. I'm only a Jew, but in the name of six million of my brothers who've been 'one to death by the Germans, I'm going to appeal to the wo ' ' o teach our persecutors how evil they are—not by visiting on them all they've given us, but by showing them the opposite way. That I take to be the essence of Christianity.'

' And so it is. You may be a Jew, sir, but you seem a better Christian than many of us.'

This opened the door to Ben Ostrion for a dissertation on the Talmud, the Chinese sages, Taoism, the Indian prophets, Dharma the Hindu Law of Righteousness, and Marcus Aurelius. The vision proclaimed by all of these, he said, was essentially the same as the Christian, and for him, Ben Ostrion, it was not merely an idealist ethic but a revelation of Reality. His lone voice went on, uttering the universal truth with power and poetry and Father Dawbeny, listening, thought, ' The voice of one crying in Wimbledon. . . .' The voice was now telling an old tale from the Talmud : how when Miriam sang her song of triumph over the drowning Egyptians—' you know : " Sound the loud timbrel o'er Egypt's dark sea "—that's Byron's version, of course—what, not Byron ? Tom Moore ? Are you sure ? ' There was an argument about this, till Ben Ostrion broke it off, asking, ' Well, what the hell does it matter ? Whether Byron wrote it, or Tom Moore, the Angels joined in, and Jehovah— this is the story—rebuked them, saying " My children are drowning. How can you rejoice and sing ? " '

' Perfect,' said Father Dawbeny. ' Thank you for——"

But he found he was interrupting an excursus on Marcus Aurelius. Mr. Ostrion was reciting whole passages from that Emperor's Meditations, and delivering them across London with such skill that Father Dawbeny suspected he must be a practised platform orator. ' Bethink thee thou hast vices of thine own, and art a sinner with the rest. If thou canst, show the sinner the error of his ways, saying, " Not so, my son : this is not the end for which we were created. True, it will harm me not ; but, child, it is harming thee." ' He was declaring his conviction that the English people, above any in the world, would respond to an appeal for such magnanimity ; that they were something very different from what their leaders and their newspapers and some of their clergy imagined, and from what their present angry words might suggest ; and in support of this he quoted, reciting it sonorously, a poem of the Poet Laureate's, in praise of the Englishman's nobler parts :

> ' A grave wise thoughtfulness and truth,
> A merry fun outlasting youth,
> A courage terrible to see,
> And mercy for his enemy.'

The voice waited for a comment from the distant audience.

' I like to think that some of that's true,' said Father Dawbeny, ' but the fact remains that, when I made my appeal, half my congregation walked out.'

' But others have walked in. Didn't I walk in ? '

' Well, that's true.'

'And am I not going to bring heaps more to your side, Piers?'

Piers! This use of his Christian name shook the father, and, hardly listening, he wondered if he was expected to respond with 'Ben.' Or perhaps 'Benjamin.' They were certainly great friends now, though neither had seen the other's face. But he really couldn't say 'Ben' yet; or 'Benjamin'; not till he'd been face to face with the man for at least an hour.

'And you *will* give me the substance of that sermon as an essay?'

'I'll certainly try to, but I know nothing about pamphleteering. I suppose you couldn't come again and tell me all about it. One evening when you're not busy. Perhaps you could have a little something to eat with me?'

'Nothing I should love better, Piers. Could I bring my wife? She's longing to meet you.'

Father Dawbeny's hand shook, holding the receiver. 'Yes, of course. Delighted to see her.' But bread and cheese was his usual meal. Or corned beef and lettuce. Or a basin of vegetable soup out of a tin. What in pity's name had he brought upon himself? A wealthy publisher and his wife, both accustomed to every luxury. 'Daddy's always a bit slow after a big dinner.' His mind, even while he spoke with Ben Ostrion, was running to Sophie and her capabilities as a cook. She could cook a joint, a cottage pie, a toad-in-the-hole. 'Of course bring your wife. I shall love to see her. Couldn't you bring Naomi too?' He made this desperate remark, realizing that one might as well drown in an ocean as a pond.

'Naomi? No, my God, no. That'd mean bringing the whole tribe of Benjamin. When shall we come, Piers? So far as I'm concerned, the sooner the better. To-morrow any good?'

'Yes, to-morrow. To-morrow, of course.'

'What time do you have dinner?'

Dinner! 'Oh, say about seven.'

'Seven o'clock. Fine. We shall look forward to that. Hey, put down that receiver half a second.' Father Dawbeny did so, and the bell rang again, and the rich voice came again. 'I did that because in common fairness I thought the Postmaster-General should get another penny for all that. We've been talking for twenty minutes and have covered the whole duty of Man. And I haven't enjoyed anything so much for a long time. I must go now and finish my glass of port. Good-bye.'

Glass of port! Heavens, what had he done? 'What time do you have dinner?' What sort of home did Mr. Ostrion imagine he'd got? Having seen the church which was filled with beautiful things, did he imagine that the vicarage dining-room would be equally beautiful instead of this long, bare, littered room? Father Dawbeny, standing motionless beside his telephone, saw a table in a mansion, garnished with silver, lace, and cut-glass—like Lady Guttree's table in her cream and green dining-room in Upper Hyde Street.

He stood, deep in thought, head down, fingers in waistcoat pockets. What in the world would he give them to eat? And Mrs. Ostrion: ought he not to get another lady for her comfort and ease? And thereupon a memory—or half a memory—sprang up out of the past when he was a familiar and sometimes photographed figure in the homes and hunting fields of society. It drove him to his old, back-broken copy of *Who's Who*. ' Ostrion '—yes—' married Jessica, youngest daughter of 3rd Viscount Achan.'

God! Lord Achan! Millionaire head of Julius Marks & Co.; munificent patron of British artists; donor of Achan rooms to art galleries in half the great towns of Britain.

His heart went deeper down, weighted with dismay. What other woman could he get to meet and (so to say) balance the Hon. Mrs. Ostrion? His sister was in Cumberland; he no longer knew any society women, except—yes, for the life of him, the only person he could think of was Lady Guttree.

But as he thought of Lady Guttree his lips moved into a smile. There were many reasons why he might approach Lady Guttree: first, that he might show in true Christian fashion (if not without a spice of mischievous malice) that he forgave her for her very rude exit from his church; secondly, because he owed her a meal, after that excellent lunch of three years ago; thirdly, because it would do her good to see that Ben Ostrion agreed with him—yes, to learn that as she walked out this powerful man walked in; and lastly because, if she was disengaged to-morrow evening, and if he made his invitation sound like an S O S, she would almost certainly come, since she was an inveterate pursuer of literary, artistic, and theatrical celebrities.

167

He laid his fingers on the telephone again. Then nodded, grinning. Yes, it would do her soul good. She would hear the most powerful publisher in Britain requesting—beseeching—the publishing rights of that sermon. She might hear him calling it a 'remarkable sermon,' a 'courageous sermon,' a 'sermon that was just the pure unveiled truth, but far too bright for most silly people.' It was simply to do her soul good, of course —at least he hoped so. His duty to her. The wandering sheep. He dialled her number.

A man's voice answered, and after half a minute—was she deliberately keeping him waiting?—Lady Guttree's voice said ' Yes ? ' and said it a little sourly.

Let him sweeten her at once. ' My dear Lady Guttree, this is an S O S. Are you ready to do a work of mercy ? You've always been ready to help me. Are you free to-morrow evening ? '

A silence while her curiosity overcame the sourness. ' Yes, I think so. Why ? What for ? '

' I've got Ben Ostrion coming to dinner.'

' The publisher man ? '

' Yes. And his wife.'

' She was Jessica Marks, wasn't she ? Old Achan's daughter ? '

' Yes, and they're both coming to dinner.'

' Dinner ? But, my dear man, what on earth are you going to give them ? You never eat, do you ? Bread and water ? You can't give them that.'

' I know. Don't make me more nervous than I am. I've got to get them something nice. I'll make it a good dinner, I promise you.'

' Is it a dressy affair ? '

' Oh, heavens, no ! Gracious, I never thought of that. They won't come dressed, will they ? '

' I should think it extremely probable they will. And won't they want Kosher food, or whatever they call it ? '

' Kosher ! Oh, my God ! . . . Do you think so? . . . Well, they won't get it. They'll have to take what I give them. If he can only eat Kosher he'll have to starve.'

' Does the man know how you live ? '

' I shouldn't think so. I've never met him. He wants me to write for him, that's all. And he's more or less invited himself and his wife to dinner.'

' Poor man.'

' And I've nobody else but you to keep his lady company. *Please* will you come ? I'll try to make it a good meal.'

' Why, yes . . . but '—clearly she didn't want him to think he was forgiven—' I didn't agree with that sermon of yours.'

' Which sermon was that ? ' This question amounted to three parts of a lie, since he knew quite well which sermon she meant.

' The one in which you said we were as bad as the Germans. I can't easily forgive you for that.'

' Well, you're not alone in that. Still, never mind me and all my seditious talk. This dinner is nothing to do with that sermon. You're coming ? That's splendid.'

Heavens, he had lied again ; so he thought as he put down the receiver. Deliberately he had deluded her. This dinner had everything to do with that sermon. Truly the tongue was an incontinent member, and man, in weak moments, was born to lie as the sparks flew upward.

Much of the rest of that evening he gave to making plans, tidying up the room, rearranging the books in more attractive order, straightening the curtains, arranging for the loan of Sophie's dining table (since he'd only the trestle table and one too small for company), arranging for the loan of four of Sophie's dining-room chairs, thinking further and indenting for Ernie and Sophie's two easy chairs so that they could stand to-morrow between his own two before the gas fire. They were two chairs which he had bought for their living-room, and they were in much better condition, and much more comfortable than his own. After the dinner to-morrow Ernie and Sophie would have to sit in their room on kitchen chairs—or go to bed.

§

He rose early next morning to a busy day. But a pleasant day, since he had decided that, all circumstances considered, it was legitimate—nay, it was his duty—to abandon asceticism for an hour or two and relapse into the old seductions of the epicure. A quick cup of coffee, and he set out for the invaluable store of Latman & Pearson's, Piccadilly. Praise God for Latman & Pearson's. But he did not wear a clerical collar this morning lest the stately gentlemen of Latman & Pearson's, not realizing that he was but doing his duty, should find occasion, as they took his expensive orders, for entertaining unworthy thoughts about the Church and its priests.

Messrs. Latman & Pearson's palatial bazaar stands on the south side of Piccadilly, and its main doors are therefore north doors ; but Father Dawbeny always thought of them as West Doors, and West Doors with capital letters. Were they not the doors of a noble cathedral where due devotion was paid, with a decent formality and a seemly ornateness, to the High God of gastronomy ? This was a cathedral in which he had often, in the old days, been one of the congregation, as a firm and indeed fervent believer. It was a church from whose services he used to come away with inspirations for the future and with fresh gifts of grace to persevere in living well.

An impressive gentleman, dressed in morning coat and striped trousers as for a solemnity, came forward to welcome him and guide his steps aright, but Father Dawbeny, with a lifted hand, declined for the moment his assistance. He was something of a prodigal son in this temple, and must learn the Faith again. To call this majestic person with his silver hair and well-groomed clothes a ' shop-walker,' or even to think of him in such terms, was something that Father Dawbeny was not so irreverent as to do : a ' senior sidesman,' perhaps, or a ' churchwarden,' or even, if the hierarchy in this particular religion carried such orders, an ' elder.' But however he was to be named, Father Dawbeny held that he was not yet fit to speak with him, and would not be for some minutes. He must prepare himself with some profound meditation. So with that lift of his hand (which might be construed as an ' Unclean ! ') he walked away from him and strode the whole length of the noble hall. Not at all unlike a garish cathedral, he thought, with its pillared aisles, its pendent candelabra a-glitter with lights, and its soft carpet designed to keep the footsteps quiet so that a suitable seriousness might be felt among the arches, and the devotions of the faithful, at this altar, or in this chapel, might be as little as possible disturbed.

' And there are altars everywhere,' he thought as he walked between the island counters with a slow step and an invisible smile. Altars laden with foods in brilliant tins ; with brilliant foods in glass bottles ; with foods in jars and cartons and boxes and baskets ; with sweets and preserved fruits in beribboned presentation cases. Here was the Cooked Meats counter, and before this altar, honoured above the rest, was a priest in linen vestments.

'And a mass at every altar,' he thought, because there was hardly a counter at which a servant of the shrine was not saying his familiar office to a congregation of two or more persons.

There were devotions in the chapels, too—in those large side rooms that opened on to the main hall and carried such sacred words as 'Tea and Coffee,' 'Cigars and Cigarettes,' 'Fruit and Flowers,' and 'Provisions.' To reach the 'Wine and Spirits' department one had to descend wide, carpeted stairs into a grand room too large to be styled a chapel. It was like going down into the tranquil beauties of the Lower Church at Assisi.

As he wandered among the brightly-coloured sights and the pleasant hammy smells the seeds of inspiration fell into his mind and germinated. The old spirit had come down upon him in power. A fine meal was like a poem, and should be built like a poem—say, a sonnet with octave and sestet and gentle, falling close. Turtle soup—but wait : one must shape one's coat according to one's cloth, and the cloth in this case was Sophie's capability as cook. Turtle soup ; that would be simple enough ; he had just passed it in glass jars. Sophie had only to heat it up, and he to put a dash of good sherry into it. Say four jars, since Ernie and Sophie must enjoy this debauch, too. Then galantine of chicken and veal, enriched with truffles, pistachio nuts and spice ; he had seen it on the Cooked Meats altar, lying there like a sacrifice. It could be served cold with a salad of lettuce, tomatoes and runner beans. No trouble here, since he was an expert in assembling and dressing a salad. But one hot dish there must be ; his sense of perfection in eating—a Rip Van Winkle now mightily alive after its twenty years' sleep—demanded this. Those slices of venison all ready for a Grenadin St. Hubert. A Grenadin St. Hubert with a Sauce Poivrade and a chestnut purée. It was within the united capacities of Sophie and himself? Yes, yes. He himself would make the sauce. He decided on the venture. For the sweet a Macedoine of Fruits ; he had seen the glass jars of *Fruits au Sirop*, all ready to be turned into a dish ; no trouble to anyone, and just as well, since the Grenadin and the sauce would extend Sophie and himself, and probably Ernie, to the utmost.

Now at last he felt, as it were, full of grace again, and fit to speak with one of the magnificent elders at the church door.

The one with the silver hair, whom he had first seen, came towards him with an ingratiating smile, just as a sidesman might to an incoming worshipper whose face was new ; and Father Dawbeny stated to him his spiritual needs—and, applied to a consultation with a gentleman of such high seriousness, the word ' spiritual ' did not seem misplaced. ' Turtle soup, sir ? Why, yes.' The gentleman took three steps and lifted down a jar from a counter nearby, and Father Dawbeny was surprised that anyone so grand should actually handle anything. But he did : he gathered and arrayed four jars for his customer. ' Galantine ? Come with me, sir.' And he led him to the Cooked Meats counter and instructed the celebrant there to oblige this gentleman. So helpful was he in his views on a galantine and how it should be served that Father Dawbeny began to feel confidential and discussed the salad which he proposed. ' A bean and tomato salad is what I had in mind,' he said. ' It is a salad recommended to go with galantine by the British and Foreign Bible Society.'

' By the what, sir ? '

' Oh, what did I say ? I mean the British Wine and Food Society. I am always mixing the two up.'

His cheeks heated at the idiotic mistake, but his guide did not so much as smile lest this should not be what the customer wished. He merely bowed slightly as if to imply that he quite understood, and it was a mistake he'd often met with.

Father Dawbeny hastened to a discussion on the Grenadin St. Hubert and such garnishings as should dress it. And immediately his counsellor took from a neighbouring counter and handed to him as a gift a copy of the firm's booklet, *Fine Eating*, wherein he would find full instructions on the making of a Sauce Poivrade and a chestnut purée. Together they selected some jars of fruits and the counsellor consented to assemble for him at the door all these assorted foods, while he visited the Wine and Spirit department. Father Dawbeny went down alone into the Lower Church. Here his task was easier because the problem of Sophie no longer delimited his choice. A dry sherry . . . a claret, but a claret of what year ? Once he used to know which were the great vintage years for the clarets and burgundies, the hocks and Moselles, the champagnes and the ports. But now—now he had forgotten almost all he ever knew ; he was getting old, alas, getting old, and his memory was growing dim ; what was he to order ? Straightway this incomparable firm placed in his hand the vintage chart of the British Wine and Food Society, and he learned that the clarets of 1929 alone received the highest marks. And the ports of 1927. Best be safe, best be safe with Ben Ostrion, and he bought a claret of 1929 and a port of 1927, and felt proud and pleased. A cognac to go with the coffee and, yes, a liqueur in case the ladies preferred it. A whisky at the end of the happy evening for the men—or at least for Ben Ostrion . . . and possibly for Ernie on his kitchen chair in his empty back room.

The pile of foods and wines was now considerable, and there was the problem of getting it from Piccadilly to Potters Dale. The firm would hardly deliver it in war-time, and in any case they had probably never heard of Potters Dale. Even if they had, he did not propose to shock them by mention of such a place. So he asked the commissionaire to call a taxi, which he did, and together he and the commissionaire loaded the parcels into the taxi's seat. Soon all was aboard, the parcels and their purchaser ; and if the commissionaire was shaken when instructed to give the driver an address in Potters Dale, he courteously showed no sign of it.

His arrival at the door of the Church Hall with the parcels and the bottles was a sensation for Ernie and Sophie, and for two or three children who rushed up to see. Sophie was pale. It was the nervous pallor of one for whom a first-night performance was only a few hours away. But the afternoon, if full, was a happy one for all : Sophie having learned that the father was going to make the sauce and the salad, and she would have to only ' hot up ' the soup and the venison. Ernie made merry ever and anon about ' half the aristocracy coming to supper.' Father Dawbeny and Ernie spread the table with a fine clean cloth of Sophie's and a mixed levy of Ernie's cutlery and his own. Much of the time between six o'clock and seven the father walked in and out of the kitchen, or up and down the passage, reading his booklet, *Fine Eating*, like a monk his breviary in the cloister. All was steaming on the stove and shining on the table as the clock struck seven.

He stood at the window looking up Greig Street and down it, waiting for a sight of the Ostrions. He wished they would come while everything in the kitchen was still in good order. But the wish was flooded with alarm directly he saw their big blue car and the big blue chauffeur, matching it. As so often with a commander planning a battle, or a murderer a murder, his elaborate and exhaustive preparations, such as made proud his heart, had omitted one thing. They had omitted the chauffeur. Where was he to be put? There was food in plenty and drinks enough, but was there even a chair for him in Ernie's emptied room?

No time to deal with this question now, however; and he had to carry it downstairs, like a burden unwrapped and still tightly packed as he went to meet and welcome his guests— Squaller the dog hurrying down with him to meet and welcome them, too. But down there on the pavement Ben Ostrion quickly relieved him of the load and placed it, so to speak, in the car.

'Ah, Piers!' he said. 'We meet. Miriam, this is Piers. Harry, take the car. Good evening, dog. Pleased to meet you. Handsome beast. Harry, take the car and park it, and have a meal at the Brewers'. Do yourself proud. Come back about ten. Yes, somewhere about ten. You'll probably have to wait while I finish talking. Is that all right, Piers?'

'Perfectly all right,' said the host. 'This way.' And, not lightly relieved, he led them up his stone stair (the dog following) and showed Mrs. Ostrion into his tiny bed-chamber that she might divest herself of her fur coat and do what she wished to her hair and face. In the front room he quickly gave Ben Ostrion a sherry that he might not, at sight of the room, be disappointed and apprehensive. It was such a sherry as should not only quiet all doubts, but even raise hopes that one was in the house of a connoisseur. (And on the whole he did not think that the shining table looked too disappointing.)

He was impressed by his visitor, and, not chiefly by the fine large Hebraic face under the curled and bunching black hair, but by the almost tangible vitality that seemed to exude from the soft, easy, comfortable figure and surround it like an aura —an aura that was at once rich, silken, pleasing, and slightly overpowering. When last night he had listened to that rich and rapid voice with its easily inspired eloquence he had thought of it as a voice in the wilderness denouncing the sins of the people, but this Mr. Ostrion was no gaunt Elijah or emaciated Baptist. Everything about him—face, figure, raiment, voice and vocabulary—was round, ample, and opulent.

Here was a man who must take command of any talk and the centre of any stage.

Mrs. Ostrion, as ample as he, impressed him, too, but rather for her chestnut hair, rosy skin, copper-coloured dress and general autumn-tinted beauty. She was as golden-brown as Ben was black. Inevitably, as wife to the dynamic and dominant Ben Ostrion, she was little more than a clerk leading the responses for him, the minister, in his rich and handsome pulpit above.

Lady Guttree had now arrived, and he presented her to the Ostrions, describing her with a mischievous eye as 'a devoted member of my congregation.' She ignored the thrust and gave herself to being amiable with the Ostrions, and especially to the man and publisher whom she'd been so eager to meet.

When he had seen their glasses filled, and their talk launched, he slipped unobserved into the kitchen to see how the campaign was going. But here he quickly learned that he'd best leave the steamed and bedraggled and unusually irritable Sophie to her saucepans, and he returned, a restless host, to the front room. He was in time to hear Ben Ostrion saying, ' You've known Mr. Dawbeny a long time then ? '

' Oh, yes,' came Lady Guttree's voice. ' For some years.'

' And I've known him for precisely twenty-four hours, and already we're buddies. A man who will stand up and without fear or favour say the true but unpopular thing is a man after my own heart. I got him to give me the notes of that sermon of his. More shall be heard of it.'

' Yes, yes,' responded the clerk. ' Ben told me all about it. Oh, I do love a clergyman with courage.'

' But, Mr. Ostrion,' objected Lady Guttree, ' if those who know much better than we do believe that the only way to win this war——'

' They don't know better than we do. They are blind, dear lady, blind. They're like schoolboys who haven't learnt their lesson yet. They've not yet grown up ; they still believe, like children and savages, that to correct and conquer evil you must give the evil man exactly what he's given you—which, of course, does no good to him but only makes him worse, and does no good to you, but just hands the victory to him. Precisely as Piers said. You have to give him the very opposite—as Piers said. I tell you, Piers knows more than all of them put together. He's grown tall, to the height of a man, and can see over the children's hedge.'

'That's it exactly,' responded the clerk. 'But the sad thing is, so few ever grow up. And it seems to me that women are the worst. It's always the women who are the most rabid. What you hear them saying !'

'But, Mrs. Ostrion, I don't see that we can do less than——'

'No, you don't see,' echoed Ben, delighted with the admission. 'That's the trouble. That's what we're coming to. You've got to grow up. You've got to mature into the good wine your Maker intended——'

Father Dawbeny hastened to the sherry bottle. 'A little more sherry ? ' he asked, and forward came Ben Ostrion's glass, without his eyes following it. He filled Lady Guttree's glass. To his surprise all his sympathy and compassion had rushed out to her, and his whole desire was to defend her from Ben Ostrion's fusillade. He was fast filling with a sense of sin for having thrown her like this to the lions.

But Lady Guttree, while accepting the sherry, wanted to continue her scuffle with the massive male lion. 'Do I understand, Mr. Ostrion, that you are prepared to lose the war rather than use the enemy's weapons ? After all, he chose the weapons.'

'Oh, my dear lady, my dear lady ; oh dear, oh dear, oh dear.' It was a sigh as for one whose mind was still infantile. It was not a polite sigh. In truth, it must have been an infuriating one. This impassioned prophet might, like his host, be unafraid of speaking the truth, but he was also, unlike his host, unafraid of offending his opponent and hurting her. He did not suffer from the weakness of wanting anyone's love. You felt that he had a love for his opponent but that this love was a prophetical fire, ready to burn if so only it could heal. 'Oh, my dear, my dear, my dear ! Why don't you try to think clearly instead of in the ready-made, reach-me-down terms of the Public Bar ? I can understand a plumber's apprentice in a pub talking like that, but we who have had the advantages of

176

education, should have brains and souls above that sort of stuff. What you are suggesting is that we should pick up all his weapons even if it means throwing away the one weapon he hasn't got at all and which is far and away, as Napoleon knew, the most powerful of all—the moral weapon. To do this is to hand him his victory on a plate. Oh, I know you can't see it, but that's because you're still blind—no—just let me finish . . . Thank you, Piers, I will : it's a very fine sherry . . . It's exactly as he said in that wonderful sermon : if we throw away all decency, then in this great moral crisis for the world we shall have lost, not so much the war against Hitler as mankind's centuries-long war for civilization. What a very fine sherry. It slips down like silk. We are watching the retreat of the world from Christianity—and you, dear lady, are the first to scuttle.'

'How is your delightful daughter, Mrs. Ostrion?' Father Dawbeny thrust in quickly. 'We made great friends over the telephone. We exchanged some very private views.'

'Naomi? Oh, she's awful, Mr. Dawbeny. She wanted to ring you up this evening about her Latin. She said you were bound to know Latin.'

'And she didn't ring me up? Why?'

'Because I wouldn't hear of it.'

'Oh, but tell her to ring me up at any time. I shan't know anything about her Latin, but I shall enjoy a quiet chat.'

'I wouldn't dream of telling her any such thing.'

'*I'll* tell her, Piers,' promised Ben, and resumed his assault on Lady Guttree. 'Piers and I aren't going to scuttle. We aren't going to abandon our colours, dear lady. Oh, no! Our colours are decency and mercy and brotherhood and we fly them as exultantly as the Nazi thugs fly their flags of evil and frightfulness and enslavement, and the communist boys and girls theirs of violence and class-hatred and war. And its only by giving as passionate a loyalty to our creed as these others give to theirs that we can win back the slipping world to the loveliest thing mankind has created, which is . . . brotherhood . . . which is magnanimity . . . which is . . .'

'Come and eat,' interposed Father Dawbeny hastily. 'All is ready.'

They sat down to the soup, but Lady Guttree who in her own rooms, as he so well remembered, normally took command of the conversation, was not yielding ground to Mr. Ostrion, without a hot rearguard action. She argued over the soup that there was such a thing as punishment, and that the whole German people merited it, because they had done nothing to stop Hitler but had rather gloried in his outrages.

At this, for one second, Mr. Ostrion laid down his spoon with a smack on his plate. Every word of that, he said, was nonsense. Fifteen million Germans had voted against the Nazis and even after the Nazi terror had begun, there were thirteen million righteous men who'd had the courage to vote against them.'

' But since then ? ' demanded Lady Guttree.

' All right : since then. No open resistance since then. Let me ask you this, Lady Guttree dear. Have you ever, *ever* in some lonely place, asked yourself what you would have done openly, if the reward of your outspokenness was torture for yourself and for those you loved ? Before you can affirm that you would have spoken up and dared all, keep quiet, please, about the silent Germans. The whole German nation guilty ? What are we to do with her, Piers ? Do get it out of your head, lady, that there's any such real and actual thing as " Germany." There isn't ; there are only seventy million folk like you and me. And in the seventy million—though I suspect there are more who have been corrupted and degraded by their vile masters than you'll find in Britain—there must be several millions of decent, kindly people, and a petty thousand or two of saints. What was that soup ? Turtle ? Oh, I wish I'd known ! I love turtle. And one and all of them, the corrupted and the uncorrupt, are my brothers, members of our common human family.'

Clearly his guns outranged the old standardized weapons of Lady Guttree, but she must fire with what she had, and fire angrily. ' I must say I believe in Justice. Law and Justice. A crime against humanity must be met with condign——'

' We all believe in Justice, madam. Justice is fine, but justice is not enough. Justice can keep the world in order, but it can't redeem it. For that you must go to religion ; and that, I take it, is why you go to Piers Dawbeny's church. Man can create nothing till he transcends Justice. Justice deals only with the things that are. Love creates new men.'

The soup had come and gone under this stormy argument, and the galantine, beautifully dressed, was on their plates. They were eating it, but barely noticing it, since their minds were in Germany. It was as if, thought the host, his proud meal was proceeding under an air-raid, a blitz : Ben Ostrion the bombing air-fleet, Lady Guttree the angry London guns. At this moment she was arguing that it would be time to forgive the Germans when they showed signs of repentance.

'And that is nonsense !' cried the prophet. 'Pure and palpable nonsense. Good God—pardon the expression, Lady Guttree, but, as it happens, it's apt because, though I'm only a Jew, I clearly understand your God and your religion better than you do——'

'Have some more galantine, Lady Guttree,' invited Father Dawbeny.

'No !' she snapped angrily, diverting a gun for one moment on to him, and then directing it back again with the rest of the artillery on the main enemy.

But the main enemy, hardly noticing the interruption, continued his bombardment and his meal. 'One forgives people and shows them love, my dear lady, *in order that they may repent*, not after they've repented, or they may never repent at all.'

'Yes, that's clearly right,' endorsed the clerk, from her place below the pulpit. 'That's obvious sense.'

'It's not,' began Lady Guttree, getting hotter and hotter. 'It's by no means sense to me. In fact I don't think I've ever heard such nonsense.'

'Oh, yes, you have,' Ben Ostrion assured her cheerfully. 'You've heard it hundreds of times in Piers's church next door. Haven't you succeeded in teaching her anything, Piers ? Good heavens, what are you serving now ? Venison ? ' He put up his glasses to consider the dish.

But Lady Guttree's temper was gone. And with flushed cheeks and a mere mask of civility she struck. She fired her most cruel gun of all. 'But, Mr. Ostrion, if I may say so, you are not English. It is possible that the English can feel things about this war and the threat to their country that are impossible to you.'

It was then that Ben Ostrion demonstrated in action all that he had been preaching. He showed no indignation, but smiled. And first he covered the painful silence with a question to his host, 'This seems a claret worth drinking, Piers——'

'Yes, I was thinking that,' his wife endorsed.

'——What year is it?'

'1929,' Father Dawbeny informed him.

'Ah, yes. '29. You know how to choose, whether wisdom or wine. '29 was *the* year for claret. What was the vintage year for wisdom, I wonder, eh. That would be an interesting subject for debate.' Then he turned to Lady Guttree. 'Dear Lady Guttree, I am an Englishman. I am not a visitor in your country but a citizen in my own. My forbears were here before the Hugenots, and I don't think you would tell one with a Hugenot name that he was not an Englishman. I think it is possible that my love for my dear country is even more poignant than yours, because she has always welcomed the outcasts of my race. I love her so terribly that I want her always to rise to her highest instead of sinking to her lowest; and, Lady Guttree, I believe that her highest—but this is perhaps just my English patriotism—is higher than anyone else's because she understands tolerance and magnanimity a little better than any other country in the world. Whatever she may say in her wrath, she is at bottom good-natured. I want to keep her good-natured. I want to keep her great and kind. I am fighting for her now. Piers and I are both fighting for her. We are going to raise up people who are capable of spiritual resistance to the evil thing that threatens us. I find it very difficult to bear when you who are my dear countrywoman, Lady Guttree, turn Nazi and brand a whole race. Don't do it, because I so want to love and admire you.'

Up to a point this quiet demonstration of the methods he believed in had its success. Lady Guttree was certainly mollified by his soft answer and gentle tribute, but she had to defend her ground a little longer.

'What I cannot understand, Mr. Ostrion, is this: the Germans have slaughtered millions of your race, and yet you——'

'The answer is simple, my dear. It is to prevent millions more from suffering in the future that I want to bring back into the world respect for human life—even the life of Germans. Oh, Piers, Piers! When will they *see*?'

After that the battle dwindled, and when they rose from the table, all fair friends, Ben Ostrion, full of good argument, good food, and good wine, put his arm along his host's shoulder and said, 'Piers, you are an orthodox Christian, I am an unorthodox Jew, and we are brothers.'

CHAPTER SIX

THAT pamphlet, edited by Ben Ostrion, raised only a momentary and limited conflagration, soon extinguished by the inrolling waves of war. Its title was a variation of Father Dawbeny's *Has the Enemy Come?*, the editor, in the maddening way of editors (that supremely self-confident race) having changed these excellent words to *Is the Enemy Here?* which he, as usual, thought better and Father Dawbeny thought worse. It received some praise from quiet voices, and some vehement invective from the loud and strident. There was an eight-day correspondence in *The Times* about it, some of it warmer than was customary in those staid columns, some of it suggesting in forthright fashion that ' this reverend gentleman, Mr. Dawbeny, would be better employed in stiffening the Christian will to war instead of deliberately unbracing it,' but all this proved but a small quarrel, local and soon lost, among the resounding quarrels of the nations. Father Dawbeny, together with other contributors received letters of praise and letters of abuse, and noted for his comfort that the favourable ones had a quiet sanity and the unfavourable an hysterical heat.

What good it may have done in an inflamed and bellicose world, what seeds of better health hereafter it may have scattered, was something out of its author's sight, something which only the angels knew. So too such dislike as it earned in the world for the name of the Reverend Piers Dawbeny was a thing hidden from him. In the Dale it could do him no harm because it was only his sermon over again, and that had already touched off and exploded the local mines of anger and hostility.

In the perspective of time he came to see that pamphlet as no more than a preliminary sortie before the grand assault which Ben Ostrion launched at the close of the war. This grand assault, this offensive all along the line, was the pamphlet *Vae Victoribus*. Few people have ever known it, but the originator of this very famous pamphlet, though certainly not the creator of its uproarious success, was the Reverend Father Dawbeny of Potters Dale. *Vae Victoribus* was a noise indeed ; and why not, for the guns were now silent. The crowds could come away from the touchlines of a world-combat and gather, with their cheering or their booing, around a domestic quarrel. Father Dawbeny may have been the father of the pamphlet (with Ben Ostrion for its mother) but he figured in it only as one of the contributors, and by far the noblest and most impressive article was Ben Ostrion's own. As a pamphleteer, a prophet whose love for his listeners was a cauterising fire, Father Dawbeny was no match for Ben Ostrion. Only in the matter of titles did the priest think himself more inspired than the publisher, but, as usual, his suggestion for a title was tossed by the editor into the waste-paper basket, and instead of the magnificent and heart-awakening words, *If Thine Enemy Hunger*, Ben Ostrion chose the surely less effective *Vae Victoribus*. But Ben Ostrion was true to all the prophets of Israel and Judah and must cry Woe, Woe to the Conquerors.

§

The priest had been moved to visit the house of the publisher in Amen Street by a rapid succession of shocks. First there had been the ' non-fraternisation ' order of the British Commander-in-Chief and his broadcast to the German nation, explaining that it had been decided upon because ' we are a Christian people.' So ! We had gone proudly to battle in the name of Christian brotherhood, and now, in the hour of victory, were proudly, pharisaically, denying it to one and all of our enemies, innocent and guilty both. Then, to shock and wound him further, came the surrender of the Western Allies to the demands of their violent Communist partners, the Soviet Union : demands for the assignation of large tracts of Germany to Poland, for the forced migration of millions from their lifelong homes, and for the vindictive demolition of Germany's industrial plants, or their plunder by the Allies (to the victors the spoils) even though this pillage reduced Germany to a pauper state in Europe. And lastly came the deliberate policy, announced with pride rather than shame, that the food ration for the Germans should be kept at a level which the experts declared to be below that necessary for normal life, labour and warmth. 'The German food-cuts have come to stay,' said the British Commander, with a disciplinarian's rigour. 'One thousand calories. That is more than they gave the inmates of Belsen.' He was a sincerely religious man, a devoted churchman, who never ceased to direct his soldiers' thoughts towards the Lord and to remind them that they were the army of a Christian people. 'Soldiers of Christ, arise.'

Father Dawbeny arose. He could stand no more. 'I did not go to war for this, or tell my people to make war for this. I told them we were defending Christianity. And the marching orders of all Christians are simple : " If thine enemy hunger, feed him." '

The vision was clear again, clear as it had been in the matter of saturation-bombing ; not a cloud on its edge anywhere ; and loud and insistent came the call to speak. He raised his protest first in a sermon, but what good was that, with only his thirty faithful to hear him? He tried to sound a louder protest in a newspaper article, but no paper would publish it ; and this perhaps was not due to the crudity or the timidity of editors, for Father Dawbeny was quite unskilled in the journalist's craft, and his article was not only burdened with far too many ponderous, abstract words, but was also, in these days of a newsprint shortage, far too long. The article either came back to Greig Street with a courteous rejection or it disappeared into one of the endless silences of Fleet Street.

So he marched somewhat angrily to Amen Street and asked what Ben Ostrion could do. What about another pamphlet ? 'Give us a platform, for God's sake, Ben—literally for God's sake.' Ben Ostrion was ready to do everything, for a similar insurrection had been brewing in him. 'My God, Piers,' he said, ' we'll put out something that'll shake 'em, and do it in record time. I'll give it priority over all my other titles.'

' And you'll call it *If Thine Enemy Hunger ;* that's the obvious title. It's what St. Paul said . . . always supposing he wrote the *Romans*.'

' Pardon me, sir,' corrected Ben. ' It's what Solomon said a thousand years before . . . always supposing he wrote the *Proverbs*. Your boy Paul was but quoting our boy Solomon. We are Christians too, my boy. Go home and write. Write me something that'll break up the hard ground of their hearts like a plough before the Lord.'

And Father Dawbeny hurried home and wrote. He wrote his article anew, both because there was room for fuller treatment in a booklet and because he had been inspired by Ben's fiery encouragement to write it better. Considered as a whole it was not a good article, a stiffness always coming down upon him when he must compose on paper, but here and there his emotion, kindling, did give him sentences that Ben himself could scarcely have bettered. 'Whatever our statesmen and generals may have done, we, the people, have not so quickly exchanged our simple idealism for a new cynical opportunism, nor shall we abdicate from our high moral position at the call of the godless East.' 'Our love of fairness, yes, and of generosity whenever possible, cannot be signed away by any statesman or general, because it pulses deep in our English hearts.' 'We have come out of the war one of the little nations, but assuredly the leader of the little nations. We can be " great " no more in terms of power, but we can be great morally. We were so for a while, and all the future ages call to us to stay so now.'

When he had finished his article he felt purged and at peace.

Vae Victoribus burst the confines of bookshops and bookstalls, so that it was sold in the streets by the vendors of newspapers and magazines. But, once again, what friends or enemies it made for the name of Father Dawbeny among its millions of distant readers is a matter beyond tracing. This chronicle is concerned only with the effects of its great popularity on his enemies in the Dale and in the regions round about.

§

The least of his enemies, but an effectual one nevertheless, was the Rev. Oliver Custance, of St. Luke's, Ledbitter. Mr. Custance did not choose to perceive that his readiness at all times to disparage, in accents of great fairness, his neighbour of St. John's sprang from his fear of a standard that was flying too high for him. This young man had talents and large ambitions, and he was not anxious to sell these possessions and give the proceeds to the poor ; and so he found pleasure in every good reason for defaming Father Dawbeny who seemed to think this was just what a priest should do. He had been pleased, more pleased than he allowed to show, when his neighbour had somewhat soiled his fame with his ' pro-German ' outburst ; now, on the other hand, he was displeased, displeased to the point of malignity, that this neighbour's name should be travelling all over Britain, and even on to the street-vendor's pavements, within the covers of this runaway success, *Vae Victoribus*.

One morning, walking along Chester Crescent, on the slope of Ledbitter Hill, he met a woman parishioner, and she must rasp and fret him by mentioning the booklet and its immense success and the Reverend Dawbeny's part in it. He replied, ' I think it's a pity he's lent himself to that sort of thing. Everyone knows that Ben Ostrion only publishes stuff like that because it has a *succès de scandale* and makes a good profit. I'm no anti-semitist, but if there is one type of Jew I cannot stand it's the fat, oily, profiteering careerists like Ostrion. They always live on the fat of the land, and it is we who have to support them. I must say I shouldn't care to have my name associated with his. No, I'm sorry Piers Dawbeny got himself mixed up with that crowd. Besides, what sentimental rubbish the book is ! Personally I agree with Field Marshal Montgomery that the whole German nation must be taught once for all that all Christian and god-fearing people have had enough of their barbarities and intend to treat them as pariahs until they mend their ways. There is good scriptural authority for this attitude—you remember : " Put away from among yourselves that wicked person." '

This, or such as this, the Rev. Oliver Custance was saying to all whom he encountered on the slopes of Ledbitter Hill.

He was a covert enemy ; Comrade Anton was an open enemy, at least in so far as he pretended to nothing but a hatred of religion and was frank in his attacks upon its ministers as druggers and disarmers of the people. It was with a fascinated disgust that he read that his old opponent, Mr. Dawbeny, was one of the *Vae Victoribus* gang who had dared challenge and assail everything that the Party Line demanded—that is, everything that the Soviet Union demanded. He summoned the eager, if grubby, young men of his cell to his bed-sitting room in Tyre Street, for a secret meeting. They closed the door and sat around in their roll-neck sweaters and slack coats, in their red ties and dirty corduroy trousers ; and they smoked their fags or pipes and talked, and were happy in the thought that they were underground conspirators and the seeds of the Future. In the great class war was not History battling ineluctably on the side of the toiling masses and the Proletarian Revolution, and was not their Party the spearhead of this historic and invincible movement ? And if this was so, and no lad there questioned it, for it was the catholic faith of his church, then, as Comrade Anton reminded them, anyone who opposed the Communists anywhere was inevitably, whether he knew it or not, an enemy of the working class. And this Mr. Dawbeny : they had read his part in that ludicrous *Vae Victoribus*. And they knew that he was hand-in-glove with that foul, fascist scum, Ben Ostrion. ' I say,' declared Comrade Anton, heating up, ' that Mr. Dawbeny, though he doesn't know it because he hasn't the brains to, and because he's never studied Historical Materialism and probably couldn't understand it if he tried, is a paid agent of the capitalist exploiters and therefore an enemy of the people.'

Loud and cordial agreement everywhere. Murmurs of agreement like the ' Amens ' and ' Praise-the-Lords ' at a Salvation Army Holiness meeting. To hell with all fascist priests ! *A la lanterne.* They went into delighted conference about it. If Mr. Dawbeny was a rock of resistance to the People's Revolution, then it was their duty to break down this rock, dynamite it, and clear it out of the way of History. How ? How could they discredit him so that his influence was destroyed in the Dale ? That was what they must attempt to do : discredit him for ever. All methods were open to them, moral or immoral ; or, rather, any method they chose to adopt was moral, since morality was not absolute but something determined by the needs of the historic moment and the Proletarian Revolution. And certainly, in their small field of action, the historic moment required that they overthrew the power of this priest whom the people, whether they agreed with his views or not, persisted in calling good.

He was not good : in Marxian eyes he was bad ; but the foolish people could not be persuaded to look at him with Marxian eyes. They must be persuaded by other means that he was not good. Had any of the comrades any ideas how this could be done ? The meeting was now a ' Down with Dawbeny ' meeting, but the only decision they could arrive at was that they must besmear his name at every opportunity. A whispering

campaign they had organized against him ever since he denounced
the bombing of German civilians, contrary to the stated views of
the Kremlin; they must now, in the vogue-phrase of the day,
'step up' this campaign, enlarge it, put some ginger in it, give
it a 'stop-at-nothing' character. Let every comrade present
vow, here and now, that he would devote himself to this secret,
and indeed sacred, task.

That was the only way they could think of at the moment, and
the meeting broke up.

But an ally was coming to their help : as open an enemy of the
father as they, even if he, like they, preferred his deeds to be
secret. This man, a capitalist in his way, and certainly in his
aims, hated Communism as heartily as he hated Christianity ;
and all this they knew, but none of it mattered to them if he
could be used for their purposes.

Mr. Albert Howden, than whom there had been no better
behaved prisoner in the country's gaols, for he had learned
wisdom in these premises before, came out of prison. He had
collected all his remission marks and earned therewith his release on licence with a quarter of his sentence unserved. And
he came into the free and open streets with a resolve in his
heart. His luxuriant hair was whiter than it had ever been,
and his face beneath it grey with the prison pallor ; his aqueous
red eyes had sunk a little deeper into his head his lips were
thinner and they too, like the eyes, seemed to have retreated
further into his face ; but beneath that hair, and behind those
eyes and lips, were the thoughts of revenge that had been his sole
comfort for five and a quarter years in prison. In a different
'cell' from Comrade Anton's, and with only himself for audience,
he had conducted many a ' Down with Dawbeny ' meeting. He,
like Comrade Anton, had considered ways and means of traducing
Father Dawbeny, and been untroubled in these deliberations by
questions of bourgeois morality.

CHAPTER SEVEN

MR. HOWDEN, on leaving prison, did not return to his tall house in Lamplough Terrace, Cremona Road. It had stood empty during the blitz, and for some time afterwards, but had recently found a tenant, a better man than Mr. Howden, but not much. This able man had seen an opening like a light: he had bought the house and now let its many rooms as furnished apartments, not to such customers as Mr. Howden's, but to young couples who could find no homes after the war. He let them at extortionate rents, but was thoroughly respectable, sitting comfortably within the ring-fence of the Law.

Besides, Mr. Howden now felt that the atmosphere of Cremona Road and the Dale would be too oppressive for him, too close. He had only one thing to do in those streets and would then forget them for ever.

During his long absence his large, lush, golden-haired wife, as capable as she was comely, and as well found in ideas as she was handsomely dressed, had acquired a high, narrow Georgian house in Lunn Street, just across the road from St. Pancras and Kings Cross stations, and was running it as a small private hotel, one of fifty such ' one-night hotels ' that stood waiting for custom near the great terminuses. She called it 'St. James's Hotel' and advertised ' Bed and Breakfast.' Why ' St. James's ' has never been known, and certainly if the apostle was its patron saint he must have disapproved of its patronne. St. James in his general epistle appealed to his brethren to keep themselves unspotted from the world, but this smoke-darkened, dingy little hostel was in no sense, neither in a material nor in a spiritual sense, unspotted from the world. Its face was grimy, its halls were grimy, and its deeds were dim. But perhaps Mrs. Howden no more believed in St. James's ' salvation by works ' than did Luther himself, who called this encyclical of St. James's ' a right strawy epistle.' Mrs. Howden gave bed and breakfast to many couples who purported to have come from one of the terminuses and were asked no further questions, but were shown upstairs to double-bedded rooms.

So Mr. Howden came to the St. James's Hotel from Parkhouse Prison, but if his body wandered about Lunn Street, Judd Street, and the Euston and Gray's Inn Roads, his spirit behind the moist, abstracted eyes was far away, moving contemplatively up and down Greig Street before the doors of its church and its Church Hall. Or it was wandering along other streets he had known, as if in search of someone. His spirit, brooding about the Dale, was in fact looking for someone : a woman whose likeness and whose name he did not yet know. Her likeness and her name changed many times as he walked and wandered and wondered.

' I wish he was dead. I wish the earth would open and swallow him up. Frame him and break him. Frame him and break him.'

Such for five years and more had been his thoughts and such they were now, day after day, week after week ; and always they ran on to one line, to be stopped by the buffer : ' Where's the woman ? ' In prison it had been frustrating, sickening, mad-making to think that he could not answer the question till years had gone by and he was out and free again.

His plan was now a fixed idea, and sometimes, like a one-stroke motor engine affixed to a cycle or a boat, it drove his body as well as his spirit to the streets of the Dale, where he walked guiltily, eyes switching left and right, even while his head was charged with thought.

Not the first woman he visited, nor the second and third, seemed to match with his purpose, and in the end he forbore to lay it before them. But time was passing ; he had been out months now ; and he must move, he must *move*. At last with Connie Beron he had his success.

Connie Beron had loved him more than any other of her men, and he had loved her more than any other of his women—or so he told himself in these later years, for like many other old sinners he became more and more sentimental as he grew riper in years and perhaps over-ripe. While he was in his fifties, and she in her twenties, she had accepted him as one of her lovers and declared she loved him best ; and he had been touched by this. And she had continued to receive him, very secretly, after she married young Tim Forrester, the fruit-and-flower boy in the Becker Street market. Always she was a great comfort to him, because she was always on his side, passionately on his side, in every complaint he took to her. No one ever made a greater fuss of him than Connie, or had been more agreeably indignant and spiteful against anyone whom he declared to have injured him. Tim had gone to the war, Mr. Howden learned, and been killed, and Connie, who had no desire to remain a widow for long, had married as soon as decency permitted, which is to say, about a year later, old Silas Beron, the Jew who had a junk stall in the same market, from which he sold at a fine profit second-hand china, brass ware, spectacles, jewellery, umbrellas, corsets, shoes—in fact anything except perishable goods. Silas was fifty-four. She had always liked men older than herself.

Mr. Howden went to the door of the Berons' home in Water Street but learned from a lady within—probably a lodger—that Mrs. Beron was out. ' She generally goes out just about this time,' said the lady ; and because it was mid-day, and because of the tone in which she said it, he guessed that her meaning was, ' She always goes out for one or two, as soon as they are open.' Yes, that would be like Connie. She had always been a sight too fond of her gin-and-water. And that was five years ago. She probably had a craving for it now. But in these post-war times, what she must spend on it ! Caw ! What did old Silas say about that ? Thinking this, he wrote a note asking her to come to Lunn Street and signing it ' Ossie,' which had been her pet-name for him, because she said he ' favoured ' Oscar Bentley the old film actor who so often played the part of some distinguished and benevolent old pianist or philosopher. Then he came out of her house door, but not before he had looked quickly up and down the street.

Connie, who had a heart as large (for her friends at least) as her conscience was small, arrived the very next morning at St. James's Hotel, happy to know that her old lover was home from ' over the wall ' ; and Mr. Howden, who had no occupation in these days but wandering about the passages or the pavements, opened the door to her.

' Hallo, my Albert,' she said. ' Not to say Ossy dear.'

' Connie ! ' He saw that her figure had grown plumper in the last five years and her hair, which was set in tight artificial waves, much fairer, and that she was expensively dressed with pearls at her ears and about her throat. No doubt old Beron was ready to spend money on adorning and embellishing his young wife for his own pleasure. She was as seductive as ever, he thought. Only a slight liquid filming over her green eyes heightened his suspicion that she was drinking far more than a woman should, and a slight drooping of her mouth at the corners, so that it was now a little hard and vindictive, made him wonder if old Beron bullied her at times and she was easily huffed with him.

' Come in, my dear,' he welcomed her, feeling fond and senti-mental. ' Come in here.' Mrs. Howden was out shopping, and he took his visitor into the ' Lounge ' which seemed exceedingly small for a hotel. He put her in a chair by the fireplace, and himself leaned an elbow on the mantelpiece. The elbow touched a silver-framed photograph of himself looking like a dissipated professor of Ancient Philosophy. It was inscribed across one corner, ' For Gracie, my dearest wife. My heart yours till death and beyond. Albert.'

' How's things with our Connie ? ' he asked.

' Oh, Silas is doing well enough. There's never been a better time for his junk—old china and glass and all that. You can get what price you like for it almost. The shops haven't any new stuff to offer. It's a sellers' market for old china, and no mistake.'

' Well, that's good. I'm glad someone's happy. Been behaving yourself, Connie ? '

' What-you-mean ? ' she laughed. ' I've always behaved myself.'

' Oh no, dear. Not quite always. You and I know that, and one or two others, eh ? '

' Oh, well . . .' she began, and was not ready with quite the right lie for Ossy, who knew so much.

He saw her difficulty and grinned. ' Well, never mind that, ducks. You look lovely.'

' Do I, Ossy ? But you don't look too good.'

' No. They've just about finished me. Five years and more in prison's no joke for a man who's turned sixty——'

' My poor dear ! '

' Yes, they've done for me.' Self-pity welled up in him so that his eyes, always moist, now swam in tears.

She saw the tears, and her womanly pity ran out to him. ' It's a shame. A wicked shame.'

He offered her a cigarette with a shaking hand, seeking refuge in this action till his mouth should cease to shake. He lit one for himself, returned his elbow to the mantelpiece, and was capable of speech again. 'Yes, my dear, it was a foul business, that. Seven years, just because I didn't see eye-to-eye with them about letting people live their own lives. I've always held, and I still do, that if people want a little fun in their lives they should have it, and it's no business of mine or the police or the parsons either. *Seven* years. Not months, Con: years. For an old man of fifty-eight!'

'It was wicked.'

'There ain't much fun and happiness in the world, I always say, and why shouldn't people have what little they can get? That's always been my philosophy; and seven years they gave me—just because their philosophy was different.'

'It was the girl's age that done for you, wasn't it?'

'I knew nothing about her age, or the other girls' ages either. Never asked them, and they all looked eighteen or more. Seven years! I who've never stolen nothing or hurt anybody. I don't believe in hurting anyone. I believe in helping them to a little happiness. And they treated me as if I'd done robbery with violence. By Christ, I'll never forgive that parson. I wish he was dead. I wish the earth would open and swallow him up. It was his doing from beginning to end.'

'I know. I've never forgiven him, either. The beast. I never heard anything so wicked in my life.'

'Yeah . . . I owe him one.'

'You sure do. Of course you do.'

'Yeah . . . I've got an account to settle with him. And if I can, I'm going to break him. Break him. It's the only thing in life that interests me now. I want to hit him as hard as he hit me.'

'It's only natural. People used to think the world of him, but he's rather done for himself now.'

'What's he done?'

'Didn't you know? He's turned pro-German.'

'*No!*' Mr. Howden was shocked. Shocked that a man could sink so low.

'Oh, yes, he says that now we've got 'em absolutely beat, we should go and help 'em. We should give over being nasty to them and share our grub with them instead.'

'What boloney! They deserve all they get. Why, they're brutes. One and all of 'em: brutes.'

' Of course they are ! '

' They're absolute beasts, one and all, and there's no changing them. The only thing to give them is the toe of your boot, and plenty of it.'

' That's what I say.'

' And he takes their part, does he ? Well, it only goes to show. He's a rotter, out-and-out. A bloody hypocritical rotter . . . Don't you agree ? '

' Naturally I do. Ever since he done that to you. At the time I said I only wish I could get at him.'

So far, so good. Get her agreement first, and then come to the proposition. But, afraid to come to the proposition, he kept silence awhile, leaving the mantelpiece and walking once to the far wall and back. He could not believe that Connie would do for love alone the thing that he wanted. No. But for love and money both—yes. Yes, possibly. Well, back to the mantelpiece, and come to the issue.

' Con. Would fifty nicker be any use to you ? '

' Fifty quid ? What are you talking about ? '

' Fifty pound. That's what I'm talking about.'

' But what for ? And why ? '

' I reckon it would be worth that to me. Yes, indeed I do.'

' What would ? '

' Just this. You do think I'm entitled to get my own back on that brute ? '

' Of course I do.'

' He got up a case against me : that's what it amounted to. He got at that girl ; and he and the cops got at the other girls. And a lot of what they said just wasn't true. All right. O.K. I'm getting up a case against him. Oh, yes ! '

' How ? ' Connie's eyes were full of interest.

' I thought you might help me, Con. There's one sure way of getting at these parsons. I thought it all out in prison. You meet parsons in prison, and generally men of his age, who've got their carpet for you know what : taking liberties with some woman or some girl in their vestries or their vicarages. . . . And even if they only get bound over, they're done for with their bishops. Well, Con, my idea was——'

He put it before her nervously because he was not very hope-ful of her consent, but, as it chanced, he had driven his pick into a richer vein than he knew. Connie in the last few years had developed a craving for, and a dependence on, the stimulation of gin, and Silas, her husband, while ready to spend money on her adornment, grudged it for housekeeping and was quite unready to see her spending any of his hard-earned profits on spirits at their present post-war prices. The result was that she had spent the rent money in the bars of the Dale and was in debt to the shops for milk and groceries and clothes. She did not dare tell Silas this, because when in the past she had confessed to even a small overspending, he had sworn and 'created' and used most shocking terms. And she was desperately afraid of his finding it all out. This sudden offer of fifty pounds, then, *fifty*, shone before her eyes like a gift extended towards her in the hand of a guardian angel. Her eyes had brightened at the mention of fifty pounds, and her hard lips parted.

Her lips might have parted, but she continued to gaze at him without speaking. There was another strong motive for accepting his suggestion. He knew too much about her. He knew things which old Silas had never been told. He knew all about her games when she was married to Tim Forrester, and it was possible, since he was a shrewd old rogue, that he knew of some adventures since she had married Silas Beron. She couldn't say how much he knew, and she didn't dare ask him. And if he turned nasty and sullen, might he not . . . but on one thing she was resolute : no one was going to spoil her marriage with Silas. She had married old Beron for security, and she was going to keep her security. No, she might be really fond of Ossy, but she didn't trust him. Connie was perfectly capable of loving Ossy heartily and distrusting him as completely.

So when Mr. Howden made his proposition to Connie Beron there was much in her heart that made a favourable tilth for it. There were need and greed and fear.

And they stared at each other, he moored by an elbow to the mantelshelf, his heart slightly apprehensive, she gazing up at him with her green, lymphatic eyes and thinking rapidly, but saying nothing.

' Eh, what do you say, my dear ? '

Almost as if the question were merely academic, she put forth a smile of incredulity and submitted, ' But Mr. Dawbeny would never fall for that,' and when he replied, ' Oh, you never know : it's extraordinary how often men of his age do, specially

if they've never been married and are starved like,' she insisted,.
' No, not Mr. Dawbeny ; he's not that kind.'

To which he retorted boldly, ' Well, to hell ! what's to prevent
you saying he did ? He got 'em to tell lies about me ? Why
shouldn't he be served with some of his own sauce ? '

Then, still staring at him, she began to justify her desire to·
co-operate. She set about justifying it with many, too many,
words. She said, ' I don't know that I should mind doing it,
Ossy. After all, he deserves something ; ' and ' He more or less
framed you, you say. Well I reckon he deserves framing in his·
turn. Yes, I do ; ' and ' If he got 'em to tell lies about you,
as you say, I don't see why he shouldn't have a few told about
him ; ' and ' Yes, I'm on your side in this, Ossy, you can be
sure of that. I said from the first that I'd like to get my hands.
on him.'

And Mr. Howden, his elbow slipped from the mantelshelf that
both hands might rest in his waistcoat pockets, listened with all
the excitement of hope, but somewhat shocked at her compliance..

CHAPTER EIGHT

THESE first two years after the war, in the new quiet world of peace, were a time of deep discouragement for Father Dawbeny. His share of the *Vae Victoribus* pamphlet had been sprinkled with humour and a gay, mordant wit, but really it had been written out of a sorrow that was like despair. It had seemed to him that not only was the Christian creed retreating from the world —this he could understand, for it was a difficult creed—but the Christian virtues were in retreat, too.

His brother clergy. He would meet Oliver Custance in the streets of the Dale or on the slope of the hill, and always the fat little man, because he was in angry disagreement with *Vae Victoribus*, would start an argument so that he could attack Ben Ostrion and see to it that some of the arrows directed at the editor hit his contributor. One enlightened priest in the north invited Father Dawbeny to address a Church Congress on the lines of *Vae Victoribus*, and he went north and did so, facing a large audience and giving them the whole strong meal, fearlessly. He sought no love from them nor applause, though he would have dearly liked both. And from that audience, composed largely of parsons, church councillors and church-women, his speech evoked far more hostility than support, and it was a hot, impatient hostility not unlike hate. But perhaps, he told himself, this had been his fault. Perhaps where he had meant to be humorous he had been only rude. He had quoted an aphorism of Archdeacon Denison that the particular Evil Spirit who had it in charge to corrupt and ultimately destroy the Church of England was Cosmophilus, the Spirit of Compromise with the World. 'Cosmophilus, it seems to me,' he said, 'writes all the leaders in the *Church Weekly*, and most of those in *The Times*. He had written quite a few of the speeches we've heard in this Congress and at this moment I suspect he's inspiring a whole lot more in answer to me. My experience of Church Congresses is that they must be joyous field-days for

Cosmophilus because he knows that it's his proposals which will emerge triumphant.'

Perhaps it had been rude. Perhaps he had sinned in yielding to the joys of pungent words instead of speaking only in love.

Lady Guttree came no more to his church, nor contributed any longer to its support. After that dinner party with Ben Ostrion, over which a certain friendship had settled at the close, she had declared, to save her face, that she didn't wholly agree with either of them and thought them altogether too sentimental, but she was prepared to ' bury the hatchet.' And she had come back to St. John the Prior's and taken her usual place in a hindmost pew. But *Vae Victoribus* had kindled all her fire anew and sent her hurrying to where the hatchet lay that she could dig it up again. Now, everywhere, she spoke as disparagingly of him as once she had gushed with adulation.

His congregation was smaller than ever. Some of them had died, some had gone from the Dale, and others, like Lady Guttree, had found his doctrines too hard for them. Nothing fails like failure, and the emptiness of his pews drove the weak away and discouraged others from coming in their place. He had no men for his choir and only two boys for servers. Men and boys, alas, were exhibitionists ever, and didn't want to perform in the high places unless there was an audience in the pews to admire them. On weekdays there was only Ernie to serve at the early Mass, and one could not ask him to do so every morning. One must not try the devoted too far. Sometimes Sophie, who said ' it was a shame the father had to do it all himself,' would come to the daily Mass, take the sacring bell to her place among the tiny congregation, hide it by her hassock, and ring it for him three times at the Sanctus and the Elevation of the Host.

Denys Flackman was demobilized from the army and home in the Dale, but he came to serve no more. Nor, if he could help it, would he come face to face with Father Dawbeny in the street. If he saw the father in the street he would turn about and go the opposite way or escape round a corner before they could meet. It was exactly what Mr. Howden used to do after he learned that the minister had discovered the worst of his sins. Sometimes Father Dawbeny saw these quick, evasive movements and knew, with no small pity, that the boy was running from him because he was remembering the dark things which he had confessed to him. Once or twice the encounter was inescapable, and then the boy's talk was rapid and embarrassed, and his eyes unstable and shifting, and it was plain that his one desire was to end the interview and get away. He would explain, while the eyes flew away, that, try as he would, and much as he would like to have some religion, he could believe in the Christian dogmas no more. He was finding his happiness now in literature and art and music. He belonged to a play-reading circle of young fellows who met at the Liberal Men's Institute, he went whenever possible to the Promenade Concerts at the Albert Hall, and he and some of his pals were making a study of the Greeks in English translations. Yes, the demobilized Denys was very much the young intellectual, nor was it only a pose, even though he wore his yellow hair a little long and walked the streets in the correct uniform of the Young Intellectuals : a black beret on the side of his head, and a fawn duffle coat with toggle fastenings and dependent hood. Father Dawbeny's heart went out to him as a vain young poseur, certainly, but something else as well : a seeker after some beauty to believe in and love, in a war-wasted world that had stripped the young of all their fathers' armour and left them naked and vulnerable.

The lad did not look happy or even healthy ; the handsome face under the fair hair looked sallow, hollow, dulled, even debauched, so that Father Dawbeny would wonder whether Denys, his late server, whom the restraints of his religion had not been able to hold back when his desires were hot within him, was now taking advantage of his intellectual freedom to indulge as he liked the lusts of his young flesh.

Just as his little church seemed typical of a dying Christianity, so did the young Denys seem typical of the new, despairing age.

Father Dawbeny was now very poor. The last of his capital had gone into the south and north walls of the church which had begun to show cracks four years after the blitz ; and it was as much as he could do to keep church and hall and Costers' Club afloat. And just as church and club were getting shabby so were his suits and his cassock and his surplices ; and this always hurt him. He had always loved (and tried to believe there was no sin in loving) a stateliness and perfection in his dress. But now he could have it no more. (He did not know that he was a more dignified and striking figure in his worn and shiny cassock than ever he had been, when it looked like an expensive garment bought only yesterday.)

There was another worry, too, but since this had reference only to himself and not to his people, its indulgence was surely sin. It was a worry about his age and his health. He was sixty-five now, and very tired ; far more weary than he ought to be at such an age. In his heart and limbs there was a treacherous longing for rest. More, in his body there was often a pain round his heart which frightened him. It had frightened him for years, and he had not dared to go to the doctor, lest the doctor should frighten him more. Sometimes he would look into the glass and be disappointed, horrified, at the wrinkled and loose flesh of his face, the melancholy, storm-beaten expression in his eyes, the death's-head hollows under those tired eyes, and the revolting stringiness of his throat, which was like (he thought) the long, pulled, empty neck of a boiling fowl. Was he really this lean, gaunt, shocking, awful cadaver ? But enough of this : this was vanity. ' God forgive me. Does the vain old Adam never die ? '

Ah, well ; so, so ! Let the depression roll on and have its way. It was partly the heart-sickness of a lonely man who had always craved love, but had been too shy and reserved to win much of it. There was the love of his few faithful, of course, but he saw them only for brief moments ; there were Ernie and Sophie, devoted friends, but never could they fill up his need of an intellectual partnership ; Ben Ostrion was the only friend who could have given him all, but Ben was the busiest of men, and months passed, and they met each other not at all. It was the heart-sickness of the artist also : the artist who feels that his public is going from him so that he is already almost forgotten, but who remembers the labour he gave to his work and knows, with all the vision he possesses, that his work was good.

§

The depression, a snowball depression, gathered size as it rolled on. Sometimes it was so great a weight that he had to get up out of his chair and wander up and down the room, trying to shake it off. The dog whose ears he had perhaps been

fondling would make one protest at this abrupt move, giving a
single low wail and a single tap of his paw on the floor. This
protest delivered, he sat on his haunches quietly and watched
his master walking up and down the long room with his hands
thrust into his cincture or halting by the window with his
fists resting on his hips. The poor, watching beast could not
know it, but his master was striving to fortify the sick heart
and the fainting will with the fine words of those who were his
heroes and exemplars. F. W. Robertson : 'Truth has not
crowns to give, but thorns.' Again and again he said this,
walking up and down the room. Liddon : 'Earth is no place
for realizing ideals or for escaping disappointments.' The same
Liddon in a grand moment : 'There can be no reason for
despondency if we really trust in God. We shall yet see the
drowned Egyptians on the shore.' But perhaps more comforting
than these, because they promised no easy relief, but rang with
truth in a man's despair, and went straight to the heart and
rooted there, two sayings : one from the old fourteenth-century
friar, John Tauler : 'Children, turn it which way ye will, the
heart of man must be bare, empty, free and poor if God is to
work therein ; ' and, grandest of all—Father Dawbeny would go
always to these words for a draught of healing when his melancholy was at its deepest—the words which Plato gave to Diotima,
the wise woman of Mantinea : 'Love is the child of Poverty.
Therefore love is always poor ; not tender and beautiful, as
most people think, but lean and gaunt ; he is shoeless and
homeless ; he lies on the bare earth without a bed and sleeps
in the open air, on doorsteps or in the street, dwelling ever
with want.'

§

He prayed often in his long upper room, or in his small bed-
chamber, but never had he known such a dryness in his prayers.
They brought little comfort. He rose from his knees unwarmed,
unencouraged. It was as if the Presence was withdrawn and
only darkness was left to him. It was so at his altar : the
Presence might be there, but he could not feel it, and deep
and deadening was the sadness when he turned to bless the
people who himself so needed blessing, or to comfort them
who himself could find no comfort.

To no one did he speak of this inward darkness ; his to hearten, not dishearten, the members of his flock and the people who were not of his flock, but stopped to speak with him in the street. If, as sometimes happened, they spoke sympathetically of his difficulties, he would only smile and say, ' Oh, we scratch along. And we shall continue to do so.'

Yes, he would continue to do so. His heart might be rebellious and completely disobedient to his desires and gone into a far country, but one could always call up the old, stubborn will and go on with the work coldly, steadfastly, unwaveringly, till the prodigal heart came home again.

§

And out of the darkness came the attack.

Connie Beron was not a little nervous as she approached the old grey police station in Lutine Street. It stood in the parts north of the Dale, and the street was strange to her. The station itself was a little frightening : everything about it was a little frightening : its difference from the houses on either side of it, its old stock bricks grimed to dark grey, its white stone dressings eroded by weather and time, its five white stone steps up which so many must have gone, not soon to return to liberty again, and its hideous word, Police, over the doorway. She had never been in the hands of the police, and they, so far as she knew, had never heard of her, but, like many of her class or type, she thought of them less as friendly helpers than as natural enemies. Her steps slowed a little, and slowed more as she drew near that doorway. Her lips were moving as she came, like the lips of an old woman, for she was muttering to herself ; she was sustaining her will with words that Ossy had said to her, and she had said to him, and with the thought of that fifty pounds.

Her conscience, undersized and a weakling, had been knocked out and put to sleep by that sudden offer of fifty pounds, but now, and indeed for the last twenty-four hours, it had most inopportunely stirred in its sleep and tried to rise. For the last twenty-four hours she had been obliged to dope it with those justifications in which she didn't really believe, and she was doing so now, rapidly, dose after dose : ' Where's the harm ?

. . . Ossy says he told lies about him, so he's asked for some of his own back. . . . He's put others on the spot ; time someone put him there, I reckon. . . . Everyone knows the cops invent what they like about us, just as it suits 'em, if they want to put someone away, and there's no doubt the cops and he got together because they wanted to put Ossy away. . . . I'm on Ossy's side in this . . . yes, every time. . . . Yes, I don't mind what I'm doing . . . not at all.'

But she walked past the station, not wanting to go in at once. Let her rehearse again the things she must say to them. Let her remember all the instructions that Ossy had given her. She was hearing his voice and seeing the cunning in his eyes (though trying not to consider it cunning) as he said, ' You must have the date and the time, see, my dear ? But you don't want to come out with them too quick. Wait till they ask you for them, and then sort of pretend to work out which day it was, see, my dear ? And you must have your corroboration ready, but there again—see—don't go offering it till they ask for it. Look as though you didn't know they'd want any. He'll just say, " We shall need corroboration " and begin asking questions, and then you pretend to think, see, and give him what he wants. And above all, you never met me in your life. I see no reason why they should mention me, but if they do—no : Albert Howden ? No, never met him. Who's he ? I knew a Mr. Howson once ; would that be he ? A nice man, only he was *Jimmy* Howson, I think. Albert Howden ? No ; the name's strange to me. D'you understand, my dear ? '

She turned back to those five steps. But however deliberately she stilled her conscience and rehearsed her words, her heart and her hands were still shaking as she went slowly up to the door.

One of the double doors was wide open. She passed through it and found she was in a long passage with a stone floor and a dado of brown tiles. The passage, dimly lit, stretched to a glass-panelled door which opened on to the old stable yard, and even as she stood there, alone and hesitating, she saw a blue police van pass across it. Bringing some poor devil of a prisoner, she imagined ; and some obscure loyalty to all such captives came as a welcome reinforcement to her resolve.

On her right was a door marked ' Charge Room ' ; on her left a door marked ' Inspector's Office.' The Charge Room was silent ; from the Inspector's Office came the murmur of men's voices and the stuttering of typewriters. But from neither door came anyone to greet her. The word 'Inspector' was somewhat alarming, so she nervously opened the door of the Charge Room. Would not this be the right door ? Had she not come to lay a charge ?

The square room was empty, and seemed the emptier for the scantiness and bareness of its furniture. Benches stood against two walls, and a high desk in the middle of the bare floor, with a high stool before it. The charge desk, doubtless, and therefore the soul of the room. The ceiling was darkened almost to black, and a more fanciful mind than Connie's might have imagined that it had been blackened by the sins which had been laid like a burnt offering on that desk. As she turned to glance at a notice-board on the wall a voice, speaking behind her, almost jumped her heart out of her body.

'Come to give yourself up ? '

The words could not have seemed a worse omen. She swung towards the voice and saw a fat police sergeant with a round, jovial face who had come through a door by the fireplace. 'Well, what have you done ? ' he went on merrily. 'Let's have it out. A little murder, is it ? '

'No,' she stammered, and again didn't like his words, for the conscience that *would* not sleep suggested that 'a little murder' was just what she had come to do. Unwittingly she gave her head a sharp little shake, as if to shake the conscience away from her. 'No, I just wanted to report something.'

'Lost your little dog ? '

'No . . . no . . .'

'Found an old gentleman's spectacles, what ? '

'No. I wanted to make a complaint.'

'Ah, a complaint ! I see. A complaint.' He seemed pleased —relieved—as if this was what they were there for, and much more interesting than a lost dog. 'Well, come this way. This is only where we charge the boys and girls.'

He led her across the passage and through the door marked 'Inspector's Office.' Now she found herself before an empty counter and saw in the wide spaces behind it a uniformed sergeant seated at a table, a uniformed constable typing at a desk and another young constable standing by a filing cabinet nearly as tall as himself. 'Lady to see you, Sergeant,' said her guide, and retired.

'Yes, madam?' inquired the Sergeant, without rising from his table. 'What can I do for you?'

'I wanted to make a complaint about something. I was told I ought to report it to the police.'

'Oh, yes?' His eyebrows seemed to be asking further details.

'Do I tell you . . . here? It's a—it's a formal complaint.'

'Is it something serious?'

She looked down on to the counter, as a modest woman should. 'Well, *I* think so. It's a case of assault.'

'What kind of assault?'

She kept her eyes down as if not liking to speak her next words before a couple of young constables. And yet one part of her, the vain part, was a little proud of the words. 'Well . . . you see . . . I think it's what you call improper assault.'

'Oh.' The Sergeant turned his face and called to someone out of sight round a corner, 'Stanley! Stan, ring up and see if the D.I.'s there.'

'Yes, Sarge,' answered a young voice.

'Or someone else from the C.I.D. office. We won't keep you waiting a minute, madam.'

'Don't mention it.' She rested her handbag on the counter and stared at the green dado round the room and the glossy green paint. The Sergeant went on with his work at the table, and the two young constables, who had not even looked up at the words 'improper assault' continued their work at typewriter or filing cabinet.

'Will you come this way, madam?' Again a voice, coming unexpectedly from behind her, set her heart hammering. She turned and saw a young man in grey flannel trousers and grey sports jacket, who must have entered from the passage.

'This is Detective-Sergeant Powys, madam,' said the uniformed sergeant. 'He will look after you.'

The information surprised her: this youth seemed too short for a policeman, too young for a sergeant, and too slackly dressed for either category.

'This way, madam.' He opened the door for her and led her along the dim, brown passage till they came to a door marked 'C.I.D. Office.' She knew well enough what 'C.I.D.'

stood for, and the words scared her. Never again would she embark upon a business like this : no, not for another fifty pounds. Better freedom from fear than fifty pounds. As he opened the door the young man said, ' I'm sorry, madam, but I forgot to ask your name.'

' Mrs. Beron. Mrs. Constance Beron.'

' Thank you.'

Now he was leading her through a large room where five or six men in plain clothes sat each at his own small table. Two of them were typing. Detective-constables and detective-sergeants ? She had no time to notice much, but did get an impression of cream walls, green-shaded lamps, and high windows whose lower panes were frosted so as to veil all sight of the stable yard. These frosted panes made her feel shut in —caught—caught by the police. She felt a little stifled, and longed to get this business over and be out in the street again.

The young man was leading her diagonally across the big room to a door marked ' D.I.'s Office,' and as they went she observed a hat-stand on which hung an assortment of hats and coats and mackintoshes, no two alike. The garments in which these sergeants and constables went out into the streets, disguised, to uncover the truth about people like her ! Her heart was now almost rattling in her breast. But they went on.

The young man opened the door. ' Mrs. Beron, sir.'

This room seemed as small as the other was large : it had barely space for the writing-desk in its midst, the small table against one wall, the small cupboard, and the few chairs.

A thin man with thick dark hair and earnest eyes rose from behind the desk. He again seemed a curious figure for a policeman : too slight and too gentle-eyed to handle some of the roughs she knew in the Dale. She did not know that this was Detective-Inspector Glower who, six years before, had come to fetch Mr. Howden from Lamplough Terrace ; and he did not know this visit was a belated sequel to that half-forgotten tale.

' Good morning, madam. Do sit down.' And he indicated the chair in front of his desk, as polite as anything. ' You have something to tell me. I am the Detective-Inspector, as I expect you've gathered.'

No one could have spoken nicer, she thought, as he resumed his seat before her. The young sergeant closed the door, and its closing interrupted the beating of her heart. She felt shut in deeper, caught in the very heart of the police station. The young sergeant was still in the room. Why? The Inspector's next words suggested that the Sergeant might be there to keep watch on the Inspector. A chaperon.

'You are a married lady, I understand; but would you rather give your information to a woman officer? Emily's here, isn't she, Powys?'

'Yes, sir.'

Mrs. Beron looked down on his desk, while she wondered what a modest young woman should answer. At first she thought she ought to say, 'Well, perhaps it'd be best if I could,' but fear of a woman officer who, she felt sure, would see much deeper into her, and be far more suspicious of her, than this pleasant gentleman, determined her course, and she replied, 'Oh no, I don't think I need trouble you all that. It's not all that embarrassing, if you see what I mean. It's just something we don't think ought to be allowed to go on. I expect you know all about these sort of things.'

'I expect we do,' he said with a significant smile. 'Very well then, madam. Let us hear.'

She told her story: it had happened in the vestry; she had gone to his service on the Sunday morning, like, and had told him she liked it no end, and asked if she might come and talk over difficulties with him one day, 'you know, difficulties about believing this and that; and what they expect you to do—like you do with a minister.'

The Inspector nodded, as if he had done this in his time.

And he had said he was always in his church to see anyone at half-past five in the evening. So she'd gone along, and he'd taken her into the vestry, as they call it, and he'd walked up and down listening to her, as she explained her difficulties because, you see, to be quite frank, she hadn't been accustomed to going to church.

So far Connie Beron's story was true. She *had* spoken with him after the service; she *had* visited him in the vestry; and he *had* listened to her difficulties, walking up and down. But now, with her heart beating treacherously, she ventured out of this safe harbour into the open and perhaps perilous sea of imagination. They were in the vestry for a long time, she said, and she couldn't help thinking he was looking at her strangely.

And he kept asking questions and talking as if he didn't want to let her go—' if you see what I mean.'

Again the Inspector nodded. Not a sign of surprise had he shewn ; no one would have supposed that he'd ever heard of the Reverend Dawbeny before. In fact, his surprise, and his shock, were total. A complaint like this of Father Dawbeny ! Father Dawbeny with whom he'd worked ! Who'd been so good to that child when they were pinning the medals on that old—what was his name ? Could one believe this woman ? He could wish the answer were, ' No, not for a moment,' but —she was a round, buxom, comfortable person, and didn't look the starved, hysterical type.

At first, she was saying, he had put his arm along her shoulder, and this she had thought just friendly like, but then he stooped and kissed her, and she was almost too flabbergasted to know what was happening. Then he put his hand down her blouse. . . .

The Inspector was silent. He looked at his finger nails. He turned and looked at the frosted window though there was nothing he could see through that. Apart from a slight dropping of the jaw, which separated his lips, there was still no trace of surprise on his face.

At last he spoke. ' And when did this happen ? Can you give me the exact day ? '

' Oh, yes, I think so. I think I could. Let me see. It was a Monday, you see, because it was the day after I went to his church—not the Monday before last, but the one before that. Yes, that was it.'

' Nearly three weeks ago ? '

' Yes. . . . Yes, I suppose so. Yes, all of that. I was too shocked, as you might say, to do anything about it. It was others who persuaded me I ought to tell the police.'

' You appreciate that this may be very serious for this man ? We shall need to know a great deal more. Did anyone see this ? '

' Well, no, how could they ? '

' No, I suppose not. . . . No. . . . H'mmm. . . .' He went into a silence, shutting his mouth suddenly and pressing up his lips. Why didn't he ask her if there was anyone outside ? Ossy had suggested that she had someone outside. And she had asked Mrs. Cooper to come along with her, pretending that

she felt ' all of a dither at going to see a minister,' but really
so that she could act shock and distress before her, when she
came out of the vestry. But the Inspector seemed to have no
idea of asking this, and she was obliged to proffer the information.

' There was a Mrs. Cooper outside, a friend of mine—I known
her for years—and I'd asked her to come along with me, as
you might ask someone to come with you to the doctor or the
dentist, like—if you see what I mean. I told *her* immediately
I come out. She said, "What's the matter, ducky?"—I
looked so flabbergasted—and I told her all about it.'

' Well, that may be some sort of corroboration. Would she
speak to this?'

' Pardon?'

' Would this Mrs. Cooper give evidence to that effect?'

' Oh, yes, I think so. She was one of the first to say I ought
to tell the police. She said so from the beginning. She's kep'
on saying it. Yes, Mrs. Cooper'd tell you anything you want to
know.'

' Do you know, have there been any other complaints against
this man?'

' Well . . . I've heard stories, you know . . . stories.'

' Why did you go to him, if you'd heard bad stories about
him?'

Her heart plumped down into a pit, even as her blood rushed
into her head. Had he trapped her? Oh, never again would
she start upon a game like this; not for a hundred, not for a
thousand pounds. ' Well, I didn't believe the stories, you see.
Not then. He looks—he doesn't look that sort at all. Do you
know Mr. Dawbeny?'

' I think so.'

' Well, you'll see what I mean. How could I believe anything like that about him? I just didn't. I thought, " People'll
say anything."'

' They will. You're right there, madam. That's why mere
stories are no good to us. Do you know anyone by name who
says she's been subjected to this sort of thing?'

' No, I'm afraid I don't. Not by name, no. But I could try
to find out, perhaps.'

' Well, if you can, do. And now, Mrs. Beron, if you don't
mind, we'll just take down in writing all you've told us.

Sergeant Powys, take down Mrs. Beron's statement, will you?'

'Yes, sir.' He sat down at the little table, accepted a few sheets which the Inspector drew from a drawer, and poised his pen to write. Connie's quick anxious eyes saw that the sheet was headed 'Metropolitan Police. Statement of Witness,' and didn't at all like seeing her story going down in ink under that head. It seemed a much worse crime, and much more permanent, written down than spoken. Could they ever find out that she'd—but no, it was always her word against his. Her word was as good as his. She could always swear black-and-blue that she said only what was true. There was nothing to be frightened about. And, anyhow, she couldn't withdraw now.

The Inspector had risen from his chair. Walking up and down behind her (which was disconcerting) he was guiding her along the lines of her previous story, as the Sergeant wrote, and reminding her of this thing and that which she had said. She didn't at all like being pushed and prodded like this.

§

When Connie with unsteady hand had signed her name on both sides of two sheets, and with unsteady heart had watched Sergeant Powys signing his name four times as a witness to her signature (which seemed to make her sin four times as bad), she was escorted to the front door by the Sergeant, and passed out into Lutine Street, quaking, confused, and apprehensive, but promising herself, 'They can do nothing to me. It's always my word against his.'

Meanwhile Inspector Glower was looking down upon the sheets of her statement. Presently he picked up one of his telephones and asked for his senior sergeant to be sent in to him.

Detective-Sergeant Shrewsbury entered, inquiring 'Yes, sir?' smartly. He was a much bigger and stouter man than his chief: a woman would have called him an enormous man. He must have weighed his sixteen stone, and this sixteen stone was always the 'anchor' in a tug-of-war team at the Police Sports. He was also a much noisier and more jocular man than the Inspector. Inspector Glower smiled often beneath his grave, dark eyes, Sergeant Shrewsbury never, because he always loosed a laugh like the bellow of a bull. The difference between that quiet smile and that loud laugh was the difference between the two men : the one humorous but cautious and thoughtful ; the other breezy and brisk, but unsubtle, and in judgment either shrewd or crude.

'Tom,' said the Inspector, 'sit down.' He fingered the statement. 'I've got a nasty one here.'

'Yes, sir,' acknowledged Sergeant Shrewsbury, unsurprised ; and he sat himself in the chair Connie had occupied, but much more comfortably, leaning back and crossing his stout thighs. And he waited to hear more.

'You know Father Dawbeny of St. John's ? '

'Do I not, sir ? He and I have been on many an incident together during the blitz. I never went along to a single incident but he was there. He was there when the V.2 rocket fell in Paisley Road and killed those women. Lor' bless you, he's just about the bravest bloke I ever saw.' The Sergeant was a man of easy enthusiasms and generous exaggerations. ' He never once took cover, even though the bombs and the shell splinters were dropping all around and poor old Detective-Sergeant Shrewsbury was safely down the nearest hole. But, of course, he was a big noise in the First War. A colonel or something.'

'Well, you saw that woman who went out just now with Stanley ? '

'Yes, sir. We all did. She was worth a glance, and I'm afraid we took our eyes off our sums for a sec. Just for a sec.'

'She's made an allegation against Father Dawbeny.'

'What sort of allegation ? '

'Oh, the usual thing about parsons.'

'*What ?* The "little trouble," eh ? '

'No, no ; not that. She alleges he assaulted her improperly —and oh hell, I can't believe it. I've known Father Dawbeny five or six years now and I should have said he was incapable of this.'

'But they nearly always seem incapable of it till they've done it, sir. That's my experience. As often as not they're absolutely devoted padres in every other respect, and then down they go, and no one can believe it at first. Everyone's struck all of a heap. You've seen it again and again.'

' Well. . . . I don't know. . . .' The Inspector handed over the statement. ' Here you are. Read it.'

The Sergeant read it, raised his eyebrows, grimaced, laid it down, said ' Well, well. . . .' and then added with an air of worldly wisdom, ' It may be true.'

The Inspector did not immediately deny this. ' It's difficult to believe she's deliberately lying,' he said. ' She looked respectable enough. They're mostly very respectable in Water Street.'

' She looked a bit overdressed to me, but perhaps that was only her compliment to the police. A few too many pearls about her for my liking, but there : I daresay she came by them honestly.'

' She's married to an old Jew who sells cheap jewellery, along with old shoes and hockey sticks and what-have-you.'

' Well, why can't the old Jew slosh the padre one, and settle the matter that way ? We're busy.'

' But do you believe the tale ? '

The Sergeant shrugged his shoulders, worldly-wise again. ' It may be true. Sex is sex.'

' And it may be completely imaginary. It's wonderful what some women will imagine about parsons and doctors and psychiatrists—anyone to whom they bare their souls——"

' Or their bodies,' submitted the Sergeant.

' Yes, well, you needn't be crude. Just lift your mind up from below your waist where it seems to dwell most of the day. I can never understand it myself, but they seem able to believe, and really to believe, that all sorts of things happened in the consulting room or the vestry or the dentist's surgery.'

' Yes, but it's generally the sex-starved old virgins who go dippy like that. This dame's a married lady, and I don't think there's much starved about her.'

' Yes, I was thinking that. But it's by no means only the unmarried who get these delusions. Remember that French-woman, Mrs. Prevost, who declared she was pregnant by old Dr. Robartes ? '

' Can't imagine a Frenchman's wife being unsatisfied.'

' Well, there was nothing to it. She wasn't pregnant at all.'

' Perhaps that wasn't the old doctor's fault.'

' Oh, come off it ! The whole thing was pure imagination. She'd probably got a pash on the doctor, even though he was rising seventy. And I'm not so sure that this isn't a similar case. I know the padre well, and I should say he's two parts of a saint.'

' Maybe, but it's the other part we got to worry about.'

Inspector Glower knocked a pencil on the desk, thoughtfully, first the point, then the top.

' It's often the saints of God who tumble worst,' suggested the Sergeant. ' They try themselves too hard.' And he quoted a limerick, apposite but lewd. ' What's his age ? '

' Sixty-five, perhaps.'

The Sergeant gave a wise, sidelong nod. ' A dangerous age. May be true.'

' There's never been a breath of scandal against him before.'

' Well, he's got to start some time.'

' Not Father Dawbeny. . . . No, I still suspect it's a delusion.'

' But why should this creature have such a delusion ? '

' Heaven knows. Sometimes their vanity becomes such an obsession that they have to rush into the limelight with stories that they're so attractive that within an hour of their visiting a man he's been after them. And they actually believe it. They believe it of chaps like us. Decent cops. Do you remember old Sergeant Cluff ? A woman charged him with coming to her house and taking advantage of her.'

' The devil she did ! We can't have that ! Poor old Cluff ! One of the best, he was.'

' Yes, and the whole thing was a fantasy from beginning to end. And yet the woman seemed sincere. Sometimes they just can't distinguish between dreams and reality.'

' They should be bloody well made to. But I don't suppose it was fantasy at all. It was probably an effort to frame him. Christ, I always say some of the women, if they're unscrupulous, are twice as unscrupulous as the men. They'll say anything. A man'll knock you down decently with his cosh, but a woman'll murder you with her tongue. Give me the man any day.'

' Well, why couldn't this be a frame-up ? '

' Because there don't seem to be any reason for it. He's got nothing against her, has he, so that she's got to hit him good and hard ? '

' I don't suppose so.'

' What's her corroboration worth ? '

'Not much as it stands. And it could be part of a frame-up too. Or she might have arranged for this other woman to be outside the church, and then acted it all before her. Women are wonderful actresses when they want to be, and their friends believe anything they want to believe. Look here, Tom. I suppose we can't just sit back and do nothing about this : an allegation is an allegation. You find out all you can about Mrs. Beron, and I'll go myself and see this Mrs. Cooper she speaks of. And if her corroboration turns out to be worth anything, I suppose I must go and see the padre. But in all my life I never liked a job less.'

§

'Inspector Glower to see you, Father.' It was not the first time Ernie had met the Inspector, and he saw nothing strange in this visit to the father.

'Come in, Inspector.' Father Dawbeny, in his long cassock, rose from the trestle table where he had been writing his Parish Paper, and welcomed his visitor cheerfully. 'Haven't seen you for a long time. Down, Squaller ! You remember the Inspector, surely ? Lie down and be a good dog, or he may run you in. How's trade with you, Inspector ? Not too brisk, I hope. Am I right in thinking the Dale is better behaved than it used to be ? '

Father Dawbeny was in a happier state than he'd been for days, and simply because yesterday he had received some praise. For several Sundays past he had observed a stranger in his congregation, a tall, dark, powerfully made, well-dressed young man ; but not till last Sunday had he managed to speak with him, because he was single-handed now and had to unrobe in the sacristy while the congregation dispersed. Last Sunday, however, he had found the young man waiting in the porch with his pretty young wife—much as Ernie and Sophie had waited for him eight years before. The girl's face seemed familiar, but he could not think where he had seen it before. The two of them, a young couple who charmed him, had declared, each taking the words out of the other's mouth, how much they had been impressed by his services and his sermons, and asked, 'Might they come and talk things over with him ? '

Together they had come yesterday evening, and the young man had identified himself as 'Maynard Hicks' and his wife as 'Alma Fry, the actress.' The name, Maynard Hicks, had astonished Father Dawbeny: he knew it well from many brilliant signed articles in the extremely left-wing review, *The Saturday Weekly*, which he used to read regularly till its almost communist angle began to bruise and sicken him. This splendid young figure was the same Maynard Hicks, and no other. And Alma—she was Alma Fry, the actress whom he'd often watched and admired from his cheap and lonely place in the Upper Circle. And here in his room Maynard Hicks was telling him that, having read attacks on him in the communist journals, he had come to St. John the Prior's, merely to study, and perhaps write satirically, about its vicar and its services, but that, as a result of the services and the sermons he had experienced 'something which he supposed you could only call conversion.' He had come to blame and stayed to bless. He now wanted to change much of his life and learn how he could best help the Church in Bexley where he and Alma lived, or in the columns of the paper for which he wrote. And Alma agreed with him in everything and wanted to learn what part she could play in the world of the theatre, or elsewhere. And Father Dawbeny, much touched by this confession, had said to them both, ' It's people like you, and moments like this, that keep us going, and our heads above water, so that we struggle on.' And all his depression of the last few days had been healed.

It was the second of such happy experiences, for only a week or two ago that woman from Water Street had come to him with a similar tale—what was her name ?—the wife of a Jew.

Perhaps, because he had struggled on with breaking tools in the stony ground, God was letting him see a little fruit from his labours.

So he was happy, and this visit of Inspector Glower was a pleasure, for the Inspector was such a likeable fellow and they'd been friends now for seven or eight years.

' Do sit down, Inspector, and have a cigarette.' He indicated one of the chairs by the fireplace, and himself took the other. ' You look as though you don't agree with me that we are almost a model community now.'

' I most certainly do not, sir. We were all pretty good during the war but are beginning to give plenty of trouble again. It's the young ones who are the worst, those who grew up in war conditions, and those who've come back from the war where we've trained them in every sort of violence and murder. We've taught them to knife and to throttle and to be smart with the gun, and now—— ! I don't altogether blame them, but few of them seem to have any scruples left, or any beliefs or hopes of any kind, so they just make a god of their own pleasure and resort to violence wherever necessary. In this last year we've had more sexual offences and crimes of violence than at any time I remember.'

'But they're not all like this, Inspector. What we're apt to forget is that the great bulk of the people, even in our Dale, are hard-working, respectable, and tolerably law-abiding citizens. Don't you agree? There's nothing so very wrong with most of them except that they *won't* come to church.' And he added banteringly, 'I don't see *you* there very often, Inspector.'

'I don't live in the Dale, sir.'

'No, but I have Evensong every day, and Litany on Wednesdays. What an opportunity for you to come and pray for all these sinners.'

The Inspector smiled at the sally, but it was a courtesy smile, and no more. He obviously hadn't thought the joke very funny, so Father Dawbeny, not lightly abashed by his failure, hastily deserted levity for seriousness. 'Did you want me to help you in something, Inspector?'

'Well, yes, sir. It's an unpleasant business.'

'I'm used to that,' Father Dawbeny encouraged him. 'Possibly almost as used to it as you are.'

'Yes, but . . . this concerns you, sir. I'm sorry to have to come with such a story, but someone has made an allegation against you.'

'I can quite believe it. What do they say I'm up to now? Some underground activity on behalf of the defeated Nazis? They call me a Fascist because I suggested we might share our food with the undernourished Germans.'

'No, sir. Do you know a Mrs. Beron?'

'Beron? Beron?' One of Father Dawbeny's secret fears— a completely self-regarding fear and therefore, he doubted not, an ignoble one—was that his mental powers were abating and senility setting in, because, as surely as he wanted to speak of someone, he forgot his name, or if someone else mentioned a name, he could not for some time associate a figure with it. Beron? Ah, yes, at last he had it! Mrs. Beron was the woman from Water Street. 'Yes, I know her. She's just joined our congregation. Her husband's a street trader. A Jew.'

'She's made an allegation against you; a very serious allegation.'

'Against *me*?' His first thought, as he frowned over this bewildering announcement, was that she must be going to promote a prosecution against him for using incense at Solemn Mass or for genuflecting before the Sacrament. 'But what's she saying?' (Could she be a spy for the Protestant Church Association?) 'I thought she and I were the best of friends.'

The Inspector told him what she had said.

'She said *that*?' Father Dawbeny's body had suddenly hunched forward in his chair. He sat staring at his informant, his brain defeated. His eyebrows met and parted, met and parted, before this defeated brain. It was as if this sudden and inexplicable blow had deranged the brain and he could not drag it into order again. He tried to remember what had happened that evening in the vestry. He had loved her because she had come to him, and pitied her, and tried to be kind to her. He had longed to touch her gently as a gesture of love and encouragement, *but his shyness had forbidden this*. But surely his words and his eyes and his smile had shown her his affection and his longing to be of help to her. And now she had done this to him. Why? Why this gratuitous lie? Why had this trial been sent to him? What was God doing to him, who had tried only to serve? 'She said *that*?' he could only repeat. 'It is, of course, an abominable lie.'

The Inspector said nothing. And Father Dawbeny rose and walked to the bright window, as he always did when perplexed—towards the light and the open streets and the sky. Why had the Inspector come? Why had he not tossed this wicked accusation into the refuse bin as a ludicrous slander or the nonsense of a madwoman? For a second he turned from the window. 'Inspector, you don't believe this, do you?'

'No, sir.' But had he spoken with conviction, or merely politely, trapped by the abrupt question? 'I just felt that it was my duty to tell you that she'd laid this information. No, sir, I don't believe it.'

'Thank you.' He turned back to the window.

The Inspector from his chair tried to comfort him. 'It may not be a deliberate lie. It may be a delusion.'

'That was not a woman easily deluded,' said Father Dawbeny to the streets of the Dale.

He did not believe it was a delusion, he believed it was a cold attempt, by some unseen forces, to murder his reputation. And this woman was their willing instrument. And wrath, a frenzy of wrath, erupted within him like the volcanic magma within the earth's crust. It flung his priestly character from him. He forgot the black cassock in which he stood. It was such a wrath as his men had sometimes seen in trench or rest-billet. The old tongue spoke within him : 'This foul and evil *bitch*. Hanging's too good for her. I hope she simmers in hell.' And aloud he said :

'This woman, if she's not mad—and she isn't—ought to be——'

Whipped at a cart-tail, he was about to say. And then he remembered. He became conscious of the cassock in which he stood ; he even looked down at it, as if to recover its memory. And there by the window, his back to the policeman, his mind became a battleground. If this woman was his enemy and trying to ruin him, then, ideally—and he felt like laughing at the ideal—he must love her, forgive her, do good to her because she hated him, pray for her because she despitefully used him, and see her all the time as a creature made in the image of God. He remembered Oliver Custance coming to this very room, and telling him to cast out young Denys Flackman because he was 'a peculiarly revolting type,' and how he had answered, 'And to me there's a glory round about him.' 'A *glory*?' said the astonished Oliver Custance. 'Yes, a glory, because the God of all the universe invests him with his love.' How much easier to say that when it was only someone else against whom Denys had sinned. He remembered preaching, there in that church yonder, that they must learn to forgive and treat again as brothers even the most corrupted Germans who had devastated their cities and mangled their children. How much easier when the sin was only that of a nation against a nation. How difficult when the ruin was

217

attempted against oneself, when a single individual was trying to lay waste one's good name.

He must feel neither malice nor hate, but pity only ; no anger with the woman herself, but only with her sin. For her only love. It was very, very difficult. It was to mortify every natural response to the grossest of injuries.

And his mind at the moment was too poisoned and sour for these high thoughts to live in it. Its soil had been stamped so hard that these seeds could only lie on its surface and take no root. He tried to break up the soil by thinking of Maynard Hicks and Alma, his beautiful wife, whose bright young souls he had touched, and who had said words of praise to him, but it was useless : their memory was a blunted tool. He began a prayer, but his anger against God dammed back all prayers. There remained only the dull, cold will. ' If it be Thy will, O God, I will take it.' ' Take it '—the words stirred an old memory, and he felt a little stronger. But it was to crucify himself ; to crucify the old and natural man. ' Crucify ! ' The word, like a distant bell, called to his loyalty.

To crucify the old, vindictive man, these were his Master's orders. He felt blinded and stunned and stupefied, but even the blinded could go on fighting. In the old war, if he'd been blinded, he'd have gone on fighting till the unseen bayonet finished him. And if he'd been struck down by a mortal wound, he'd have risen to strike one more blow. *Debout, les morts !*

He felt wounded to death now, but never mind ; he'd hold his ground . . . somehow . . . blindly. He'd obey his difficult orders, since there was no doubt about them. Even if no one else had ever obeyed them, or believed in them, he'd try to obey them. He turned to the Inspector ; and his tall body was upright again, his hands in the cincture of the cassock. ' I did not do this thing, Inspector, and I don't know why she should say I did. I did not even put an arm on her shoulder because that is something which, though often my heart longs to do it, I never seem able to do. I never seem able to show by any outward action how much I love—how great is my affection for these people when they come with their troubles to me. Often I feel I would like to put an arm along a weeping woman's shoulder, but nearly always something inhibits me. I shall, of course, fight this accusation in any court that it may come to, but I must try to forgive the wretched woman. Will it come to court?'

'That I cannot say, sir. I shall try to persuade the woman that she can hardly hope for a conviction——'

'My God, I should hope not!' interrupted the father. 'A conviction, indeed!'

'No, her corroboration, in my view, is altogether too thin. But if she insists in applying for a warrant, I shall have to go with her to the magistrate——'

'Yes. And then?'

'And then I imagine he'll say to her that, unless she can get further evidence, she'd much better withdraw the case.'

'I see,' said Father Dawbeny; and added suddenly, 'Or perhaps I might go and see her.'

CHAPTER NINE

ALL that day he was considering, almost as an intellectual exercise (for his heart would not follow his head, but lay like a dead thing behind it) the question, If he was to obey his Commander's orders exactly as they were given him, what must he do?

Presumably he must find the woman and say without hate, ' Why have you done this to me?' He might rebuke her sternly and tell her of his firm intention to defend and clear himself, but he must not threaten her with reprisals. Unless there were no other way to rebut the lie, he should not threaten her with actions for slander, libel, or public mischief. He must try to overthrow her malice by showing her only patience and forgiveness—and, yes, love. Ha! *Love!*

Of course, as the hours passed, and the shock lessened, and the wound healed a little, he did this—or tried to do it. He set out for Water Street and Mrs. Beron's door. There was no knocker on her door, and he tapped on it with a knuckle. It was she who opened to him. But no sooner had she seen who stood on her threshold, and heard him saying gently, 'Mrs. Beron, could I speak to——' than she cried, 'No, No!' in a kind of vertigo, as if he were fire on her doorstep, 'I don't want to see you,' and slammed the door in his face.

For a second his anger sprang up fully armed to overthrow all the good resolutions with which he had come. 'Intolerable woman! Am I to take this? I won't. I can't. God asks too much.' But he recollected himself, and the purpose which had been good, and walked slowly away. Once he turned and looked back at her house, and he saw that she was watching his retreat from behind the curtains of an upper window.

Useless to attempt another visit. What other way could he see her and achieve his double purpose, to save himself from her, and to save herself from herself? He would try to meet her in the street. Most of the wives went out early to the shops; and soon Father Dawbeny found himself leaving his daily Mass, where he took in strength for his purpose, and loitering near the approaches to Water Street. Once, crossing the mouth of the street, he saw her on its pavement and turned at once and walked towards her. She saw him, and he tried to suggest with a faint smile that he was not come to revile her. But she turned about and fled into her burrow like a shivering rabbit which had glimpsed the eyes and the long slim body of a ferret.

And he knew that she was in terror, and that her terror was not of his wrath but of his forgiveness. Let not his forgiveness come close and reduce her to repentance and reparation. Keep away! Get thee behind me, Charity, for thou savourest the things that be of God. He must not make her repent and declare her crime to the police and suffer the consequences.

Yet another time he met her, and this time he was in front of her before she could turn and escape. Her eyes were now the rabbit's before the snake's, fascinated, terrified, her body unable to move; and he had time to say, ' Mrs. Beron, why have you done this to me? Are you going to withdraw this wicked charge? ' but she pulled herself together, and cried, ' No, no! ' just as she had done at her door, ' I don't want to speak to you,' which was the sincere truth; and she swung about and hurried away.

§

The charge did not come to court. All fell out exactly as the Inspector had foretold. She had insisted on going to the magistrate to institute proceedings, not that she wanted to do so, but that she must save her face. The magistrate, having read the application in his private room, summoned Inspector Glower and asked him, ' Does this woman really insist on going on with this very skimpy case? It looks pretty cock-and-bull to me. She does? All right then. Let me see her. I will see what I can do to soothe the lady down.' And when she came in, he said to her, ' I will grant process if you insist, but, without prejudging the case, I must say that unless you can get further evidence, your hope of a conviction is small. Why not leave the matter with the Inspector, who'll keep observation on this man, and if there are other complaints, we may call upon you to support a much stronger case.'

Connie pretended some disappointment, but accepted this advice with relief, only too glad to be rid of the business at last. Now let her forget it for ever, for ever. If only she could leave the Dale and lose sight of the Reverend Dawbeny for ever.

So far had his forgiveness undone her.

But in the meantime rumours and reports of the story, like the winged seeds of sycamore or pine, had dropped everywhere in the Dale. They had drifted on excited winds and fallen beyond the Dale in all the regions round about. Connie had talked of her case, at least till she came to be afraid of it and hate all mention of it. Mrs. Cooper whose conscience was clear, had spoken of it ceaselessly and fluently. People had told how they'd seen the police going to Mrs. Beron's house, to Mrs. Cooper's house, to the Church Hall. The first impact of the story was so stirring and stimulating that everyone stopped everyone else in the street to speak of it; street-sweepers left their trucks to give it to the uninformed; shopkeepers discussed it with their customers, and the waiting queue of shoppers did not protest because they were listening avidly. It was discussed in every public house, and discussed precisely as it had been by Inspector Glower and Sergeant Shrewsbury, a few refusing to believe it, but most following the Sergeant and remarking that it wouldn't be the first time a celibate clergyman had fallen like this. Some declared over their pots, ' He was properly frightened after the police come to question him. He went and begged her to withdraw the case, and when she banged the door in his face, he tried to waylay her in the streets.' Others, with even thicker heads, answered knowingly, ' Yah, if he'd been a poor working man, it'd have come to court all right, but he's got money and probably squared 'em. Don't forget his brother's a duke or something big. They know how to pull the strings, these dukes.' Mr. Howden, visiting his old haunts one day, said exactly this. He simulated a great surprise when he was given the story that was all over the Dale. ' What's this I hear? Well, who'd have thought it? Mr. Dawbeny! Well, well, well. But doesn't it go to show: isn't it exactly what you'd expect? He was able to get up a lying case against me, because I was a poor working man, but do they proceed against him? Not on your life! He's a rich man, with friends in the House of Lords. But even if the police won't act, let's hope his old Bishop will. I hope the Bishop unfrocks him: that's what I say.'

The tale fell like a very acceptable gift into the lap of the Rev. Oliver Custance on Ledbitter Hill. The young man had conscience enough not to mention it first to any of the laity, but he longed for them to mention it to him. And when they did allude to it, he thought it becoming in a minister to say, ' We can only hope it is not true. After all, it hasn't been proved, and don't you think we ought to give him the benefit of the doubt ? ' But when, as nearly always happened, they offered the thread-bare comment, ' Well, you know the saying : there's no smoke without fire,' he merely spread his hands helplessly and forbore to submit that while this was certainly true about smoke, it had never been true about slander. With his brethren, the clergy, he felt no such hesitation about introducing the story ; on the contrary he made a point of introducing it sooner or later to every brother he met. ' Have you heard,' he would ask, ' this unhappy story about our brother of St. John's ? '

He played his part in sowing the tares.

But if it was a pleasing gift to Mr. Custance, what was it to Comrade Anton and his cell in Tyre Street ? They seized upon it as a fine, effective weapon in the class war. Comrade Anton, and one or two of his lieutenants, were not among those who were sure they believed the story, but what did that matter ? The recoil from giving false witness was an out-dated bourgeois weakness to which the brighter boys and girls, those who had grasped the principles of Historical Materialism and were on the side of History, had long risen superior. It was their piety to publish lies about the enemies of the Revolution, and the greater the slander, the higher, perhaps, the sanctity. Go to it, comrades. Lose no opportunity of spreading this splendid tale. Bring it into prominence wherever you can. Don't wait for people to mention it ; mention it first. The Line is simple : he did this thing ; he begged her to drop the charge ; and when she refused he got his rich and powerful relatives to pull the necessary strings. Justice ? There is no such thing ; there is only the defence of Capitalist interests. The Capitalist class is completely unscru-pulous in defending its own. A poor man assaults a woman. Prison, and scathing words from the judge. The hired servant of the capitalists, an aristocratic parson, does the same. Hush it up. This sort of scandal is a danger to religion, the dope of the people. That's the Line. Say it everywhere.

They said it everywhere ; and the damage to the name of the Vicar of St. John's was quite as complete as if the charge had been heard in the magistrate's court and reported at length in the local press. At first. Till Ernie heard of it.

CHAPTER TEN

THE story first came to the ears of Ernie in the public bar of the Brickmakers' Arms, into which he would sometimes wander on a Saturday evening, having long ago ascertained from the father that he had no objection to his verger being seen in a pub. When he entered on this Saturday night, there' were three or four men by the counter and three or four round the dart-board. One of those at the counter was Bernie Streeter, the young vanman from the Swandown Steam Laundry, a dark, good-looking, good-hearted, conceited young man; and Bernie promptly greeted him, 'Hallo, Ernie boy. Nice vicar you've got.' His cigarette drooped and wagged at his lips, as he said this. 'I hope you're proud of him now.'

'Wha'd'you-mean?' snapped Ernie, and his face turned very white. It flew a white flag, not of peace, but of war. 'Mild, please, miss. What the hell are you getting at?'

Bernie explained what he was getting at, while the other men, to whom the story was of high interest, stood around listening.

Ernie, after listening, stared for a few seconds in a white-faced silence, and then said, 'It's a *lie*.' His mouth was square and ugly as he breathed this at them. 'It's a wicked lie. Who ever dared say such a thing?'

'On no, it isn't,' Bernie maintained, shaking his head over his glass. 'It's no lie. It's the truth.'

'It's *not*—it's—what right have you to say it's true? How can you know it's true?'

'Everybody knows it's the truth. The police were going to act on it, but he got round 'em not to. Ask anybody.'

'Look.' Ernie put down his glass on the counter and faced Bernie. His head was trembling, his lips were trembling, and his hands, hanging straight at his sides but not yet closed into fists, were trembling. The men watching were amazed to see that tears—'tears like those of an angry kid'—had made his eyes moist and brilliant. He was squaring his mouth and turning his lower lip into his teeth, to control those tears. 'Just you stop. You don't know what you're talking about. And, come to that, you don't know who you're talking to. I've known him a sight longer than any of you. I've known him thirty years, ever since we were on the Somme together. And you can take it from me that this is a dirty lie. The dirtiest lie ever. And you'd *better* take it from me ! Say it again, any one of you, and I'll shove it down your throat.'

'There's no smoke without fire, Ernie,' one of the bystanders reminded him.

'And of all the bloody silly remarks that's the silliest,' declared Ernie, swinging round on the commentator. 'Have *you* never been accused of anything you never done ? Why, gawd-a-mercy, I was up before my O.C. once for pinching a blanket from the Quartermaster's dump, and I hadn't touched the thing—not on that occasion I hadn't. Another bloke confessed. "No smoke without——".' He substituted a word for 'fire' that was unbecoming in a verger ; but he was not a verger as he spoke ; he was back in the Army.

'Didn't the cops come to his house ?' demanded Bernie. 'Didn't old Glower himself go there ?'

Ernie remembered the Inspector's call and for a second was at a loss : not shaken in his faith, but in his line of defence. 'Of course he did. And not for the first time by a long chalk.' Here in his heat he lied rather freely, for just as the Communists believed that their great end, the triumph of the Proletariat and the classless society, justified all lies, so did Ernie feel (in so far as he was thinking at all) that his great end, the defence of his master from a dirty lie, justified anything and everything that leapt to his lips. 'The cops are always coming to us. Maybe three times a week, you bloody fool. Sometimes it's to get some help for some poor cove on two years probation—like it might be you, one day—and probably will be—or some poor girl in trouble— yes, after you've been up the lane with her. What's more, the Inspector's a personal friend of the father. Comes often to see him. Why don't you talk about things you know something about ?'

'I do,' Bernie affirmed with some dignity. He did not like being regarded as ignorant of anything. 'I do,' he repeated, relying on the dignity rather than on any substantiation of his statement.

'Well, you're talking a damned lot of hooey now.'

' *Is* that so ? ' sneered Bernie.

' Yes, it is,' Ernie announced, and after taking a drink from his beer, added, ' Get your facts right before you start throwing your silly mouth about.'

Then he went into a sullen silence and sipped his beer. But further thoughts came to him in the silence and he had to give them voice. ' I wonder you dare talk like that. A man who's given up everything he's got for all of you in the Dale. He was a rich man once, and I happen to know he's barely enough to live on now. I wish I could tell you what he done for me at one time.' The passionate, infantile tears were almost in his eyes again.

Another of the bystanders sought to comfort him. ' We ain't saying he hasn't been a good boy in the past, Ernie.'

' No ; and you'd better not. Nor say anything else against him either. Not to me, at any rate.'

' For my part,' proclaimed Bernard, still sore at having been called ignorant of something, though he could no longer remember what that something was, ' I'll say what I like.'

But when he said this, Ernie had plunged back into his silence and it was a little while before the defiant remark sank down to him. When it did, he saw it and pounced upon it. ' If anyone comes with that story to me,' he announced to the shelves and the bottles and the mirror beyond the counter, ' he'll get my fist in his jaw. I'll knock it down his gullet and three of his teeth with it. Yes.'

' Oh, you would, would you ? ' demanded Bernie, who was feeling combative too.

' Yes, mate.'

' You'd bash his face in if he so much as whispered that this tale was true ? '

' Absolutely, chum. Got it right first time.'

' I see.'

' Nobody's saying it's true in my presence.'

' Aren't they ? Well, that's where you're wrong. I say the story's true. I say it's absolutely—'

But he never finished that sentence. Straight as a piston-rod from its cylinder, Ernie's right arm and fist shot into the midst of Bernie's face. It crushed his lipped cigarette on to his cheek, driving sparks from it. The cigarette fell to the floor and back came Bernie's furious fist into his assailant's face with all the vigour of a powerful young man behind it. It caught Ernie on

226

the chin and sent him reeling backwards on to a high stool ; he snatched at the stool to save his balance, but it only went down with him as his hindquarters and one elbow hit the floor. In a second he was up on his feet, and his head was down towards his waist, and he was coming like a he-goat at his young opponent : he was back in the Montebello Road.

'What's this ? What's going on ? ' The landlord's son, a burly ex-marine, had heard the crash of stool and customer and hurried across the brief segment between saloon and public bars. The bars of the Brickmakers' Arms were organized on interior lines of defence so that the garrison could speed from one threatened breastwork to another, ' Now then, stop that, you lads ! Stop 'em, boys.'

' It's Ernie and Bernie,' explained one of the ringside spectators who'd been watching happily with his hands in his pockets and his overcoat thrust back. ' They're having a little hernie-bernie together.'

' Yes.' Another watcher offered a ringside report in greater detail. ' Ernie gave him a fourpenny one right in the middle of his target, and Bernie replied on his chin with sixpennorth of the best. At that point Ernie went down on his arse, dragging half the furniture with him.' He drank from his beer to sustain himself in this business of reporting, and wiped his mouth with his knuckles so as to be ready for further speech. ' It's all about Mr. Dawbeny. You mustn't say anything against Mr. Dawbeny to Ernie Matters if you want to keep your nose in front of your face instead of behind. I, personally, am not saying anything. Don't want to get hurt.'

' Well, stop 'em now, for the Lord's sake,' begged the landlord's son.

Two men held Ernie, panting, by the arms, but spoke to him kindly. ' Now then, Ernie lad, that'll do. Spare him. Why, good lord, he's old enough to be your son.'

' Let him say it's a lie then,' panted Ernie.

' Say it's a lie, Bernie, for Jesus's sake. Anything for peace and a quiet life.'

' All right, all right, all right,' soothed Bernie. Having seen his man on the floor, with a stool beside him, he felt satisfied ; indeed proud. ' It's a lie.'

' And don't forget, Bern,' added the peacemaker in a whisper, ' the guy's a bit lame.'

Bernie *had* forgotten this and was shamed. He made instant amends. 'All right. Ernie wins. It's a lie.'

Ernie relaxed ; and his two moderators loosed their hold. He was glad not to have to defend his honour, and Father Dawbeny's, any further against that terrible young fist. He contented himself with reaffirming, 'It's the wickedest lie ever. Anybody who knows Father Dawbeny'd know that.'

'That's right, Ernie,' said one of the two moderators, appeasingly, not to say affectionately. 'And now have a drink to cool yourself. Have it on me. Give 'em both a drink, miss. A half o' mild to damp down the fires a bit.'

'Ta,' acknowledged Ernie ; announcing to the company, however, that he was only accepting appeasement on conditions. 'But I'm not listening to that from anyone.' He turned to Bernie and asked gruffly, 'Where did you get that daft tale from ? '

'Charlie Partridge.'

'Well, he's a bloody red. Or if he isn't, he's next door to one. He's one of their mutton-headed fellow-travellers.'

'I know he is,' agreed Bernie.

'And I heard it from another red,' a man who hadn't yet spoken suddenly informed the general assembly.

'Who was that ? ' asked Bernie.

'Steve Knox.'

'Crimes ! ' said Bernard, as if Steve's credit was not good. 'We'll he's a hundred-per-cent red. He's quite a big noise in the party, I believe.'

'Yes, it suits the reds all right,' continued the man, pleased to have provided a new piece of evidence. 'They're just feasting on it like flies on jam. They hate him ever since he said their Party Line was all ——' he used the brief syllable which Ernie had used in place of ' fire.'

'Well, there you are ! ' Ernie had suddenly seen a great light, and in that light he was ready to love them all again. 'It's a lie of the reds. You know they'll say anything, true or not, to down anyone who dares disagree with whatever their Party Line is at the moment—though Lord knows it's seldom the same two minutes together. They'll tell you they glory in a lie if it'll help their rotten Cause. Now we know where we are. They've always been out to down him. Remember their " Down all Fascist priests." They're at their dirty games again.'

228

'Well, there's something in that,' assented one of the listeners. 'Maybe the reds are making the most of it, even though it's never been proved. Maybe the cops wouldn't act because they're pretty sure this woman imagined it all. Christ, *women*! I once knew a woman who——'

'There's no "maybe" about it,' asserted Ernie—and that tale of a woman was never told. 'That's what happened. It's a dead cert. Unless, perhaps, she was a communist stooge, put up to frame him. Might be that, come to think of it.'

'Yes, I wouldn't put that past the reds,' said another. 'Reds'll do any damned thing. They stop at bloody nothing.'

'You're right there,' came from more than one voice. 'And they've never loved Mr. Dawbeny.'

Thus once again did the hot participation of the communists in the attack on Father Dawbeny, and their blind, bull-headed, methods of propaganda, bring him less harm than help.

§

Ernie took the story home to Sophie, and she was as shocked as he, and as furious. 'What people will *say*!' she breathed in a low voice, as if it were not a matter that could be spoken of in ordinary tones.

'It's the reds,' Ernie explained.

But Sophie, having a greater understanding of women than of politics, and a far greater interest in them, held another view. She said, 'I know what happened. I bet your life I know. The creature fell in love with him, like so many of them do, and when she did her come-take-me stuff, and he showed her that he wasn't that sort, and never had been, she turned nasty and invented this about him. It often happens like that. It happens again and again. The hateful creature!'

'That may be how it began,' Ernie allowed, 'but a lot of the boys and I suspect that it was all a put-up job of the reds, and she was just their stooge. Yes, that's what I'm inclined to believe. But, anyhow, it's the reds that are putting it about now. Doing their best to publish it everywhere. It's wicked. It's evil.'

And during the next few days Ernie and Sophie, in their back room a few feet from where the father sat, discussed often the extreme whiteness and sadness of his face, and his unbroken silences, and his restlessness in bed at night ; and how Ernie, going into him with his meals, would see him either standing by the window and staring out miserably, or sitting in his deep chair with his book fallen to his lap, as if his mind could deal with one thing only, and he found it impossible to read or work.

' I just can't bear to see the awful whiteness of his face,' Sophie said one evening. ' It's like the whiteness of a hunted man.'

' Yeah, it's hit him.' Ernie nodded profoundly. ' It's hit him harder than he'll ever tell anyone. I know him, you see. It isn't as if I hadn't known him for thirty years. He's scorning to say a word in his own defence. He's going to treat it with a proud disdain, like. He's as proud as a king, really, is Father Dawbeny. But he can't get it out of his mind. Not for five little minutes.'

' No, and the trouble is, Ernie, as long as he's like that, one can't offer him a word of comfort. Sometimes I feel I'd like to rush in to him and say, "Look, Father : there's nobody that knows you as believes it." I'd like to say, "Nothing on God's earth'd ever make Ernie and me believe it ; you can be sure of that. And that goes for everyone else that knows you ; " but, you see, I wouldn't dare.'

'No ; but it's what we all ought to say. And I've talked to plenty of chaps who'd like to say exactly that. If only there was a way of saying it without saying it—if you see what I mean. Some way of showing what we wouldn't say. See what I mean ? '

' I wish there was,' said Sophie.

How to show their faith in him without saying any words he wouldn't wish to hear—this question recurred to Ernie next morning when he carried in the father's breakfast of coffee and toast and saw him standing and staring at the map over his table, but assuredly not seeing it. Ernie glanced up sideways at his face, so white, so deathly white. ' Oh, if only there was some means of showing him—' he thought, as he arranged the coffee pot, cup, and plate, and a few seconds later, in that six-foot of dark passage between the Vicar's room and Sophie's kitchen, Ernie's idea was born. He entered the kitchen and said, ' Christ ! ' and the word was perhaps not altogether a blasphemy, since his idea, at bottom, was to bring to the afflicted a cup of consolation in that Name. ' Sophie, I got an idea ! It's just twenty years since he come to St. John's. He come in December, '27. Couldn't we get up a testimonial for him, pretending it was to celebrate his twenty years, but seeing as how it wants about six months till he's done his twenty years, he'll see at once what we're up to. Christ, it's an idea. Here, where's a sheet of paper? Or better, a notebook. Where's that old laundry book of which we only used the first two pages? Where the hell is it? I sor' it the other day.'

Out of the dresser drawer he dug a sixpenny notebook with a glossy black cover. He tore from it the pages that had been used, removing them tidily, and here before him was an apparently new and empty cash-ruled book.

He rushed to the table, dragged a pencil from his pocket, sucked its point, scratched his head with its point, poised the point over the book and said at last, ' Look, Sophie. Come here. God knows where it's coming from, but Mr. and Mrs. Ernie Matters are going to head the list.' And somewhat laboriously, for he was never an easy writer, he wrote,

' Testimonial to the Revd. P. L. Dawbeny after twenty
years' service :

| Ernest Matters | - | - | - | £1 | 0 | 0 |
| Mrs. Matters | - | - | - | £1 | 0 | 0 |

' But, Ernie ! ' exclaimed Sophie, a little pale. ' We haven't got two pounds to spare.'

' Then we'll sell something. Things are fetching big money now. We'll sell a bit of furniture or some china.' And because he was in a lively mood, and because his liveliness all too often blossomed into the ribaldry of the Montebello Road, he suggested that they might sell a china vessel from their bedroom . . . ' It's a thing we could do without at a stretch,' he said. Then he jumped up. ' I'm busy for the rest of the day, lady. The church'll have to clean itself. Or stay dirty for a bit.'

He went out with the intention of visiting every member of the Parochial Church Council. But, knowing the ecclesiastical ropes, for he had now been a verger for nearly ten years, he went first to the Vicar's warden, Mr. Sandeman, the greengrocer, in his shop. Mr. Sandeman was delighted with the scheme, for he was as loyal to his vicar as Ernie himself, but he pointed out that, if it was to be in good legal order, a committee would surely have to be formed to promote it. And he sent Ernie to collect men and women, instead of money, that day. The men and women, mostly members of the P.C.C. met two evenings later in Mr.

Sandeman's parlour, over the shop ; and from that parlour the scheme was launched into the Dale. All added their names to Ernie's and Sophie's in the subscription book, though some ' couldn't run to a quid,' and Ernie was allowed to go forth and canvass the parish. Ernie went. He limped to the door of every member on the Electoral Roll, and there was not one who said ' No ' to him, though the subscriptions of some were small. He approached every member of the Costers' Club, and here he gleaned a very fine sheaf of full-eared corn. The street traders of the Dale were in the big money just now, when there was a post-war shortage of most things, from ladies' suits to saucepans and tea cups and hairpins. They were reaping a plentiful harvest and could afford to scatter a little by the way. Many gave him a dollar, and some, not to be outdone by Ernie's own subscription, said ' O.K., mate, I'm good for a quid.' It was not that they, one and all, believed the minister innocent of the charge whispered against him, but that those who didn't were tolerant men and didn't take it as seriously as perhaps they should have done. Also the communists had put a powerful trump card into the collector's hands. Ernie had only to expose his suggestion that the whole thing was a communist trick, for these trading gentlemen, who believed with an incandescent fervour in private enterprise and the profit motive, and were in the way of becoming capitalists themselves, to demand his sub-scription book and sign on the next vacant line, all hesitation shed away.

On the very first day of this ingathering Ernie acquired a helper and field-worker no less enthusiastic than himself. This was Denys Flackman. Denys was still the young intellectual whose religion had fallen from him ; no church saw him now except his little group who called themselves the Liberal Ration-alist League ; he was still reluctant to meet Father Dawbeny in the street, but he was as indignant as Ernie at the whispered slander and, like Ernie, his thoughts ran back to an hour when Father Dawbeny, hearing of his sins, uttered no word of condem-nation but was instant with help and affection and faith in him. He leapt with a young man's abandon at Ernie's scheme ; he almost snatched the standard from Ernie's hand ; instead he made himself a standard of his own—that is to say he made him-self a subscription book like Ernie's ; and he set off with it in his duffle coat and beret in one direction, while Ernie went in another.

Ernie, collecting in the street, stopped dead one afternoon, halted by a new inspiration. He remembered Lady Guttree. Straightway he hurried home, sought out her address from an old electoral roll, and set off for Upper Hyde Street. He was not a little disconcerted by the mansion in which Lady Guttree lived, and by the butler or footman, or ' whatever the guy was,' who opened the door to him. Lady Guttree, wondering what on earth could have brought that little verger limping to her door, consented to see him, and in her alarming white-and-gold drawing room he told her what business he was about, but did not speak of the scandal. But Lady Guttree had already heard of it, and, however disgusted she might be with the father's gross sentimentality about her late enemies, she was quite as disgusted, and even more so, at this calumny upon his name, for she was sure he was a good man, if a fool. So she perceived at once what was behind the little verger's game. And when she opened his glossy black notebook, much thumbed now, and saw the first entries, ' Ernest Matters, £1.0.0., Sophie Matters, £1.0.0.,' her heart, parts of which were of the best, swelled within her, and she said as coolly as you could imagine, ' Well, yes, Mr. Matters, I'll do what I can. You can put me down for fifty.'

' *Fifty* ? '

' Yes. Fifty pounds—'

' Chri—'

' I'm afraid that's all I can manage. But that'll help a little, won't it ? '

' Will it ? I'll say it will ! I—well—well, thank you, Madam —thank you like—thanks a lot.'

And Ernie came out into Upper Hyde Street, staggering beneath the weight of this excitement. He could collect no more that day but must hasten home to share the lovely burden with Sophie.

Thoughts of Lady Guttree reminded him of that dinner which had so ' put Sophie about ', and he saw at once the portly, genial, but withal overpowering figure of Mr. Ostrion. His success with the lady encouraged him to attempt a like success with the gentleman ; and next morning he limped very rapidly to Amen Street, and stood looking up at the fine façade of Testament House, the offices of Messrs. Ostrion, Hart and Company. Soon he was in the large and splendid room of the managing director, and when Mr. Ben Ostrion was ready to look up from his great desk, Ernie told him the whole story, scandal and all, since he was a man and needed not, like a lady, to be protected from the filth of the world. Nor did he omit to mention the wickedness of the reds, and this proved as good a card in the offices of Ostrion, Hart and Company as in the street markets of the Dale, for Mr. Ostrion did not like the red philosophy and ways.

' " If the red slayer think he slays," ' he began to quote, ' " or if the slain think he is slain . . ." ' but he perceived that his visitor was a vessel ill-adapted to Emerson's verse ; so without further comment he took Ernie's glossy black notebook on to his desk and studied the entries, beginning with the subscriptions of Mr. and Mrs. Matters. Then he asked, ' How much have you got so far ? '

' Over eighty—' Ernie was going to say ' quid ', but in this room, and on this carpet, he translated it to ' Over eighty pounds, sir.'

' I congratulate you. Why, that's fine ! Was it your idea ? Wonderful ! It appeals to me, Ernie. That's your name, isn't it ? Yes, this is very fine. He has cast his bread upon the waters and now he's going to find it, after many days.'

Ernie didn't know what in the name of sense the gentleman was talking about, but he said, ' Yes, sir.'

' The bread upon the waters ! And you say there's another lad collecting some of it ? '

' There's another chap collecting, yes, sir. Denys Flackman. He was our verger once. But he won't get any fifty quids—fifty pounds—like I did. Only shillings and a half-dollar or two.'

' How much do you think you'll get altogether ? '

' Well, I begin to think now we may get over the hundred. But not much more. No, not much more.'

' And what are you going to buy with it ? '

' Haven't thought about that yet, sir.'

Ben Ostrion studied again the entries in the notebook. ' If it's true that he's given away about all that he had, it might be a good thing to give him money. He isn't getting any younger. But I suppose you can't really hope to get enough to be of any real help to him.'

' Afraid not, sir.'

' No . . . ah, well . . . does the father know anything about this ? '

'Heavens, no, sir ! It's Top Secret from him.'

'But I suppose he'll see this subscription list one day ? When you make the presentation ? '

'That's for the subscribers to say, sir.'

'Well, look here, Ernie.' Ben Ostrion paused and, rising from his desk, walked up and down his carpet for a while. 'Look here, Ernie. I don't mind my name appearing—I think I should like him to see it—and if you have a party to make the presentation I hope you'll let me come.'

'We'll have a party all right,' assured Ernie.

'Yes, have a nice party, and let him know the names of a few who love him, but this is my point : I don't want the amount of my subscription stated.'

'Very good, sir. I see. I'll see he don't know anything about it.'

'No. You can just say that an anonymous subscriber promised to give ten pounds for every pound you collect.'

Ernie turned pale. As he said afterwards, he even felt a little sick. Sick with joy. Out in Amen Street he was incapable of anything but rushing home to Sophie. And before he could tell her the story in full, though its climax was disclosed in the opening sentences, for Ernie had no narrative skill, she was telling him that the Nonconformist minister, the Reverend McClewer, of the Baptist Church, had come to call on him and left the message that he'd ' like to be associated with any tribute to Mr. Dawbeny.'

'Would he, and all ? ' exclaimed Ernie. ' Oh, Lord, I must go round and see him before he loses his enthusiasm. He may be good for a quid. We've only got to get ninety-one pounds, Sophie, and we'll top the four figures ! Crikey, these Yids do things in a large way. A thousand ! Then we'll have such a meeting in our own Church Hall, with the Bishop and the Mayor—that's what I've in mind—and certainly the *Ledbitter and Potters Dale Chronicle* there. Gee, Mrs. Matters, we shall have dished the reds then ! We shall have shown them what we think of the father and their mucking lies about him. A thousand blooming quid ! Gee, I've never handled so much money before. Do you think I'm to be trusted with it ? I wasn't the last time, you remember.'

Ernie had swept the Church Hall for nine years, but never with such interest or so thoroughly as for this meeting on a June evening in 1947. He had decorated it sometimes for whist drives, dances, and social gatherings, and with an especial goodwill and many pleasant fancies for the children's treats, but never had he worked on its embellishment in so inspired a manner as now. His inspirations blossomed as luxuriantly as the blooms of the hydrangeas which he laid along the platform's edge. It had been his idea to borrow tall palms and potted flowers from the barrow-men in Becker Street. And now he placed the palms at the corners of the platform and the flowers wherever else he could array or mass them. Where possible he hung flags. Denys was his willing mate in this labour, holding the ladder, handing up the hammer, and stepping back to tell the artist whether his handiwork was a success or needed such and such improvement. It was Denys who suggested that they must hang a banner with a slogan on the wall behind the platform, and he who found the best and simplest words for it. Ernie had suggested all sorts of phrases that to Denys, now a student of the Greeks, seemed a little vulgar in their over-emphasis. He instructed Ernie on the virtues of under-statement, a new idea to Ernie which did not penetrate his intelligence at once. But Ernie did at last perceive the effectiveness of Denys's phrase, and together they painted it in red on white calico and hung it high for all to see. It was simply, ' Thank You, Father.'

By seven o'clock there were many voices outside the closed doors of the hall, and it was a proud Ernie who flung open the double doors and let the people in. They poured in, and he felt that they, too, were his creation. He and Denys acted as stewards, showing them to their places and bringing fresh chairs, which were soon necessary, from all the other rooms in the building, including Sophie's kitchen and Father Dawbeny's study. Denys was not afraid to come close to the father to-night because he knew that his presence would be diluted by that of a few hundred others. Soon the hall, not very large, was crowded to doors and walls and window-sills. Denys left the broad double doors wide open, and in the warm June evening, still full of daylight, more people stood there in a crowd, looking in. When it was quite impossible to pack another person in the hall, Ernie went and sat at the back alongside of Sophie. His work was done.

Miss Maud Ayer, the church organist, played airs on the old piano, and when she modulated into some tune they knew well, the people, led by the men who were determined to be jolly, sang it in full chorus. They even started some choruses of their own, and then Miss Ayer did her best to pick up the tune on the piano and accompany, or possibly correct and re-direct, the straying performance. They sang ' Roll out the barrel, roll out the barrel of rum,' and nobody felt that Father Dawbeny would object to this intemperate song. They gave of their best to ' The Lambeth Walk,' jigging in their seats, beating with their feet, and conducting with their hands. ' Any time you're Lambeth way, Any evening, any day, You'll find them all . . . Doing the Lambeth Walk.'

Precisely at half-past seven the Bishop stepped on to the platform, followed by the Vicar, the Mayor, the churchwardens, the Rev. Atholl McClewer from the Baptist Church, Captain Fowler from the Salvation Army Citadel, and a portly, handsome well-dressed Jewish gentleman whom they supposed to be con-nected with the Millan Street synagogue, but who was really Ben Ostrion. At the first sight of Father Dawbeny in his familiar black cassock and cape (both a little tarnished and shiny now) the whole audience rose to its feet and cheered and cheered, and adorned the cheers with brilliant whistlings ; for most of the Dalesmen, as we have striven to show, have hearts rather larger than their consciences, and the hearts of the Dales-women, for the most part, are even larger and softer than the men's. The women waved the hymn-sheets which they had found on their chairs. Ernie, standing with the rest, watched the father and saw that, on entering, his eyes had shot up to those words on the wall, and then instantly dropped. They remained dropped, and his hands trembled as the people cheered and cheered. His worn face was not white now, but red as that of a shy woman suddenly shamed.

The Bishop, a small man but imposing, with his crown of light-steel hair, his silk vest and his shining pectoral cross, rose from the chairman's place and motioned to them all to be seated. And he began, ' Ladies and gentlemen, there is no need for me to describe what this meeting is about. The splendid welcome which you have just given to Father Dawbeny expresses that infinitely more eloquently than any words of mine. You have made it plain that we are here to do honour to one man only, a priest who for twenty years has fought in your midst for the faith that is in him—fought against odds and not light odds ; odds determined by poverty, bad housing, and, I'm afraid, by crime '—' Hear, hear,' from a humourist—' by the malice of the King's enemies, and, what is worse than that, far worse, by misrepresentation and detraction and even sometimes '— he waited and then added in a dropped voice, ' by cold and wilful slander from very sinister quarters.' This was his first indirect reference to the real thing which all knew to be at the base of this meeting, and the words fell into a pool of significant silence. ' He has fought always, I say, for our ancient faith, and I am therefore going to ask you, before we do anything else, to rise and sing together " Faith of our Fathers." ' There was a rustling everywhere as the people sought and opened their hymn-sheets, and the Bishop quoted the first lines of the hymn, ' Faith of our fathers, living still, in spite of dungeon, fire and sword.'

They sang it not less heartily, not less mightily, than they had sung, ' Roll out the Barrel,' though few of them believed any of it. They sang, they roared, ' Faith of our fathers ! We will love both friend and foe in all our strife ; and preach thee, too, as love knows how, by kindly words and virtuous life,' and sat down, no more disposed than before to do what they had just undertaken to do.

All the time they sang Ernie, singing not at all, was staring at the Bishop with his golden cross and the Mayor with his golden chain and the Salvation Army captain in his uniform, and all the other gentlemen on the platform, and thinking with amazement that it was really *his* achievement.

The Bishop called upon the Mayor. And the Mayor, Colonel Burkestone, a squat, square-shouldered man with a bald head and a squat, square black moustache, cleared his throat and rightly decided that it was his task to be funny.

' My lord,' he said, standing erect, at a half-right turn so that he could address both the Bishop and the people, ' as I look out upon this magnificent audience, all come to do honour to their vicar, I cannot help wondering how many of them were at church last Sunday. (Laughter.) I cannot ask those who were to put up their hands because it would embarrass the others, and because, quite frankly, I couldn't put up my own. (Laughter.) I couldn't give them the lead as their Mayor should do. Father Dawbeny, sir, had you that excellent piece of furniture which is so prominent in my friend Captain Fowler's citadel, the penitent stool, I would now go to it. But may I say this to you by way of a small penance? You probably feel disheartened sometimes, as all the padres I meet say they are, by the meagreness of church congregations to-day, but such a sight as this, before your eyes this evening, must show you how much buried affection and admiration there is for you and your work—how much buried worship (I might almost say) for that which you preach and exemplify. I have seen but little of your vicar, ladies and gentlemen, but, by heavens, I've heard about him! In the old heroic days of the London blitz—I was not Mayor then, but only a councillor and a hopelessly confused corporal in the Home Guard (laughter)—but in the Town Hall we knew all about Father Dawbeny of St. John's. We knew that the rescue parties, the demolition squads, the stretcher-bearers, the firemen would say, directly they got to an incident, "Where's that old sky pilot?" (Loud laughter and cheers.) "We can't have an incident without 'im." And, as far as I know, they never did—not in the Dale. Sooner or later he was there, and generally sooner, rescuing the casualties, digging out the buried, demolishing the houses, putting out the fire. . . . Well, this is a very different incident to-night, a much happier incident, and there he is, in that old black cassock. (Laughter.) He used to run *towards* those other incidents; he looks as though he'd like to run *from* this one to-night. But we aren't having any yellow stuff from him. My good friends, Captain Fowler and the Rev. Atholl McClewer, both powerful fellows, are there to collar him at the first sight of a cowardly desertion. Strange to think he was once a colonel like me. A colonel, as we all know, is a figure of fun, only one degree less comic than a sergeant-major. While they are still in the army they are not, perhaps, so much of a joke, but once they've retired they're a perfect scream. Either they are peppery, plum-faced old die-hards, always talking about tiffin and the memsahibs, or they are tiresome old councillors who oppose every legitimate aspiration of the people, want all the bad boys flogged, and, alas, have to be made Mayor just once before they pop off. (Much laughter.) Well, I've known many retired colonels, and some were certainly like that. I've known some who came to bad ends, believe it or not, but, ladies and gentlemen, I've never known one who came to end up like this one here : a devoted priest, in an old black cassock, surrounded by the love of his people. I can only say that I am glad it was in my term as your Mayor that to-night's little ceremony fell and that mine was the privilege to bring the blessing of the whole borough upon these happy proceedings and to associate the whole borough with your " Thank you " to Father Dawbeny.'

The Bishop now rose and said that, since these gifts to the Vicar came from his parishioners and not from his bishop, it was fitting that the presentation should be made by the senior churchwarden rather than by this evening's chairman, and he called upon Mr. Eric Sandeman.

Mr. Sandeman rose. A short, rotund, outspread little man, with a ruddy weather-tanned face (his greengrocer's shop in Cartwright Street was open to the air in all weathers), he was not unlike one of the more russet English pippins which he displayed before the public. Well accustomed to speech in council, he was little accustomed to platform oratory when there were ' nobs' like the Lord Bishop and His Worship the Mayor beside him, and he had accordingly brought a manuscript filled, as he hoped, with suitably ceremonious words. Mr. Sandeman's aspirates were never accurately disposed, and on a nerve-shaking occasion like this they leapt about and changed their seats, almost as if they were panicking behind his mask of ease.

' My lords, ladies and gentlemen,' he began ' we are gathered together here in the sight of God '—these had seemed good words when his pencil was in his hand, and he thought them his own, forgetting that he'd heard them, time and again, in the Marriage Service—' to do honour to how'er good vicar, as his lordship the Bishop has said '—he was glad of this parenthesis, which was added impromptu and enabled him to look up from his script—' but before I tell you what form our tribute is taking, I feel that I ought to tell the father something about how the idea horiginated. It all originated, sir, with our good friend and excellent verger, Mr. Matters—Hernie to most of us, I think. (Applause.) He come to me and says, " Have you forgotten that the Vicar completes twenty years of service to

240

St. John's this year, and didn't we ought to do something about it ? " Hi, of course, agreed at once, and we got a committee together, but I don't think any of us, least of all Ernie, expected the seed which he had sown to grow into quite such a 'andsome tree as it 'as. We was amazed at the way the subscriptions came in. After all, the Dale is a place where a shilling is a shilling, and not easily given away—at least that's what it used to be like, but now everybody seems to have money but me.' This parenthesis, uttered on the spur of the moment, drew a fine laugh, and he was greatly encouraged and began to be truly at ease instead of only pretending to be. ' 'Undreds of people we'd never heard of arst to be associated with our gifts— and not only from the Dale neither ; people from far and wide —but don't suppose that this sort of result is achieved without donkey-work, and nearly all the donkey-work, let me tell you, ladies and gentlemen, and you, Father, was done by Hernie, ably abetted by Mr. Denys Flackman, whom some of you older ones will know. They worked so well that the business began to look like getting out of hand, and it was then that we waited on the Lord Bishop to arst his advice and to invite him to preside at any function we might organize. That, I may say, was Hernie's idea, too. It was his lordship who made the suggestion that we should give the father two presents : one to him as a priest, which would remain in his church as a memorial of his ministry, and one to him as a man and a friend and a neighbour, which he could keep for his'self. To him as a priest, then, we offer '—he began to uncover something which had been hidden under a red cloth on the table—' this silver chalice and paten suitably hengraved. And to him as a man and our friend we present this illuminated address, containing the names of all who have subscribed, and in addition a capital sum of money '—unlike Ernie, Mr. Sande- man had some narrative sense and had kept his climax to the end ; and now he gave it emphasis by pausing before he spoke it—' a capital sum of one thousand one hundred and eighty pounds.'

Father Dawbeny looked up, startled—even perhaps horrified. The people, no less astonished, but beyond measure delighted, burst into an uproar of cheers and clapping, the men studding the cheers with whistlings and cat-calls and stampings of their feet.

' Perhaps I ought to correct that last statement,' pursued Mr.

Sandeman when he could speak again. 'We all knew that Father Dawbeny was not to be trusted with a capital sum—he'd only spend it on the church or on us—so we've bought with it for him a small hannuity. (Laughter and cheers.) So now, Father'—Father Dawbeny had risen, and into his hands the greengrocer put the chalice with the paten resting on its top— 'we ask you to accept these gifts and the address which accompanies them as a small proof that your twenty years of labour amongst us has not been altogether wasted, and certainly not unnoticed. I have had many 'appy hours as your church-warden, sir, but this is my 'appiest. When you use this 'ere chalice will you please always think of it as evidence of our gratitude, our faith in you, and, yes, the real love we bear to you?'

Ernie at the back saw the trembling of the father's lips as the cheers beat about him, and he suffered with him, but very happily.

As the father stood there, holding the chalice and waiting for the cheers to subside, the Bishop rose, and his rising and his up-raised hand quietened the storm. 'I want to say one thing only, and it is this,' he said. 'The chalice has always been the symbol of the priest's office, and, ladies and gentlemen, as I saw this beautiful vessel passing into the hands of your vicar the thought came to me that though it may be used at the altar long after we've all passed away, it will never have more priestly hands to hold it.'

There were few but understood why he had said this.

He continued : 'Before I ask Father Dawbeny to reply there are others who have expressed their desire to be associated with this tribute, and I am indeed happy to ask the Rev. Atholl McClewer, of the Cremona Road Baptist Church, to say a few words.'

Mr. McClewer, a tall, broad Scot with brown curly hair, a long brown curly moustache that seemed to belong to Edwardian days, and eyes as mild as his frame was muscular, was not afraid to speak in scriptural words that neither the Bishop nor the Vicar, nor probably any Anglican priest—and certainly no Anglican layman—could have used. He began by saying that though the sair'vices in his church were very different from those in Mr. Dawbeny's he knew a sair'vant of the dear Lorr'd when he saw one, and he knew that Mr. Dawbeny, in spite of all his incense and candles and banners, was as fair'vent an evangelical as he was, preaching the simple gospel of our Lorr'd Jesus as forthrightly and as powerfully as any nonconformist minister in the land. Then, turning to Father Dawbeny, he said, ' I am here simply because we want you to feel that, whatever trials and tribulations may beset you, we of the free churches will endeavour to be always on your side. The guid Bishop alluded to misrepresentations from sinister quarters. There is only one wairr'd to say about that, and it is the wairr'd of our common Master, and I hope you will not think it impair'tinent of me to recall it. " Blessed are ye when men shall revile you and pair'secute you, and say all manner of evil against you falsely for my sake. Rejoice and be exceeding glad." To those grr'and wairr'ds I will add only, but from the verra bottom of ma hairt and I know I speak for every soul here, the wairr'ds of the prophet Daniel, " O man, greatly beloved, fear not, peace be unto thee, be strong." '

At a glance from the Bishop, Ben Ostrion rose, and to some of the humourists who knew him not, it seemed that he, with his massive head and large Hebraic nose, might be the prophet Daniel himself. His eyes twinkled at the audience as if he suspected they were thinking something like this. ' Ah, yes,' he said, 'I see you are all thinking, Who is this? He is not one of us. He is a Jew, and we don't have things like that in Potters Dale. (Roars of laughter.) What is he doing at our party? Well, my good friends, it is true I invited myself, but I think my presence not wholly unseemly for three good reasons : first, because I am able to represent the many outside your parish who've wanted to make their small contributions to these gifts ' —Ernie at the back grinned at the word ' small '—' secondly, because, having heard a nonconformist praise your vicar, it seems good that you should hear a Jew endorse every word he said ; and thirdly because I want you to know that a Jew can believe passionately in the full Christian ethic which Father Dawbeny has always so fearlessly taught you. He and I have fought side by side for that real Christian behaviour, and heavy has been the abuse which has sometimes been heaped upon us. So I just couldn't bear not to be at his side when, for a change, a little praise was laid at his feet. Thank you for allowing me to sit among you and hear it. I have been uplifted by all that has been said about him. And now let me make way for him who is the one you really want to hear, and to cheer.'

Father Dawbeny was now standing before them, with his eyes down as they cheered, all having risen to their feet, and gave him musical honours. And when he lifted his eyes as they sat down again it was not to look at them, but at the ceiling. A great silence awaited his words. And he began : ' It is part of my weakness as a priest, my dear friends, that I can never speak easily the words of love. But, believe me, I do feel it—I always have—and never so much as at this moment.' He brought his eyes down and faced the people with a faint smile. ' Perhaps this weakness is due to my training in the army with its outcome that I became, as the Mayor has said, a colonel ; and it is not on record that colonels, as a rule, address those in their charge in the language of love. (Laughter.) They do not, as a rule, express adequately their affection to the defaulters in the orderly-room or to the battalion on parade. I have never heard of one who said to his defaulters, " My dear fellows, you can't imagine the source of happiness and comfort you are to me, nor that I could not live without you." (Loud laughter again.) But that is exactly, word for word, what I'm struggling to say to you now. These gifts and the thoughts behind them are a spring of comfort—" comfort " in its exact meaning of strengthening—to one who was beginning to fear that he'd made a mess of things. It is a great comfort to be shown to-night that kindly thoughts and words can travel as fast as evil ones. Thank you for so helping me. Thank you all—except perhaps Ernie Matters. I'm not sure about him. But I'll have it out with him later. He's definitely for orderly-room to-morrow. (Laughter and cries of " Seven days C.B. for Ernie "). It is news to me that he is behind this generous deed, but if he's not listening I'll say I'm not surprised, because for the last nine years he has been my support—almost my crutch.

' My dear people, these are darkening days for our Christian ethic of which my friend Ben Ostrion spoke. The progress of knowledge everywhere is most unevenly balanced by those other things needful, vision and faith. Evil is strengthening itself everywhere against all faith and holiness. But I take comfort in the thought that God sitteth above the waterfloods, and it is a simple absolute certainty that the gates of hell can never fully prevail against that element of Ultimate Truth which sits in the heart of man. There will always, always, be this remnant of truth in the hearts of spiritual men, and therefore there will always be a remnant of Israel in the world——'

' Speak up, sir,' called a voice from the back.

And others, encouraged by this brave man, called, ' Can't hear you, Father,' and ' We're not getting you back here, sir. Too much interference.'

' I am sorry.' He raised his voice. ' Sometimes when I look from my altar or my pulpit at my little remnant of faithful people I think immediately of, and take heart from, that conviction of the Hebrew prophets—Mr. Ben Ostrion's prophets— that the remnant of Israel will always be there. Do you remember? " And the remnant of Jacob shall be in the midst of many people as a dew from the Lord, as showers upon the grass ; " and " I will also leave in the midst of thee an afflicted and poor people, and they shall trust in the name of the Lord. The remnant of Israel shall not do iniquity, nor speak lies ; neither shall a deceitful tongue be found in their mouth, for they shall feed and lie down, and none shall make them afraid."

' And what I am thinking now is if my little remnant can so bestir itself for me and achieve so much for me, what might it not do if it would work with equal love for my Master ? What you have done for me is proof that you are all capable of love. And my message to you—as taught by the Master of us all— has always been : let that love spread out—far beyond your neighbours and friends, even so far as is possible *over your enemies*.' He was resolved, even on this occasion, to state again the hard saying which had antagonized so many of them before, even though it might cost him some of that which for the moment he possessed, and so longed to possess—their love. ' Try to let it go forth everywhere, so that it can play its part in saving the world. I don't know how long I shall be with you, but if I am remembered for a while after I am gone, I should like to be remembered as having given you always the full message, difficult though it may be to take. And the full message is just this : love must always breed love as surely as hate breeds hate. Forgiveness and mercy seem foolishness, but they raise goodness : wrath and retaliation seem sense, but they raise evil. The blood of the lovers, the forgivers, the martyrs who will die rather than return evil for evil, is the seed of the Church, but the bombs of a Pearl Harbour are the seed of an Hiroshima.' He had come prepared with nothing more to say, and his speech, after a hesitation, ended abruptly and lamely.   He just repeated with a smile, ' Thank you again, all of you, with all my heart.'

The meeting over, the people crowded round him to shake his hand and then funnelled out into the night.

Ernie was the last left in the hall because he was its caretaker. He closed the wide doors proudly and animated by a feeling of accomplishment, as a painter lets a curtain fall over a picture completed, or an author closes the cover upon a story to which he can add no more.

PART III

CHAPTER ONE

FOR a long time the memory of that evening stood in Father Dawbeny's thoughts like a little shrine which he could visit in search of comfort and strength. There was much to dishearten him in the next months. Sometimes at Sunday evensong there were but fifteen people in church ; that year he had but five candidates for confirmation, though he could remember a time when he had forty ; even the baptisms and weddings were far fewer than they used to be. In the old days, if some of his parishioners came to church at no other time, they came to see their children baptized or their daughters married in white. Now the intellectuals' rejection of baptism as a superstitious rite akin to a witch-doctor's magic seemed to be invading the streets of the unintellectual poor, and if the young girls still wanted a white wedding, whether or not their virginity entitled them to it, they seemed to want a handsomer church than his. When all these symptoms of failure weighted his heart he would often go into the solitudes of memory and re-create that scene in his hall, with the people crowded to the doors and even listening and cheering in the street beneath the warm June sky. He would repeat to himself those words which *he* could never have uttered, but which McClewer, the Baptist minister, had undoubtedly spoken : ' O man, greatly beloved . . .'

' Greatly beloved '—the man had certainly said that.

But then the priest in him, the man of penetrating vision, would whisper that all this loyalty had been offered to him as a man and a friend, not to the faith which it had been his life's work to meditate, or to the practice which he had spent himself in preaching. It had been given to him, not to his Master. And to that extent he had failed. Was it not proof of his failure that the congregation, after that meeting, had not increased

247

by one face, and that with the passing of time, as the old people died, it grew only smaller ?

So, gradually, the blessed anodyne which the memory of that meeting had been, lost its virtue and even worked as a mild poison, heightening his melancholy. The people might have applauded his fight that day, but was not the position almost lost ?

And two years after that meeting it seemed to be certainly lost. He received the first intimation that his headquarters might command him to abandon it.

Out of the sky, like one of those V.2 rocket projectiles which in the last year of the war came without warning or sound of their approach and exploded a war-head of two thousand pounds, destroying a whole block—or a church—there came a formal letter from the Diocesan Reorganization Committee to him and his Church Council announcing that it was proposed to close St. John the Prior's and ultimately to demolish it.

To demolish it ! He stood by his trestle table with the nails of his long fingers beating upon the letter. He looked down and read it a second time, a third time, and a fourth. The committee, under its new chairman, the young and vigorous Archdeacon Harries—a Pharaoh who knew not Joseph—having pronounced his church redundant, recommended that its work and its income should be shared between St. Luke's, Ledbitter (Oliver Custance's church) and St. Anselm's, Lode Street. And St. John's be demolished. They were going to do what all the bombs of the enemy had failed to do. His church to cease to be ! A factory, perhaps, or a tenement block to rise on its site ! All that he had spent upon it, his whole private fortune, to be given to the waste or drained away.

Oh, he could see the arguments for this shattering decision. St. Luke's, Ledbitter, was a larger and better built church ; it had a larger congregation and larger collections because it was set among fairly well-to-do middle-class streets, and it was from the middle-class and leisured people that the Church of England could still draw a small following. Moreover, the streets around it had received no direct bombs and were now all inhabited again. It had no waste places or condemned houses at its side like St. John's, and the fine church itself was in stout condition. Admirable sense to economize in man-power and money by letting one church do the work of two. Was there not a great shortage of clergy and of candidates for ordination? Admirable sense to concentrate resources and strengthen the position of St. Luke's (and to a lesser degree St. Anselm's) by endowing them with the small income that came from St. John's two properties, the Church Hall and the Costers' Clubhouse, and, ultimately, with the proceeds of the sale of St. John's, a valuable building site.

Admirable sense on paper. But to Father Dawbeny it seemed that the able and business-like young archdeacon and his obedient committee were dealing with arithmetical figures rather than with flesh and blood, with stones instead of souls.

He had to persuade himself that his instant resolve to fight for his church, back to the wall, was not merely a matter of sentiment, but of sense. He and his council had been invited to lodge their objections against the proposal, but his principal and most worthy objection was one that he could not state aloud : it was that he knew in his heart that if he surrendered his charge to Oliver Custance he would be handing over his few faithful to an unworthy priest. Oh, Oliver up on his hill must be no little pleased at this prospect of an addition to the size of his parish, to its income, to his congregation, and to his stipend. Since this could not be spoken to committee or to council, he must submit that even if he had only a few adults he had a large and exceptional number of children, few of whom would ever cross that strange boundary between the Dale and Ledbitter Hill ; that however poor on paper his fruits might look he knew there were many who in an emergency would go to no other priest but him ; that his Costers' Club at any rate was a success ; that he had a small income, and if they would leave him his church he would now work there without remuneration ; that if the Bishop thought that a more vigorous and eloquent man might succeed in winning people where he had failed, he would willingly serve as his unpaid curate, so long as the church stood ; and lastly that the waste places would one day be built over again. . . .

But while he managed to make all this convincing to himself, he could not believe that it would influence the Archdeacon.

And it did not influence the Archdeacon, or his committee. The committee did not consider the objections valid ; they were determined to act, and they asked the Church Commissioners to prepare in legal form a scheme for the demolition of St. John's.

And then Father Dawbeny began to fight. His teeth set

together and his will closed like a vice on the determination to fight. He summoned a protest meeting to the Church Hall; he, with the angry assistance of Ernie, organized a troop of children to thrust through every letter-box and to fly-post on every grit-bin and available wall (how the boy scouts enjoyed this!) a leaflet announcing the meeting and headed 'Save St. John's.' And when the day of the meeting came he encouraged a dream that the hall might be crowded and a great triumphant battle begun; and for half an hour before the advertised time he was looking from his window into Greig Street, hoping to see the people of the Dale approaching in good numbers. But he did not see them; he saw only the faithful and one or two others (on whom be praise and blessing) dawdling towards the hall. And when with a sigh he went down the stairs and across the alley to the hall, he found about forty persons there. And in the depths of his heart he wondered how this little platoon, composed of elderly women, three or four working men, and a few young girls, could hope to defeat the heavy cannon which the Archdeacon could deploy. But let the forlorn battle begin. And let it go on to the death, without surrender offered at any point, not even at death. Revealing no disappointment, and no doubts, he arranged with this small audience that they should organize a petition, visiting every house in the parish and indeed in the districts beyond, and enlisting the support of other church councils. Everyone there, including the oldest of the women, promised to carry the petition down the length of one or more streets. And with a prayer he sent them forth to the battle; but if his will was iron-hard and unshakeable, his hopes were weak.

§

That was the situation, no one knowing whether the church would be razed or saved, on the night he heard the sudden scream. It seemed to come from the very midst of the church. It was as if the church itself had screamed. The time was about ten o'clock on a January night and, easily tired in these days, he had dropped asleep in his chair by the gas fire. He woke with a horrid start, his heart having leapt from its seat. The cry, or scream, had stabbed into his mind as he slept there, and it had sounded like the cry of a girl-child in terror.

He sat up and waited for it to come again. A child does not cry only once. But not a sound came from the streets. They were silent in the darkness and chill of the winter night.

He rose and went to his side window. It overlooked the flagged alley between hall and church. The church stood there, a dark shape, with no light in any window and its doors closed. He went to the front window and looked down into Greig Street. Nothing to be seen anywhere except the zig-zag procession of the street lamps, marching away into the night. Wondering if he had imagined that cry, he turned and walked into Ernie and Sophie's kitchen. Had they heard anything? No; but then their wireless was playing loudly as they sat together by the fire.

He returned to his own chair and fire, deciding that it had either been the scream of a child having a nightmare in one of the neighbouring houses or had happened in an unremembered nightmare of his own.

In the cold morning, while it was hardly yet light, he crossed over to the church to take the daily Mass, and, as with some difficulty he undid and thrust open the west doors, he remembered his absurd fancy that a scream had come from inside this securely locked and dark and silent place. He had the same thought as he unlocked the vestry door for the server (it was a saint's day, and he had a server coming). Then he thought of it no more.

That day, a saint's festival, he had to leave London for a preaching engagement in the north. His Dale congregation might be small, and his preaching unskilful, but he was strangely in demand as a festival preacher in ' Catholic ' churches all over England. He was not home from this engagement till the early afternoon of the next day. It had been pouring with rain and as he threw off his wet mackintosh in his upper room he inquired of Ernie, laughingly, ' Anything interesting happened while I've been away? '

' Only Mrs. Lancellotti came to see you yesterday afternoon. She seemed kind of worried.'

' Mrs. Lancellotti.' At the name he saw a large, square, excitable woman of forty with blonde hair and high-coloured cheeks, an Englishwoman married to the dark little Italian ice-cream and hot-chestnut vendor, Paolo Lancellotti, generally known in the streets as ' Polo.' Always he had wondered that

251

this little coarse-featured, blue-chinned and barely literate Italian should carry the name of one of the princely families of Italy. ' What did she want ? '

' I don't know, Father. But she was quite a lot put about. When I said you wouldn't be back till to-day she said, " Oh, oh, oh," and just left me standing there. She walked back along the street wagging her head like she was going daft.'

' She does get into states, doesn't she ? '

' I'll say she does. She'll throw a fit about anything and fling her arms about and scream. Comes of being married to an Eye-tie, I suppose. Yes, she went along that there street, shaking her head and moaning for all London to hear. _I_ don't know what it was all about.'

Father Dawbeny nodded and shrugged in a similar ignorance. This untamed and unbraked behaviour of Mrs. Lancellotti, venting her full grief or full fury in a public place—wagging her head, wringing her hands, rolling along a pavement in despair or storming along it in wrath—was always a strange display to him who could so rarely uncover his feelings, even in a private room.

' Oh, well,' he said, ' I suppose I had better go round at once and see her, rain or no rain. Anyone else ? '

' Not yesterday, but this morning Inspector Glower rang up.'

' Glower ? ' The name, because it reminded him of the dark slander three years ago, was always a thrust of pain. But of course he showed no sign of this to his servant. ' What did Mr. Glower want ? '

' He didn't say. I told him you should ought to be back about three, and he said he'd ring up again.'

Father Dawbeny glanced at his clock. It was six minutes after three. He walked to the window and looked at the rain. ' Well, I suppose if Mrs. Lancellotti is in distress she must have priority over the Inspector. I'll go round and learn what her trouble is. If he rings——'

But at that moment the telephone rang. ' Hallo,' he said into the receiver.

' Is that you, Father ? This is Inspector Glower. Remember me, don't you ? '

' Do I not, Inspector ? And how are you ? '

' I'm all right, thank you, sir. You know Mr. and Mrs. Lancellotti in your parish ? '

'Very well indeed. She's one of the few who still come to church. She's even been known to bring her husband, and he's a Roman Catholic, officially.'

'Well, I'm afraid I've a very unhappy piece of news for you.' The Inspector's tone quenched all humour. 'You know her little daughter Christina?'

'Surely. She's one of my girl guides. A charming child, and one who's going to be very beautiful.' As he spoke, the child, Christina Lancellotti, stood before his mind : dark Italian eyes, pink English skin, dark hair in a straight fringe over her forehead and in a bob over her ears ; hardly thirteen years old, a slip ripening early into beauty because of her southern blood ; a child at that lovely point when she is neither the young brook nor the full stream. Sometimes the straightness of her nose and the wide spacing of her eyes had made him wonder if the features of the princely Lancellottis were appearing again in this daughter of the ice-cream vendor. 'There's nothing wrong with Christina, is there?'

The Inspector delayed the direct answer. 'The night before last, at about midnight, her father came round and reported her missing. She'd gone to a cinema with her auntie, but ought to have been home long before. Her auntie parted from her on the steps of the cinema, and that was somewhere about half-past nine. Since then there'd been no sign of her. We took every sort of action '—he sounded almost apologetic— 'more than usual, because the C.I.D. is always immediately interested if the missing person is a young child or a young woman. We sent an S.O.S. message to all surrounding stations and notified all the policemen on their beats, especially the women policemen, but none of them found anything that was of any help. This morning, however, a tramp, turning into one of those bombed houses in Despard Street to get out of the rain, as he says, but heaven knows what really for, went into the back cellar and found her body there.'

'Oh, my God? Dead?'

'Yes, sir. Dead.'

'Murdered—murdered, of course?'

'Oh, yes.' There came a sigh along the wires. 'Not a doubt about that. Superintendent Collins, who's taken charge of the case, telephoned at once to C.O. and got authority to summon Dr. Galston from St. Mary's Hospital. He was there in a few minutes, and he reports the usual thing : she was strangled.'

' Oh, my God, my God ! And assaulted, too ? '

' Not criminally assaulted, no, sir. That's an odd feature of the case. Very odd.'

' When does Dr. Galston think it happened ? ' Suddenly a memory had bounded into his mind.

' He thinks she must have died somewhere about ten o'clock the night before last.'

Ten o'clock ! The very time ! But Despard Street was half-a-mile away ! On the extreme border of his parish.

' Did anyone hear anything ? Any scream or anything ? '

' No, sir. But that's understandable. The houses all round are bombed and condemned as dangerous structures. There's no one living near the house where she was found. As you know it's practically a dead street and almost certainly deserted at ten o'clock at night. That makes us think that the man who lured her there was a local man and knew this neighbourhood well.'

' It looks like it. And no one reports having heard anything ? '

' Not yet, sir. But the reports'll come in.' He seemed to have laughed sardonically. ' We shall soon be having plenty of letters from dreamers, clairvoyants, theorists and other pests.'

Clairvoyants ! The word, so pat to his thought, hit the listener like a displeasing blow. He had been asking himself, daring to ask himself, whether it had been some form of clair-audience which had enabled him to hear from half-a-mile away the cry of one of his children as if it had come from the heart of his church. Those church doors had undoubtedly been locked—he himself had found them locked in the morning—so clairaudience or coincidence it must have been, and perhaps it was better not to speak of it now lest he were numbered among the pests.

' Have you any clues at all, Inspector ? '

Again the Inspector gave no direct answer. ' It's early yet, sir. What I wanted to know was, will you go and see poor Mrs. Lancellotti. I understand from Lancellotti that she turned to you when the child was only missing. Now she's prostrate with grief. Can you help her ? '

' I'll go at once. Thank you for telling me.'

He seized the mackintosh and hurried out. Hatless, he hurried through the rain to the small low house in Platman

Street where the Lancellottis lived. All the way he was wondering what he could say to them, wishing that he was not always so awkward and tongue-tied, and praying to God to give him words. ' Help me to help them. O God, help me to help her.' Outside the house was a small cluster of women, gossiping with each other or just gaping at windows and door. They gaped at him as he went up to the door, but gave to this coming of a priest the courtesy of silence. Strange that they could so mix reverence with a gaping curiosity.

An unknown woman opened to him: some good-hearted neighbour, doubtless, who had come in to help the stricken household. She, however, knew him by sight and, opening the door of the front room, said to someone inside, ' Father Dawbeny to see you, ducky.'

He went in and saw the heavy square figure of Ada Lancellotti slumped in a wicker chair by the fire. Her up-thrust breasts were lifting and falling and the half-closed hand on her broad lap oscillating and jerking like an old man's palsied hand. Her eyes only stared and stared. This usually excitable woman, voluble with words and quick to gesticulate, sat there like one in a trance, motionless, speechless, as he came towards her. She who so usually flung head, arms, and body about in her despairs was still—still as a staring, cataleptic figure. Sometimes her heavy flesh quivered—and that was all. Her eyes did not blink as she stared. So might a mad person stare in fear at a face approaching. ' Oh, help me to help her.' His eyes were so held by her, and by his longing to help her, that not until Paolo Lancellotti rose to welcome him, had he noticed that he was sitting in the other wicker chair opposite her.

' Make-a yourself comfort, Father. Sitta down, please. Ecco,' said the little dark Italian, pointing to the chair he had vacated. ' Polo ' Lancellotti had been twenty years in England, but his speaking of English was still no better than if he had come from his native Calabria but a month or two ago. And perhaps in this day of distress he had lapsed back towards the language of home and childhood. ' I go to get you something. Some-a tea, no ? '

' No, no ; please not. And don't move from that chair. I shall not be long.' Oh, wicked, this longing to be gone, this desire to escape from the presence of this pain, from the need to minister to it, and from his sickening inability to do so.

O God, help me. There must be no self-saving retreat, no betrayal of his priestly task. Speechless as the mother herself, he took Polo Lancellotti's hand in one of his and placed the other over it and pressed. O God, give me words.

Mr. Lancellotti shook his head sadly and jerked it towards his wife. 'What are we go to do, Father? She can't take-a it. It is too much. I am not understanding what to do.' He lifted his shoulders and his outspread palms. 'I am beaten. See, my Ada, it is the Parroco.'

Father Dawbeny walked towards her, went down on a knee beside her and took her hand. 'What can I do for you, my dear?' he said. So difficult for him as a rule to say 'my dear,' but to-day he couldn't *not* say it; so difficult to do anything demonstrative, but to-day he had knelt and gathered up her hand in both of his before he knew what he was doing.

She did not answer him. Her mouth was a little open, the jaw fallen.

'Tell me anything I can do for you.'

Her voice came hoarse and deep, like the voice from a sick bed. 'Find the man that done it.'

'*Si, si.* That is it,' said her husband, standing by. 'Find-a da man, and letta me get my hands on him.'

No moment this to speak of forgiveness; and the tongue-tied priest did not know what else to speak of. Not even in this room would he preach vindictiveness. But for the present he gave it the countenance of silence.

Polo Lancellotti walked to the window and looked out into the street. '*Si*, tell me where I can find the man that does it. He is somewhere. He is somewhere in the Dale because my little Christina does not go with a man she does not know. Just take-a me to where he is. Putta me up against that dog of a man. That is all I am asking now. Or don't tell me where he is because, if I see him, no police, no law of the land, no nothing stop me from killing him. I am a naturalized Englishman, *si*, but I come from Calabria—Calabria, yes?—and in Italy, *Dio mio*, we pay our own bills. We pay. *Ma si! Senz' altro.*'

'My little girl . . .' Ada Lancellotti's hand was trembling in his. He stroked it, and this wordless sympathy broke down some resistance in her and she moaned, 'Oh . . . oh . . . oh . . .'

'Listen,' he began, but just then, looking up in his helplessness at the wall above the mantelpiece, he noticed a square, unfaded patch from which a framed picture had been removed. And he remembered that an enlarged photograph of Christina at five years old used to hang there, taking pride of place in the room.

' *Si*,' said Polo Lancellotti, following his eyes. ' I take-a itta down. She is not able to look at it. I place it upstairs and shutta the door. One day we are able to look at it again.'

Rising from his knee, he drew a chair from the table and sat by them. ' Listen,' he began again, and, still holding her hand, he told them that almost the only actual words of Christ that the world possessed, the only syllables that actually came from His lips, were ' *Talitha, cumi*. Little maid, I say unto thee, arise.' He told them the story of Jairus's daughter, twelve years old, reminding them how Christ had said to her father, ' Be not afraid ; only believe ; ' and how he had said to the crowd loitering before the house : ' The little maid is not dead, but sleepeth.' And he tried to reassure them that Christina was still alive in another world and waiting for them. He went so far as to say, ' I promise you that you will find her again.' And he prayed beside them, holding the mother's hand. And when, dissatisfied with his ministration, deploring his inadequacy, he went from them into the street, he hoped that they believed all that he had said in his talk and in his prayer. And he hoped, hoped, that he believed it all too.

§

This murder of one of its children shocked and rocked the Dale like that ' land mine ' which, in 1940, fell upon this same Despard Street and killed it. It was as much the subject of shocked conversation in the streets, on the doorsteps, and in the bars. It was more so, because that old disaster stood against a background of war and after twenty hours or thirty hours people spoke of it no more. But they spoke of Christina Lancellotti for day after day.

And not in the Dale only. The eyes and thoughts of the whole country were now directed upon these streets in which Father Dawbeny had worked so long. It was January ; Parliament was in recess ; news stories were scanty ; and all the newspapers, even the sober *Times*, reported for many days, on their principal page, all the developments in the story of

Christina Lancellotti. Their pictures of her, with her wide-spaced, dark eyes, bobbed hair and ' gym ' tunic bearing her school's monogram on the breast, stirred the pity of all and the wrath of all. All longed for an arrest, and they read with a virulent satisfaction, with a vengeful hope, that ' detectives were flooding into the neighbourhood ; ' that ' the whole resources of Scotland Yard were being employed in an effort to bring to justice this brutal murderer ; ' that there had been ' a notable response to the appeal of Superintendent Collins for all who might have any helpful information whatsoever to come forward ' ; and that ' already over a thousand statements had been taken from persons, not in Potters Dale only, but in many other parts of the country.'

Christina Lancellotti, dead, was a national figure. Even in *The Times* the headline was always ' Christina Lancellotti.'

One morning, Father Dawbeny, seated at his breakfast, read in his *Times* : ' Christina Lancellotti. Much information is now in the hands of the police with reference to the murder of this London schoolgirl. They now incline to the view that the child was not murdered in the place where her body was found, but elsewhere, possibly in a motor car into which she had been lured, and that the murderer, having done his fell work, conveyed the body to a street which he knew to be ruined and deserted and dumped it in the back cellar of the house. It is a notable and curious fact that the body had been laid down very gently.' In a motor car ? Was this perhaps the explanation of the nearness of that cry ? But there had been no car in Greig Street when he looked from his window. The street had been empty, quite empty. And the cry had seemed so close. Almost the other side of his window.

After five or six days the story sank lower in the newspaper columns, or disappeared from them altogether, and the world went its usual way towards forgetfulness. But not the Dale : the Dale waited and talked in clusters and hurried new rumours from lip to lip. And on the tenth day the papers suddenly elevated the mystery to the top of their pages again. ' Christina Lancellotti. New Information. The mysterious death of the London schoolgirl, Christina Lancellotti, continues to occupy the attention of the police. After eight days in which the whole resources of Scotland Yard have been employed in trying to solve the mystery, without any apparent success, and with no potential suspect in view, new information was yesterday obtained by Superintendent Collins, and fresh hopes were raised of an early solution. Certain articles are in possession of the Home Office for expert examination, and it is believed that valuable evidence will result from microscopic tests. The police have now little doubt that the body of the child was conveyed to the ruined house in Despard Street by car, hand-cart, or truck of some kind. Anyone who noticed any such vehicle in the vicinity of Despard Street at any time between the disappearance of the child and the discovery of the murder are requested to communicate immediately with the police. A circumstance, however, which may or may not militate against this theory is as follows : Yesterday in the course of their inquiries officers were told a detailed story by two women who declared that they heard the loud scream of a child in the neighbourhood of Despard Street on the night the child disappeared and at exactly the hour when the medical experts believe her to have been killed. The police have carried out experiments in the back rooms and cellars of Despard Street to ascertain if cries for help could be heard at the place where these women stood or in any of the nearest inhabited houses, and the results are pronounced negative. The matter is further complicated by the fact that other persons have spoken of hearing a child's cry at the relevant time, but in places far apart from one another and at considerable distances from Despard Street.'

Could it be, thought Father Dawbeny, reading this, that Christina's cry for help had been heard across the distances, and in many different places by people who, unknown to themselves, had some psychic power ? Could it be that it had come to him because she had loved and trusted him as her priest ? He remembered suddenly that his dog, Squaller, who had been lying at his side had not stirred, or raised an eye, when that cry seemed to sound in the night.

What mystery was here ?

Next day the papers began to speak of a ' man ' who was a potential suspect. They must mention no name, but they pointed very firmly to a figure whom the police were watching and whom the whole Dale could recognize. The whole Dale, devouring its papers, saw the tall, overdressed, black-haired figure of this man and named his Jewish name. ' Seldom,' one paper was bold to say, ' have the police had so much evidence and yet been unable to make an arrest. Numerous reports have been received about the conduct of a man who lives in the Potters Dale area and is alleged to have spent much of his time trying to get children to accompany him by offering them toys and sweets.' That was a morning paper ; on the same day the *Evening Star* reported, ' Officers in charge of the case are convinced that the answer lies in the district where the child was known and that the man they are seeking will be found there. While they have a suspicion as to the identity of this man, a local resident whose conduct has lately been the subject of much local gossip, they realize that unless the information they need is forthcoming, they will be powerless to proceed against him. He is, of course, entitled to the protection of the Law, and he has been favoured so far by the fact that no evidence finally incriminating him has been received.'

' Favoured so far.' This surely, thought Father Dawbeny, was saying a good deal, and indeed rather more than it was legitimate for a paper to say. It stated pretty frankly, and despite the absence of ' finally incriminating evidence,' that the man was probably guilty, but lucky.

Father Dawbeny knew, of course, who this man was. How should he not know when either Ernie or Sophie came every few hours into his room with further information about him ? He was Matt Rubens, the son of old Lew Rubens who had the dusty little junk shop in Cartwright Street and who would travel the roads with his pony and cart, crying his melancholy syllables which told the housewives that he was ready to buy anything from old bedsteads to old bones. Matt, the son, lived with his parents but worked as a garage hand at the big Red Circle Garage in the high road, and when he was not in his greasy overalls he was a far smarter man, far more the gentleman, than his rusty, dingy and, to say the truth, somewhat reeky old father. Tall above most, with a high coif of black hair, a prominent Jewish nose and large mischievous brown eyes ; well-dressed, if you didn't mind a little ostentation such as a pearl tie-pin, a yellow waistcoat, and a diamond ring, he was a clean, burnished and striking figure to come out of that dusty and smelling little store in Cartwright Street. But never had Matt Rubens so arrested the eyes of all as now. All knew that the police had visited the shop many times ; that they had taken him to the station and detained him there for two days and nights ; that they had made inquiries about him of his workmates at the garage and of all who knew him in the streets ; that they were ' on '—on like bulldogs—to two facts : one, that he was wearing a bandage on his finger at the time of the murder, and the other, that he knew Christina Lancellotti and had sometimes spoken with her.

This was enough, quite enough, to convince them all that he was the man. Probably there was only one person in the Dale, apart from his parents, who still declined to affirm his guilt ; and this was Father Dawbeny. Had not he himself been pronounced guilty by a great many people, three years before, just because the police had visited him and had made inquiries about him of Connie Beron and her friends ? And he had been completely innocent.

Matt Rubens did not run from the neighbourhood. He stood his ground, declaring to his confidants with much gesticulation and a fire in his brown eyes, ' I am innocent of zis terrible t'ing, absolutely innocent. I know nutting about it, no more dan vot anybody does, and I am not going to run. I am not even going to stay indoors. I go out and face them all. They can stop and stare at me as if I vos dirt, they can lynch me if dey like, they can string me up to a lamppost, but I don't run. I'd no more have hurt zat little girl dan I'd have hurt my mother : she vos a darling, and I spoken often with her, yes, because she vos so beautiful.' And so he walked the streets every night, just as usual, his head high and his lips tight—but he was very pale, his face was a sick white wax under the glossed black hair, and it was plain that he walked with terror at his side.

People said that if the cops didn't do something soon, the Dale'd take the Law into its own hands and something'd happen to Matt Rubens. The wiseacres said, ' Mark my words, the cops'll arrest him soon on some paltry charge, not only so as to have him where they can find him, but also to give him protective custody—yes, protective custody, see.' ' Protective custody ' was a phrase they had become familiar with during the war, and they were proud of it.

Help and sympathy had beaten like a flooding tide about the little house of the Lancellottis in Platman Street. Flowers, fruit, offers of money, and even offers of a home away from it all, had poured through its door, coming not from the Dale only but from all parts of England. Some balm these kindly mercies brought to the broken home, but Ada Lancellotti tended to rest for comfort and hope on her priest, Father Dawbeny. As Polo Lancellotti would say to his mates, ' You know-a what it ees ; you know-a what women are. Dey don' listen to their husband at a time like this. I say plenta t'ings, but it don't never do much good ; she don't listen to me. It's wotta *he* says that gets her. It's a no good my saying anything. Alla right. I stoppa da talk. She joost believe everything he tell her, and she ask him again and again to say that our Christina is still alive somewhere. He say it for her. *Bene.* She stoppa da crying. You see, with women, it's the priests or nothing at a time like this.'

Father Dawbeny, knowing what a funeral meant to people like Ada Lancellotti, had been resolved that the Church should do for her all that it would do for the greatest. On the day of Christina's funeral he had celebrated a Requiem Mass for her ; and for the first time in a dozen years his church held a congregation that filled every pew and stood along the walls. For once he had all the clergy, acolytes and choir he needed for a perfect Mass. Only a few of the packed congregation knew what a Requiem Mass was, or what was happening up there at the altar, but they watched in silence and with a great reverence. After the Mass the first part of the Burial Office was said in the church, and then choir and clergy and congregation took the child in procession to the New Cemetery. The police escorted them through the traffic and marshalled the reverent crowds on the pavements. The choir sang hymns as they went along ; and when the cemetery gates came into view they began to sing ' There's a friend for little children ' ; an incident of which they speak in the Dale to this day.

Many of the Potters Dale and Ledbitter clergy were present at that Requiem Mass and walked in that procession with the child's body, but Oliver Custance was not one of them. And when next day he saw pictures of the procession in the papers, with the tall robed figure of Father Dawbeny the most conspicuous figure of all, he declared with a show of sad disapproval that ' he feared his neighbour was publicity-hunting as usual,' and that to him, personally, ' the whole orgy of emotion was repellent in the extreme.'

CHAPTER TWO

FATHER DAWBENY offered to go with the trembling mother to the adjourned inquest, the final hearing at which all the evidence would be disclosed and the matter brought to a verdict. And she begged him to do so : ' Yes, oh yes, Father, *please*.' So he and Polo Lancellotti (dressed in his best, with stiff collar and cuffs) walked on either side of Ada Lancellotti (also dressed in her best since ' one must go decent ') to the square, grey isolated building in Endown Road which was the Coroner's Court.

There was a crowd outside the doors : all those who could not get in because the public seats were few, and those who had come to watch the arrival of the witnesses—the mother, Dr. Hubert Galston, the famous pathologist, Superintendent Collins and the other famous detectives, and, above all, the one against whom they might murmur, Matt Rubens. They recognized the parents and Father Dawbeny, and a whispering ran among them like a sudden breeze in tall corn; then stillness and a staring silence. As Father Dawbeny took Mrs. Lancellotti's arm and led her up the steps, the women spoke sentimentally about him. ' Where there's trouble, there the Father is. He's hardly left her for a minute, they say ; it's him that's kep' her alive.'

The court room was very full : the only empty places being the platform under the arched window, which held the coroner's desk and throne-like chair, and the raised witness box on its left, waiting to hold the drama of the morning. By each of these important places stood a tall policeman like its guardian. At the press table immediately beneath the platform sat ten reporters in their overcoats ; other reporters had sought writing room at counsel's table just behind. The jury box held nine men of whom only three appeared to be men of education ; the rest, elderly grey men in frayed collars or mufflers looked as if the coroner's officer had gathered them from street corners. The public benches were filled to discomfort, except the two front ones which had been reserved for witnesses. And there in front sat Matt Rubens, all eyes turning to him again and yet again. He was very pale—pale as a man who had kept company with a death-threat for weeks—but his back was straight, his head upheld, and his eyes defiant. His large hands with the diamond ring on one little finger and a gold ring on the other lay clasped on his knee, thumb stroking thumb. Could those be the hands. . . .

The warm atmosphere of the room pressed upon one's face, coming from the overheated radiators and from the crush of people. But crowded though the room was, it housed hardly more murmuring than one would hear in a church.

Suddenly the policeman on the platform called out, ' Rise, please, for the King's Coroner. O yea, O yea, O yea,' and before he had finished, the Coroner had entered, bowed to the Court, and taken his seat. He was a small man of fifty with soft, rounded, pleasant, easy-going features, but keen and steady grey eyes. He was both a doctor and a barrister but looked like neither. So mobile and collapsible were his rubbery features, so bright his eyes, that Father Dawbeny, who'd sat under him more than once, always thought he looked more like a character actor who would be cast for genial comedy parts.

' Will the court be seated, please,' called the policeman.

And when all were seated, and when the nine jurymen had been sworn, the Coroner, turning towards the jury box, as if none of the rest of the court mattered much, and speaking in a low soft voice but with the clearness of an actor, began to re-hearse for its occupants the familiar story. He spoke of little Christina's disappearance into the darkness of that January night, and of the discovery of her body in the ruined house thirty-six hours later. Not a person in the room but knew every detail of the story, yet they listened in silence, glancing sometimes towards Mrs. Lancellotti and sometimes towards Matt Rubens. Then the silence deepened, and their eyes stayed fixed upon the Coroner, because he was now beginning to disclose facts which hitherto had not been known or had been only the subject of rumours.

' Now, gentleman of the jury, it will be your duty to say how, when, and by what means this child met her death. All her relatives and friends describe her as a shy child who would have been quite unlikely to speak to strangers or walk away with any-one unknown to her, and so there seems to be a high probability that she was decoyed away by some person, or persons, familiar to her. The police are satisfied that the crime was committed in this district but not in the place where she was found. Her body, they believe, was conveyed there, perhaps in a car, perhaps on a handcart or barrow. There were no signs of disturbance in the brick dust and plaster beneath her ; they lay there just as they must have lain for months—even for years. Her body appeared to have been gently—almost reverently—laid down. The stump of a candle lay at a little distance from her, and a few spots of candle grease had fallen on her breast, as if the murderer had held the candle and looked down upon her for a little while, or even for a long while, before leaving her there. On the other side of the child's body was a torn fragment of the *Daily Express* newspaper, rolled into a wad and slightly smeared with candle grease, as if he had tried to wipe these stains from her breast before he left. In the pit of her right arm a fragment of boric lint was found and some strands of a material such as is used to make bandages. Both the lint and the threads still retained a faint smell of petrol.'

At the word ' petrol ' eyes swung towards Matt Rubens whom all knew to work in a garage. He was staring straight before him. His eyes did not move, nor his tight-closed lips, nor the large hands that gently played with each other on his knee.

' In the early hours of the Tuesday morning a woman walking to her work at a laundry saw a man pushing a barrow in the direction of Despard Street, and she states that on it was something wrapped in, or covered by, a red cloth with a fringe, like a tablecloth. And these—the candle grease, the piece of newspaper, the lint, the threads from a bandage, the smell of petrol, and the statement of this woman are the only clues which the police have had to work on during the last seven weeks. They have taken over a thousand statements from people in this district and elsewhere. Now, of all the people who would have been familiar to the child one alone was known for certain to have been wearing a bandage on his finger at the time of the murder or at any rate up to a few hours before it. Moreover, he was wearing it on the middle finger of his left hand, and if we are to assume that the fragments came from the hand of the man who laid her in the brick dust, then, since they were found under her right arm pit, it is likely that they were dragged from a left hand. This man, Matthew David Rubens, lives in this neighbourhood at the house of his parents in Cartwright Street. Since his return from the army, which he left with an excellent character, he has worked as one of the many hands in a large garage on the main road. The police, of course, questioned him at great length and took away certain things from his home for expert analysis. These things included candles in his room, some lint and bandaging material from his mother's kitchen, a red tablecloth with a ball fringe and certain of his clothes. The candles were found to agree with the stump that lay by the child's side ; the shoes to retain traces of brick-dust and plaster ; and the clothing to be stained with petrol. Other issues of the *Daily Express* lay in a cupboard in his room, but not that of the same date as the fragment found in the debris on the site of the crime.'

Not an eye from public bench or jury box but had swung towards Matt Rubens as the Coroner enumerated these discoveries. ' The only clues '—but surely they were enough to weave the rope for that strong, full neck, now bedizened with big black tie and big pearl pin. What doubt could there be of Matt Rubens' guilt ? He was still staring at the Coroner. He had not moved.

But the Coroner, almost as if he had apprehended this too-ready judgment, began to warn them against it.

' These facts justify some suspicion against Rubens—even, if you like, grave suspicion—but let me remind you, suspicion is not enough. It is conceivable—quite conceivable—that each one of these facts, suspicious though they appear, could be explained as a coincidence : a most unhappy coincidence for this man. We must remember the vast possibilities of coincidence in a crowded neighbourhood like this, where nearly all the people are working folk handling similar materials and where the children play in the streets. Mr. Rubens knew this child and had often spoken to her, but so had a great many others. He seems to have a habit, certainly, of loitering about and talking to children, but he is not the only one to do this ; young men—and older ones—do it, some from the friendliest motives, I am sure, but others, alas, from motives that are secret and dark and shameful. The police receive all too many allegations of this kind of guilty approach. The candles in Mr. Rubens' house agreed with the stump found in the rubble, but so would the candles found in half the houses in this district. And we must not forget that this candle may have nothing to do with the murder ; it may have been left there by some vagrant like the man who found the child. Mr. Rubens had been wearing a bandage, but this is a district where the majority work with their hands, and it is an important point that the Home Office analyst (from whom you will hear) has pronounced that the materials taken from Mrs. Rubens' kitchen are *not* identical with those found under the child's arm. Of course Mr. Rubens may have got a new bandage from some chemist or friend, but we have no evidence that he did in fact do so. His clothes were stained with petrol, yes, but how many friends of little Christina drive vans, have motor cycles, work petrol-driven engines of various sorts, or use petrol to remove stains from their clothes? There were traces of brick dust on his shoes, but this is a bombed area, and how many of its residents cross the rubble-strewn waste places as they go to or return home from work? A man is seen pushing a barrow on which is a bundle, covered with a red cloth, towards Despard Street, but, gentlemen of the jury, in all London I suppose there is no district where, because of the street markets, the rag merchants, and the scrap-metal and waste-paper merchants, and the many second-hand dealers, more men can be seen with barrows laden with strange objects.'

Some titters affronted the silence here, and the policeman on the platform, the coroner's officer, called out 'Silence, please!'

And the Coroner continued, 'Mr. Rubens senior is himself a general dealer and possesses a pony and cart. Finally, three points which seem to operate in favour of Mr. Rubens: first, the woman has been shown the red tablecloth from the Rubens' home and, while thinking it similar to the one on the barrow, she declines to say with any certainty that this is so; indeed she is inclined to think that the fringe is different. Secondly, she has twice been given an opportunity of identifying Mr. Rubens as the man with the barrow, and on both occasions has failed to do so. Indeed, when the police placed her where she could see all the mechanics leaving the garage, and Mr. Rubens who is not an inconspicuous figure—' again the eyes turned to his lofty head with the massed and glossy black hair—' came out with the rest, she declared emphatically that the man she had seen was not among them. And thirdly, not all the researches of the police have produced a single person who saw Mr. Rubens in any place where Christina could have been on that fatal night. . . . Well, there are the facts, gentlemen, and you will see that this case is one of great difficulty, and I must remind you that such verdict as you find must be based, not on things that look suspicious, but on an adequate chain of facts, all proved in evidence before you.'

The silence was complete when his low voice stopped. The people were confused by this entry of doubt, and probably disappointed since they liked things simple and plain and did not like to be deprived of a confident and agreeable indignation.

Fifteen witnesses followed : police with plans and photographs, the parents, the aunt, the tramp who had found Christina, the Divisional Police Surgeon, the famous pathologist, the Home Office analyst, the big detectives, and workmen from Matt Rubens' garage. Of these only two held the eyes of all in a fascinated gaze ; the mother and the pathologist ; the mother as she affirmed, with flooding eyes, that her little girl never spoke to strangers, and that there was no grease on her school uniform when she left to go to the pictures with her auntie because she herself had made her nice and tidy (came a sob at this from the back of the court) ; and the pathologist because he bore so famous a name. With the rest the people were impatient, because they were waiting for Matt Rubens to enter that box. There was a flurry of heads, a stirring of bodies, when at last the coroner's officer called, ' Matthew Rubens.'

§

Smartly, briskly, but with a face as white as the summer dust, Matt Rubens walked to the witness box, all heads swaying to watch him. Some persons even rose from their seats at the back to see him go. Very deliberately he put his black velour hat on his head and took the Pentateuch which the coroner's officer handed him and held it high in his right hand as he said, ' I swear by Almighty God that I will tell the truth, the whole truth, and nothing but the truth.'

He handed the little volume back to the officer, braced his fine shoulders, threw out his breast, and, refusing to glance at the people, bent his eyes on the Coroner. An all-defying expression looked from those eyes. Gesture, voice and carriage were all a little overstressed, but he was an ostentatious man. The blue silk handkerchief peeping from the breast pocket of his jacket, the bright blue shirt, the purple pullover, the jewellery about his person were all on parade for this audience. Only the white face and an occasional drumming of his ringed fingers on the ledge of the box showed that he was less unafraid than he wished to appear.

'Mr. Rubens,' began the Coroner in his soft, courteous voice, 'it is my duty to caution you and to tell you that anything you say will be taken down in writing and may be used against you. You understand?'

'I understand vot you say, sir. Perfectly.'

'It is not incumbent on you to give evidence. You know that?'

'I do, sir. Yes.'

'But all the same, you wish to do so?'

'Zat is so, sir.' His answers were as crisp as a soldier's to his officer.

'Very well. You knew Christina Lancellotti?'

'I did.'

'You have spoken to her sometimes?'

'Many times.'

'How is that, since her parents did not know you?'

He hesitated; looked down; then threw up his head, as one who would say the truth. 'She vos a very charming child, and I was attracted to her. By her beauty, her great beauty. It vos a pleasure just to speak with her.' He confessed this haughtily, as if saying, 'Take that, and make what you like of it; I am not ashamed of it.'

'She knew you quite well by sight?'

'Oh yes. I have played with her in the street. I have picked up her ball and played with her.'

'Now listen to me, Rubens. You will know what I mean. Are you rather given to approaching children in the street?'

'It may be.'

'And has there been gossip about you, and once or twice a complaint from parents?'

'Yes, sir. Zat is so.'

'Why should parents have complained?'

'I can imagine vot they are t'inking, but they would be wrong. I would never have hurt their children.'

'There was nothing at all, then, in all this gossip?'

'Nutting, sir ... Or only that I have been very unwise.'

Father Dawbeny, watching him, heard himself saying, ' This man is speaking the truth. He is innocent.' But he did not know whether to trust these affirmations ; he knew himself, and knew that of late years he had always felt driven to hope the best and plead the cause of the man in the dock, as surely and irrationally as many other men, and most women, were driven to believe him guilty and wish justice on him.

The Coroner was now questioning the witness about his movements on the night of the murder.

' You left your home, you say, about seven o'clock ? '

' Yes, after my tea.'

' Where did you go ? '

' It vos a lovely night, and I went for a walk. I went wandering in the Vest End.'

' Alone ? '

' Alone.'

' Why alone ? '

' I walk much alone. I always have.'

' What time did you get home ? '

' About midnight.'

' Were you wearing a bandage up to a day or two before this night ? '

' I vos.'

' When did you leave it off ? '

' I t'ink—two days before that date.'

' What did you do with it ? '

' Threw it into the fire.'

' One of your workmates declared in evidence, very unwillingly —I had to drag it from him—that you were wearing it on the day of the murder.'

' He vos mistaken.'

' Where did you get the bandage ? '

' From my mother. My mother.'

' And you got no other at any time ? From a chemist or a friend ? '

' I did not, sir.'

' But surely it got very dirty at your work ? '

' I would renew it.'

' But you have just said you didn't ? '

' No, no—pardon—I meant I did not renew it from any source but my mother's materials. I renew it sometimes, of course.'

The words had scarcely left his lips before Mrs. Lancellotti, whose head had been swaying in anguish from side to side, shivered the court by crying out, ' That man is telling lies, sir ! Lies, lies, lies ! '

The coroner's officer by the witness box took two steps towards her but, perceiving whose voice it was, halted.

Father Dawbeny laid a hand on her elbow.

' My little girl,' she screamed, 'my little girl ; ' and, plunging her face into her hands, moaned into them, ' Oh, oh, oh ! ' so loud that the court could not continue. It was as if she was protesting to the court, ' Condemn him. She is dead, and you must find someone to die too.'

Father Dawbeny drew her hand down from her face and held it sympathetically between both of his. His touch and his nearness calmed her, and she just sat there, swaying her head from side to side in a public despair, and letting the sobs tear up her body, behind the huge breasts.

' Mr. Rubens,' the Coroner resumed, ' did you borrow or find or in any way obtain a barrow on that night or the next night ? '

' No, sir. I needed no barrow. Vot for do I want a barrow ? '

' You know, of course, where you could get a barrow if you wanted one ? '

' Yes, sir. There are many places—in Becker Street, in Greig Street, and in the Montebello Road.'

' A barrow could be abstracted from a yard without anyone knowing ? '

' Yes, sir. Easily, I t'ink.'

' There is a yard stacked with barrows—a Mr. Fowler's I think —at the corner of Greig Street and Cartwright Street near your home. You did not take one from there ? '

' No, sir. I needed no barrow.'

' Your father has no barrow, I understand ? '

' No, sir. Only a pony and cart.'

' And you made no use of that, of course ? '

' No, sir. My papa—my father—has already assured the police of that.'

' Would it be possible to take a car from your garage with nobody knowing ? '

' It would be possible, but difficult. And, of course, wrong.'

' Wrong, certainly. Rubens, do you swear that you did not meet Christina Lancellotti on this night ? '

Matt Rubens appeared to have been waiting for this question, or one like it. He picked up the Pentateuch and raised it as high as his head. ' I swear it. May the Lord God of Israel strike me dead, before my father and mother here, if I saw her that night.'

The gesture offended Father Dawbeny to the point of acute discomfort, but he reminded himself that Matt Rubens was no constrained and undemonstrative Englishman like himself, but an Oriental to whom such strong declamation and such striking pantomime were normal things and seemed good.

' And do you swear that you wore no bandage that day ? '

' I swear it.' The book was still held high.

' And that you are innocent of this terrible crime ? '

' Absolutely innocent. As innocent as you, sir, or as anyone else in this room—*so far as I know*.' As he said these last words he turned and swept the public benches with his eyes.

' Very well, then. Thank you, Mr. Rubens.'

The Coroner's summing up was not long. He touched again upon the facts which seemed to direct suspicion towards Rubens, and, perhaps with greater emphasis, upon those other facts which must make them wary of an easy decision. They had no evidence, in spite of a thousand statements taken by the police, that anyone had seen him in the company of the murdered child ; no evidence that he had got a new bandage from any quarter but his home ; no evidence that he had temporarily possessed himself of any barrow, hand-cart or car. ' I am bound to tell you, gentlemen of the jury, that you must not record a verdict of guilty in this case unless you are satisfied beyond all reasonable doubt that these various points which seem to indicate that he is the guilty man form a chain of circumstantial evidence so strong that, were it a matter of business to you, and of serious consequence to you in your affairs, you still could come to no other conclusion. If you are not so satisfied, then there is nothing for you but to record an open verdict of murder against some person or persons unknown. Will you now tell me what verdict you find ? You may leave the box if you wish and retire to your room for your deliberations.'

The jury did not leave the box. They conferred among themselves, their heads nodding wisely, or their shoulders shrugging in doubt, or their eyebrows lifting in despair of a confident answer. And in less than three minutes the foreman, a lean and tidy man in a morning coat, who looked like a draper's shop-walker or a *maître d'hôtel*, rose to speak, but the Coroner, who had been watching them, spoke first :

' Mr. Foreman, have you come to your verdict ? '

' Yes, sir.'

' And how do you find ? '

' We find an open verdict of murder against some person or persons unknown.'

Instantly, sudden as a squall from the sea, an angry murmuring rose from the public benches. A man called out, ' No ! He done it ! Every time ! ' And some excitable women, encouraged by this bold shout, called out too, ' *No !* He's guilty. He ought to hang. It's wicked;' and ' Persons unknown ! Did you ever ? *We* know who done it, and it's that man there.' A low voice muttered, to be echoed by others, ' Dirty Jew.'

' *Silence !* ' roared the coroner's officer on the platform, while the other officer made a menacing approach towards these extraordinary demonstrators. Both officers were shocked. Never before had either seen anything like this in their quiet and seemly court. The loud voice of the one and the approach of the other allayed the momentary storm, but, even before it had subsided, the Coroner, his voice as soft and untroubled as if he had observed nothing unusual, had begun to repeat the jury's verdict and to write it down : ' . . . and we do further say that she was murdered by some person or persons unknown.'

' Rise, please ! ' called the officer by the witness-box. All rose, and their silence was like a broad, hollow vessel waiting to receive what he was going to say. ' O yea ! O yea ! O yea ! ' he called. ' All manner of persons who have nothing further to do before the King's Coroner for this county, at this court, and ye good men of the jury, having discharged your verdict, may now depart hence and take your ease.'

§

The people thronged out, now muttering angrily again. Everyone went, except the jury, who must sign a document, and Matt Rubens, who, standing in the gangway, had picked up a paper from a seat and was reading, or pretending to read it.

Was he afraid ? Afraid of the street ? Was he delaying till the majority of the incited people should have turned homeward ?

Father Dawbeny observed him halted there, and wondered this, but he and Mr. Lancellotti were now supporting Ada Lancellotti, one on either side, as she went out towards the street, throwing back her head and weeping hysterically. 'It's wicked ! It's wicked ! ' she bewailed. 'Is no one to be punished ? Is no one to suffer ? '

Outside Father Dawbeny saw the people waiting, and not only those who had been in court, but a crowd of others, who had been lingering near the doors to learn the issue. Many of these were loutish lads with sour and determined faces. Others were women with turbulent, stupid eyes, hard, shrewish lips, and disorderly hair. He had no doubt that, one and all, they were waiting for Matt Rubens.

'You take her home, Mr. Lancellotti,' he said. 'I must go back for something. I have left something.'

'Alla right, Father. Come along, dearie. If the law don' do its part on him there's plenta others that will—no ? You will see. Come on home.'

Father Dawbeny went back into the court-room. Except for the jury in their box, who were signing their document, one by one, and Matt Rubens, who still stood by his seat alone, the room was empty. It was as empty as a vat from which the strong wine has been drawn, leaving only the dregs.

'Mr. Rubens.'

The man looked up. 'Yes, Mr. Dawbeny ? '

So then he, like all the rest, knew him by sight and name.

'Mr. Rubens, don't think it impertinent of me, but I want you to leave by a side door. It can easily be arranged. There is a crowd out there, and I don't know what they may have in mind to do.'

'I leave by no back door. I have done nutting.'

'Well, then, will you let me go with you ? May we go together ? '

'Vy should you go with me ? I do not understand.'

'Because I think they will stay their hands for me.'

'I look after myself—but I t'ank you. I'm not afraid of nobody.'

'I'm sure you're not. But what can one single man do against a crowd ? '

' If it come to dat, vot can two do ? '

' I think they will respect my cloth. That is something they always do.'

' But you don't want to be seen mit me. I am a dirty Jew. It is just because I vos a dirty Jew that they believe all zis about me from the first. You are a Christian minister ; you don't want to be seen about with a Jew.'

' Don't be absurd. Mr. Rubens, listen to this : some years ago I, too, was wrongly accused, and it was one of your faith that came and stood by me.'

' You believe I am wrongly accused ? '

Father Dawbeny did not know how to answer this with complete truth, so he looked him straight in the eyes and said only, ' I am on your side.'

' I t'ank you. Mr. Dawbeny, you are the first person, except my parents, who has spoken one kind verd to me since the police throw their suspicion on me. I am a Jew, you are a priest, but may I say this as if I vos confessing to you before God : I never done this thing. Before your God and mine, I never done it.'

' I accept that from you, Mr. Rubens.' And, indeed, so far as any man may convince another of his innocence, Matt Rubens had convinced his listener. ' And since that is so, will you not let me walk at your side so as to show them all that I believe you're wronged ? '

' I take no exception to dat, Mr. Dawbeny. No, it is kind of you. I have no objection to dat at all.' Perhaps, despite his brave show, he was glad of it. ' But I am not afraid of them ; not afraid at all.'

' Let us go, then.'

' Yes, let us go. I don' want them to t'ink I am skulking from them. But you're sure they vill not hurt you ? '

' Quite sure.'

' Then I am most villing to have your company. T'ank you. I value very much that you believe in me.'

Together, two men equally tall, they went out on to the pavement. Most of the people, seeing the father at Rubens' side, were so surprised that they made no move. But some of the young roughs surged forward with clenching fists and ugly, glaring eyes. Instantly Father Dawbeny raised his hand. ' Stop ! ' he commanded. It was the harsh, rasped command of a battalion commander in the days of the old dead war. It was sharp, sudden and straight as a bullet among mutineers. It startled him as well as them, so that he changed his tone. 'My dear fellows, don't be stupid and silly lads.'

'He's guilty. He ain't getting away with it. He's the man that done it.'

'Try to be sensible. How can you know that? Can't you see, didn't the coroner tell you, that it's more than possible he's the victim of a terrible misunderstanding? I for one believe he is. Let us pass, please.'

'You believe he's innocent! Come off it!'

'I do. . . . Please . . . let us pass.'

They fell back and made an avenue for them. Laying his fingers gently on Matt's elbow, Father Dawbeny guided him through the staring, frustrated, impotent people, and beyond. And at his side he walked with him to the door of his father's shop, some of the young roughs and hostile women following at a distance, sullenly. There, having shaken hands with him before them all, he turned about and, as they were now close, said to them appeasingly, 'Come along now, all of you. Use your sense. We must all know a lot more before we pronounce anyone guilty. Think what these poor people have endured if he's innocent—as I believe he is. Come, leave them at peace.'

So he drew them away from Matt Rubens' door, but, to save their faces, they grumbled as they came behind him, 'He done it. He done it right enough. And he's not getting away with it.'

CHAPTER THREE

'By person or persons unknown.' Was this to be the verdict for ever? The disappointing close to the story? It seemed so as the weeks passed, and the long silence suggested that Christina Lancellotti was being forgotten. But however hamstrung the police might be, however doubts and scruples might impede the law, the people had brought in their own verdict. Matt Rubens walked in daily peril of grave molestation. But he walked the streets none the less. He still refused to leave the Dale. He still lived with his parents behind the little shop in Cartwright Street, though neither he nor his parents were ever certain that the shop might not be wrecked by hooligans or that a body of men might not come one night to 'take him for a ride.' More than once the shop-front bore in the morning the crudely chalked question, 'Who killed Cristina Lanciloti' and old Lew Rubens would come out with a wet rag to wipe it away.

Neither father nor mother wished him to go, even though his presence somewhere behind the musty old shop was like a maleficent ghost haunting it; even though they were Jews with a love of money and knew that his presence frightened business away. 'He's our boy,' old Lew would say, 'and he's innocent. We know dat, even if all the rest of the verld don't. We are standing in with the boy, even though I lose money, even though I lose one hundert, two hundert pounds. Maybe we have to sink; vell, we all sink together.' And sometimes he would add, 'His mother's sure that God vill do right by him some day. She says she's waiting upon God. I only hope she's right, but I don' know: it don' look to me as though there vos a God or justice anywhere. The minister, Mr. Dawbeny, approves of vot he's doing. He says he reckons the boy's right to stand his ground. It's vot he'd do himself, he says. You know, ever since that day when he come home with Matt from the inquest he's been coming to see us regular and I t'ink, and I say to Mrs. Rubens, I t'ink he goes out of his vay to let people see him coming to the poor old Rubens' home. He'll stand at the shop door and let people see him talking vith me or with Matt. I say to Mrs. Rubens, you'd t'ink we vos members of his congregation instead of dirty Jews.'

No one would employ Matt Rubens. The manager of his garage requested him to leave because the other men had said they would not work with him. They had announced this to a man. Even the workmate who had been so unwilling to provide incriminating evidence about the bandage was over-awed by the others—he was only a lad of nineteen—and he stayed silent, defending Matt Rubens no more. Matt nodded to the manager, said ' I understand,' and walked out. He found work in another garage far away in the East End, but like a faithful hound the story followed him and leapt up at him and licked him. What else could happen since he had refused to change his name ? ' My name is a good name,' he said, ' and I am not ashamed of it. I have done nutting to spoil it. I do not change it. My name is Matt Rubens.' But he had to carry that name, good or bad, out of this garage and out of another. Then he declared he would ask employment of no man any more ; and he picked up a living—not a bad living, for he was an able fellow and had the blood of smart traders within him—as a pedlar of stockings and cheap orna-ments in the big shopping streets. The police had willingly enough granted him a licence, and he was often to be seen with his handsome head and his tray of wares before the great shops of Oxford Street.

Because his profits were not bad he was able to compensate his parents for the blight his presence inflicted on their little business. The business in the shop, never robust, was sick unto death now, but there were people in the Dale and people beyond who were willing to deal with old Rubens when he came with his pony and cart, ' whatever his boy may or may not have done.' So the Rubens family remained solvent and afloat behind the grimy shop window in Cartwright Street. And of an evening Matt would come out of the shop door, tall, well dressed, with head uplifted, to walk the streets, a solitary, sad, defiant figure ; and all eyes would turn to stare at him, but no man spoke to him. His few familiars, if they saw him in the distance, turned quickly and went another way. It was not wise to be seen talking with Matt Rubens. Only Father Dawbeny encountered him sometimes and stayed to talk with him in the public view. Resolutely, and as of right, Matt would push open the door of a public-house and walk up to the counter, but he drank his pint there alone, in the midst of a little island of silence.

§

After a time the matter faded from Father Dawbeny's thoughts. That had happened which evicted Matt Rubens from his mind and kept it tenanted with a bitterness of his own. All day his thoughts were beating and breaking about a heart-sickening but seemingly indestructible fact : the Church Commissioners, after considering the representations and objections lodged by his Parochial Church Council, had certified their approval of the scheme to demolish St. John the Prior's and to sell the site.

This—one could believe no other—was the end. The scheme would go before the Judicial Committee of the Privy Council, and here indeed the incumbent and parishioners would have a further opportunity of submitting their objections, but even if there was any hope that this remote Judicial Committee would be any more sympathetic than the Diocesan authorities or the Church Commissioners, where was the money to be found for briefing counsel ? The congregation had none and the vicar had no more. Certain now, therefore, that St. John's would be extinguished. The Judicial Committee would prepare a bill to be laid on the table of the House of Commons, and after two months, no one objecting, the bill would become law.

In a *Memorandum* to the Commissioners Father Dawbeny and his little council of petty shopkeepers and street traders, plus a lady organist, a verger and his wife, had gathered together all the small objections they could find and offered them as a little sheaf to the harsh face of authority ; they had ' respectfully submitted ' that modern flats would be built by the borough council one day on the bombed sites and the population of the parish be thereby increased ; that even if the congregations were small, the people looked to St. John's for the baptism of their children and the burial of their dead ; that St. Stephen's alms-houses stood in the parish and the seventy old people who lived in them, worthy citizens of the borough, could not, or would not, make their way up the hill to St. Luke's, Ledbitter, or so far as St. Austin's, Lode Street ; that a hundred years

279

ago both site and church had been given by a devoted church-man to the people of the Dale, and it seemed a terrible thing that such gifts should be so lightly regarded and the conditions of those gifts so easily set aside.

These paragraphs of the *Memorandum* had been hammered out by the council in session, but its last paragraph had been written by the Vicar and only acclaimed by the rest. ' We are loyal Church of England communicants,' it said, ' and we appeal to the Church Commissioners to see that our rights are respected and our faith vindicated as early as possible, and we ask them to use their utmost endeavours to see that this siege imposed by the Diocesan Reorganization Committee is raised as soon as possible. Far more people than the Diocesan Reorganization Committee realize, or can realize in the serene seclusion of their committee-room, with their eyes fixed upon a map, and their minds upon statistical or financial arithmetic, have an affection for St. John the Prior's which may not be outwardly demonstrated by their regular attendance at its services, but is nevertheless there. It is difficult to put upon paper in such a way as will impinge upon the Diocesan Re-organization Committee the emotions of shock and distress with which these people view the proposed destruction of St. John the Prior's, Potters Dale, which to them has been and is still, in time of joy and sorrow, a landmark in their lives. *P.S.*—A copy of this letter has been sent to the Diocesan Reorganization Committee.'

But not for many minutes together had the writer of these words believed that they would soften the heart or weaken the will of the Commissioners, and he had even less hope now that they would shake the Privy Council or disturb the House of Commons. And if he was frank with himself he felt, deep in his heart, that the men who would demolish his church and turn its site into good round money had a case difficult to answer. On the surface of things, and as far as good-natured business men could see, St. John's was only one of a thousand churches, all over the country, in working-class areas, for which there was too small a demand.

But even if he felt that the position could not be held against the forces threatening it, he could not bring himself to be the one to abandon it. He must fight for it blindly, hopelessly, unreasonably, romantically. He must fight for it as a mother for a child whom the doctors have given over to death. As he told his Church Council, 'According to the Pastoral Reorganization Measure, these proposals cannot come into operation so long as the benefice is full, unless the incumbent filling it—and that is me—gives his consent in writing. I do not propose to write that consent. (Applause.) So far as I can understand the law it appears to me, ladies and gentlemen, that as long as I stay here this little ship cannot be taken away and broken up. I therefore propose to stay in the benefice, and in the Church Hall, and in your midst, till death us do part. (Loud applause.) I only wish that I were much younger and likely to keep my health for a much longer time. You see, this is what will happen if I go : no one will succeed me ; no captain will be appointed to a condemned ship ; on Sundays and holy days a priest, commonly called a " guinea-pig " (laughter) will be sent to take duty, and this will go on till such time as the shipbreakers are ready to come and tow your church away.'

So he said to them, and they applauded him, but they did not know—it is known to few even now—that the Bishop, the same little bishop who had commended him so highly at the Testimonial meeting—had offered him attractive work elsewhere and a prebendal stall in the cathedral in recognition of his long service to the Dale. 'My dear Dawbeny,' the Bishop had written, 'I am writing to ask you whether you will accept a prebendal stall in memory of your twenty-five years of devoted labours at St. John the Prior's. It is a great pleasure to me to offer you the stall, and I very much hope that you will accept it. I feel sure that it will give great pleasure to your many friends in all parts of England if you do so.'

To this Piers Dawbeny replied, 'My dear Bishop, It would be a pleasure to me to do what would be a pleasure to you. But I couldn't be a prebendary. I shall never forget your kind thought and wish in the matter, but there are many reasons, more than I can put in a letter, why I do not wish to be a cathedral dignitary. Between ourselves, I think my ministry is closing. My age and certain symptoms point to this ; and I want it to close in the service of St. John the Prior's, Potters Dale. I ask only one thing of you, and of those who are so good as to wish me well, and it is this : to let me slow down quietly into the terminus and come to rest on the lines that have held me so long. You will, I hope, think of me as very grateful and take this as final.'

CHAPTER FOUR

NONE knew what was happening to Father Dawbeny in his solitariness now. In the eyes of the world he seemed to be conducting the fight for his church with gaiety and courage and like a man of stable faith. No one knew that in his mind's secret chamber the lights were nearly out. Only hopelessness, or something very like it, sat there in the dark; trust and joy and the quietness and confidence of a faithful man had gone so far away that he could hardly descry them any more. No one knew that, so far from being full of faith, he was feeling like one fallen overboard and near to drowning in a sea of doubt; that in church, in street, in his room, and in his bed, he was keeping himself afloat by clutching and clinging to the words, 'I believe, I believe, I believe . . . help thou mine unbelief.'

It was not that he had any doubt about the ethics of Christianity; his vision was clear as noon on a cloudless day that they alone could save the world from itself; it was the ancient dogmas on which these ethics were based, their sanctions in heaven, that had veiled themselves in black clouds of doubt; one and all of the dogmas: whether there was any God anywhere; whether, if there was, He was a person and a father; whether that young Levantine artisan whom his mates knew as Joshua or Jesus was more than a young man of fine vision and great courage, such as humanity had produced in its thousands; whether there was any purpose in the stars or in the souls of men; and, as a corollary of this, whether there was any Hereafter where he would meet his mother again or where Mrs. Lancellotti, as he had so firmly promised her, would one day find Christina.

These doubts in a priest! In a priest at his altar as he consecrated wafers and wine! In a priest in his pulpit where he must act for his people's sake an unshakeable faith! In a priest in the homes of his people whose faith he must sustain!

They were with him now, these shackling doubts, every hour of the day, but he struggled on with his work and with his fight to save the church ; struggled on, because of that within him which would never surrender nor show fear to the men of his command. Saying no word of all this to any living soul, he walked among the people, gaunt and melancholy and smiling.

§

But one evening, when never had he felt so dead in spirit, when the doubts seemed to be sinking him finally, he was suddenly seized by a desire to take them into his empty church and lock the door on himself and them. It seemed the only place where he could properly pray when encompassed by such despair. His room only exacerbated the despair : the very bareness of the walls seemed the picture of a world bare of meaning ; the very daylight in the room offended the darkness of his soul ; the very sounds made by Ernie and Sophie in their kitchen lunged at his solitariness and seemed to profane it. His heart would stop at each sharp sound ; it would miss a beat, and then beat too quickly. He longed for the peace of a total silence and the balm of a half-darkness.

And another thought : here he stood in the robe of a priest, and he felt naked of faith, naked of hope—only, perhaps, not quite naked of love. To go into the church would express the only sure truth within him : that he *wanted* to be a good priest, that he *wanted* to believe all things and hope all things.

He went quickly out of the room, told Ernie and Sophie that he was going across to the church for a little while, and went down the stairs. The dog had risen to come with him but, bidden abruptly to remain at home, it stood at the top of the stairs, watching him and whining.

It was March, and a low twilight filled the street. He walked, not up the alleyway to the vestry door, but along the pavement to the front of the church and stood looking up at it : its three-arched porch, twin turrets, rose window, and steep roof. An ugly little church of a style long dead and despised, but he'd spent himself and his substance on it. And soon not one stone would stand upon another. How perfect a symbol of his failure.

The doors were locked. 'The church is open from First Mass to Evensong,' said the notice board at his side, and he had closed and locked it, west door and vestry door, nearly an hour ago, after saying Evensong to himself in the empty chapel.

He put his hand into his cassock pocket and drew out the church keys. Opening the door he passed in, and the door shut on a spring lock behind him. Since the vestry door was also locked he felt secluded from all the world, and the grey church with its wan light seemed like an enlargement of his mind's secret chamber into whose dim solitariness he had so often taken his problems or his doubts or his desolation. Because its narrow lancet windows were dimmed by their coloured panes or their London grime the church housed a gloaming deeper than the dusk without. Through this half-darkness he walked up to the altar rail and knelt there. This rail was an alabaster balustrade with tarnished gilded gates leading into the sanctuary. His arm resting on the alabaster and his hands clasped, he gazed for a minute at the altar, then closed his eyes, laid his arms along the alabaster wall, and sank his forehead on to them. '*Eloi, Eloi, lama sabachthani* . . . My God, my God, why hast thou forsaken me?'

How long he knelt there, how often repeated these words, he did not know. They were the only words in all the Bible which seemed strong enough to hold him fast to his Lord. God be praised that the young commander, to whom he had given all his loyalty, had once uttered that cry. '*Lama sabachthani*. . . .' He did not move, save only at times to lift his head from the pillow of his arms and look at the altar and then drop his head to its rest again. And, meanwhile, the half-darkness around him became something very near to the darkness of night.

'O God, what is the meaning of this that thou hast done unto me? Art thou there? Do not let me feel absolutely forsaken. I am not strong enough for that. Give me faith again that thou art there and I have not striven in vain.'

And as he said those words he heard a step. A step between him and the darkness of the altar wall. His heart stopped a beat—with a sickening fall. One such lost beat, it seemed, and he must have died where he knelt. A step? The step of someone who had come from vestry to sanctuary? How could this be? He himself had locked the vestry door. But there *was* a figure there—a tall figure peering through the darkness into chancel and nave. The figure discerned him kneeling there, and approached.

Denys. Denys Flackman. Father Dawbeny sprang to his feet. What was happening? Was he apprehending some danger to Denys far away, and seeing his phantom there? He recalled how he seemed to have heard Christina's cry when she was in danger; heard it at the moment of her death.

But this figure of Denys spoke. 'Father,' he said, 'they told me you were here.'

'Yes?'

'Can I talk to you? I must talk.'

'Of course, my boy. But how . . . how did you get in? I know I locked the vestry door.'

'I've had its key on my ring ever since I acted as your verger.'

Father Dawbeny said nothing. Said nothing because, even in this darkness, he could see that Denys's face was haggard with anguish and grey-white. It was like one of the faces carved on the corbels of the chancel arch.

'I should have returned it long ago, but I didn't. I've always meant to, but I've always forgotten. It's just stayed on the ring with the others.'

'I see . . .' To a youth so distraught he could offer no laughing comment. 'You wanted to see me, Denys?'

'Yes . . . oh, yes.'

'Well, put on the light.' He smiled gently. 'You of all people know the switches well enough. Put on the chancel lights.'

'No . . . oh, no . . . let's talk in the dark.'

'Very good, my boy. Where? Here in the choir?'

'No, no.' He said it almost as if what he wanted to say was unfit for chancel and choir. 'Let's go down into the nave.'

'Come along, then.' They went down into the nave, and Father Dawbeny sat in the front seat of all which was but half a pew because it was unenclosed; it was but a seat with neither hassocks nor prayer-book shelf before it. Denys sat beside him. His head was drooped and his elbows trembling, but for one second he glanced up at Father Dawbeny.

'Well?' The priest gave him an encouraging smile.

'I want to make my confession . . . but I must talk first. May I ? '

' Of course, of course.'

' Father . . . I must speak to someone. And you are the only person in all the world—oh dear, oh God ' —here he sank his face into his hands.

Father Dawbeny laid his hand on the suffering youth's shoulder. ' You have something very serious to confess ? '

' Yes, yes, and you are the only one who'll forgive. You won't understand—you'll never understand—but you'll forgive, I think—only you in all the world.'

' I shall try to understand.'

' I believe God will understand. He can see everything.'

' God will understand.'

' You believe that He is there, and——"

' I know that He is in you now. I know it must be He who is moving you now. Who else ? '

' You are sure ? '

' Yes. I trust my life to whatever is moving you to speak . . . Yes . . . and to whatever, my boy, is filling me now with His love for you.'

' You are wonderful.'

' No, I am not. But the love He pours into us sometimes is wonderful.'

' You believe He will forgive the worst of sins ? '

' I believe it absolutely.'

But Denys did not speak for some time. Plainly he could not speak of some ' worst of sins,' so after a minute, Father Dawbeny said, ' I am a sinner and weak . . . like you.'

' Oh no, no : you don't know *me*.'

' You have always told me all about yourself. I think I know you.'

' I don't know what I should do if you were not here. I have thought of killing myself. If I can save myself at all, it will be because you were here.'

Ever hurt by praise, Father Dawbeny turned his face quickly aside.

And Denys spoke on. ' I should love to have been like you, Father. There's something in me that would have liked to be everything that you are. Instead . . . instead . . .'

' What is it you want to tell me ? Have no fear.'

286

Denys rose from his seat. He walked a few steps away, with his arms shaking at his sides. He returned and faced Father Dawbeny, and now the trembling hands felt for one another, and the fingers fidgeted together.

' Father, I——"

' Yes ? '

' Father, it was I who killed Christina Lancellotti.'

As before when, not ten yards from where he now sat, he had heard Denys's confession, the priest showed no sign of any feeling at all, though the boy's words had been like a bullet against his brain. He said only, and at once, and in an easy voice, ' Tell me all, my boy.'

' I killed her here in the church. In the vestry there.'

So then ! There had been no miracle in that cry. He nodded as one who understood.

' I brought her here to be alone with her.'

' I see.'

' I knew her quite well—though nobody knew this—I used to play with her sometimes in the street. She was so beautiful that I used to like to be near her and talking to her. And I longed to kiss her—kiss her many times—nothing more : I would not have hurt her more. That night I was out in the streets wandering about and hoping to meet some girl who would let me take her to some dark place—you know how I have told you I sometimes feel driven to do such things ? '

' I know, and I understand. I, too, have been young.'

' I—I saw Christina walking home. She was dancing off the kerb and into the gutter and back again. I loved her, Father ; I tell you I loved her. I told her I'd walk home with her and see her safely—oh, my God ! God !—and she seemed pleased and smiled. She was fond of me—and all the time I was wondering where I could take her and kiss and kiss her. I knew she went to your church, and I talked about you, and I bragged that I had the key of the vestry. She said she loved the incense, and I saw my chance at once and told her that if she came with me I'd give her a little for herself to play with. She was pleased and skipped and skipped with pleasure. I brought her here ; and no one, it seems, saw us . . . if you remember, it was a cold night and dark and the streets were empty. No one *could* have seen us, because if they had, the police must have come to see me. But no policeman has been near me from that day to this. Yes, and I was wearing a bandage, but it was not on my finger, it was round my wrist : I'd slightly cut my wrist one day, putting my hand through a broken window : it was the broken window of an empty house where I wanted—but never mind that. I brought her into the vestry and shut the door. And there in the dark I said, " But you must kiss me first," and I caught hold of her and began kissing and crushing her against me madly, and she screamed in panic. I was terrified, and forced my hand over her mouth —no one must hear a scream like that—and she struggled hysterically, and then I realized what I had done, and what people would say I was going to do, and how the story—and I—oh, *no !* '—he turned from Father Dawbeny and ran to the aisle, as if he were running from what he must say.

Father Dawbeny, rising, said, ' Come back, Denys, I am on your side.'

Denys flung himself on to a row of chairs in the aisle, sinking his face into his arms.

Father Dawbeny came and stood by him, laying a hand upon his shoulder. ' Come, Denys. That you are suffering so is good. You are not lost. God still loves you. I still love you.'

' I killed her to save myself,' he mumbled into his hands. ' It was no accident ; I only wish to God it was. I decided in my terror that anything was better than exposure. I had been in the hands of the police once before—years ago. Years ago. I—I—it was a kind of madness of self-preservation. Oh, Father . . . I decided that she must die so that no one would ever know that I—oh, God, I destroyed her life to save mine. I see now that to do such a thing is to be evil—evil utterly. It is the last and worst of sins——'

' No, my son—it is not quite the worst. You did it in terror, not coldly and deliberately. . . . There are worse——'

' No, no, no ! Nothing worse—how can there be ? There is no pardon for me. Not for me. It is too awful what I have done. Not even God can forgive me.'

Father Dawbeny laid his hand upon the boy's head. ' By His authority committed unto me I absolve thee from all thy sins.'

' No, no ; not after this ; not after what I have done.'

' Listen : The son said unto him, Father, I have sinned against heaven and before thee, and am no more worthy to be called thy son. And the father said, Bring forth the best robe and put it on him.'

Denys lifted up his eyes and looked at him as he spoke. Father Dawbeny sat in the chair at his side. The church was quite dark now except for the light of street lamps shining through the uncurtained windows. Denys sat with his head drooped and his hands clasped and quivering.

' But, Father, it comes upon me—I can't live with it—she is destroyed—she is nothing now, nothing at all, and I put her out of existence—just because I was terrified and nothing mattered but myself. Oh, that awful night after I'd left her. I was in terror, I could do nothing but think of her lying there and at last I knew that I must hide her so that she would not be found in the morning. So I stepped out at about four o'clock and took one of those barrows from Mr. Fowler's yard. It was not the barrow which the woman saw, for I covered her with an old grey blanket and my old duffle coat and my waistcoat and an old ground sheet. I hoped it would look like old cast-off clothes on a barrow. And I pushed her through the streets in an awful terror, but whistling and humming most of the way, lest anyone was looking from a window. I thought if any policeman saw me and stopped me I would leave her there and run and climb somehow to a roof and fling myself down on my head. But no one troubled about me. I had thought of those condemned houses in Despard Street where no one ever goes, and I got her there and put her in that ruined cellar at the back. I had brought that piece of candle with me so that I need not turn on the light in the vestry ; it was in my pocket, and before I left her, I lit it and looked down upon her. I felt compelled to do this, so that I should know for ever what I had done. Something *made* me do it. I looked at her for a long time, because I knew there was no one near. I could not easily blow out the candle. Something seemed to be making me fix the sight of her on my mind for ever. And as I looked at her I seemed to know that my life was over too and it could be only a little while before I ended it. . . . How can I live all my life remembering ? I can't. I want to die . . . and soon . . . quickly.'

' Listen : take a little comfort from this. That you can feel like this shows that, whatever you may have done, God is still on your side and fighting for you. We all deface the image of

God in us—you have defaced it—but He is helping you to restore it. He is helping you to rebuild it again.'

'But nothing can restore *her*. . . . Oh God! Nothing can give her back to her mother. And nothing can ever make me forget what I have done. Oh, why didn't I see all this in that terrible moment when I tried to save myself? I saved nobody. I just brought everything to an end.'

'Nothing is at an end whose issue is in eternity.'

'Eternity! Have I to live with this for all eternity? I want to make amends and die. Perhaps if I could make amends I could live with it in eternity. I have thought and thought for days and days, and I think I know what I've got to do. I've got to do it for that man Rubens' sake, and for her parents' sake. I suddenly saw last night that it would ease their pain if the man who did it confessed and was punished.'

'God is indeed working in you, my boy.'

'And last night I thought I would first come and make my confession to you and then, if you said so, I would go straight to the police.' He shivered. 'That would have to be your counsel, wouldn't it?'

'I don't know. Not quite that, I think. I don't think a confessor may order a penitent to convict himself. He might counsel this as reparation, if another man were accused. But if no one was in any danger I think he would counsel him to live a life of penitence for his sin.'

'But Matt Rubens *has* been accused. If not by the police, by everyone else.'

'Yes. That is so.'

'And there is her mother. I want to do what little I can to help her. It's little enough. It may be some happiness to her to know that I couldn't bear what I had done. It all seemed clear to me last night. . . . You have always told me that I must make satisfaction after a confession and undo what I can of my sins. This is all I can do, but I must do it—I want—I want to do it.'

Father Dawbeny remained in thought for a long time; and at last he said, 'My counsel, Denys, will be that you obey the light that is in you.'

Denys shivered at the word, but said, 'Yes. Yes, Father.' And later, for there was still weakness in him, 'That means that I shall die. In a few weeks, in a matter of days, I shall be dead too. There will be no mercy from any jury for me.'

Father Dawbeny offered no easy denial of this, but left a silence between them. And Denys, who had been fidgeting with finger upon finger, ceased and lifted his head. 'When shall I go?'

'Not now. Not to-night. I should like to give you your absolution and then . . . I should like you to go home and give one night more to thought. And in the morning, if you are still sure that God is showing you the only thing to do, come to me.'

'Yes, Father.'

'I shall be waiting for you, and if you like we will go together. But do not come because I told you to. Only if God in your heart tells you to.'

'Yes, Father.'

'And don't think that, if you don't come, I shall think any of the worse of you, or that it will make any difference in my affection for you. As soon as I have given you absolution I shall know nothing of what you have told me. It is God's part to forgive and mine to forget.'

'Yes, Father.'

In that north-east corner of the church, under a dim transept window, where often before he had heard this youth's confession, Father Dawbeny vested himself in surplice and violet stole and extending his right hand over the penitent kneeling at his side, pronounced the absolution and said the Last Prayer, thinking as he did so of what this boy would almost certainly do in the morning, 'May the passion of our Lord supply all the defects of this thy confession; may it supply to thee strength in every good work, grace to overcome all thy temptations, and perseverance until thou reach the land of everlasting life.' And in the morning Denys came to him.

CHAPTER FIVE

It was early, only a little after nine, when he heard the diffident knock at the door of his room. This must be Denys : in the old days he would always walk through the unlatched door of the Church Hall and straight up to the father's room. No doubt he had come early, driven by the thought that if this thing had to be done, it had best be done quickly.

'Come in.' Father Dawbeny made his voice sound as kind and encouraging as he could.

Denys entered. He could have looked no whiter had he been going then and there, pinioned, to the executioner's floor. But he had dressed in his best, his collar clean, his tie carefully tied, his fair hair carefully anointed and brushed. Had his face looked happier he might have been going to his Sunday service or to a wedding. The dog had risen and barked at his entry, but recognized him as a friend of the father's and a companion of his own, long ago in the sacristy, and lay down again.

'Come in, Denys. You have thought it all over ? '

'Yes, Father.'

'And you want to make a clean breast of it ? '

'Yes. I can't think anything else is right. I have tried to, but I can't. I know I shall never feel right again if I don't do it.'

'Have a cigarette.' Father Dawbeny, having risen from his chair, extended his box of cigarettes. Denys took one with shivering, fumbling fingers.

'You look tired,' said Father Dawbeny as he lit it for him.

'I didn't sleep much.'

'Would you like Ernie to bring you a cup of coffee ? '

'Oh, no, no. I want to go. I want to get it over.'

'I'm sure you do.'

'Father, will you tell them why I have not gone to work ? I didn't know what to do about that.'

'I will go and tell them something.'

'And would you—is it asking too much?—would you tell my parents? I haven't dared say anything to them.'

'Of course I will.'

'Break it to them gently before they see it in the papers.'

'I will tell them all that I think of you.'

'Thank you. And give them my love.'

'Yes.' Father Dawbeny smiled so as to appear confident, but within he was recoiling from this heavy, this almost un-liftable, task.

'And, Father . . . I know I am finished, but . . .'

'Yes, my boy.'

'Could I send a message through you to the Lancellottis—that I am terribly sorry—and that I couldn't bear it and gave myself up? I don't know why I feel it would soften things for them, but I feel I am right.'

'I'm sure you are right. I will go to them.'

'Thank you.'

'Denys . . . would you like me to say a prayer before we go?'

'Yes, Father. Yes, please.'

So they knelt together by the long trestle table, still littered with the papers of the parish, and Father Dawbeny, after resting his face in his hands, raised it and said, 'Father of mercy and God of comfort, look down upon this Thy well-loved son——' Upon the words 'well-loved son' he lingered. 'I thank Thee that Thou hast renewed in him whatsoever has been decayed by the malice of the evil one or by the frailty of his young spirit. And forasmuch as he now putteth all his trust in Thee, impute not unto him his former sin, but fill him with strength and courage to do what seemeth to him to be Thy will. Preserve and continue him in the unity of Thy Church and, delivering him from all doubt and fear, lay the light of Thy countenance upon him and give him peace.'

They rose, and Father Dawbeny said to him, 'If you will just go down into the street and wait for me I will follow you.'

'Yes, Father.'

Denys went from the room, and when his steps sounded no longer on the stairs Father Dawbeny lifted the telephone and dialled a number.

The answer was prompt. 'Ledbitter 1119. Police Station. Lutine Street.'

'This is Mr. Dawbeny of St. John the Prior's speaking. Could I speak to Inspector Glower?'

'Yes, sir.' A click in the dark invisible distances, and immediately a voice. 'Detective-Inspector Glower speaking.'

'Good morning, Inspector. This is Father Dawbeny.'

'And good to hear from you, sir.' The pleasant Scotch voice was very cheery. 'After all this time.'

'Inspector, I have a lad here who wants to confess to a crime.'

'Is it anything serious?'

'Very serious.'

'Is it by any chance something that's been in the papers?'

'Indeed it has.'

'I only ask because if it's some notorious case the confession may not be a genuine one. You feel it is, sir?'

'I'm quite sure it is.'

'Well, then, I expect you're right. We always say that you parsons—' and the pleasant voice laughed, its owner all unaware of what was coming to him—'can see quite as deep and possibly deeper than we old cops can. And in any case we shall have to hear what he has to say. Of course, you'll know that we get dozens of people who're a little daft confessing to crimes they've read about but certainly haven't committed.'

'I only wish that were the case here, but——"

'Well, we shall soon know. We have ways of making sure of that. We soon know. The daft ones very soon show that they got their facts from the papers and nowhere else. Ten minutes chatting with them, and we——'

'Look. Could I bring this lad round at once? It would be a kindness to let him get it over.'

'Certainly, Father. Bring him along. I'll be waiting for you.'

Changing his cassock for jacket and overcoat that he might draw no eyes in the street, he went down. Denys was waiting on the pavement, his hands gripping and pressing each other behind his back. Once more Father Dawbeny offered a cigarette, this time from his pocket case, but Denys refused it with a shake of the head and without words. And without words they began to walk northward, in the direction of Lutine Street.

They walked through the dry, clear morning, the March

294

sun bright, but not yet high above the housetops : it cast the house-shadows, long and oblique, across pavement and camber. The long vistas of the streets ran into luminous hazes that were the pale grey-blue of watered milk. The roadways beneath the thrown shadows were ochre in the sun, and every one of them led to the world of sun-flushed freedom for all in the streets—except this boy. He was losing freedom for ever They passed the fat street-sweeper, Mr. Handel, with his truck, who touched his cap and said, ' Morning, sir.' They passed women with shopping baskets or string bags, who said ' Good morning, Father,' and sometimes ' Good morning, Denys,' or ' Good morning, Mr. Flackman.' And Denys would reply ' Good morning,' but there was a catch in his voice as he said it. The morning was good for them, not him.

Once or twice, as they walked on, Father Dawbeny knew that his companion had gulped. All the time he was thinking, ' This boy in his twenties is walking to his death. What can I say that is of help ? Nothing. There are no words. Every word is unworthy.' What he said, he said to God, hardly ceasing from prayer all the way.

They were in Lutine Street now, and Denys gulped again. They came to the five steps of that old grey police station which Connie Beron had once visited to lay an information. Father Dawbeny led the way up them. They encountered Inspector Glower in the long tiled passage between Charge Room and Inspector's Office.

' Oh, there you are, padre,' he greeted them. ' I was waiting for you. Come straight to my room.'

Like Connie Beron they followed down the corridor, through the large C.I.D. office, and so to the door marked ' D.I.'s Office.' The Inspector ushered them in and came after them, shutting the door. He went to his chair behind his desk, saying, ' Sit down, Father,' and ' Sit down, son.' And when they were seated, Denys on the chair this side of the desk and Father Dawbeny on the one against the wall, the Inspector said to Denys, ' Well, what is on your mind, old chap ? '

' God help him, help him,' prayed Father Dawbeny.

' I want to confess to a murder—the murder of Christina Lancellotti.'

Father Dawbeny saw that the police officer was as well-trained as he to hide all surprise and shock. ' Wait, son,' was all he said. 'Do you really mean this? You realize what it involves?'

'Yes, sir.'

'I must then formally caution you. You know you are not obliged to say anything . . .' and he continued with the familiar words.

'I understand, sir.'

'Very good, son.' He rose, went to the door, and called, 'Sergeant Baily.'

'Yes, sir,' answered a brisk, untroubled voice.

'Come in, will you please. I want you to take down this young man's statement. Padre, I think you'd better leave us, if you don't mind.'

Father Dawbeny, rising, laid an encouraging hand on Denys's shoulder and passed to the door. The Inspector went through with him into the C.I.D. office and there explained, 'He'll speak more freely, if he's alone.'

'I may wait?'

'Surely. Wait here. Sergeant Cutler, look after the padre, won't you. It's not the cheeriest room in London, a C.I.D. office, sir, but these are good fellows—or some of them are—and they'll do anything for you. We may be an hour or more, though these chaps who volunteer confessions are usually much quicker than others. They're so full of it that they speak faster than we can get it down.'

'I will wait.'

This Sergeant Cutler, a burly, friendly fellow, brought forward a chair from the only unoccupied table, and Father Dawbeny sat on it against the wall, by the door of the D.I.'s office. He sat there for an hour and a quarter. At first, thinking of nothing very clearly, he gazed round the room, at the cream walls, the green-shaded lamps, the large notice board hung with papers, the detectives' little tables, and the high windows with their lower panes frosted to obscure the irrelevant activities of the uncriminal world. Like Connie Beron he noticed the branched coat-hanger in its corner and its crowding assortment of overcoats and hats, and he thought of the duties these detectives would go out to when they put on these garments again—sly, secret duties, but necessary to the peace of the State. He watched the big clock above the notice board ticking the past away, its rhythm as regular as the clit-clatter of the detectives' typewriters.

Ceaseless, this industrious chatter of the typewriters, like the chattering of teeth in a deathly air. Then, thinking of what was happening on the other side of this wall behind him, and how Death was a fourth presence in that room, he prayed and prayed for his spiritual son who was taking Death by the hand, and hoped that the prayer might somehow brace and uphold him, through the wall. 'Help him, help him. . . .'

He remembered his next duty, to carry the catastrophe to Denys's parents, and his heart, recoiling, began a sickly beat. He felt pain there, and the timid valetudinarian, who was always within him, wondered how long he had to live. God grant that he did not drop dead for a few months yet—not till he'd done all this boy's business and helped him through. . . .

After an hour Sergeant Cutler brought him a cup of tea and a cake, and said, 'Do smoke, sir, if you'd like to.' But he declined, smiling. To interest him, the Sergeant took him to the finger-print apparatus by the far door and showed him the printed form for the impressions, the copper plate, and the finger-print ink. For the fun of it he took the father's impressions, wiping his fingers with a petrol-damped cloth and when Father Dawbeny presented his thumb above the ink-filmed plate, exclaiming, 'Why, you know all about it ! Have you done it before ? When was you last " in " ? No, I'll press. Not you. No, chaps, he hasn't done it before. For a minute I thought you must be an old client of ours. There you are, sir. There are your dabs. Would you like to keep them for a Christmas card, or shall I tear them up ? '

His offer rejected with a smile, he tore them up, laughing, and Father Dawbeny went back to his chair.

The clock had registered an hour and eighteen minutes when the door of the D.I.'s office opened, and Inspector Glower emerged, like a doctor coming from an invalid's room. 'Well, sir,' he said, as the father rose, 'I propose to detain him but not charge him yet. I just want to make a few further inquiries to verify all he's told us. You said you'd like to have a word with him before I take him to the cells ? '

' Please. If I may.'

' Come along then.'

Denys was standing before the Inspector's desk, his task accomplished. On the desk was the written statement, the death warrant, which Denys had initialled and signed with his own hand. And now his whole body was shaking, and the death-to-be, as if already practising its handiwork, had drained all blood from his face. His eyes looked unusually large in the stone-grey face, as he turned them to the father. So clean-cut and handsome that young face, and it was for the discard to-morrow.

Father Dawbeny took his hand. 'This isn't good-bye, Denys. I'm told I can come and see you as often as I like. That is so, isn't it, Inspector?'

'That is so, sir.'

'Thank you, Father. I feel much happier now.' But he stuttered as he said it.

'Leave everything to me. I will see to everything for you. I will go now to your father and mother and do everything for them, and I will tell them it was you that sent me to do every-thing. And every morning at Mass—remember—I shall be offering it for you. Remember that.'

'I will, Father. Yes, I shall like to think that.'

'Just till to-morrow, then. Keep a stout heart. You have done the right thing, and God is with you all the rest of the way.'

CHAPTER SIX

WHEN Denys was condemned to death, and the news received with applause in the Dale, people saying, 'Well, thank heaven for that,' and 'Yes, but hanging's too good for him,' then Father Dawbeny set out alone for the little home of the Lancellottis in Platnam Street. He found them at home in their front room : it was evening. They were sitting in the same two wicker chairs, on either side of the fireplace, as when he had come to them after Christina's death. Polo Lancellotti got his little body out of his easy-chair that he might offer it to this visitor, but, as before, Father Dawbeny declined it and, drawing a chair from under the dining-room table sat on it between them. Glancing above the mantelpiece, he noticed again that blank, unfaded space where once the enlarged photograph of Christina had hung so proudly. Not yet had the parents felt able to replace it. It was upstairs, hidden, with its face to a wall.

'No, let the father have the comfortable chair,' protested Ada Lancellotti, and Polo rose again. 'He looks absolutely wore out.'

'I am quite happy here,' smiled the visitor, and Polo sank back into his cushions.

Mrs. Lancellotti pressed on to the arms of her chair, as if to lift her large heavy figure out of it, and the chair creaked under her great weight. 'Would you like me to nip out and make you a cup of tea, Father ? You look that tired. It wouldn't take me above a minute.'

'No thank you, Mrs. Lancellotti. I am not so tired. I've just been sitting in the Old Bailey. You've heard the result of the trial ? '

'Yes.' Her tone had changed at once. It had been full of friendliness for him : now it held only a hard steel hate for the man condemned. The expression on her big face had changed with it : from a sympathetic solicitude to a dour enmity. 'Mrs. Brookfield come in and told us.'

'Have you read any accounts of the trial ? '

'No, and I don't want to.'

'No, we don' wanna see any of da papers—*ma no!*' agreed Polo, who in this matter of resentment was an echo of his wife, but a softened echo.

'Well, just let me tell you a little about the trial. Only a little. It was a very strange trial because he refused to let his counsel call any witnesses or to speak in his defence. So it was all over very quickly. The counsel for the prosecution told the whole story according to the prisoner's statement to the police, and then the defending counsel just stood up and said he'd had a long talk with his client, but his instructions were definite, that he was to put no argument before the court and to call no witnesses. That made only one verdict possible. There was nothing for the jury to do but to find him guilty and nothing for the judge to do but to sentence him to death.'

'And I wish,' said Mrs. Lancellotti, from squared lips, her body unmoving, 'that he could die a thousand deaths.'

'Yes, a t'ousand,' said the echo.

'Now, I want you both to try not to think like that any more. He has made what reparation he could.'

'What's the good of that?' demanded the woman. 'It won't give Christina back to me.'

'No, dat's true enough. Reparation's justa no possible after murder.'

'Yes,' she hissed. 'Let him keep his reparation. It ain't no use to me.'

Father Dawbeny sighed. The obstacle before him seemed immovable and insuperable. On the black woollen hearth-rug at his feet was a single loose strand of the black wool, and he picked it up and twisted it, his elbows on his knees. And at last he said, 'He was deeply penitent. I have seen him nearly every day in prison, and I know that, whatever he was before, he is a bad man no more. I am going further; I am going to say that now he is good.'

'Ah, *no!*' cried the woman indignantly, and for a moment he feared she was going to break like a sky-rocket into one of her frenzies; in which case he might abandon the hard but lofty boon he'd come to seek, for she would listen to reason no more. 'Good! I like that! No, I don't listen to that, even from you, Father. No, no, *no!* A man who can do a thing like what *he* did can never be good.'

'That's where you are wrong, my dear,' he said in his gentlest voice, to stay the threatening storm. 'Have you been one of my congregation all these years and not learnt anything from me? Haven't I tried to show often and often that the sinner whom God breaks down is often His best material for making something good. Have I failed so badly?'

'You haven't failed, Father. *Ma no,*' Polo made haste to comfort him.

'It's a bit late to be good now,' grumbled Mrs. Lancellotti. 'It won't bring Christina back.'

'Yes, it's a bitta late,' said Polo. 'It's alla a bit too late now.'

'Do you know: all the prison officers, from the Governor downwards, though they had nothing but hatred for him at first, have little but pity for him now?'

'Let them. They didn't lose their child.'

'No, it's a easy for dem, ha? Yes, I t'ink so.'

'Yes, it's easier for them. Mrs. Lancellotti, it was you he had in mind when he gave himself up. He thought that if he took his punishment, it would comfort you.'

'They'd have got him in any case.'

'I doubt it. Even if they'd found any reasons to suspect him—and they didn't!—there was no real evidence against him except what he provided. No one had ever suspected for an instant that the crime was done in the church. The church was locked, and no one knew—*I* didn't know—that anyone else but Ernie and I had a key. He gave himself up to help you and to save the man Rubens. That was something, wasn't it?'

She shrugged unwillingly. 'Something, I suppose. But where's my little girl?'

Father Dawbeny sighed again, because of the difficulty of his task: no blow of his pick would make the rock-face yield. He continued fiddling with the strand of black wool. He tied it into knots and untied it. 'Mrs. Lancellotti and you, Polo—if I may call you that——'

'Calla me what you like, Father.'

'Thank you. Polo . . . and Ada . . . I had an idea when I came to you this evening. Directly the trial was over, I was surrounded by newspaper reporters who wanted what they called a "story" from me. They had known, of course, ever since the hearing at the magistrate's court, that Denys had come to me first and that we'd gone together to the police, and now that they were free to write what they liked about the case they wanted all I could tell them. I managed to escape from them without saying anything, but ever since I got home, they've been ringing me up with the same request. I've been refusing them but all of a sudden this idea came to me and I got in touch with them again and told them they could come and see me this evening. They'll be with me in about an hour from now.'

' Whatta was de idea ? ' asked Polo, who was more capable of dispassionate interest than his wife.

' I thought I would give them a story that would surprise the world. And help the world.' He turned towards the mother. ' But I can only do this with your help.'

He saw some curiosity in her eyes, even though she gave him no encouraging word.

He put out a hand and touched her. ' Do you want your little girl's death to be of help to the world ? Wouldn't you like to feel that we brought some good out of her death ? '

' How ? ' The syllable was low and hoarse, her voice sounding as it had sounded when she had said, ' Find the man that killed him.' It was hoarse and hostile.

' Let me try to explain.' He paused while he raked for words and assembled them. ' Human nature loves vengeance, doesn't it ? That is plain for all to see. It's first leap is always for some weapon of retaliation. But the extraordinary thing is that there is also something in human nature which can fall in love with the very opposite of vengeance. With compassion and forgiveness and the magnanimous refusal to deal in evil, even if your enemy does. Don't you think it quite extraordinary that whenever the great saints—of all religions—have set up this ideal, the people have always bowed before it and worshipped it, whether or not they've obeyed it ? Don't you think that's proof that while human nature loves vengeance it can't worship it ; it can only worship the exactly opposite idea, that one can only overcome evil with forgiveness and with good ? '

' If you're trying to suggest . . .'

' I know, I know, my dear.' Again he laid a hand upon her arm. ' One's vindictiveness is so very, very difficult to overcome. But it *can* be conquered. It *can* be exchanged. *You* know that. You were among the few who remained with me when I preached against treating our enemies as they had treated us, and so many of my congregation left me. You stayed. You didn't go from me. Do you remember ? '

' Yes.'

' It is a wonderful moment in life when you fall in love with this new and better ideal. You are so much happier because so much of your bitterness falls away, and a measure of understanding comes in its place. . . . Yes, it is one of the most difficult, but, when done, one of the happiest things, to forgive.'

' Are you asking me to forgive this man ? '

' I am, dear; and more than that. I want to ask a great thing of you. Of you both. For Christina's sake. That her death may bring forth good.'

' What is it ? '

He hesitated because it seemed so much to ask of them. And because it seemed so much, he could not look straight at them, but kept his eyes upon his fingers and the twisted wool between them. When his words were ready, he said, ' I want an example from you before which the people can bow. Whatever people may do, or may not do, I know that in their heart of hearts they will bow before a compassion large enough to pity and help a man who has killed your child.'

There was silence. They offered no resistance, and he wondered if he was moving them.

' But what I want to ask of you is more for the world's sake than for his sake. I have little hope that he can be saved from death. The world is not ready, its people are not tall enough, to deny themselves the blood of a man who has killed a child. But even so, and chiefly for the world's sake, as I say, I want to start a petition for his reprieve, and I want to tell these reporters in an hour's time that the first two names, heading it, are Christina's mother and father.'

They were staring at him, but they offered no immediate or indignant refusal, and he prayed within himself, ' O God, give them to me. With Thee all things are possible.' And he went on, ' I want to tell them that you said, " One death is enough." That you said you knew he had repented and you wanted him to have a chance of repairing his life. That you said you wanted to do what you could to save another mother and father—*his* mother and father—from suffering what you have suffered. That you said, " One such suffering is enough." '

Now he looked up at them ; and still they did not say No. Could this mean that, though they were not yet able to say Yes, they were no longer able to say No ? He prayed passionately within, steadily, importunately, hammering at the Gates of the Kingdom, to get them in : ' With Thee all things are possible. With Thee all things . . . .' Aloud, and with eyes averted from them, he said :

' I am quite sure this action would be spoken of everywhere and praised by nearly all and so do its little to help our poor, half-blind, and blundering world. It would sow its seeds here and there, in places that will never be known to you. At the present moment, Ada—and Polo—you have the power to teach the world something. Christina gave it to you as she died. Don't let it lie unused. Use it for her sake.'

Waiting, and wondering what else he could say to persuade them, he noticed again that blank space above the mantelpiece. And, looking up at it, he asked of Mrs. Lancellotti : ' Am I wrong, my dear, but wouldn't you be able to bear Christina's picture again, if you could always think, as you looked on it, that her death brought, here and there, a little more goodness into the world ? '

' Well . . .' she began a little grudgingly, because one does not like to abandon a resolution too quickly, ' Of course I'd like to think that. Naturally.'

' Will you do it ? May I let it go forth that you did this ? I feel it would do more good than all the sermons I have ever preached.'

It was then that Polo said, ' Lets'a do it, Mother. Lets'a do what the father say. He's right. Dere's been evil enough. Dere's no sense in hurting nobody any more.'

But it was a very long time before Mrs. Lancellotti spoke ; to Father Dawbeny, sitting there, it seemed like a long half-hour, though probably it was no more than six or eight charged and over-full minutes. He sat there hoping that the very length of the pause meant she was not quite as adamant as she had been. And at last she said with a sigh, and with no full conviction showing as yet—this, he believed, would come with time : ' All right. . . . If you think it's right. . . . if you think it'll do any good. . . . Yes, for Christina's sake. . . .'

Father Dawbeny hurried home to his upper room, hurrying with the happiness of something accomplished ; and there he gave the reporters a story that, in its own way, rang about the world.

CHAPTER SEVEN

DENYS made no appeal against his sentence, and there was no reprieve. Even though the story which Father Dawbeny had told the correspondents was tossed about the world and touched the hearts of some, breaking ground here and there for finer seeds, there were not many who were ready to say with Christina's parents, 'One death is enough.' As Father Dawbeny had said, the people were not tall enough yet to disclaim the blood of a man who had killed a child; and the function of the Home Secretary was to express the people's will.

So Denys died between the platform and the pit. Father Dawbeny, by special consent of the Prison Commissioners, was with him every day of the three weeks before he died, and stayed a long time with him on the evening which was the vigil of his death. And the next morning he rose early to be with the father and mother at the hour when their son had this early appointment with justice and death.

Because of this remarkable story of a petition for clemency led by the murdered child's parents, and because of his daily visits to Denys at the end, the name of Father Dawbeny was once again in every newspaper; indeed it won a wider circulation now than ever before; and up on Ledbitter Hill, the Rev. Oliver Custance commented to his intimates in slightly brackish tones, ' Some people certainly have an astonishing talent for getting into the news. Dawbeny never seems to be out of it. If it's not one thing, it's another. How does the man do it? It's not a talent I've ever possessed myself, and I don't know that I particularly want to.'

Which, of course, was absurd, because there was nothing he would have liked better.

And Mr. Custance went on: 'Years and years ago I told him to turn away that boy because he was a wrong'un, rotten through and through. But he thought himself far too clever for that. And now see what has happened.'

This succouring of Denys and his parents was almost the last act of Father Dawbeny's twenty-five years ministry in the Dale. The strain of that last visit to the condemned youth, when he struggled to keep Denys's heart filled with the comfort and even happiness of his faith, and his young unsteady hand in the strong grasp of God, was almost too much for him. It drained him of his own strength, and he came out of the prison into a street too bright beneath the sun, with his breast like an empty chamber and his heart beating unnaturally. He slept hardly at all, and in the morning he had to go and give more —more than his body and spirit seemed to hold—to the mother and father.

He discharged his week-day duties and conducted his Sunday services for a few weeks more, and then one night—a night which held all the midsummer beauty in its arms and crowned it with stars and a fine moon—he said to Ernie and Sophie, ' I think I shall go for a long walk, the night is so lovely. Don't sit up for me.'

' Right you are, Father,' said Ernie. It was not strange for the father to take a long lonely walk through the streets of London at night. ' We'll be making for bed. You can have the night, Father, so far as me and Sophie are concerned ; have it and keep it.'

' Thank you, Ernie. I will. Good night. Good night to you both.'

' Good night, Father.'

The dog stood waiting, panting, with a high hope. His master summoned him and together they went out into the warm air and the moonlit and murmuring dark.

Father Dawbeny walked towards the bright glow in the east. Eastward from the Dale, but in the language of the Dale, ' up West.' He wandered, as he often liked to do, about that blithe and brilliant fairground, London's West End, looking at the laughing theatre crowds who could not be other than lively on such a night as this, and at the young people, dressed for self-display and gaiety, alighting at the vestibule of dance hall or night club. He trod the sober pavements of Pall Mall and St. James's Street, looking up at the great Italianate façades of the London clubs which once had known him so well. They were mostly closed now and darkened for the night. And so at length he came homeward along Piccadilly, now almost empty except for the women in the shadows. He and the dog walked along the broad, quiet thoroughfare from lamplight to lamplight. It was long past midnight when he left the sleeping parks behind him and reached the stilled and emptied streets of the Dale, with the dog trotting unwearied at his side.

And as he came along Greig Street and saw his little condemned church, the thing happened. Without warning of any kind, without preparation, without graduation, there possessed him an extraordinary, inexplicable, irrational sense of joy, contentment and peace, a sense so real and active as to be an ecstasy. His body might be walking in a dark street, but his mind or soul was immersed in light.

No words in being could contain the moment. The light seemed one with bliss, and one with knowledge. Knowledge? Aye, a certitude that behind all the warring elements of this world there was one thing only and it was Love; that the final good of all was assured; and that the existence of his basic soul in the bright stillness of eternity was as sure and undeniable as his existence in this grey, dark Greig Street now.

He had often read of this experience. 'Illumination' the mystics of a dozen faiths called it, or 'Recognition.' 'The Brahmic Splendour,' said the Hindus; or 'The Brahmic Bliss.' But he knew also that it sometimes ushered in the onset of the epileptic's fit and that something of a like character could be induced by opium or hashish, so he had never been sure whether it was an illusion or a glimpse, Heaven-granted, of the Ultimate and the Immutable—never till this moment when he could no more doubt its truth than he could doubt his existence and still live.

'If I doubt this, I must doubt everything.' It seemed like a Heaven-granted answer to all those terrible despairs which had so nearly laid him low, only it did far more than merely balance them, for they had been incomplete, but this was complete. It was more complete than anything he had ever known, even more complete, if such a thing were possible, than his consciousness of himself and his belief in the word 'I.'

It may have lasted a second, ten seconds, this visitation, this possession; he had not crossed three flags of the Greig Street pavement before it was over and he was as he had been. But the afterglow was in him, suffusing memory, and he felt a need to be alone with it, in a darkness and on his knees. So he drew the church keys from his pocket and, opening the West Door, turned in ; and the dog followed him. That no one might disturb him, he closed the door, and it locked behind him. He put on no light. Light would have offended this exultation just as, before, it would have affronted his despair. And in any case the church was light enough for him to see his way because the high moon was shining through all the windows on the south side. The single lamp in the sanctuary, burning gold like a single eye, called them towards it, and he and the dog walked up between the shadows of the pews to chancel and sanctuary rail. Here at this alabaster balustrade he knelt on the communicants' step, almost in the same place as when Denys had appeared like a ghost in the sanctuary. The dog, taught to be quiet in church, lay down on the chancel carpet at his side, with his sooty jowl between his extended paws. Sometimes he closed his bloodshot eyes; sometimes he opened them to look at his master.

The church might be dark, but Father Dawbeny, with his eyes shut, saw only light—the afterglow of that light which had seemed one with bliss and knowledge. He was unspeakably happy. ' Where is happiness like this ? ' But words were not possible. They belonged to some world in Time, and this light belonged to no earthly place and no earthly time. He was understanding now, as never hitherto, the stories of saints who had prayed on their knees through a whole night and yet spoken no word. His arms lay along the alabaster wall, and he left his head upon his hands.

§

Perhaps an hour later the dog rose and came towards the kneeling figure. He looked at it but did not dare to bark, and instead lay down a little closer to it. The summer night wore on, and the moon, going to its bed, left a midnight darkness in the church. The dog, anxious, rose and put his feet on the alabaster rail, wanting to lick his master's face. He could not reach it, and lay down again. And he watched by the kneeling figure, the only light to help him now being the sanctuary lamp in its hanging cup, a single golden fleck, sometimes astir. He watched for a quarter of an hour, half an hour, and at length, dissatisfied, put his paws on the rail again and, stretching his great head along his master's arm, licked his cheek. His master did not respond. He did not move. And the dog lay down again.

For a long time, lying there, he did not dare to howl. This was the church, and he had been trained to keep quiet and still in church. But gradually his distress became too great, and he broke the habit of a lifetime by emitting a low whine, and then, gently, a howl—a low howl such as was perhaps permissible in this place. A grey hint of daylight visited the church and, the distress overturning the last of his discipline, he cried to Heaven—but no one heeded. Ernie and Sophie slept across the alley, and if his intermittent howling worked into their dreams, well, the sound of a dog baying the moon, or complaining in a kitchen yard, was no unusual night-sound in the Dale. The forlorn crying drew a policeman and his torch across the road to the church doors. He tried them, found them locked, and muttered to the silent street, ' Dog shut in there all right,' but he saw no reason to bring anyone from his bed at so dark and cold an hour, for the night had turned cold as it met the morning. The morning was at hand.

§

And when the sun was high enough, and the day's work was beginning, this policeman's ' relief,' who had come on the beat at six o'clock, knocked on the door of the Church Hall.

This constable, waiting at the door, was P.C. Baldry, a familiar and popular figure in the Dale. A big man, heavy with fifty years, thirty of them spent in the Force, he was still no more than a constable because he had never been able to pass the examination which would qualify him for promotion but which required such impossible skills in composition and arithmetic and such excessive information in geography and general knowledge. But, as Inspector Glower had once said to Father Dawbeny, he was ' one of those seasoned old cops who are the salt of the earth and the real mixing grit of the Police Force, because he knows every bad lad in the division—and every bad lassie too—and (rather like your God) lets his friendliness shine alike on the just and the unjust.' P.C. Baldry was very big because his enlistment went back to the misty days when police had to be tall, and 'Big Baldry' was his nickname among his mates, and, of course, 'Jumbo' and 'Tiny' among his clients in the streets or the cells. Many were the jokes in the station canteen and in the streets about his size and his comparative senility.

Ernie, in flannel pyjamas, opened the door to him, saw the blue helmet and broad blue breast and immediately exclaimed, 'Caw-lummy, what'a we done now? No, I didn't do the job, straight I didn't, guv'nor, I been in bed with my missus all night. Ask her. It wasn't me. It was the other chump.'

To this P.C. Baldry replied, 'Very funny. Very funny, mate; ever so witty; Dan Leno ain't in it with you; but that don't alter the fact that there's either a dog or a ghost shut up in your church. Listen. You ain't buried anyone under the floor who's a bit restless—have you? Listen.'

Ernie listened and P.C. Baldry listened, but, as so often happens when one asks another to listen, no sound came.

'Just wait,' begged the constable.

And then the dog's unhappy howl beat against the church wall. It was like a voice crying for someone to come.

'There y'are!' said Mr. Baldry triumphantly. 'There it is again.'

'Well, how's that?' said Ernie, amazed. 'I locked the church myself. But you're right, guv'nor. And it sounds like our Squaller. What time is it? Hah' pass five?'

'Fifteen minutes after seven.'

'After *seven*?'

'That's right. And you ain't outa bed yet. You vergers do lead the cushy life. Wonder you trouble to get up at all.'

'Seven; and what day of the week, is it?'

'Friday, o'course. What d'you think?'

'Friday and fifteen minutes past seven. Oh, well, I won't wake the father yet because he's not taking Mass till eight. There's the dog again.'

'Shouldn't it ought to be got out, hollering like that?'

'Beats me how it got in,' laughed Ernie. 'But wait a mo and I'll get the keys.'

He ran upstairs for his keys, and for his trousers and a jacket, and then the two of them, one tall and heavily rounded, the other small and half-dressed and limping, walked together to the West Door. 'Yes, locked,' said Ernie; and he put in the key, and pushed open the door.

At the sound of the key, and of the door's creak, the dog ran to meet them. The look in his sad, bloodshot eyes was full of appeal and he led them, impatiently halting and turning his head, towards the chancel. The sun was now shining through the East Window and by its ample light they saw the kneeling figure with its head upon its arms. Straight to its side went the dog, and then turned its inquiring, appealing eyes upon them.

Frightened, very frightened, Ernie went close too and said, ' Father ? '

No answer.

He touched the father's shoulder but drew no more response than if he'd touched the clouded-amber top of that low alabaster balustrade. The dog whined.

' Could he be in a trance ? ' he asked, not daring to ask a larger thing.

The policeman, trained in first aid, touched the kneeling man's hand, shivered away from the touch, for the hand was colder than the alabaster on which it lay, and then felt for the radial artery at his wrist.

'He's dead,' he said. 'His body is cold.'

' Oh, no ! ' pleaded Ernie. And the dog, as if listening and understanding, looked up at them and whined louder.

' Afraid he's dead,' repeated the constable. ' I'm sorry, mate. He must'a been gone some time now. To be so cold.'

' Gone ! Father Dawbeny ! '

' Yes, he's gone. He's passed on. We've had him.'

' Oh, no ! ' Ernie's mouth began to shake, and his breast too. ' Oh, no ! '

The constable saw this taut trembling, and tried to comfort him. ' Never mind, mate. He ain't suffered ; you can see that. It must'a been his heart, I expect ; and it's a grand way to die. He's gone where the good men go, you can be sure of that, because if ever there was a good man, it was 'im. One of the best. One of the absolute very best.'

Ernie turned and looked at him. ' I know. He was my colonel in the Great War,' he said.

CHAPTER EIGHT

All this happened not very long ago, and the people of the Dale remember it well; indeed it will be a long time before they forget it and cease to talk of Father Dawbeny. Many good men, many good priests, have served their neighbours well and died, and no legend has lived after them, but there were many seeds from which the legend of Father Dawbeny of Potters Dale could spring and flourish. News of his death had hardly swept like spores upon the wind into every home, shop, warehouse, and factory before the legend began. There was the strange fitness of his death—alone, on the steps of his own sanctuary, and with his face to his altar. The Dale has its good people as well as its sinful ones, and both tribes are very sentimental; the sinful, probably, the more exceedingly sentimental of the two. Thus the whole of the Dale was ready to declare that he had worn himself to death in the service of his church and parish, and that the blow which killed him was the sentencing of the church which he had loved to demolition. Then there was the dog, and he was perhaps the most potent collaborator in the creation of the legend—the dog which had been the only friend and watcher by the side of him who had so often ministered to the death-beds of others; the dog who had sounded his only passing-bell all through the night, and in the morning summoned helpers and guided them to his side. Then there was the great and crowded funeral service and the words of the Bishop, which all said were 'unforgettable'; and, after it, the wonderful procession through the streets of London, when they took Father Dawbeny from Potters Dale, with clergy and choirs and singing, on one of his own coster's barrows. And there was the hymn, so unexpected and yet so strangely apt, which the procession sang through the streets. Lastly there was the book, the life story of Father Dawbeny, which Ben Ostrion published; but it is a question whether the book would have had so wide and enduring a public, without that death at the altar step, and the dog, and the barrow.

§

Within the ringed boundary of the Dale the news of his death, quite unexpected, fell upon the people almost as the announcement of a prince's death might fall upon his little principality. People everywhere, who had hardly given a thought to him for years, now felt as if they had lost a father whom they had loved. They could not understand why their sorrow was so poignant and so personal. Women—and some men, too—could not understand why they had to wrestle with tears, and why their voices tripped and were treacherous, as they spoke of his death to one another, on the pavements, at their thresholds, and by the shop-counters.

For two days and nights the coffin lay on trestles in the chancel under a black and white pall on which rested the father's biretta. Tall candles gleamed about it, and the flowers stood massed against the choir stalls and along the chancel steps. The stale, dusty air hung heavy with their scent. Since the Dale was a kingdom of street traders, many of whom sold flowers and fruit, some fifty or more of them were their own best customers that day, and some of their offerings were large indeed. One of them, from the Potters Dale Street Traders Association, was in the form of a huge cross—and this, it must be thought, was more of a compliment to his faith and practice than a statement of their own. Other tributes were but small —cheap wreaths or little bunches of flowers—but the cards attached to them often carried the simple poetry of the London streets. One said, ' To the Father, from a backyard in his Dale ' ; and another, written in a clumsy, illiterate and slightly disguised hand: 'From one who been in prison and you give him work. Goodbye, Father.' No one knew whose this was; not even Sophie. Ernie knew. The official wreath from Mr. and Mrs. Matters was something very much larger. It was one of the largest of all.

Towards mid-day on the Wednesday, which was closing day in the Dale, Father Dawbeny drew for the last time a great congregation to St. John the Prior's—far greater than it could hold. Priests and choristers from other churches in the Deanery celebrated for him a Solemn Requiem, and the Bishop spoke to the people. It was summer, and the West Door was open, and the Bishop, a little man with no great voice, tried nevertheless, to send his words out to the large crowd standing there and peering in.

This is a little of what the Bishop said.

'My friends, this should not be too unhappy an hour. Your good priest, Piers Lygon Dawbeny, was ready and waiting, I believe, for this call. It is already many months since he wrote to me saying that he thought his ministry was closing and that he wanted it to end at St. John the Prior's, Potters Dale. So we may believe that he felt death approaching for many months past. Now you will remember how in the days of the great London blitz, night after night he fought with the rest of you against Death, but I think he always honoured that ancient enemy and in the end was able to smile at him as at an old friend. Can we doubt that the manner of his death was a thing that he could have wished but dared not hope ? Oh, yes, God granted him a life of hard struggle, wherein he could perfect himself, and then a very perfect death. You may perhaps think it sad that no priest came to him with the last sacrament, but I suggest to you that we think of Death as God's High Priest who brought him very gently a bread of his own, not hard or bitter, at the very place where the Blessed Sacrament is administered and received.

'It is thought that he died about two o'clock. If so, he knelt there for some six hours like a statue of all that a priest should be. Which reminds me, my friends, that he once told me of certain words of counsel which his spiritual director gave him just before he was ordained, and which were his secret guiding line all through life : " Live and labour so that at your death, you may return to God the office of an earthly priest." All this he did. He set before you the very difficult Christian life and, if one aspect of it more than another commanded his loyalty, it was the Christian life as a life of forgiveness, of overcoming evil by love, of abandoning all harsh judgments for ever, because all judgment tends to be self-righteous, and we are all sinners. Some of you, I know, thought he asked of you forgivenesses that were impossible ; yes, I have known priests and bishops who were impatient with him and maintained that he asked impossible things ; but, my friends, these things are not impossible, and Piers Dawbeny has shown us they are not. If you really do ceaselessly try to love the whole world—as a priest most certainly should—then each individual soul is to you as a child to its mother, who cannot but try to understand, forgive, and help it. That was what he believed himself commissioned to preach, and Piers Dawbeny was never one to desert his commission. It is all so simple, really : a priest should lead his people in growth ; and people have only to grow into the loving and generous adulthood of your Father Dawbeny, for the world to be saved.'

The Bishop then turned his face towards the coffin in the chancel. He had seen, and been moved by that mysterious bunch of flowers from the one who had been in prison. And he quoted its simple farewell : ' Goodbye, Father. Your people here thank you for having never failed them in your message or your struggles for them ; and I, your bishop, thank you for having discharged your commission so faithfully and so fearlessly.' He brought his eyes back to the people. ' My brothers, this little church of yours was always a sacred place, but it seems to me that it has been hallowed for you now, as never before, by the memory of that figure kneeling there, and by the life of a good priest which he there rendered up to God.'

§

After the Mass they said the first part of the Burial Office, and then the procession formed to pass out into the street where the coster's barrow waited. They went with crucifix, lights and incense ; the greatly enlarged choir following the incense cloud ; then some thirty priests in their surplices and a half-dozen of nonconformist ministers in their black gowns ; then the coffin borne by eight costers, grizzled men for the most part ; then Ernie alone ; and then the relatives and friends led by old Lord Strathpenny, who, tall and gaunt, had startled all by his likeness to his brother, their dead priest. After these privileged mourners came a large contingent from the Costers' Club, a patrol of boy scouts, two sisters of mercy, and lastly the people. The procession formed in Greig Street ; and when the coffin was on the barrow, with the pall on it, and the biretta on the pall, and when the eight old costers had taken their stations on either side of the barrow, the procession moved off, the choir singing to the surprise of many, till they saw that every word was true and fit :

> ' Come, ye thankful people, come,
> Raise the song of harvest home.'

So they took him through three miles of London roads to Euston Station that he might go back now to the great home of his fathers among the mountains of Cumberland. There were big crowds in the Dale to watch the procession go by, and the tradesmen stood at the doors of their shops, which they had shuttered since the morning. Mr. Gus Chambers, the wardrobe dealer, who had never been to church since his first child died, spoke for many when he said, ' I didn't agree with him in everything because I don't like high-church myself, but he was a good man, and he sweated his life away for the old Dale, so I for one will put my shutters up.' The Salvation Army, officers and congregation, stood arrayed upon the steps of their Citadel in Morden Street and bent their red and blue standards to the ground as the barrow went by. ' Wheat and tares together sown,' the long white choir was singing. ' Unto joy or sorrow grown ; First the blade and then the ear . . .' From every threshold and shuttered shop door the Dalesmen watched ; watched as he passed from their view. They stayed very silent and still, only moving their hands to lift their caps or perhaps, if they were women, to touch their mouths or eyes.

A very conspicuous figure among the following people was Ben Ostrion, holding his silk hat in his hand all the way from St. John the Prior's to Euston. Ben Ostrion was perhaps the only publisher in England who because of his political activities was as much ' news ' as some of his more celebrated statesman-authors, and whose splendid Hebraic head, therefore, was known to many from newspaper pictures. Not a few, watching the procession, recognized his face at once, and wondered. An inconspicuous figure, unknown to any, small and lost in the following ranks, was Polo Lancellotti. Not far behind him walked Matt Rubens and his father: two companions, one tall and dark and handsomely dressed, the other short and shabby and grey, and both marching thus close to the man who at one time wanted to kill Matt. A lonely but proud figure, limping along behind the barrow was Ernie—proud of this honour paid to his master, proud of his own black robes and place in the procession, and thinking

sometimes of a trench in Murder Wood, and sometimes of a cell
in a prison.

> ' So, thou Church Triumphant, come,
> Raise the song of harvest home ;
> All is safely gathered in . . .'

It hushed the streets of London wherever it went. Who was
this, they asked from sidewalk and window, on omnibus, lorry,
wagon and dray ; who was this that they were carrying on a
barrow, in triumph, the incense praising God ?

Who could it be ? The few who knew the answer told those
who did not ; these told many others ; and the story caught
the ears of Fleet Street, so that it was told in the national newspapers the next day. And thus the legend broke new ground
far away from the Dale and began to prosper there.

§

Lastly the book.

A few mornings after the procession Ben Ostrion came to
Greig Street and knocked on the door of the Church Hall.
Ernie, answering that knock, wanted to show such a distinguished
visitor into the empty, and now very tidy, sitting-room of Father
Dawbeny, but he insisted on coming into Ernie and Sophie's kitchen
and sitting there on a hard chair while Sophie got on with the
peeling of potatoes and the scraping of carrots for their dinner.

And he talked, and he talked. Ben Ostrion's talk was usually
as voluble as a river in spate, but because it coruscated with
humour and vision and bright similes, you could listen and listen
as he talked and talked.

' I have an idea, Ernie,' he said. ' It came upon me as I
was walking through the streets behind your good father. It
was one of those ideas that I couldn't doubt was right. It just
came and commanded me to get busy and act on it. It didn't
argue with me, it just told me. I imagine our old prophets felt
rather like that when they suddenly appeared before the kings
and announced what they purposed to do next. There are
times, Sophie, when I feel sorry for the kings.'

' Yes, sir,' said Sophie, and she brought her basin of vegetables
from the sink to the bare kitchen table, and sat there to hear better.

' What was the idea, sir ? ' asked Ernie, who'd already sat

himself down with no notion of doing anything else but listen.

'Someone ought to write the story of his life so that its effect may not be transient——"

'Not be what, sir?'

'Transient—fleeting—forgotten like the pictures in yesterday's newspaper. Did you see that picture in the *Illustrated London News* of our procession in the Euston Road? Who got that I wonder.'

'Yes, they were showing it around at the Brickmakers' Arms last night.'

'Well, I don't want his life's work to be a nine days' wonder. We've got to do something about it, you and I, Ernie. We've got to preserve it from too rapid decay. And that can only be done by a properly written story.'

'Oh, I think that would be nice,' said Sophie over her bowl.

'Yes, but who's going to write it? I imagine you don't feel like writing it, Ernie?'

'Gawd-a-mercy, no, sir.'

'No, Ernie wouldn't be no good at that,' said Sophie with a wife's readiness to put a visitor at ease by a depreciation of her husband so that the visitor can feel larger than he. '*He's* never written nothing.'

'No, I rather thought he'd be diffident about it. But the only other person I can think of who could be trusted to do it adequately is myself. I'm only a Jew, I know, and really only a publisher of better men's work, but I've done a certain amount of scribbling, and I feel I could write it with some gusto because he was a man who stood for most things I believe in. Perhaps it wouldn't lose point if a Jew wrote it.'

'I'm sure you'd do it beautifully,' Sophie encouraged.

'Yes, and I've had to pilot the work of other men—politicians and such who rarely know the first thing about writing books— I've had to guide them through waters whose rocks and shoals I know all too well—from many a mishap, many a horrible sandbank, many a disastrous foundering and total loss. Now I shall have to pilot my own ship.'

'Yes, sir,' said Sophie, anxious to play the hostess and take her share in the conversation, 'but it shouldn't ought to be difficult to a gentleman like you.'

'Ah, that's all you know, Sophie! Wait till you write a book. I've talked to Lord Strathpenny about it and he's given me authority to proceed and promised me access to all his brother's papers. So far, fine ; but it's his life in Potters Dale that is the heart of the story and especially these last years when you were with him, Ernie. So you've got to give me all you know. After all, he was a lonely man, and you were nearer to him—and, I think, dearer to him—than anyone else. You and Sophie.'

'Oh no, sir,' Ernie deprecated, while Sophie lifted her apron to the corner of her eye—and then went on peeling.

'Oh, yes, sir ! Neither you nor Sophie can dodge that. And nobody can help me as you can, Ernie. You will help me, won't you ? You will be my best collaborator ? '

'Well . . . sir . . .'

'Of course he'll do all he can,' assured Sophie, as wives do, never quite trusting their husbands to say the right thing.

'You see the idea, don't you, Ernie ? You and I preserve his story for the sake of the world. He, being dead, yet speaks —eh ? '

'Yes, but what's going to become of us, do you think, sir ? ' asked Sophie, who as a homely woman was more interested in next week's meals than in the salvation of the world.

'I have an idea about that,' answered Ben Ostrion. 'You hold on here. Just hold on. It'll be a long time before they can demolish the church, and in the meantime it must be served.'

'It's a wicked shame to demolish it,' declared Sophie.

'That's rather my idea,' said Ben Ostrion.

'I don't know how they dare do such a thing.'

'Perhaps they daren't. We shall see.'

It was nearly one o'clock, and Sophie, after some minutes of hidden and exceedingly difficult deliberation, the text of which was, ' Seeing as how he's all that friendly,' said timidly, ' I suppose you wouldn't care to stop and have a little something with us, sir ? It won't be long now. I'm afraid there's only soup and potatoes for dinner and some of yesterday's jam tart which I'm going to hot up—things are so difficult these days.'

'There's nothing I should like better, Sophie. I've tasted your cooking before. Eh, what a meal that was ! Galantine and venison and macedoine of fruits. I remember it all. Yes, I shall enjoy sharing your meal but only—only, my dear—if you'll let me help wash up afterwards.'

'No, Ernie will do that.'

'Ernie and Ben will do it, Mrs. Matters. It's time you had a rest. Ernie and I will clear up everything and leave everything tidy. You see, Ernie : it's my firm conviction that a man can't live a life like his without little miracles happening around it, and I want it to go on working its small miracles for a while.'

§

The book appeared within a few months of Father Dawbeny's death. This was a notable achievement, for the times were bad, but then Ben Ostrion was always a thruster in the publishing trade, a beater-up against the tides, one who, if he wanted to, would force a book through the presses by some sorcery which his competitors did not understand or commend. It was a good book. Ben Ostrion, so excellent a talker, was also a good writer so long as he wrote as he talked, straight out of a full and effervescent heart. But he was a far greater publisher than writer, and he put the whole power of his house, Ostrion, Hart and Company, behind the promotion of this 'title' (which is a publisher's word for a book). And because this story of a Christian priest was written with fervour by a Jew, and because it was promoted with such adroitness and strength, it conquered a large public and changed the name of Father Dawbeny from that of a struggling and apparently unsuccessful priest into a name of some power among men. If the legend of Father Dawbeny was largely created by the dog and the coster's barrow it was certainly enshrined by Ben Ostrion in a little chantry-chapel of good words.

It saved the little church in Greig Street. Soon that ugly little ark, with its triple porch and cheap rose window, was hardly known any more as St. John's but nearly always as 'Dawbeny's Church' or 'The Church of the famous Father Dawbeny', and had the Church Commissioners pursued their scheme to demolish it and sell the site, they would have raised something like a national outcry.

It became a chapel-of-ease to St. Anselm's, Lode Street ; and sometimes—not often, but now and then in the daylight— strange wanderers may be seen in Greig Street, staring up at it and then passing through its unlocked door to walk through its silences and gaze about them and come away. They are people who have been moved by Ben Ostrion's story.

It cannot, alas, be said that the Dale people attend its services in any larger numbers than before, but they are proud of it ; and all those who knew Father Dawbeny, even if he only spoke with them once or twice, make a little boast of this ; and the biggest of these boasters is Ernie, verger and caretaker of the Church. So the legend still lives in the streets of the Dale, and Father Dawbeny still resists the assaults of such as Comrade Anton, Albert Howden, and others within or without the Church, upon the things for which he stood.